A Novel

the

TEAHOUSE
BY THE TRACKS

Eric Schoeniger

The Teahouse by the Tracks

ISBN: 0615529607
ISBN-13: 9780615529608
Library of Congress Control Number: 2011915011
CreateSpace, North Charleston, South Carolina

For their friendship, inspiration, or help, the author thanks Jill Colford Schoeniger, Charles Burkhart, Donald Marks, Maria Marks, Tom Schultz, Jenny Schultz, Janet Colford, Anne Brumfitt, Chris Bursk, Stan Heim, Muriel Spark, Megan Goldblum, Leyra Ryan, Carolyne Van Der Meer, Kathy Baumgartner, Richard Bowditch, Drew Landis, Alix Ohlin, Kelly McQuain, Edna Ng'eny, David Oestreicher, Jami Cooper, Robert Pruecel, Nancy Kovel, Elizabeth Lippy, Jane Goldblum, Fabian, Zuzu, Bonobo, and Cabbage.

For Jill
Sine qua what's-it

the
TEAHOUSE
BY THE TRACKS

1

"Tinkle," said Janet, eying the little brass bell on the top of the door. But the bell didn't tinkle. It hung silently, its tongue mute with anticipation, waiting for the door to open.

My first day, she thought. My grand opening. But no customers. Not yet.

Henry would have liked this place. Not the work of it, not the setting up and the serving and the clearing away. Not the brewing and the baking and the scrubbing up afterward, the shelving and the organizing. Not the planning and the scheduling and the coming up with ideas for tea sandwiches and lemon cakes and teas, all the lovely teas: black tea, green tea, white tea, oolong; Earl Grey, Darjeeling, Ceylon, lapsang souchong; cinnamon, chamomile, rooibos, yerba-maté. But the meeting of new people, the greeting of old customers, once they had become that, the idling and the chatting and the gossiping, Henry would have liked all that. And the counting of the nickels and dimes, Henry would have liked that, too.

Tinkle, thought Janet, wishing the bell to quicken.

And then: *Tinkle.* The door swung open, and the little bell leapt to its feet.

As did Janet. "Good morning!" she fairly shouted. "I'm sorry," she added more evenly. "You're my first customer."

"Have you just opened for the day, then?" the first customer asked in an unfamiliar accent. "It's already half-ten."

"No, I mean, you're my first customer. Ever. I've only just opened the place."

The customer pulled shut the door behind her under a din of tinkling bell. She leaned her ample weight against it, once it was shut, as if it were a relief to be inside. Outside the sky was low with October clouds, roiling and looming, that invaded the air with damp chill. Inside was warm and bright.

"I'm sorry, I missed that. Did you say you've just opened?"

"It's my grand opening," Janet said. "And maybe also my grand closing, depending on how things go," she added cheerfully.

"Oh, how delightful. The opening bit, I mean, not the closing. I'm honored to be your first customer."

Janet took in the woman who stood at the door. She was about her own age, early to mid-sixties, with wire-rimmed glasses and a neat gray bob that perfectly suited her round face. Her raincoat and the clothes beneath it were rumpled — shabby genteel was the term Janet thought of, though perhaps the woman had simply been traveling. She had no handbag but held a worn paper shopping bag by its looped handles, and she carried a folded umbrella against the threat of rain. Her clothes seemed vaguely foreign, but there was something about her face that was oddly familiar. Janet's first thought, which she instinctively had about anyone she might recognize, was that the woman had been one of her school students; but she instantly rejected the notion, as they were obviously contemporaries. The woman set down her shopping bag, which Janet in the same instant realized was labeled Marks & Spencer and was heavy, and glanced past Janet at a table by the window.

"Well, now I'm just letting you stand there, when I should be inviting you in to sit down," Janet said. She turned her body toward the table the woman had been eying, as if to guide her there.

"Thank you very much," the woman said, taking the hint and making her way to the window seat. She unburdened herself of her bag and umbrella and, with a few deft motions, removed her raincoat. "I'm Ann, by the way. Ann Firth. Do I order at the counter or just here at the table?"

"Oh, either, whichever way you want to do it," Janet said, and in response Ann took her seat. "I'm Janet Charbray. Can I get you something to eat or drink?"

"Do you have something like a menu?" Ann asked, vainly searching the room for chalkboard or billboard or any other kind of posting that might give some indication of what was on offer.

"I'm afraid I haven't gotten around to that yet. But I don't have so much yet that there's really a need for a menu. There's lemon squares, which I just made myself last night. And I picked up some scones from the Safeway, though I couldn't find anything like clotted cream. I never think to have it myself, so I wouldn't even know where to start looking. Have you ever seen it? I'm not even sure exactly what clotted cream is. They had regular scones and scones with raisins, though I've never been a big fan of raisins in scones."

"A lemon square sounds lovely," Ann said, looking a bit overwhelmed, which made Janet realize she had been running on. "And do you have tea? Only the sign said 'Teahouse.'"

"Oh, of course, I'm forgetting the tea. We have all sorts of tea, pretty much anything you'd like, if it isn't too unusual."

"Just some English Breakfast, if you've that. English Breakfast with milk and sugar, and a lemon square."

Janet stepped behind the counter and put on water for tea. She could just see Ann where she sat by the window, gazing out at the clouds that had begun to release tentative heavy drops of rain. The ancient sashes, sagging a bit and in need of fresh paint, let in a hint of the gusting autumn wind, which faintly stirred the blue-and-white-checked curtains. Ann hugged herself against the draft. From where Janet stood she perceived Ann's face in three-quarter profile, but from the rear, so that she saw mostly the shroud of Ann's white hair. But there most certainly was something familiar about it, the face, if not the overall carriage of Ann's round body. Ann might have been described as fat, were she still young, but at her age most people would just see her as a woman at the tail end of middle age. Janet sensed that Ann had always been slightly rounded, if not fully round, and that perhaps what she recognized was a younger version of her. Could she be a former classmate? It was unlikely, all these miles from where she grew up, from where she went to elementary school and high school and then college, but it was certainly possible. She couldn't remember a classmate named Ann, though, not one who looked like the woman in the window seat. As she set a lemon square on a plate — the plates were new, white with a green curl of strawberry vine and two plump red strawberries, bold and simple, as if they had been stenciled, and Janet liked them so much she felt newly satisfied every time she looked at them — she saw Ann turn and glance at her behind the counter. Ann smiled politely and shifted her gaze across the room, thoughtful, and it seemed to Janet that Ann had looked at her not in expectation of tea and cake but in searching, as if she, too, felt a hint of recognition. As Janet made the tea she decided she would brew some for herself. She likewise noticed that one of the lemon squares had come out rather smallish and thought she might as well help herself to it.

When Janet brought the tea and cake to Ann she found that the two of them had turned shy and said nothing. She retrieved her own tea and cake and, removing herself by a short distance, sat at the table she had occupied when Ann came in, as if it were the official place to await new customers, which she then realized it would probably become. The table was uneven and rocked a bit as she set down her cup and plate.

Janet took a bite of lemon square and a sip of tea. Ann ate her lemon square with appetite but then drank her tea distractedly, mostly gazing out the window at the rain, which couldn't seem to make up its mind, and occasionally stealing glances at Janet, which Janet couldn't help but notice. Finally Ann said, "Can you tell me how to get to Norristown? I'm afraid I've lost my way."

"Do you mean by car?"

"No, I've come on the train. I've come on the train from Philadelphia, but I fear I've got on the wrong line, which I have to say is rather unlike me. When I realized my mistake I got off at the next station, which is how I ended up at your door."

"Oh, yes, Norristown is the R6, I think. We're the R5. Or at least it used to be. They recently changed the names of all the lines, which is probably why you got confused."

"I'm just here to see my son, you see," Ann said. "He's taken vows at St. Antony's, and I wanted to pay him a visit. Do you know it?"

"I think so. It's Orthodox, isn't it?"

"It's Coptic, which is a kind of Egyptian Orthodox. It's Christian, anyway, but I have to confess I don't know much more than that. But that's why I've come over, to visit him at the monastery."

"You've come from England, then?" Janet asked. She thought she had detected a British accent, and it had given her an idea of why she might recognize this stranger.

"From Scotland, actually," Ann said. Janet felt a stumble of disappointment: the person she had been thinking of wasn't from Scotland. Well, she hadn't been named Firth in any case, though of course Firth was probably a married name. Ann continued, "Logan — my son — was engaged to be married, but he broke it off, and the next thing we knew, he had joined the Coptic Church. Which surprised us immensely, because we've never been religious."

"When you say 'us,' you mean your family?"

"My husband and I. Well, I mean my former husband, or I should say, my late husband. Lionel only just died last year."

"Oh, I'm so sorry."

"No, really, it's all right," Ann said, but then she surprised herself with a single sob. "Look at me," she said, reflexively crumpling a paper napkin and bringing it to her face.

"It's completely understandable," Janet said, getting up from where she sat and crossing over to Ann. She placed a hand on Ann's shoulder, a bit awkwardly, and then withdrew. She had never been very comfortable with physical contact. "I only lost mine two years ago." And then Janet teared up as well, she wasn't sure whether from being reminded of Henry or because she recognized her own pain in Ann or a little of both.

"Look at the two of us," Ann said, smiling instead of weeping.

Janet took the seat across from Ann. "Henry died in a plane crash. He was a commercial pilot, you see."

"How awful. Were there others, then?"

"Oh, no, he was by himself. He had this antique plane that he used to fly on the weekends, an ancient thing that scared me to death. So it was just him."

"Pulmonary embolism," Ann said, referring to her husband. "Lionel had developed a blood clot in his liver, somehow. He spent months in hospital, while they tried to figure out what the trouble was. And then just when it looked like he was going to recover, the blood clot migrated to his lungs, and just like that he was gone."

Janet had a sense of much more needing to be said, of a long conversation, or conversations, about losing their husbands, but that this would take place at some time in the future. For now their deaths were merely the facts of their last moments.

"And then your son decided to join the convent? Or monastery, I guess."

"Well, it was all happening at the same time. I couldn't really even think about Logan, with Lionel being so ill, and my having to care for him. And then right around the time he died, Logan announced he was moving to the States."

"Won't he miss Scotland? Well, I guess a monk doesn't think about where his home is. Is he a monk?"

"He's a brother, I think they call it. Anyway, he's just starting out, so he's the equivalent of what a novice would be to a nun, whatever they call that in the Coptic Church, and for a man. But no, Logan won't miss Scotland, will he?

7

We moved around a bit, between London and St. Andrews. We were from London, originally."

"Oh, I didn't think your accent was Scottish."

"No, it isn't, of course, but then I'm not sure I sound very British any longer, either. Moving back and forth seems to have muddled me."

"And you say you were from London?"

"Lionel and I settled in London when we were first married, yes. But I grew up in Winchester, which is south-west of London."

"Winchester, yes!" Janet said. "It's what I thought. Were you Ann Wright?" She didn't wait for Ann's reply. "It's Janet. Janet Guernsey."

"Yes, I thought you looked familiar," Ann said, not quite believing.

"But how can it be that we cross paths after all these years?"

"Well, people are so mobile now, aren't they? It's both more likely and less likely, I suppose. I ..."

"You must tell me what you've been doing," Janet interrupted, "since, since ..."

"Since secondary school."

"Since our last letter."

And so they began to recount what they both knew: how Janet's high school, in her native Massachusetts, had instituted a pen-pal program with "sister schools" in England; how Janet's class had been matched up with a school in Winchester; how Janet and Ann had drawn each other's names and had started writing letters; how they had instantly felt a connection, a camaraderie, across an ocean, through words inked on a page; how they had exchanged photos and ambitions and secrets, safe in the knowledge they would never be revealed to anyone to whom they would matter; how they had both finished high school and gone off to college and forgotten about each other, the way people do, and lived entire lives each without knowledge of the other.

"Oh, but I've thought of you so often," Janet said. "I've always wondered what happened to you, and whether there was a way to find out, to find you."

The door opened again, and Janet was met with her second and third customers, a man and a boy, maybe seven years old, who was clearly the man's son. Shouldn't he be in school? They shuffled to the counter, where they peered at the lemon squares and scones in their glass cabinet.

"That's all they have?" the boy asked, obviously disappointed.

Janet watched them absent-mindedly, till Ann prompted her: "Should you be serving them?"

"Oh, right," Janet said. "I haven't quite got used to the idea that I run the place."

She left Ann at her table and circled behind the counter, asking what she could offer her second and third customers.

"Is that all you have?" the man echoed his son.

"We also have tea and coffee," Janet said — the boy made a face — "as well as hot cocoa," she added, at which he looked at his father brightly and nodded.

"We'll have two hot cocoas," the father said. He turned to his son and said, "That's pretty cool, huh?" at which point Janet realized the man was divorced from the boy's mother and had him for the day: it explained his ordering the same drink, his over-enthusiasm at the prospect. The man paid, and the pair made their way to a table, where they sat without speaking, familiar yet awkward, in the mode of so many post-divorce father-and-son relationships.

Janet returned to Ann and resumed their conversation as if it hadn't been interrupted, giving her an abridged version of the past, what was it, forty-four years? Forty-four years, then. A lifetime, practically; in an earlier age, in another place, more than a lifetime.

Some of it Ann already knew. Janet had grown up on the Massachusetts South Shore, in Plymouth, right on the water. She was meant to be the oldest child, but after her mother miscarried what would have been her younger sister she became an only child. Somehow this placed her in a separate, vaguely pitiable category; people uttered the words "only child" as if it were a shame or even a thing to be ashamed of, whereas to Janet it simply meant she had no siblings. She finished school in 1966, at a time when it still wasn't necessarily assumed a young woman would go to college. Her father was opposed to the idea, but it was agreed she could attend Bridgewater State College, a teacher's school, less than an hour away. The prospect of becoming a teacher was pleasing to Janet, who had enjoyed school and liked children and felt she would have a knack for teaching, which, as it turned out, she did.

She was already teaching and living at home with her parents when she met the man who would become her husband. Henry, at thirty, was eight years older and eager to get married. He was a pilot for a private airline, the kind that fly corporate jets. He was originally from Nova Scotia but was brought to southeastern Massachusetts when his company began operating out of Boston. They stayed in Plymouth, where Janet taught sixth-grade social studies. It was close to her parents and an easy commute for Henry to Boston. It never occurred to Janet that she would live anywhere else, certainly nowhere outside New England.

"And that's it, really," she said. "I retired from teaching early. I had just grown so tired of the parents, all their hovering and demanding. Henry was already retired by then. I thought we were going to have our retirement years together."

A customer banged into the teahouse — the wind had grown more forceful — looking for cappuccino, which Janet didn't have. He banged out again, apparently offended by the lack. The father and son by this time had also slipped out, leaving their dirty mugs and crumpled paper napkins and rings of cocoa on the table behind them.

Janet realized she had been talking for almost an hour. "You'll be wanting to get off to see your son," she said to Ann.

Ann peered at her watch, a tiny square-faced thing she could just make out in the soft fold of her wrist. "Well, I don't know that I should bother, at this point. It's nearly lunchtime, and I don't know what Logan does there for lunch. Maybe I'll just put it off till tomorrow." She appeared to find relief in the idea. "Yes," she decided, "I'll go tomorrow. I can look at the train schedule more carefully, in any case."

"Will you head back to Philadelphia, then?"

"Yes, I'm just at the Latham Hotel, right in the middle of town, I guess it is."

"But you haven't told me about yourself. You've let me do all the talking."

"That's all right. I'll be here for a week at least. I'll see Logan, of course, but I love history, and I've always wanted to see Philadelphia. The hotel's a bit dear, but ..."

"Then why don't you stay with me?" Janet said, the idea just occurring to her. "Why don't you stay with me here?"

"I couldn't impose myself like that. Could I?"

"Absolutely. I'd like the company, actually. I'm all alone here."

"You never did say how you ended up here in ... where are we, actually?"

"Lower Slaughter. Isn't it an awful name for a place? I have no idea where it comes from. I suppose there must have been a slaughterhouse here at some point, or perhaps it refers to some Indian massacre."

"I think it's an Old English word," Ann offered. "I think it comes from *slough*. You know, like a mire, a muddy place."

"Well, we're right on the Wissahickon Creek here," Janet said, "so maybe it has to do with that. Which is in fact an Indian name, Wissahickon. It's odd, though, most of the names here are Welsh. There's Lower Gwynedd, Upper Gwynedd, Gwynedd Valley, Gwynedd Heights. I've never understood how there can be so many town names in Pennsylvania. Every other street corner is a different town, not that anybody pays any attention to it; they're mostly just forgotten names on old maps. But there's only Lower Slaughter: no Upper. I wonder how they ended up with an English name in the middle of all the Welsh ones."

"Well, there's a Lower Slaughter in south-central England," Ann said, "in the Cotswolds. It's right next to Wales, actually."

"That must explain it. Not that I know of any Welsh people here. It's mostly German: everyone I meet here seems to have been German, originally. But of course you never can tell what people are."

"No, not any longer," Ann agreed. "Not that you ever could, I suppose."

"But 'mire' is about the size of it," Janet continued. "After Daddy died, Mother met a man from Philadelphia. They decided to get married, and George — that was his name, George — brought her down here to live. I never dreamed my mother would leave New England. I never dreamed *I* would leave New England; the whole reason we settled in Plymouth was to be near Mother and Daddy. George died just a couple years later, though he was quite venerable when Mother married him. And then right after Henry died, she had a stroke. She couldn't stay on her own, and it seemed too difficult to move her back, and there was nothing keeping me in Plymouth. So I came here, to live with her."

"Then are you sure you'll have enough room for me? But no, you said you're all alone."

"That's right. I no sooner got settled in here, and Mother had another stroke. I couldn't care for her at that point, so I put her in a home. It's horrible to put it like that, but it's the truth of it."

"And now here you are in Lower Slaughter."

"And now here we are in Lower Slaughter."

2

Janet and Ann agreed that Ann would return to her hotel
for the night but check out the next morning and, once
she had seen her son at the monastery, come to stay with
Janet for the remainder of her visit. After Ann left, Janet
wondered why she hadn't thought to invite her to lunch.
But of course she had the teahouse to see to, and while
there were few customers in mid-afternoon, things grew a
bit hectic at the end of the day, with commuters stopping in
on their way from the train to their cars. Most of them were
just curious to check out the new store that had gone into
the old train station, though some were looking for coffee
for the drive home or pastries they could take to their families. She hadn't thought of that, that people would expect
coffee even though it was a teahouse, that they would want
to take quantities of things to go, rather than stay for cake
or a scone. Her sales for the day were miniscule, scarcely
enough to cover the cost of the ingredients to make the
lemon squares, never mind all the other overhead. But
she hadn't expected immediate success and was happy to

begin slowly and try things as she went along. Still, there was so much she wasn't sure of: when, exactly, to open and close for the day, how much to charge to ensure a profit while keeping prices reasonable, how to know whether she were actually making a profit. She had looked at a couple of how-to books at the Barnes & Noble, though she didn't actually bring them home, and had spent many hours on her underpowered computer, scouring the Internet for tips on running a café. But it was hard to make sense of it all without actually doing it yourself.

She would never have been so ill-prepared with a lesson plan. But being a good middle-school teacher didn't necessarily qualify her for much else, it seemed. And she had always found that while she was particularly adept as a teacher, organized and hard-working, on top of the material and in control of her students, she was never able to extend that competence much beyond the classroom. The house got cleaned only when it absolutely needed it. The bills got paid only at the last minute; with Henry flying so much, the daily finances fell to her. Buying a cheap laptop computer, just in the past year or two, figuring out how to get on the Internet, were minor miracles, as was her ability to care for her sick mother, and so soon after Henry's dying. But the big things, the important things, she could usually manage. It was the day-to-day details that got away from her, like a favorite earring slipping from her fingers to clatter once, twice, in the basin and then disappear down the waiting drain. It sometimes felt as if life were nothing so much as a repetition of unscrewing watery traps and fishing what was wanted from out of the slimy mess.

People — friends, colleagues, what little family she kept up with — had sometimes commented on this apparent incongruence in her personality, the rigorous structure in one area, the sloppy, seemingly lazy and half-hearted nonchalance in others. But people were nothing if inconsistent, it seemed to her. How many students she knew were rigidly shy in one circumstance, bold or gregarious or effusive in another; how many men were nearly telepathic with their dogs, for God's sake, yet tone-deaf to their wives; how many bleeding-heart do-gooders were expansively otherfocused while volunteering, while feeding the poor or healing the sick, yet entirely in their own orbit when backing out of a parking space or running you down with a shopping cart in the grocery store? Their only consistency was in their inability to change, in the sameness of their incongruence from day to day, from year to year, as experience and influence were shed from them like the rain from the slate roof of the teahouse, rain that dampened, darkened, but didn't penetrate.

She turned around the sign in the door so that Open faced inward and Closed outward. It seemed like the next logical action would be to pull down a window shade, as if switching off the day, but there was no shade to pull, only the old wooden door, a bit battered by age and use, with its large glass pane. She would have to think about getting a window shade. It occurred to her that this probably wasn't the most secure setup, a wooden door that was almost one-half glass. But even if a burglar smashed the glass he would still be unable to unlock the deadbolt, which was operated by a key, and his only option would be to completely break out the pane and then somehow squeeze through without injuring himself in the process. In any case there wasn't much to steal, yet, just a few tables and chairs and a mostly empty cash drawer. Maybe she should think about having some sort of alarm system installed.

She stood with her back to the door and gazed about the teahouse, at what she had wrought, as she thought of it. The first thing you noticed, when you came in the door, was the counter, set across the room, a thick slab of smooth black slate that contrasted with the white plaster walls and the pale green of the wood trim. The wood trim was broad and flat, substantial, in a way wood trim hadn't been for probably a century. It was painted a pale green the color of mint ice cream: on the baseboards, the chair rail, the molding at the ceiling; across the tongue-and-groove wainscoting under the counter; around the deep-silled windows, tall and narrow. The heavy sashes were bisected into two panes each, the glass old enough to have begun sagging, slightly warping the view. She hadn't bothered to have the place repainted. She had a notion that the colors were the original hues, and for some reason this pleased her. She thought the blue-and-white checked curtains would be a nice contrast, but they didn't quite work. She sensed that she would soon grow accustomed to them but that anyone seeing them for the first time would think them out of place.

The tables and chairs had fortuitously been left over from the former owner. The tables were mostly antique sewing machines, the kind with wood tops and cast-iron legs. The machines themselves had been removed, leaving behind broad metal treadles that still turned but no longer served a useful purpose: a player piano without strings, a grist mill bereft of stone. There were two larger, square tables that could accommodate parties of four. The chairs where simple and wooden, the backs fashioned of horizontal panels, save for one outlier that was identical but for vertical slats. The chairs were stiff and upright yet surprisingly comfortable, except that most of them had warped with time so that their four legs no longer sat evenly on the linoleum floor: one leg was inevitably shorter than the rest. Your immediate inclination was to begin rocking against the short leg, and it occurred to Janet that she'd have to extend the short legs with those little caps you could attach, lest the tap-tap of the rocking chairs drive her to distraction. Yet another thing she'd never get to, she realized. The building had been the Lower Slaughter train station, a one-story stone structure with a steeply pitched Victorian roof and broad overhanging eaves. But there was no longer need for a fully functioning station building at this far reach of the Philadelphia suburbs, and it was as defunct as a lock on the Delaware Canal. Train commuters were now served by a tiny structure set just down the tracks, though they still escaped the weather under the building's generous eaves. The transportation authority had leased the building for a time to an ambitous but unlucky local man who hoped to put in a restaurant. He replaced the original benches and ticket booth with a tiny kitchen and makeshift front counter but ran out of money before he opened for business, apparently. The building sat idle till it was sold to the owner of the adjacent property. When Janet toured the place with the real-estate agent she found it almost as it had been left, the tables and chairs still poised for diners, the kitchen stocked with unopened supplies. It almost seemed a shame to disturb it, she remembered thinking.

Through the dark glass of the front door Janet could see the rain was now falling steadily, its regular patter against the flagstones accented by heavy drips off the eaves. She locked the front door and collected her coat and handbag. She would leave through the back door, which faced the lot where she had parked her car. But when she got to it she found the door wouldn't budge. It was designed to open inward, so there was no way for her to put her weight into the effort; she just tugged at it futility, the knob slipping out of her hand. The wood must have swelled in the wet weather, she thought. She'd have to go out through the front door.

There was a window by the back door, and she peered out it, as if to glimpse what was preventing the door from opening, though she had already as good as answered the question. She could see the slick of asphalt in the penumbra of overhead lights, as well as the few cars that hadn't yet been collected by commuters. Beyond the parking lot was the property of her landlord, the man who owned the teahouse building. She could just make out the house and, beyond it, an imposing stone barn, both shrouded in trees and overgrown shrubbery. The house was Victorian, like the teahouse building, but in deep-orange brick instead of stone. It was a handsome structure, quite large, but tall and narrow, so that it had a sort of lightness and elegance to it. The windows and front porch and gingerbread trim were painted in two shades of green, light and medium, the medium green like the fine coating of moss, or maybe it was a sort of algae, that softened the orange brick, the light green the same shade as the mint-ice-cream trim of the teahouse. But the brightness of the contrasting greens was tempered by ponderous black shutters and a heavy slate roof, so that Janet couldn't decide if the house looked cheerful or dour.

She had met the owner, Charles Grapnel, only twice; all the official business of leasing the teahouse had been handled through the real-estate agent. He was tall, with lanky limbs and a girthy middle, and his hair was prematurely white. He had been charming the first time she met him, when she had come to tour the building, gracious and erudite, and had made her feel that he was genuinely interested in her. But he had acted aloof on their second meeting, after she had signed the lease and was just beginning to set up the teahouse. He seemed almost to resent the idea that she would be using the building. When he spoke to her — he used a lot of italics when he spoke, to emphasize key words — he looked past her, as if gazing at a distant horizon unseen by others. The realtor had told her that Dr. Grapnel had been a professor at Grier & Buchanan College, out in mid-western Pennsylvania, but was no longer. But he appeared to be only in his mid-fifties, surely too young to retire. His gazing past her, or through her, more like it, had seemed designed to conceal, or at least to avoid. Like his house, Dr. Grapnel was difficult to gauge, Janet decided.

She could only imagine what the house looked like, inside. Dr. Grapnel dressed in his own singular style, wearing a brown suede sport coat, apparently vintage, both times she met him, and what were obviously pricey calfskin loafers. But the cuffs of his white oxford shirt were frayed, and there was a stain on the thigh of his khaki trousers. She imagined the interior of his home to be the same mix of self-conscious artiness and tired tradition, contemporary artwork and Eames lounge chairs competing with antique sideboards in heavy oak. In any case it would have to be more sophisticated than her mother's second-floor condo, which was all pastel walls and off-white carpeting, Winslow Homer prints and laminated furniture. She still didn't think of it as her own house, a year after moving her mother to a nursing home, in part because of its anodyne demeanor, as she thought of it. Everything was designed to be convenient and serviceable but was utterly lacking in character, like a hothouse tomato or an appliance salesman. There was nothing wrong with function, she reminded herself, especially in the kitchen, now that she would be making fresh pastries every night to supply the teahouse. She began to think about what she should make for tomorrow. Lemon squares were a possibility, of course, but she didn't want to offer the same thing every day. Fudge brownies were certainly easy to whip up, as were chocolate-chip cookies, and she probably already had all the ingredients she needed. But she had to come up with things that more said "teahouse." Her plan had been to offer a full afternoon tea, with traditional items like crust-less cucumber sandwiches and petit-fours, but by the time she was ready to open all that had seemed so complicated as to be beyond her, so she had decided she would try it in some eventual future. For now she thought it best to get the teas and pastries right and see if she could win over some regular customers.

She left the back door where it was stuck and recrossed the interior of the teahouse. She kept an umbrella in the car, but she had left it there, not thinking of the possibility of rain. She would have to hurry out from under the eaves and around the back to the car; there was no question she would be soaked by the time she got to it. When she opened the front door the wind yanked it from her grasp. The teahouse filled with the night's presence, the curtains billowing, a stack of paper napkins scattering from the counter. The little brass bell clanged as the door thrashed against the outside wall. It had sounded so cheerful when it announced Ann that morning. But now, to Janet, it rang dolorous, as ominous as the livid sky.

3

How strange, Ann thought. How delightful but how strange, to meet Janet again after all these years, to literally walk into her life. And all because of getting on the wrong train, something she hadn't done in years, if ever. She would never have recognized Janet. She didn't recognize her, in fact, though she had sensed a kind of familiarness. It was like having a thought and then realizing someone else has just said the same thing, and that's why you thought it. Janet was so tall, for one thing, though of course she had only ever seen her in photographs. But more than that she had such a presence, large and loud and bustling, and that unmanageable, undyed gray hair. She never would have thought of Janet's running a teashop, but then how could she have predicted anything Janet would do, knowing her as she did by letter, and forty-four years ago? But the teaching part didn't surprise her at all; Janet had loved school. And a teashop seemed like the sort of thing one might do in one's retirement. Still, it seemed to Ann that Janet had left out some key event, or events, in telling her life story, something that all the bustling was meant to conceal, or at least keep at arm's length. Isn't it strange, she thought, how you expect to know someone after so many years? You think of yourself as decades older, or decades different, at least, but expect others to somehow have remained the same.

Ann settled into her seat. American train cars were so dismal, compared with their European counterparts, and seemed to have been designed a generation ago, with unforgiving seats and grudging windows. And there was never a buffet car. She had never been enamored of trains anyway, or any sort of public transport, for that matter, trains and coaches in particular, but also planes and even cabs. But she enjoyed travel so, and living in Great Britain, there was only so far you could go by car. Plymouth was the farthest she had driven from St. Andrews, it just occurred to her, and wasn't it funny, now that she thought of it, that Janet had grown up in Plymouth, Massachusetts. Her American friends were always surprised to learn she didn't like trains, as if all Europeans were supposed to like any sort of public works, their dependent, socialist souls comforted by the rocking cradle of the railway. Ann preferred to have her hand on the wheel.

She was missing her lunch, she realized, and she rummaged through her Marks & Spencer bag till she found a tin of biscuits. They were Logan's favorites, and she had intended to bring them to him as a treat. But she had brought lots of other things for Logan, and he wouldn't miss them. So she might as well open the tin and at least tide herself over till she could get a proper meal at the hotel.

She gazed out the window at suburbs that grew thicker as she approached Philadelphia. She had always preferred traveling alone. You could achieve a sort of efficiency of movement, parking the car at the airport, checking in and making your way through security, settling into your seat on the plane, getting through customs at the other end, figuring out the train schedule or, more ideally, finding the rental-car agency. She found the minimizing of steps, the shaving off of a few minutes here or there, so thoroughly satisfying. She had got the planning of a trip down pat, all of it completed on the computer, all of her personal information already entered into her online accounts. Travel was so much smoother when there were no surprises. And yet she liked, every once in a while, not to plan one portion of the trip, not to book a hotel or schedule a flight or find out ahead of time whether there was a train out of town, just to see how efficiently she could live on her wits in some small way. There was something pleasing about the unexpected when everything else was going to plan, like striking up a conversation with a fellow passenger and discovering you both had an inexplicable interest in mangoes, of all things, and comparing the different varieties you had tasted in different parts of the world, like the intensely sweet Alampur Baneshan she had tried in Bangalore. Such a thing never happened when you were traveling with someone. You limited your conversations to your traveling partner, never venturing outside the nimbus of your established relationship. And then of course you had to find a loo, because your companion needed a wee, at the exact moment you could have gotten ahead of a group of Japanese tourists. And do you want to stop for lunch now or later? And would a cheap-and-cheerful be OK, or were you hoping for something more formal? And now, sorry, I need a wee, too, and why do I feel the need to apologize for stopping at the cloakroom? No, it was much better to travel alone.

Not that she had ever traveled extensively. But one or two long trips a year, in the summer months, and to what she thought of as exotic places, Sydney or Johannesburg or Tuscany. She managed to establish friendships in the places she visited, as well, so she had people to keep in touch with and revisit and invite to stay with her in St. Andrews. It was odd how her only friends were the people she met while far from home; she had no friends in St. Andrews itself. Lionel had been skeptical, at first, as if her lone holidays were a symptom of a marital ailment. But he grew to accept them and, she suspected, even look forward to her going away, for the chance to be at home alone and uninterrupted with his history books and with their ancient tabby, Gerald. Yet he resented her foreign friends coming to visit, strange women in the house, often in pairs, leaving half-drained teacups on all the side tables. He could never fathom why someone would want to stay at a stranger's house rather than in a hotel.

But then after Lionel died she hadn't felt like traveling. Just when she was finally free to keep her own schedule and go where she pleased, all the pleasure was drained out of it. Had she been running, all those years, from Lionel, from the cold and dank of St. Andrews? She didn't think so, not really. She and Lionel and been perfectly suited, like those handmade trinkets, serving trays or little wooden boxes or whatever, that are asymmetrical but designed to fit snugly together. The romance had gone out of their marriage, it was true, and she had never quite accepted that fact. But she didn't think she was trying to escape it. It occurred to her that coming to see Logan was her first real trip since Lionel died.

The train squealed into the station. It was just a few blocks to her hotel. Ann lugged her Marks & Spencer bag up the steep stairs and out onto the street. The city was already growing dim, the yellow streetlights reflecting palely in the slick asphalt. She hunched her shoulders against the wind and walked, traveling again at last, but hardly going where she wanted.

**

Ann stood on the gray stone steps of St. Antony's Coptic Monastery. It was the morning of the next day, a Tuesday. She shifted her Marks & Spencer bag, which had grown heavy, to her other hand. Norristown was an inconsequential, forsaken city northwest of Philadelphia, squalid and cramped, at least from what she had seen on her walk from the train station. Main Street had been gentrified, the broad sidewalks newly laid, the building facades scrubbed clean. But beyond the main street, beyond the marble courthouse, it was all derelict terraced houses — what she thought the Americans called row homes — and red-brick warehouses, seemingly empty, with faded, generations-old paint on their sides announcing MEN'S HATS or FINE CIGARS or SCREWS, BOLTS, TACKS. Several black men paused on the corner, talking, and two or three stood in doorways up and down the block. Why an Egyptian monastery here? Were the neighborhood men Egyptian? She doubted it. A carton of empty beer bottles lay against the building. There were slots for six bottles, but one of the bottles was missing.

She had no idea what to expect. The man on the phone had sounded kind enough and said that everything would be explained when she came to visit, though she was instructed to dress appropriately, whatever that might mean. Logan had told her so little, about his beliefs or what his daily life would be like or what he intended to do in the long term. The double doors in the front, gray and peeling of paint, were locked. There was a side door with a buzzer, which she rang. The door was opened by a stooped, elderly gentleman of indeterminate ethnicity, with a bushy, albescent beard. He gazed at her expectantly but said nothing. Ann assumed he was one of the monks.

"Yes," she said, as if answering his unasked question. "I'm Ann Firth. I'm here to see Logan Firth. I'm his mother. I called earlier to make arrangements."

The monk nodded once and turned without speaking, with the implied suggestion that Ann follow. He had a surprisingly springing step, for as stooped as he was. He led her down a narrow, dim hallway to what appeared to be a sort of welcome center. He stepped aside and bent further, as if to guide her into the room. He smiled now, for the first time, through his beard, and then, still silent, turned and walked away.

Ann entered a room brightly lit with morning sunlight. There was a round table in the front, spread with what appeared to be religious books and pamphlets. Behind it were four desks, arranged facing one another. Three of the desks were unoccupied, but at the fourth sat another monk, hunched over an ancient, hulking desktop computer. He was younger than the first monk but similarly bearded.

"Welcome! Welcome!" he said quietly but with purpose.

"I'm Ann, Ann Firth."

"Yes, of course. We spoke on the phone."

"I'm here to see Logan."

"Yes, Brother Mikhail is expecting you."

Ann was about to object that she didn't want to meet with Brother Michael, but it occurred to her that Brother Michael might in fact be Logan. She thought it best to simply nod and follow along.

"I'm Father Anastasi St. Antony," the monk said. "Do you know about the Coptic Church? Our beliefs are based on the teachings of St. Mark, who brought Christianity to Egypt in the years after the Lord's ascension."

"Yes," Ann nodded in a way she hoped wouldn't encourage further discussion. Under more usual circumstances she would have been quite interested to learn about the Copts. But she really just wanted to see Logan. She really just wanted to get it over with, she admitted to herself.

"We don't normally allow women to visit the monastery unaccompanied by a priest," Father Anastasi said. "But when a parent is visiting, we make exceptions." He smiled benignly.

"I've brought some things," Ann said, almost apologetically, and lifted her bag. "For Logan."

The monk looked as if he was about to object, or at least question what was in the bag, but he stopped himself. "That's fine," he said. He led Ann down another dim hallway and through a door to a broad enclosed courtyard. The sun had risen above the low buildings and was warming the dampness from the October air. The grass of the courtyard was a luxurious green, in stark contrast with the gray-plastered architecture. Ann realized that the monastery occupied a full city block, its various buildings and annexes ringing the courtyard. Within the courtyard the city sounds were muffled, seemingly distant.

"We suffered terribly at the hands of both the Romans and the Muslims," Father Anastasi said incongruously. Ann had read as much on the Web sites she had consulted after Logan announced his conversion. Why this obsession with things that had happened eons ago? She nodded to be polite. "Come," the monk continued, "let me show you to Brother Mikhail."

They crossed the courtyard and entered a small room like a sitting room. There was an upholstered chair and a bookshelf, mostly empty of books, and an electric kettle for making tea, though it was unplugged and seemingly unused. There was also a wooden chair in the corner. On one wall was an image of a smiling, white-bearded man wearing what appeared to be a giant black pin cushion on his head. Another wall held a sort of metal grate that looked into an even smaller sitting room.

"Brother Mikhail will be with you," Father Anastasi said absently, as if their meeting were already over. He turned and disappeared through the door.

Ann was reminded of when she had to leave a urine sample at the doctor's. The nurse let you into a little room, and you weed in a cup and left it on a sill. When you were done, a technician on the other side of the wall would open a tiny door and collect the sample from the sill.

She sat in the upholstered chair and grew restless, counting the ticks of an imaginary clock. She took off her glasses, cleaned the lenses on the hem of her shirt, and replaced them. She was about to get up and go search for Father What's-His-Name, when Logan appeared on the other side of the metal grate.

"Hello, Mum," he said, and then, as if correcting himself: "Good morning."

"Logan!" She hadn't expected to see him across the grate, the purpose of which she now understood, and she felt a surge of emotion at this physical isolation. She stood as he sat down. "Can't I even give you a hug, then?"

"It's Brother Mikhail, now."

"I'm not calling you Brother Michael." She took her seat again and paused. "Are you to be a monk, then? Or a priest?"

"I'm just a novice, for now. I may become a monk in time. Not a priest; I have no plans to become a priest. But perhaps a monk. Or I may simply remain a novice. Some are called by humility to remain a novice."

"You haven't taken a vow of silence, at least."

"No." He smiled the benign smile of Father What's-His-Name. "Of obedience, yes. Of poverty and of chastity. But not of silence."

Ann took a moment to accustom herself to the idea that she would have to speak to her son through metal bars. She saw that he wore a sort of tunic in black burlap. He had started to grow a rather optimistic beard, sparse and red.

"Why a Coptic monastery?" she asked. She wanted to ask: Why this make-believe?

"It's the earliest monastic tradition in the Christian church. When a person loves God with all his heart, he wants to spend all his time with Him."

"And why here? I would have expected a Coptic monastery to be in the desert somewhere. And on the Nile, I suppose, not on the Delaware, or whatever river it was that George Washington crossed."

"The Schuylkill."

"No, I really think he crossed the Delaware."

"I mean, we're on the Schuylkill River. And it is a desert out there, if you hadn't noticed."

With that she couldn't disagree. As she had walked the streets of Norristown she had the distinct sense of being on the ugly train in *Stardust Memories*. "So you're here to help people?" she asked.

"I'm here to pray without ceasing, to meditate on the Word of the Lord. To discipline the self through fasting, vigils, the subduing of fleshly desires. The renunciation of worldly concerns."

Lord, it's like he's reading it from the brochure, she thought. "This is what you want for yourself?"

He sat up straighter and drew in his breath through his nose. "And what do you want for me? Earthly pleasures? Material things? They didn't do Dad much good, now, did they?"

31

Ann flinched at this reference to Lionel. So that's it, she thought. It's a repudiation of us, then. As simple as that? It seemed like something more befitting a much younger person. "I've brought some things for you," she said, "only I don't exactly know how to give them to you." She held up her Marks & Spencer bag so that he could see it through the metal grate.

"Things?"

"Treats and things. And some papers of yours I found at home. I got some of those Danish butter cookies you like from Tescos, but I have to confess I ate them on the train."

"We fast two hundred and ten days of the year. We take no animal products during fasts."

Ann suppressed an urge to ask exactly what a fast was meant to be if you could eat for its duration, even if the food was of the non-animal variety. "I'll just leave the things here, then," she said, placing down her bag, "and you can make use of what you can." She rose to her feet. "Goodbye, Logan," she said.

"Goodbye, Brother Mikhail," he said.

4

Janet was in a bit of a tizzy. She had left the brownies in too long, the night before, and while they didn't actually burn, they had become dry and hard enough that they weren't sellable. As a consequence she had had to stop at the Safeway again to pick up pastries and scones. And now the commercial coffee maker she used for heating the hot water for tea, which she had purchased and had installed at considerable expense, was leaking. Water was seeping out the back of it and running across the counter and, once it had pooled there for a while, pouring in a fine stream onto the floor. She was less concerned about the water itself than about the possibility that it could get into the wiring and cause some sort of electrical short circuit. Meanwhile, throughout the morning there had been a steady stream of customers so that she didn't even have time to look up the plumber who had installed the thing. She wasn't even certain she remembered his name. The receipt was in a pile somewhere.

But the teahouse seemed to be a hit; she couldn't help but notice that. All the regular commuters who had seen it open the day before must have allowed extra time to stop in this morning. It was one person after another, and she scarcely had time to keep the water hot for tea, and now the scones and cherry turnovers and croissants were running low. It was a good thing she had thought to start brewing pots of coffee, which seemed to be equally popular as tea, at the start of the rush. She hadn't thought of decaffeinated, though — she never bothered with decaffeinated tea or coffee for herself, though of course some teas just naturally had no caffeine — and several disappointed customers had requested decaf. Another lesson learned.

But why hadn't she thought of needing help with the preparing and the serving of the tea and coffee? She had pictured hiring help, if necessary — a waitress or whatever — at some point in the vague future. But clearly if she were going to do enough business to make a go of it, to make a profit, she would need more than one server. And she had figured that if she were sick or wanted to take some time off, she could simply close for a few days. But she now realized that customers would expect her to be open every day, at least every weekday, and not only when it was convenient for her. At one point at the height of the morning rush there had been a line of customers out the door, and several had to abandon their places in line to catch the train. I'm really not this daft, she told herself. It's not as if I haven't managed the big things like the electricity and telephone and health inspection.

What a relief it was when Ann appeared, wheeling a large suitcase. "You've come back," Janet said, as if she might have doubted Ann would. She came around the counter to greet her.

"Yes."

"And you've been to see Logan?"

"Yes."

"And how did it go?"

"Actually ...," Ann said, and left the word hanging.

"Well, we'll talk about it. Your timing is perfect, because I've just gotten rid of the last of the lunch rush, such as it was. I suspect it will be quieter now till the end of the day. I actually expected you before lunch."

"Well, I had to go back to the hotel for my things. I didn't feel like lugging my bag all the way to the monastery, and the only other alternative was to bring it here first, which didn't seem to make sense. And there's no easy way to get from there to here, without taking the train nearly all the way back to the hotel anyway."

"I would have offered to drive you, but I'm just not comfortable driving in the city," Janet said. "I've never been one for driving very far."

"Well, I'm here now anyway. And I'm ever so grateful for your letting me stay with you. How have things been going, then?"

Janet rolled her eyes. "Very well, in that I've had no dearth of customers. But I'm out of scones, I'm out of half-and-half, and the coffee maker is leaking all over the kitchen." She sat down at a table, newly overwhelmed. "Really, I'm not sure I can manage."

Ann glanced around the room. "Why don't you go to the market, then, and get whatever supplies you need. I can stay here and watch the shop."

"Are you sure?" Janet asked, but she was already making a mental list of what she needed.

"I'll just need to know the prices of things."

"Oh, the pastries are marked, but they're all two ninety-five. And the tea and coffee are just one size for people eating in, and two sizes for people taking it to go. It's one seventy-five for a small and two twenty-five for a large. There should be enough change in the cash drawer." Janet fetched her pocketbook from behind the counter and left Ann in charge.

"'H-m-m-m ... the first thing to do,' murmured Horton, 'Let's see....'," Ann said aloud, quoting *Horton Hatches the Egg*; Logan had loved Dr. Seuss. She went back to the kitchen to check on the coffee maker. Water had spread across the counter and floor, and there were wet shoeprints over the tiles where Janet had trod through the puddle. Ann peered behind the coffee maker and spied the source of the problem. Water was fed into it through flexible copper tubing, which was joined to the machine with a flare nut. It was now dripping from the flare fitting. Ann reached around and turned the nut to tighten it. It seemed to be enough to stop the leak.

She noticed, then, that the kitchen was freezing cold, and realized there was a gap at the top of the window that let in the outside air. It looked as if the sash had sagged in such a way that the window no longer closed properly. Well, she thought, there's nothing I can do about that; that's really Janet's business. She pulled her cardigan more snugly around herself and returned to the front counter, where it was warmer.

When Janet returned from the Safeway, laden with plastic shopping bags, she found Ann waiting on a line of customers. At one table sat an elderly couple with cups of tea and a cherry turnover, which they shared. At another were what appeared to be three high-school-age girls, though it was the middle of the school day. One of the people in line was a woman Janet recognized from her mother's condo community. Janet often saw her walking her dog, a little Bichon Frise named Andy. She was friendly in that she often spoke with Janet, but whatever she had to say always seemed to be negative or medical or both. Just the week before she had told Janet in excruciating detail about a fellow neighbor's hemorrhoidectomy.

"Oh, Emily," Janet said. "How nice to see you here." At that moment she actually meant it.

"Oh, do you come here?" Emily asked. "I didn't even know the place existed until yesterday. Do you think they've had it health inspected? I've read about places like this, shady places that go in and don't have the proper certificates."

"Actually, I own it. It's my teahouse."

"Really? Well."

"And what brings you here? Are you taking the train somewhere?"

"No, I have no business on the train. I merely came to inspect the place."

"Janet," Ann called to her.

"Oh, I'm sorry, I should introduce you," Janet said. "This is my neighbor Emily, Emily Reaper."

"How do you do," Emily said, to no one in particular.

"No, I mean, Janet, have you brought the things from the market? Only people are asking for cream, and we haven't any."

"Oh, right," Janet said. She brought the things to Ann, who quickly dispatched the people in line. Emily sniffed at the pastries in their glass case and left without making a purchase. Janet wandered back to the kitchen. "The coffee maker has stopped leaking!" she exclaimed.

"Yes, there was a nut in back that needed tightening. But we'll need a spanner to do it properly. Do you think you have an adjustable spanner at home?"

"A spanner?" Janet asked, coming back out to the counter.

"A wrench, I guess you call it."

37

"Oh, I don't know. I'll have to look. But I can't believe you fixed it. That's simply amazing."

Ann mentally rolled her eyes.

"You know, I wish I had someone with your … practicality … to help me run the teahouse," Janet said. She noticed that Ann said nothing but seemed to pause in what she was doing.

Following the burst of after-lunch customers there was an extended lull. Ann put on more hot water, got pots of coffee ready to brew, tidied up the pastries in their case, put the cream and milk in the refrigerator. She wiped down the tables and changed the full rubbish bag. How had Janet managed to fill this enormous bin already? "Where does the rubbish go?" she asked.

"There's a dumpster around back," Janet called from wherever she had gotten to.

Ann tried the back door but found it wouldn't open.

"Oh, that door sticks, I think," Janet said, hearing Ann struggle. "I think you'll have to go around front."

Ann leaned her weight against the doorknob in the direction of the door's hinges and then gave it a yank. The door lurched open with a satisfying *shunk*. "It's all right, I seem to have managed," she called to Janet.

After Ann had finished clearing up, she and Janet found themselves seated at the uneven table, where Janet had first welcomed her the day before. She told Janet about her morning visiting Logan, about his altered appearance, about having to speak to him through a metal grate.

"It's not so much that I don't understand his new-found interest in religion, or his need to embrace it in so rigorous a way," she said. "It's just that he was so distant. So … detached. It wasn't like speaking to my son at all. Which in some ways makes it easier, perhaps. And in some ways maybe he isn't my son, any longer. Maybe our adult children are never really our children any longer, or at least the children we knew. But I have to say, it bothers me immensely. It pains me, do you know. But equally, there just doesn't seem to be anything I can do about it."

Janet was never sure what to say to people in situations like this. The typical cluck-clucking of women, the "oh, I know"s and sort of mindless commiserating, seemed so pointless and unhelpful. Of course, sometimes that's what people wanted. But then if you tried to be encouraging, if you offered some platitude like "things aren't so bad" or "everything will be all right," you risked a backlash. But the worst, probably, was when people countered one tale of woe with another, a sort of "can you top this?" of misery. Which, she realized, was what she was about to do.

"I haven't told many people about this," she started. "But in my last year of college I had a son and gave him up for adoption."

Janet paused and Ann nodded.

"You don't seem surprised," Janet said.

"Well, it's hardly a scandal, Janet. People have children out of wedlock all the time."

"His name is Joseph Furze now. When he was a young teenager he decided he wanted to get in touch with me. His mother — I mean, his adoptive mother — somehow got my information. I got a phone call one day, and it was his mother saying he wanted to speak to me. I couldn't say no. And of course I wanted to speak to him. I was curious, for one thing, but of course you never stop thinking about your child."

"That must have been ...," Ann started to say.

"Well, I felt like my life was upending. I mean, Henry and I didn't have any children, and by that time I was beginning to realize we weren't going to. People — you know, relatives and friends — were beginning to make comments or ask sideways questions. People seem to act as if couples who don't have children are to be pitied. Or they'll say something backhanded, like how they don't think childless couples are selfish. I mean, truly. Why would they be? How is not having children selfish? I think it's selfish when people have children and then give every indication they don't actually want them. Of course, I'm not sure I've ever understood the instinct to have children anyway."

"How did your husband respond to all this?"

"Of course, maybe it's because I actually had a child. Maybe I didn't feel as if I fit into the childless category, because I had this child all along that people didn't know about. Oh, Henry was livid," Janet said, answering Ann's question. "Who was this interloper coming along to interrupt his life? And of course the idea not only that I had been with another man but also that I had had a son with him."

"So what happened?"

"Well, I saw him from time to time, over the years. They lived in Worcester, which is about an hour and a half west of Plymouth. I gave him birthday presents, and I gave him money from time to time. The mother seemed to resent my existence, so I really didn't have to deal with her very much. You could see some resemblance to me, and to his father, I suppose. But he really didn't look at all like what I expected. He had this thick, blond, wiry kind of hair, which no one in my family ever had, and kind of a slouched way of carrying himself. I always find when you meet someone over the phone, say, and develop a sort of mental image of them, that when you finally see them in person they never look like what you expect."

"Yes, I suppose that's true, often."

"Anyway, we had a good relationship, I think, if a little awkward at times, and I truly was pleased to be getting to know him. He decided not to go to college, when he finished school, which was a disappointment to me. But of course college isn't for everyone, and he was just an average student. But I always sensed a bit of resentment on his part, or mistrust, I guess. And then he just broke it off. He said it was too upsetting to see me, and he didn't want to see me any longer. I sent him a birthday card for several years. And then one year my card came back as undeliverable, and that was it. I lost touch with him. I sometimes wish I had never been in touch with him.

"Anyway, all this I guess is to say that I can understand how you feel about Logan. About being estranged from him and not knowing what to do about it."

"Yes," Ann said.

Janet sat quietly. It was a relief to have told someone about Joseph. Relief wasn't quite the right word, she thought. It felt so natural talking to Ann, comfortable in a way it wasn't talking to other people, even though she could have an easy conversation with pretty much anyone. She felt a kinship with Ann that she felt with so few people.

Ann was surprised to find she felt no urge to go tidy up in the kitchen but rather preferred to simply sit quietly with Janet. She didn't usually like to hear about other people's problems, stories from their past or things that were upsetting them. For one thing, there was never anything to say. But she didn't mind at all listening to Janet. It was nice to feel a connection, something she hadn't really felt with anyone since Lionel died.

"When do you head back to St. Andrews, again?"

"The plan was to go back next Tuesday. I was thinking I would see a little of Philadelphia. But I also sort of assumed I'd be seeing more of Logan. But I can easily change the ticket to go back sooner."

"Oh, no, I was thinking just the opposite. I was hoping you might want to stay longer."

5

Janet and Ann had already fallen into a routine with the teahouse. Janet continued to make special desserts, lemon squares and fudge brownies and rainbow cookies, while Ann took on the task of making sure there were enough other supplies, pastries and tea and coffee, cream and sugar and cinnamon sticks, napkins and coffee filters and cleaning supplies.

"Are you sure this is what you want to be doing on your vacation?" Janet asked, though only half-heartedly, as she hoped the answer was yes.

"Well, what else am I going to do? I'm enjoying the activity. And the company, for that matter."

Already they had begun to recognize regular customers. The first of these was a young couple they christened the Mochas. They must have been in early middle age, but as they were a good twenty years younger than Janet, they seemed young to her. They came in every day after the morning rush and sat by a window, talking quietly. They were freelance writers, whatever that meant, and had no

43

children but a pair of cats. The husband sat in one of the warped wooden chairs and tap-tapped as he rocked against the short leg. The wife had family in New Hampshire; a fellow New Englander. Janet found she had a knack for drawing people out, for learning about them without seeming to pry. She had no idea what mocha was when they first asked for it. They explained that it was a combination of espresso, steamed milk, and chocolate syrup, but it turned out it wasn't as straightforward as that. Simply adding chocolate syrup or powdered cocoa to the espresso resulted in something that was rather less than drinkable. Janet and Ann had spent several evenings experimenting till they came up with a combination of baking chocolate, Dutch cocoa, vanilla, and caster sugar that seemed to do the trick — and, according to the Mochas, was better than what they were accustomed to at Starbucks, that ubiquitous symbol of suburbia. Janet took an entrepreneurial pride in this accomplishment.

She had trouble with the countertop espresso maker, however, which she had picked up at the local kitchen-gadget store. It became Ann's job to make the espresso, though it was impossible for her to keep up with the demand for espresso drinks. Janet would have thought people would understand that a place that billed itself a teahouse would serve tea, not a multitude of types of coffee. But she supposed she would have to serve whatever people asked for, as much as she could.

"The thing is, what am I going to do when you go back to Scotland next week?" They had just closed for the day and were putting things away for the night, cleaning up and turning off machines and emptying the cash drawer, which was wonderfully full of bills, not that there was anything much in the way of actual profits yet. Janet dropped herself into a chair at the uneven table, where she sat whenever there was a lull in customers.

"Well, truly, you can't run the place on your own," Ann agreed. She had extended her stay for another week, and while she was enjoying visiting Janet, and didn't have any immediate desire to get back to St. Andrews, she couldn't afford to change her flight yet again.

"I think I'll need to hire someone," Janet said. "Except that I don't know anything about that."

"Well, surely there are books you can read. Or pamphlets from the government that tell you about pay rates and taxes and what-not."

"But I wouldn't even know how to go about finding the right person. Although I do think I'm a good judge of character. I could always tell almost immediately which of my students were going to be good students, and which of them were going to go on to be successful, for that matter. But hiring someone to work for me, that's a whole other story."

A train announced itself to the evening darkness with a screeching of metal wheels and a heaving roll to a stop. Trains came and went pretty much on the hour throughout the day and well into the night. Janet was growing accustomed to the clang of the crossing signal, the rumble of the approaching cars, the releasing hiss of the brakes. There was also the gentle *ho-oot hoot* of the horn as the train crossed Station Lane, the road that ran past the teahouse: before rolling up to the station on the way from Philadelphia, after leaving on the way back.

There was a sudden knock on the front door, and a strange face pressed up against the glass. It appeared to be a girl, or maybe a young woman.

"I'm sorry, dear, we're closed for the day," Ann called to her.

"Oh, maybe she needs something," Janet said. She got up from her chair and went to unlock the door. The little brass bell tinkled as she opened the teahouse to the person outside. "Can I help with something?" she asked.

"My car is dead, and so is my cellphone," the person said cheerfully, in an accent that sounded like it could be Spanish. "And I was wondering if I could use your phone."

"Oh, certainly, by all means, come in."

The person's stepping into the light of the teahouse revealed her to be a young woman with brown skin, a prominent high forehead, and a smile, however unlikely under the circumstances, that quickened all her features. She had dark, kinked hair that she wore tight to her scalp and pulled back in a bunchy ponytail. Janet's first thought was that she was black, though she had a rather pointed nose, so maybe she was Hispanic and dark-skinned, or of some sort of combined ancestry.

"I'm sorry about your car," Janet said. She led the woman around the counter to where the phone was. She must have been in her early twenties. Actually, she looked sixteen, but to Janet everyone under thirty looked sixteen, so she was guessing early twenties. Like her smile, everything about her exuded warmth and energy.

"Do you have someone to drive you? I'd be happy to give you a ride myself, if it's not far."

"No, that's OK. My boyfriend can come pick me up."

Janet stood awkwardly and pretended not to listen while the woman called her boyfriend. Ann busied herself with straightening up.

"... No, it won't start. ... I'm at the train station. ... No, I'm using the phone in the café. ... Yes, there is. ... Well, there is now. ... No, I'm OK waiting here."

"I called my boyfriend," she said after she had hung up. "He should be here in about ten minutes."

The three women smiled at one another.

After a pause, Ann said, "Do you know what's wrong with your car, then?"

"It wouldn't start. When I turned the key, it would not do anything at all."

Janet and Ann both nodded as if this explanation were meaningful.

"Will your boyfriend know how to fix it?" Janet asked.

"Maybe. No, actually, I don't think so. I'm not going to worry about it for tonight. I will come back tomorrow when it's light, and try to figure it out then." The young woman seemed tired, suddenly. She seemed almost a girl.

"You look like you've had a long day," Janet said. "Can I offer you something to eat or drink? It would only take a minute to heat up some water for tea."

The girl shook her head in response. "I've just had a really bad day. I had a job interview in Philly."

"How did it go?"

"I didn't get it." She seemed deflated for a moment, and then she smiled her kinetic smile, and then in another moment she looked newly dejected.

Janet wanted to say that she was sorry, but it seemed trite. Finally, she said, "I'm Janet, by the way. And this is Ann." Ann smiled hello.

"I'm Paula."

"Now where are you from originally? Your accent sounds Spanish to me."

"I'm from Brasil. From Rio. But I have spoken English for a long time."

"I've always wanted to go to Rio de Janeiro," Ann said. "It looks so lovely."

Paula smiled. "Some of it is nice, and some of it not so much."

"And then what brought you here?" Janet asked.

47

"After I finished college I got a job at Globanaut?"

"Oh, they have an office right near here, don't they? They're computers or something."

"Yes, it's their headquarters. I worked at their office in Rio for about a year, and they had a program to let certain employees come to the United States. So I came to work here."

"That sounds like it would be very interesting, to go work in another country," Ann said. "But no, you said you're looking for work."

"Well, I worked there for about six months, and they helped me get an apartment and everything. Then they had a big layoff, and I was one of them."

"Oh, that's just terrible," Janet said. "Have you been out of work for a long time now?"

"It has been about two months."

"Now what about your work visa?" Ann asked. "Won't you be out of status?"

"I was out of status as soon as I was laid off. That's why I need to find a job. And it has to be the kind of job I went to college for."

"What kind of work is it that you do?" Janet asked.

"I was a communications specialist. My degree is in social communication." Paula glanced around the room and smiled. "In Rio, when I was in college, I was a barista at the cyber café."

Janet couldn't imagine what it would be like moving to another country and then losing your job. She actually couldn't imagine what it would be like losing your job, period, since she fortunately had never faced the threat of a layoff in all her years as a teacher. But now she heard of so many people being laid off and not being able to find work. It was ever since the economy had tanked, more than a year ago now, first the real-estate market and then all the banks. Or had it been the other way around? She had tried following it in the news, in articles in *Time* magazine, but she always discovered about halfway through that she was just reading words and not really absorbing the details. It seemed enormously complex, and all the experts, the policymakers and the bankers themselves, seemed to feign shock, or maybe they were genuinely surprised. But of course people had been saying it was too complex for years, or there weren't enough regulations, or the right kind. And then every normal person with normal common sense could see it was a house of cards, people charging tens of thousands of dollars on their credit cards that they couldn't pay off, and buying these enormous houses at horribly inflated prices, unable even to afford to furnish them, and having no use for even half the rooms. And then their adjustable-rate mortgages adjusted on them, and then the market crashed, and they had no retirement savings and owed more on their houses than they were worth. They seemed so shocked. Not to sound insensitive, Janet thought, but didn't they know what an adjustable-rate mortgage was? The rate changed; that was the whole idea.

The thing was, you heard about all this on the news, about people put out of work and losing their homes. And there they were on the television screen, weeping and telling their truly sad stories. But she couldn't think of anyone she actually knew who had been affected, who had lost their job or their house or all their retirement savings. Friends of friends, whom she scarcely kept up with, yes. But no one she actually knew. And the people around her still drove their luxury cars or hulking S.U.V.'s, and still ate at overpriced restaurants, and still shopped at the mall. She never saw anyone at the Safeway using food stamps, even though more people were supposed to be using them than ever. But they used a card now, she had heard, and not stamps, not actual pieces of paper; so maybe people were using them and she didn't realize it. Maybe the people in their luxury cars and fancy restaurants and large suburban homes were still all living above their means. Maybe it was still all a house of cards.

And then here was the evidence right in front of her, this beautiful, energetic young woman, full of enthusiasm and ambition, given a promise of a new life in a new country and now unable to find a job through no fault of her own.

"Did you say you had worked at a café?" Ann asked. She glanced at Janet.

"Yes, the whole time I was in college. I became the store manager."

"Janet," Ann said meaningfully. "Paula, is it? Paula has managed a café."

"I'm sure you'll find work soon," Janet said. And then her mind went in a new direction. "Oh, was it like a teahouse? Because I'm hoping to hire someone to help me run the teahouse."

The door swung open, and a young man stepped in. "There you are," he said to Paula.

**

Paula gazed out the passenger-side window as her boyfriend pulled out of the parking lot. Her own car, parked in the corner of the lot, receded from view. The aging Toyota looked lonely in the pallid, yellow glow of the overhead lights, and derelict. Nothing about its appearance had changed, of course, but now that it wouldn't start it looked sickly, somehow. It occurred to her that this was the first time Ash had had to pick her up, had had to come to her rescue. She felt a strangeness between them, and she realized, with a twinge of unease, that it was also the first time since she had met him that Ash felt a bit like a stranger.

She couldn't believe, sometimes, that she was going out with a boy named Ashford. Ashford E. Billington. The Fourth. Thankfully, everybody called him Ash. Or maybe Ash was actually worse than Ashford, but in any case that was his name. She also couldn't believe how quickly they had met and started seeing each other and actually talking about a life together, a future. It wasn't anything she had done before, rushing into a relationship. Was it because she was eight thousand kilometers from home, in a strange place and all alone? Was Ash just filling some temporary need? No, she didn't think so. Yes, she felt a certain amount of loneliness. But everybody did, at least sometimes. And she felt excited to be living in America, to be getting her own apartment, to be starting her career, not that it had lasted very long. But she was sure she would find a new job soon. She had always thought of herself as an optimist.

She had met Ash at Globanaut. He worked in the media department, making marketing videos. He just started talking to her in the cafeteria one day, the week after she started. He was flirting with her, she was sure, or at least interested in her in the way other guys who flirted with her were. But he seemed so sincere in the way he talked to her, or even naïve, as if he didn't realize he was flirting. And he had that confidence that people with money have, without the haughtiness that always seems to go with it. They discovered they both had an interest in music. He seemed to know where all the cool places were in Philly, brewpubs that had just opened and bands that no one had ever heard of but that were really good and were in town for only one night. He still lived at home with his parents, which was unfortunate. But Globanaut had already set her up in her apartment, in a comfortable if rather boring complex, so they escaped there. He spent the night there after only their second date, though they didn't have sex. She had been exhausted from a long week of work and had fallen asleep on the couch; he curled up next to her on the floor. He got a stern lecture from his parents for staying out all night without telling them he wouldn't be home. Ash's parents. They were everything he was not, and not in a good way.

That was, what, only six months ago? But it didn't feel as if things were moving too quickly, only that they were moving naturally. They spent all their free time together, and now Ash was staying at her place as often as not. And as uncertain as the future might be, she felt more certainty about it than she had at any other time in her life. But it gnawed at her, this idea that she was turning to Ash out of some emotional need. That it might somehow make their relationship less valid, or less stable in the long term.

The women in the train-station café had said something about wanting to hire someone to help run it. What had they called it? A teahouse. She had been noncommittal, but she told them she'd consider it. Ash had seemed not to be paying attention to the conversation. Did she want to work at a teahouse? For one thing, she didn't know how it would affect her work visa. But she needed to earn an income. She had been so hopeful about the job she interviewed for in Philly. She had run out her cell-phone battery telling Ash about her failed interview on the train ride home.

"Hey, Parchy," Ash said. "Watcha thinkin'?"

Ash was big on nicknames. He called her "Parchy" for her last name, Pereira. It meant "pear tree" in Portuguese, and "Parchy" was a reference to "a partridge in a pear tree." That was typical Ash.

"I'm thinking I might have a new job," she said.

6

Janet sat at the uneven table and sorted piles of paper: receipts, bills, unopened letters, torn-open envelopes. She often found herself placing things in piles, meaning to get to them later. There was a pile for bills, a pile for junk mail, a pile of notes to herself of things she needed to do or people she needed to call. But she was forever mixing up the piles, or misplacing them, or losing an important bill among the detritus of catalogs and coupon mailers and solicitations from the local chamber of commerce. And then when she finally sat down to sort them all out, it just seemed too overwhelming, and she ended up mostly shifting papers from one pile to another, without actually achieving anything. She had heard there was a list you could get on — or was it a list you got off? — to stop getting junk mail. There must be a way to find out how to get on or off the list. This morning she had switched a load of laundry from the washer to the dryer, only to discover she had washed her cellphone. Not that she had anyone she wanted to call, necessarily, or anyone who wanted to call her. But she liked having a cellphone in case of emergencies, in case her car broke down or her mother's nursing home had to reach her. She had tried the still-dripping phone, just in case, but no, not surprisingly, it didn't work. It was wonderfully clean, though. And it had given Ann a good laugh.

It was Saturday, a good day for going through things and catching up. She had planned to be closed on Sundays anyway, but she was extending that to Saturdays, as well, after she and Ann found that not enough people took the train on Saturdays. In any case, it gave her two days off. Which I desperately need, she thought. What was I thinking, thinking I could run the place six days a week?

She had dropped Ann at the airport that morning. She was truly sad to see her go and had felt surprisingly weepy when they hugged goodbye. They had done so much catching up over the past two weeks. Well, catching up isn't quite the term for it, she thought, because they hadn't even known about each other for forty-four years. They had agreed they would see each other again soon, and at least on Janet's part she truly meant it, but it wasn't much more than something to say. Ann could come and go as she pleased, now that she was on her own, but it was expensive to fly all the way from Scotland. And Janet surely couldn't go to Ann, not after having just opened the teahouse.

She had hoped to see that young woman, Paula, her name was, when she came with her boyfriend to pick up her car. But they must have come for it while she was dropping off Ann, because the car was gone by the time she got back, and there had been no sign of them. She was a little skeptical of the boyfriend, who seemed so WASPy and spoiled and *pale*, for God's sake. He certainly didn't seem a likely candidate for a beautiful young Brazilian girl. On the other hand he seemed to wear his designer clothes lightly — she couldn't tell one designer from another, but clearly they had been designer clothes — as if they were merely the mantel he had been given and not the one he would have chosen for himself. And he and Paula did seem to be so in tune with each other, solicitous and tactile and happy to be in each other's presence, the way people newly in love often were. In any case, she wanted to speak to Paula further about working at the teahouse. Paula had seemed hesitant, or at least ambiguous, though that was often the case with young people, and you couldn't be sure what their inclinations actually were. She certainly hoped Paula would decide to take the job, because she needed help desperately, now that Ann was gone, and she couldn't even think about what running the teahouse would be like now. And if Paula didn't work out, she'd have to figure out how to advertise for the job and interview candidates and then decide on one to hire. Surely there would be a lot of paperwork, to run the classified ad in the newspaper and for tax purposes, and there must be legal and insurance implications, as well. Would she have to offer some kind of health insurance? And then there was the fact that Paula wasn't actually a U.S. citizen. She wondered if she'd be able to pay Paula under the table till they figured out the work-visa confusion.

She wandered back to the kitchen to make herself a cup of tea. The sun had dipped behind the tops of the bare brown trees, and through the window by the back door she could watch the gathering gloom. She gazed out absent-mindedly while her tea steeped. She had been careful to buy only high-quality loose teas for the teahouse, and she hoped eventually to be able to offer actual pots of brewed teas, as opposed to individual cups, to customers who ate in. But for herself it was easier just to use a teabag. She could just make out Dr. Grapnel's house, in the ebbing light, and it was a few moments before she became aware there was movement on his front porch, a shape gliding through the darkness and then a door silently opening and closing. It wasn't the set of double front doors in the middle of the porch, but a side door she hadn't noticed before, at the edge of the facade. It threw off the symmetry of the house, and she wondered if perhaps it weren't original but had been added later. After a moment the window at the gable end of the house, high near the roof's peak in what must be a third-floor attic, was illuminated from within. Oh, I see, Janet thought, the third floor must be an apartment and the side door the way in. She thought she had often seen more than one car in Dr. Grapnel's driveway, and had wondered about it. He never mentioned a third-floor tenant, when she first leased the teahouse, but then why would he?

She carried her tea back to her piles of paper. She hadn't switched on the front lights, and the teahouse was illuminated only by the fluorescent tubes in the kitchen. The dimness, the blanched, brittle quality of the light, gave her a vague feeling of sadness. Through the darkened windows at the end of the teahouse she could see a red Novembering sky above train tracks that disappeared to the west. White, widening contrails mirrored the tracks and receded to an imagined vanishing point. The contrails made her think of Henry.

There was a noise outside, almost-silent footsteps that snapped her to attention. The footsteps gave the impression of coming from the parking lot — a shape passed below one window, another window — and then rounding the teahouse. Suddenly there was a face in the glass of the front door, almost spectral in the pale glow of the kitchen light. Janet felt a quickening of heart and breath at the same time she told herself it was simply an old man, probably perfectly harmless, standing in her doorway. She was about to cross the room to the door, when the man pulled the door open. The bell rang out.

"Oh!" Janet exclaimed, placing a hand to her chest. "Oh! I didn't realize I had left the door unlocked."

"I'm sorry," the man said, smiling shyly. "I didn't mean to frighten you."

Now that he was inside the teahouse Janet could see he was much younger than she had at first perceived, perhaps only thirty. He wore horizontal black glasses and a faded blue tee shirt, despite the chilly weather. "It's all right," she said. "You gave me a start, is all."

"I thought the lights looked awfully dim, but then I saw someone inside and I figured you must be open. Also, the sign on the door says Open. But apparently not."

"We're closed on the weekends. I was just here taking care of some paperwork." Janet glanced at the sign, the Closed side of which faced her, and sighed. "I'm always doing that, turning it around so that when Closed faces me, I think it's facing out. Anyway, can I help with something?"

"No, not at all, I'll leave you to it. It's just that I live across the way, and I've been meaning to check the place out since you opened, and this is the first chance I've had."

"When you say 'across the way,' do you mean at Dr. Grapnel's?"

"At Charles' house, yes."

"So you're the man in the attic."

"Yes, I suppose I am. Ben Shriver."

"Janet Charbray. I only just realized Dr. Grapnel had a tenant. Do you call him Charles?"

"Well, we've known each other for a while now. I didn't call him Charles till he told me that's what Proust calls him, which of course was his way of telling me to call him by his first name. No, I was a student of his at G&B. I kind of lost touch with him after I graduated, but when I finally got around to graduate school we crossed paths again. I needed an apartment, and he had one on his third floor, and it all worked out."

"So you're a graduate student?"

"Yes, at Maximus?"

"Now what do you study there?"

"Native American studies?"

"Oh, now that sounds interesting. And you say you knew Charles when he was at Grier & Buchanan?" She wanted to ask if he knew the story of what had happened, of why he had retired so early.

"Yes." He could tell she wanted more details. She must have heard about the scandal, he thought, at least enough to know something had happened. He wanted to tell her, in spite of himself; he always wanted to talk about Charles; but he said no more.

Janet sensed that Ben had shut down, that the conversation was as good as over. He's discreet, she thought. Or shy. "Did you say 'Proust'?" she asked.

"Charles' cat."

"Oh, I didn't realize he had one."

They stood facing each other, silent. He *is* shy, Janet thought. I'm never at a loss for words, except with shy people.

"So you're only open during the week?"

Well, he's trying, she thought. "That's right."

"There's no listing. On the door, I mean, there's no listing of your hours."

"Oh, I haven't gotten around to that yet. I don't even have a real sign, yet, for the teahouse. I had planned to do that before I opened, and then there were so many other details to see to, and I wasn't even sure where to get a sign made. And then I realized that anyway I hadn't even thought of what to call the place." She had settled for a white sandwich sign — an A-frame sidewalk sign, the Staples store had called it — with changeable black letters that spelled out TEAHOUSE.

"Believe it or not, I did some sign painting when I was working my way through college," Ben said. "I'd be happy to make a sign for you, if you'd like."

"Really? Oh, that would be wonderful. It's definitely something I need. I mean, truly, the place needs a real sign. Oh, that would just perfect. Well, now, where would we put it?"

She bustled Ben out the door and under the broad-hanging eaves. They decided the easiest option would be to hang the sign from the rafters on two short lengths of chain. They found a spot that was out of the way enough that people wouldn't walk into it but exposed enough that they'd be able to see it from both the train platform and the parking lot. Ben was relieved that Janet had settled on the hanging-sign idea. He hadn't considered, when he made the offer, that after painting the sign he'd also have to install it. He didn't exactly relish the idea of having to dig holes, pour concrete footings, set posts — but wait, no, she had already decided on a hanging sign. It was just a matter of setting a couple of eye bolts.

"What would you charge, though, to paint a sign?" Janet asked.

"No, I won't charge you for it. We're neighbors, now. If you can just cover the cost of the materials, I won't charge you to paint it."

"Oh, now, that would be lovely. Thank you so much. I mean, truly, you can't imagine how much it's costing me to get the place up and running, and anywhere I can save at this point is probably a good idea. Do you know, just the other day my coffee maker started leaking, and I didn't know what it was going to cost to have it fixed. But then Ann was able to — Ann is my friend, she was helping me with the teahouse, but she had to go back to St. Andrews — anyway, Ann was able to fix it, and I was so grateful." She stopped, realizing that Ben's eyes were glazing.

"What would you like me to paint on the sign?" he asked.

"You're right, I guess we're getting ahead of ourselves. I still don't know what to call it."

Ben stepped back and regarded the station building. He glanced down the tracks, at the paired cordons of steel, silver in the almost-darkness. "How about 'The Teahouse by the Tracks'?" he said.

"Yes," Janet said, nodding. "That's it, isn't it? The Teahouse by the Tracks."

7

I wonder what I've got myself into, Ben thought. While it was nice to be able to do someone a favor, making a sign would hardly be trivial: going out and buying the lumber and the hardware and the paint; putting the thing together, sawing and gluing and bracing and sanding; and then painting it, first a coat of primer, then the background, white, probably, and finally the lettering, black, he thought best, something simple and easy to read. But he should probably add an artistic element, something to give a feel for the place. Maybe a teacup, maybe in something like the shade of green inside the teahouse. It was going to be a lot of work, and time-consuming. But there's no turning back now.

He'd also have to find a way to manage it in his tiny third-floor apartment. Lugging the stuff up two flights of stairs would be a hassle, though none of it would be too heavy or unwieldy. And he'd have to be quiet about the sawing and drilling and sanding; Charles probably wouldn't be wild about his turning the apartment into a temporary workshop. He thought he already had most of the tools he needed: T-square, handsaw, F-clamp, power drill, orbital sander. He'd have to pick up a few good ox-hair brushes.

He had crossed the parking lot and the expanse of Charles' damp front lawn, which had grown long and tufted since its last cutting in mid-October. He stepped onto the front porch and fitted the key in the knob lock. There was no deadbolt, and he was reminded anew that it would be easy for someone to break in; a good whack with a hammer or even a firm kick, for someone strong enough, and the knob would fall to pieces, allowing the door to swing freely. Not that he had much of anything worth stealing. And he wasn't concerned for his safety, not out here in the suburbs. The apartment in Charles' house was the first place he had ever really felt at home in, including the house where he grew up.

The apartment wasn't actually that small, at least in terms of square footage, not for just one person. But it was meant to be an attic, and the steeply pitched roof cut into all of the four rooms, reducing the usable space by almost half. At the top of the stairs was a small vestibule, which really was wasted space, though it would serve as the sign-making workshop. Off the vestibule, through four equally spaced doors, were a kitchen, living room, bedroom, and bath, all about the same size, which meant a largish kitchen and an enormous bath but a rather small living room and bedroom. There was no dearth of what a realtor would play up as charm, though, broad-planked pine floors and generous wood trim and tall Victorian windows. The attic had been converted to living quarters long enough ago that the walls were of plaster. But Charles had rerouted the stairs, closing off the original stairs in the middle of the house and installing a new stairway along an outer wall, so that the third floor was directly accessible from the outside.

It was strange, he thought, how he managed to be committal with the small things, with the inconsequential areas of his life, and yet seemed unable to summon the certainty to finish his education or get a real job or sustain long-term relationships. He could promise to build a sign — and he would finish the job; he wouldn't have offered if he didn't intend to do it. But the more important decisions, the choices that would affect his life in the long term, were somehow beyond his grasp. He sensed that Janet was the sort of person who often asked favors, or somehow got people to do favors for her without her even asking. It occurred to him that making a sign for the teahouse could become only the first in a never-ending stream of favors requested, or hinted at, or at least expected, that his life could become unpleasantly tied to the teahouse, to this woman he had just met. She was right next door, after all, always present, inescapable. The sign he would hang could well be around his own neck.

He would enjoy making the sign, though. He hadn't done much in the way of manual work for years now. He had worked a number of odd jobs while he was at G&B, as a sign painter, a carpenter's helper, a maintenance man at a condo community. He had hated most of them, the mindlessness of the work, and the dirtiness of it, and the way so many customers treated working people as if they were dimwitted. And he never had the knack for manual labor, for things like electrical work or plumbing or car repair. He had grown up in a family of working people to which such things apparently came naturally, and he had always felt inadequate in his persistent inability to deftly set a nail or solder a pipe joint or run a bead of caulk. He approached such work the way a retiree approaches a computer, with a resigned certainty, born of experience, that something, somewhere in the process, will go irreversibly wrong.

But the sign painting he had always liked. A sign was a self-contained creation with a start and a finish, with neat boundaries and a clear purpose, and it ceded a sense of satisfaction, of completion, when the final brush strokes were applied. It said something; it communicated with the world. Over the years he had acquired a small collection of good-quality tools, handsaws and nail sets, bevel squares and wood planes, which he would use to fashion the sign for the teahouse.

He crossed the kitchen and opened the half-door of a small closet that had been squeezed into the eaves and where he stored his tools. He found it satisfying, every so often, to survey them. They were a tangible reminder of where he had been and what he had done, the meager artifacts of his life, validation through accumulation. He had few other personal belongings: an old bureau and nightstand; a kitchen table with mismatched chairs; a coffee table fashioned from one-half of a dining-room table turned sideways on its pedestal legs and cut down to sofa height; a hastily constructed bookshelf crammed with a professional student's collection of textbooks. It was a small passel of possessions, to be sure, but it seemed bountiful compared with his previous apartment, the first place he had lived after moving out of his mother's house. At that apartment he had slept for weeks on a bare wood floor, till his grandmother gave him a twin mattress and box spring. It was the bed his father had slept in as a boy. He hadn't spoken to his grandmother in years, and it had been awkward going to her house to collect the mattress, in his father's borrowed pickup.

His relationship with his family had always been awkward. His parents had divorced, with acrimony, when he was a young teenager. He had two older brothers and a younger sister, none of whom he felt at all close to or even particularly related to. His siblings remained friendly with his parents and with one another, though they had long since moved away. His mother once told him that she and his father had planned to have only three children. At first he thought she was telling him that his sister had been a mistake. But he quickly realized that what she meant was that after two boys they had wanted a girl, that after he was born they had kept trying till they got one. So he had been intended to be the girl, the last child. Which made him, what, expendable? An extra son, in any case.

Why was he mired in the past so? *Ruminant* was the word he word he kept thinking of, lately. Gnawing again that which he had already ingested. Maybe the past is simply more interesting, he thought, likewise the future, for that matter. The present is just brushing your teeth and cleaning the tub and buying turnips; it was a line from a poem or something, "buying turnips." It's the past and the future that occupy us, that captivate us, the future because it's unknown, the past because it's unknowable. The future is possibility; the past is impossible — to understand, to come to terms with, to leave behind.

If he had a present, beyond his graduate-school work, it was Charles. Charles had been his first professor in college, the first person in his life, really, to recognize in him a potential — for what? It didn't matter for what; just a potential. And then to renew their friendship, years later, and now to be living upstairs from him: it was like finding the solution to a problem you didn't know you had, like first seeing Oz and realizing, all at once, that Kansas had been black and white.

He had been pleased, too, at least initially, to find a place practically on the banks of the Wissahickon Creek, which flowed about twenty-five miles from its headwaters till it joined the Schuylkill River in Philadelphia. The focus of his graduate work was Native American studies: he had a particular interest in the Lenape tribe, who had lived throughout what became southeastern Pennsylvania and New Jersey, on the banks of the Delaware and Schuylkill rivers. He had hoped that easy access to the Wissahickon would afford the opportunity to uncover Lenape artifacts. But he soon learned that while the area now occupied by Lower Slaughter had certainly been Lenape hunting ground, no Lenape settlements had ever been found this far north on the Wissahickon, and other than the odd arrowhead no local trace of the Lenape remained.

He wondered if Charles, too, were possessed by the past, inwardly still embroiled in the scandal that had cost him his job at G&B. He had never discussed it with him, never heard the story from Charles' point of view. It had happened after he graduated, and he wasn't even aware of it till sometime after the fact. He had heard there was some controversy with a professor and had wondered vaguely if it were someone he knew. He was shocked to learn it was Charles, even more so when he found out Charles had resigned over the affair. Where had his students been, and his colleagues? He had been so well-liked on campus, or seemingly so. But then Charles had always been aloof, not someone with whom students formed lasting attachments, with whom fellow professors developed close friendships. His urbanity, his sharp wit, kept people at arm's length. Would he have come to Charles' defense, had he been there?

He shut the half-door of the kitchen closet and turned his gaze out the curtainless window, which was open a crack, even though it was early November; the heat from Charles' house rose to the third floor, leaving his apartment overly warm. He could see the old train station, which was now a teahouse, beyond Charles' lawn and the station parking lot. The building was dark now; Janet must have left for the evening. He had noticed that with the window open he could hear the tinkling of the bell, as customers came and went, but now it was silent. The parking lot was illuminated by a few tepid sodium-vapor lamps. He found the sickly salmon glow of streetlights depressing, though from this vantage point they were fairly innocuous, and he had come to find their constant presence almost comforting. The sky had grown overcast with clouds, which were starting to mist, and in the cast of the lights the parking lot appeared to be rolling with fog. There was a thin cloud of fog above the teahouse, as well. It appeared to be coming from the window of what must be the kitchen.

Oh my God, he thought, the building's on fire. The teahouse is on fire.

8

It took a good fifteen minutes for the fire trucks to arrive. Ben called the local fire company directly, rather than dialing 911, and the phone rang a dozen times before the dispatcher picked up. Apparently they already had an ambulance out on call, and volunteer staff was in short supply. Fire emergencies were announced by an outdoor siren, which ran through repeated cycles, despite that the firefighters surely were alerted to calls through a myriad of electronic means. You could aurally follow a call through the process: first the long cycles of the outdoor siren; then the rush of neighborhood pickups as they raced to the station; then the wail of the fire-truck sirens, shorter and shriller, and the grunt of their diesel engines, punctuated by the throaty, sputtering blast of the air horn as the truck crossed an intersection; and, finally, siren and engine receding into the night. Why did fires always happen at night?

Ben had watched from the window for what seemed like several minutes, uncertain what to do, as smoke billowed from the teahouse window. The smoke was white, almost pellucid, and he saw no flames: a small fire, then, probably. But surely it could spread quickly, in such an old building. He found himself rushing down the stairs, out across the lawn, and up the three wooden steps to the back door of the teahouse. He couldn't make out anything through the glass of the door. He touched the brass knob tentatively, but it wasn't hot, and, surprisingly, it turned in his grasp. The door wouldn't budge, though; of course it would be locked. Should he break the glass? He leaned his shoulder into the stile to the right of the pane. *Shunk*: the door popped open. It hadn't been locked after all.

The teahouse was thick with smoke, up around the ceiling, more smoke than he would have imagined, and it surged out the now-open door. It had a smell like burned toast and smoldering plastic. There was just enough light from the parking lot to let him find his way into the kitchen. And there it was: a commercial toaster oven, sitting on the floor but plugged in, presumably left on, smoke cascading from its rear like exhaust from a steam locomotive. The first thing to do was to unplug it, he thought. He had a vague idea that if he achieved this quickly and deftly enough he would be safe from burn or shock, though he was aware he had no evidence to support the notion. Yet here he was reaching forward, grasping the cord and yanking, breath held and eyes clenched. He dropped the cord, which was searing, and fled the room.

He thought he should go back in — why? to see if the oven were still burning? — but he had lost his resolve. It's not like I have a hose to put the fire out with, anyway, he thought. And then, thankfully, joyfully, he heard the approach of the engines.

Rather than congratulatory the firemen seemed irked that he had rushed into a burning building, unaided and unprotected. Mostly they seemed disappointed not to find a blazing teahouse. They brought three engines, in all, including an enormous ladder truck, which hardly seemed necessary for a one-story building and in any case had arrived ten minutes later.

The fire had remained localized to the oven. One particularly burly fireman, clad in his impervious uniform, strode into the teahouse and emerged with his arms wrapped around the still-smoking appliance, which he heaved out the door. An examination of the building revealed that a gap at the top of the kitchen window had let the smoke pour out, making it look as if the building itself were on fire. The inspection also confirmed that there were no insidious flames lurking behind the walls or in the ceiling. After that it was just a matter of writing up a report. A fireman leaned against one of the trucks and filled in a form on a thick metal clipboard. Ben was giving him a statement, explaining who owned the building and who leased it, when he realized he should be contacting both Charles and Janet. Often Charles spent Saturday night at the Philadelphia Orchestra, to which he had a weekend subscription for one, but he had left the house early, so he must have had other plans. In any case he never bothered to carry his cellphone.

Ben remembered, then, that he had Janet's home number. He had entered it in his cellphone when he agreed to make the sign for the teahouse; he was supposed to call her with an estimate of the material costs. He glanced at his left hand, which was smarting. There was a line across a portion of his palm and through the pads of his index finger and thumb from where he had grasped the electric cord. The skin wasn't quite blistered, but it had a red sheen, and it stung. It occurred to him that he had a fire extinguisher, under his kitchen sink, but he hadn't thought to use it. He dialed his phone reluctantly. How was it that he ended up having to be the one to deliver the bad news?

Janet arrived just as the first of the fire trucks was leaving. She was nearly in tears, despite Ben's reassurances that nothing had really been damaged, other than a decades-old toaster oven. She let herself in the front door, followed by Ben and the fireman with the metal clipboard, who was trying to complete his paperwork. Once she saw that the building was still intact she settled down and was surprisingly nonchalant about the whole thing.

"I must have left it on," Janet was explaining to the fireman. "I had just been talking to Ben about making a sign for the teahouse, and then I went back inside. This is Ben, here; oh, you know that, of course. He's going to make me a sign for the teahouse. Anyway, I went back inside to organize some piles of paper I had, and I got to thinking that I meant to try out the toaster oven. It was left over from the former owner, you see, and it was in the bottom of one of the closets. Well it looked like it had hardly been used. And I figured it would be just perfect for heating up pastries and things. Anyway, it was too heavy for me to lift up onto the counter, so I just dragged it out onto the floor and plugged it in, to see if it worked.

"Oh, now I remember," she continued. "I turned it on, and it seemed to work. And then I got to thinking I should put something in it, to test it out. I had a box of old scones left over from the day before, and I just put the whole box in, because I didn't think it would get hot enough to burn the cardboard. But then the phone rang, though it was just one of those automated reminders from the exterminator that they're coming next week. And I simply forgot I had left the box in the oven. Although come to think of it, the box had one of those plastic windows in the top, so I probably shouldn't have put it in anyway."

The front door swept open, and the bell rang out. In the doorway, framed in the spotlights of the one remaining fire truck, stood a white-haired man in khaki trousers and a suede sport coat.

"Hello, Charles," Ben said.

"Dr. Grapnel." Janet's voice quavered.

"What's going on here? Why are there *fire trucks?*"

"There was a small fire, Charles, but it's OK now," Ben said.

"I'm so sorry, Dr. Grapnel," Janet said. "It's all my fault."

The fireman consulted his report. "Are you the owner?"

Charles ignored him and crossed the room to Janet. "Ms. Charbray, are you *all right?*"

In response Janet began to weep.

Charles wrapped his arms around her in an engulfing embrace. "Come now, Ms. Charbray. Do you intend to douse the flames with your own *tears?*" He patted her back, then, and stepped back from her.

Janet smiled wanly at his humor. "But it could have been so much worse. The entire building could have been burned to the ground. Oh, I truly am sorry."

"The important thing is that you're *unharmed.*" Charles turned to survey the room. "But it smells absolutely *dreadful* in here, doesn't it? Surely you'll want to air the place out." He looked hopefully to the nearest window.

"I just need to finish my report," the fireman interrupted. "And there's the matter of the service fee. We usually send it to the owner."

"Yes, well, whatever you do," Charles said.

"Oh, no, Dr. Grapnel," Janet protested. "I really should take care of that."

"Now, Ms. Charbray, I won't hear of it," Charles said to her. "That's *that* settled," he announced to the room. The fireman took Charles' signature and left.

"I really am so appreciative," Janet said. "Every extra cost feels like a setback."

"Yes."

"And please do call me Janet. You make me feel like one of your students when you call me 'Ms. Charbray.'"

Charles looked at her. "Yes."

Janet waited for him to return the favor and ask her to call him Charles, but he seemed mentally to have moved on. Outside she could hear the beep-beep of the fire truck, backing up, followed by the rumble of its engine as it pulled away.

"You're right," she continued, hoping to conceal her feeling of awkwardness. "I don't know how I'm going to get rid of this smell of smoke. And the kitchen is just covered in soot."

Their small party, Charles and Janet and Ben, made its way into the kitchen. Fronds of soot reached up the back wall, behind where the toaster oven had sat on the floor, and across the ceiling. The broad panes of the kitchen window were black with it.

"Well surely you can get someone in to take care of that," Charles said.

"Oh, I really can't afford cleaning people, or whatever," Janet said.

"Well ...," Charles said, waving his hand vaguely.

Ben began to feel he was about to be asked to help out in some way, and simultaneously began to feel the tug of the door. This was exactly what he was afraid of happening, of being drawn into involvement with Janet and the teahouse, of having to manage yet another relationship not of his own choosing. Was it too soon to excuse himself, to slip out while there was this lull in the conversation, or would he be perceived as rude or unfeeling, given the circumstances? Well, it didn't matter: he would have to do it now, or the moment would pass.

"Well, then, I suppose I'll be off," Charles announced.

"Well, then ...," Ben began a beat after Charles. Damn it, he thought, now I look like an idiot.

"Are you leaving, then, too?" Charles asked, implying that one of them should stay, but not him.

Ben stood silently while he sought a tactful reply.

"No, truly, both of you go," Janet said. "There's nothing more I can do tonight in any case. I'll sort all this out tomorrow. I'm just going to lock up here, and then I'll be off myself."

"If you're certain," Charles said, already turning to go.

Charles and Ben walked to the parking lot without speaking. Charles stopped at his car, which was parked close to the building, while Ben turned to make his way across the lot and Charles' lawn.

"Good night, then," Charles said.

"Good night."

Inside the teahouse Janet was already switching off the lights. Charles turned the key of his ancient Mercedes-Benz sedan, which sputtered to life, and drove off.

9

Who are these people? Charles thought. It was a rhetorical question, of course, and one that didn't entirely make sense in the given context, but it was a thought he had frequently, and the one he had now. He meant: how did I come to be involved with this person Ms. Charbray, Janet, my tenant, who seemed so clever and creative and delightful, the few times he had met her, and yet almost willful in her repudiation of common sense; how did I come to have living in my house this young man Mr. Shriver, Ben, also my tenant, and not so young, actually, who was so thoughtful and bright and promising and yet so resolutely diffident. These were not the people he would have chosen for himself, and yet here they were.

He pulled into his driveway and gazed across his property at the now-dark teahouse. A daring, dramatic escape, he thought sarcastically of his journey from one driveway to the next. But drama wasn't something he particularly sought, these days. He had had enough of drama over the past couple of years. The fire in the teahouse, or near fire, at any rate, was reminder enough of that.

He let himself into the house. Proust was waiting for him near the door, as he almost always was, and came forward to drop onto his side, as he almost always did, with an enormous *thump*, at Charles' feet. Charles switched on the light to reveal a stretched-out cat, his back arched, waiting for his fat, gray tummy to be rubbed. "Hello, Marcel," Charles said.

It felt good to be home. He didn't know why, really, because he spent all his time at home, now, and he had only been out for the evening. In fact, lately he had begun to feel a bit closed in, or maybe simply bored with his surroundings. So it was welcome, reassuring, to feel pleased to be home, because it was a sensation that had become less familiar. He inhaled deeply. His house had a particular aroma he delighted in but couldn't quite describe. The closest he could get was a combination of wicker and old books and pipe tobacco, not that he smoked a pipe, though he had smoked cigarettes back in the mists of time, back when everyone did. But that was before he lived here, of course. He didn't recall noticing the aroma — smell? odor? *aroma* was the more appealing word — when he moved in, but by the time all his belongings were in place, there it was, a permanent fixture, apparently. He wondered if others noticed it. Well, whom had he had over to visit? Not many.

He went to the kitchen, followed expectantly by Proust, and dropped his keys on the kitchen table. He picked up the remote and turned on the portable television he had had installed high up near the ceiling. Then he went to the sideboard in the dining room to retrieve a bottle of vodka, returning to the kitchen to fix himself a drink. Normally by this time of year he would have switched to scotch, but he had been in the mood for vodka martinis since early summer. He had started buying the big bottles of Stoli, because they were cheaper, and because he went through the smaller ones so quickly, but it occurred to him that he should probably switch to a cheaper brand. He decided not to bother with vermouth. He fished a few ice cubes from the freezer. He carved a bright twist of peel from a lemon while CNN nattered in the background. When had he started habitually switching on the television? There wasn't anything he actually watched, just the occasional PBS special. And yet somehow the television always ended up on, and always tuned to CNN. He carried his drink back to the table and turned the volume down to zero. He sat and took a long drink. For that matter, when had he started drinking vodka martinis instead of gin? Proust leapt onto the table and stuck his face in Charles'.

How quickly things had developed, and how quickly, too, they had ceased developing. He never expected to find himself living in a suburb, a non-city, like Lower Slaughter, but then he had never expected to live in an indistinguishable town like Falmouth, on the banks of the Susquehanna, and teach at an undistinguished college like Grier & Buchanan. He had grown up in Baltimore and earned his degrees at the University of Maryland, though he secured a Rhodes Scholarship and spent two years at Oxford. He had ever since felt regret for having chosen Maryland, at the not entirely explained insistence of his father, but he tried to console himself with something he had been told by a professor long ago, that you could do fine academic work anywhere. It was while he was at Oxford that he came to assume he would spend the rest of his life in an international city, as he thought of it, London or New York or, in a sort of worst-case scenario, Philadelphia. He likewise assumed he would be teaching at a prestigious university. But he had finished his Ph.D. in the early 1980s, just as the nation's economy was emerging from a deep recession, and there were few good teaching jobs available. Had he been able to wait another ten years he could have slipped in behind the retirements of those professors hired to teach the burgeoning ranks of G.I.-Bill students. But as they were still firmly ensconced in their tenured strongholds, he had had to take the offer from Grier & Buchanan.

It was also in London where he had established friendships that would keep him returning regularly, for a quick visit around the holidays or to rent a flat for the summer. And it was in London where he had met Alain. Dear, sweet Alain. He didn't want to think about that now.

But he had come to truly enjoy teaching at Grier & Buchanan, even if he didn't particularly relish the idea of living in the middle of Pennsylvania, in the middle of Alabama, it might as well have been. The local residents defended Falmouth with comparisons to Lancaster, the nearest place that passed for a city, as in, "Our restaurants are just as good as Lancaster's" or, "Our theater rivals that of Lancaster." The joke, to Charles, was that people in Lancaster claimed their restaurant scene or theater or whatever was as good as Philadelphia's, where people insisted their cultural attractions were as good as New York's. So, living in Falmouth, Pa., pop. 2,466 — not counting the 1,800 Grier & Buchanan students — home of the Falmouth Goat Race, every third week in September, was the cultural equivalent of, say, residing on the Upper East Side. But he had come to care deeply for his students, for their aspirations and expectations, their career worries and financial woes, their romances and petty conflicts. He had his share of spoiled rich kids whose grades couldn't get them into the Ivy League but whose parents' money could park them at Grier & Buchanan for four years, who seemed to think their tuition fees paid for good grades as well as an education and who couldn't be bothered to come up with even the most flimsy, see-through excuses for why their papers wouldn't be handed in on time. But he also had come to know so many earnest young people for whom college was nothing less than a transformational experience, who approached literature with something like the respect and dedication he had once felt for it himself. Ben had been one of them, till he chucked it all for anthropology, surely the wrong choice for a misanthrope in the making.

And then it had all gone awry. The scandal, as people seemed to refer to it — "the ignominy" was the way he thought of it — the abandonment of his colleagues, the seeming indifference of his students. He didn't want to think about all that right now, either.

The one thing he had never liked about Grier & Buchanan was the on-campus faculty housing, little bungalows set in the woods where tenured faculty were encouraged to live, a hare-brained attempt to make a provincial, neglected college feel like some kind of distinguished academy. The house he ended up with was low and dim and damp, last updated long before avocado green gave way to harvest gold on the decorator's palette. For his first ten years there he didn't have enough of his own things to make the house feel at all like his. But even after he inherited Alain's treasured antique furniture and artwork, there was no room for more than a small fraction of it, and the place resisted personality. Most of Alain's things had remained in storage.

When it became clear he would leave Grier & Buchanan, when he had started looking for a place in Philadelphia, he stumbled across the property in Lower Slaughter quite by chance. He had taken a drive out to Chestnut Hill, at the city's farthest reaches, to see what sort of neighborhoods might be found there. He had gotten off the turnpike and

turned the wrong way — he had always been terrible with
directions — and found himself in a sprawl of suburbs. And
then, while trying to get himself turned around and going in
the right direction, he saw the realtor's sign at the end of the
driveway. It was a stunning house, really, in a deep-orange
brick like overripe persimmon, with tall, elegant windows
and high-peaked gables. It was close to the train station, but
not uncomfortably close, as it was set back across a broad lawn
and behind a century of shrubbery. And its proximity to the
station lowered the asking price; he would have just enough
of Alain's money to afford it. When he stepped through the
double front doors with the realtor, the very next day, and
saw the sweeping front stairs, the high-ceilinged drawing
room and library, the Turkish-marble fireplaces, he was as
good as decided. That the property included a large stone
barn, set some distance beyond the house, only added to its
appeal. Perhaps he didn't need to live in an international
city after all. And here he would have privacy and relative
quiet, despite the passing trains. In any case it was available
and he could move in immediately, and he needed to get
away from Grier & Buchanan as quickly as possible.

He instantly felt at home, as if this were where he had
always intended to be, and where he would stay. He reno-
vated the third floor to make a small apartment — he had to
re-route the stairs; he certainly didn't want a tenant tromp-
ing through his living space — and expanded the cramped
Victorian kitchen with a bank of windows and a cozy sitting
area, where he had the portable television mounted. It had
taken some searching to find a small television. He hadn't
bought a new one in more than ten years, and in the intervening decade they all seemed to have grown to industrial
size.

He had an abundance of time to renovate and decorate, now that he wasn't working. And he could take all of

Alain's things out of storage; there was more than enough room for his exquisite furniture and brick-a-brack, more than enough wall space for his artwork. Charles' favorite, perhaps, though a bit out of place under a Victorian roof, was an eighteenth-century Chippendale secretary desk, all doors and drawers and tiny compartments, which Alain had always referred to as his *secrétaire*. The artwork, mostly oils on canvas, he had to admit he didn't know much about. They were all originals, and by artists reputedly of repute, at least at one time, but the only one he was sure of was an elaborate collage by the American artist Addie Herder. Some of Alain's more dour pieces, including twin busts in late eighteenth-century biscuit of Louis XVI and Marie Antoinette, he left in storage. Alain had had firm ideas about decorating, most of which had been established in the first half of the twentieth century and many of which Charles rejected. One bit of Alain's advice he followed, though, was to adorn each room with a gilded mirror, which provided varying angles of line and light and which allowed visitors to catch glimpses of themselves as they rose from a sofa, say, or passed into the central hallway. For Charles the mirrors functioned more as a stand-in for Alain, his vacant visage, his proxy portrait, in every room of the house.

He had time now to write, as well, though he made little progress and soon abandoned the effort altogether. Just before he left Grier & Buchanan he had started a book on the British novelist Muriel Spark, with whom he had corresponded off and on, and who, sadly, had just died. All her books were about disconnected characters at the mercy of their omniscient narrator. What was the word he wanted? Alienated. But as part of his leaving academic life he rejected all things academic, including literary criticism. He instead tried to return to his first love, writing fiction, but found he lacked the concentration for it, and probably the talent, if he were honest with himself. Which is why he had become an English professor in the first place: if you couldn't write fiction, you could at least write about it.

He needed some source of income, though. The inheritance from Alain covered most of the purchase of the house, and his antiques and artwork would help secure his retirement. But he had nothing to live on in the meantime. The rent from the third-floor apartment would be a start, whenever he got around to leasing it, but it probably wouldn't be enough. He began to think he might want to invest in real estate; he had always felt more comfortable with tangible investments like buildings than with gaining some vague involvement in commerce through stocks, say. But it seemed easier to do something with the real estate he already had. And so he had started to convert the barn, dividing the first two floors into two townhouses, each with an upstairs and downstairs, and the hayloft above them into a tiny efficiency. He went to the bank to tap the equity in his house and hired a carpenter to oversee the conversion. They put on a new roof and fitted windows into the vacant openings in the stone walls. They put up the interior walls and ran the plumbing and electricity. But the process got bogged down, somehow, and the final bits and pieces never seemed to fall into place.

Then the train station went up for sale. It seemed to make perfect sense for him to acquire it, as it was adjacent to him and would have the effect of just about doubling his property, and he would be able to rent it out without the need for additional renovations. He envisioned it as a potter's studio, something of that nature, a quiet place for a quiet soul. The bank was reluctant to give him yet another mortgage, but he found a direct lender that was much more open-minded, and with the remainder of his savings, plus some clever financing options suggested by the helpful loan representative, was able to buy it.

In the meantime he still had needed to rent out his third floor. It was about that time his path recrossed with Ben's. He was in the Safeway buying food for Proust, cans of Flame-Grilled Chicken Liver and Savory Flaked Fish and who knows what, Paddlefish Roe in Yak Gravy, probably. There was Ben walking down the aisle toward him. They nearly passed each other without speaking; he wondered if Ben would have continued past, as in a scene by Ionesco, if he hadn't said hello. He wondered, too, as they chatted, if Ben had heard about the scandal, the ignominy. Ben gave no sign of knowing but likewise expressed no surprise to learn Charles was no longer teaching. Ben was attending a seminar at the suburban campus of Maximus University, apparently. It transpired that he was also looking for an apartment, and the cogs slid into place.

About an inch of liquid was left in Charles' glass, mostly water with a faint flavor of vodka, plus the remains of the ice cubes. He tilted back the glass and drained it. Too quickly: the water was freezing cold, and he was struck with his own peculiar version of an ice-cream headache, which didn't involve his head at all but rather centered at the top of his sternum. Fuck, he thought, angry at himself for the mistake. He leaned over the table on his elbows till the pain subsided.

So now here I am, he thought, the pain leaving his chest but still at the back of his throat, with Ben upstairs and Janet across the lawn. He wasn't quite ready to be involved with people again, two years after leaving Grier & Buchanan. He had spent the evening driving in the November darkness, trying to rid himself of an attack of anxiety. He was supposed to have been at the home of an elderly woman in Chestnut Hill, whom he had signed up to visit and read tc, through a local charity service, on Saturday evenings. But he had panicked, just as he turned down her street. It wasn't the first time he had felt nervous at the prospect of meeting someone, certainly. But he had never experienced anything like *this*. He had lectured at Oxford, for God's sake, presented to distinguished colleagues, taught classes for twenty-five years. And now he couldn't face an old woman, failing of sight, who wanted to hear the words of *Howards End* read to her on a Saturday night. He remembered, then, Forster's epigraph: "Only connect." Only connect what?

He poured himself another half-glass of vodka and added two clouded ice cubes. He shut off the kitchen light and shuffled upstairs, leaving the news to play silently behind him.

10

Janet wrote in her looping, slanted, upward-climbing hand:

Dear Ann,

You won't believe what has happened at the Teahouse. There was a fire! Fortunately, it was contained to the toaster oven, but there was such a kerfuffle, with smoke everywhere, and the fire department sending trucks out. Oh, and I thought Dr. Grapnel would have a coronary. But he was sweet, actually, or as sweet as he probably gets.

The real hero of the day was Ben, the young man who lives on Dr. Grapnel's third floor. I had just met him that very day. Well, he noticed the fire and called the firehouse, apparently, and even came over afterwards to make sure I was okay. Oh, and he's making me a sign for the Teahouse.

I'm going to go over there later today to sort things out. I expect I'll be closed for a day or two till I can get the place cleaned up. I haven't heard back from that young Brazilian girl we met. I certainly hope I do, or I don't know what I'll do.

Have you thought about what you want to do? Long-term, I mean. We didn't really talk about it, but we both sort of hinted that you could run the Teahouse with me. I don't suppose that makes any sense, since you'd have to give up your home and move to a foreign country. And you did say how much you like to travel.

I know we only just got back in touch, Ann, but I miss you so. I start each day feeling overwhelmed and think, What would Ann do? And then of course I fail to do whatever that might be. But I am trying.

Much love,
Janet

She closed the card, which she had purchased before Ann left, knowing she would write to her. On its front was a Japanese print of a cat peering around a door at a tiny spider. She had a notion that it was what Ann's cat, Gerald, had looked like, though now she thought of it Ann had said Gerald was a tabby, and the cat on the card looked more like a Siamese. She thought of something else she wanted to add, so she turned the card over and wrote on the back:

P.S. Do you remember where you got the coffee filters, the last time you got them, or which ones you got? We ran out, and the ones I got to replace them are too fine, and they don't brew properly.

She realized she was forgetting her cup of tea, which was steeping on the table beside her. She removed the spent teabag and, as she did, dripped on the back of the card, three irregular brown spots that crinkled the paper beneath them. "Oh, shit," she said. She dropped the teabag and tried to wipe off the spots with her hand, which had the effect of adding three brown tails to the three brown spots. She thought momentarily about writing a new note but, sighing with resignation, instead slipped the card into its envelope.

She would have to get an overseas stamp from the post office. First, though, she'd have to look up Ann's address. It was in a pile somewhere. Well, it was Sunday anyway, so she wouldn't worry about it till tomorrow. She wasn't in the mood to make herself breakfast; instead she would drive to the Dunkin' Donuts, which was a bit out of the way, really, for a breakfast sandwich. Should she think about offering breakfast sandwiches? No, it was supposed to be a teahouse, with scones and finger sandwiches and dainty desserts. She didn't want to sink to the lowest common — what was the word? "Lowest common" was what she meant, in any case. Denominator.

At the teahouse things still smelled of smoke. And in the light of day she could see the high ceiling was an offer-white, more gray now than the cream color it had been. She would have to think about having it repainted, but for now it was passable. She went to open a window and got an even stronger odor of smoke. She put her nose to the curtain: that was it. She would have to launder all the curtains. She noticed a film of soot on the tables and chairs.

The kitchen was even more a shambles, the walls and ceiling black with her carelessness. This she would have to take care of as soon as possible, because after all customers could see into the kitchen from the front counter. She peered out the window and spied the oven, charred and derelict where the fireman had left it. She wondered if she could get Ben to toss it in the dumpster for her. Well, she thought, time to get to work. She went to the closet for her cleaning supplies.

She had never been much of a cleaner. In part it was because she had worked full-time. But even with Henry away all the time, and herself alone in the house in the evenings and on weekends, she never seemed to get around to cleaning. She had her summers off, it was true, and she always imagined she would do more thorough cleaning during the summer months, taking down the curtains and washing the windows and clearing out closets. But by that time of year the house had grown so cluttered, and the summer humidity was so oppressive, that the best she could manage was shifting around her piles of things, moving them from one room to the next, or slipping them into bureau drawers and out of sight. Eventually the drawers grew so heavy they became difficult to open and close, or worse, in the case of the cheaper furniture, they fell off their runners, and she was forced to empty them.

She was determined to keep the teahouse clean, though. It's one thing to have a mess in your own kitchen, she thought, to simply rinse out a tea-stained cup and sweep leftover crumbs off the table and onto the floor. But she was repulsed by other people's messes, and particularly public messes such as left-behind napkins or spilled sugar or, perhaps most disgusting, used Kleenex. Her sixth-grade students had been decidedly less than conscientious with their own personal hygiene, and it was with unfortunate frequency that she was, say, sneezed on by a ten-year-old boy who had stopped by her desk, distressed over the poor grade on his lackluster book report. The thought of it still made her shudder.

Her mother was of that generation for whom house-keeping was a way of life. Her clearest childhood memories were of her mother stripping old wax from the kitchen floor, beating out rugs hung over the back fence, running laundry by hand through a wringer washer, ironing shirts and trousers and sheets and underwear, for God's sake. The mechanization and automation of modern house-keeping solutions didn't so much render housework less onerous and time-consuming as make it an afterthought, at least for Janet, so that it was not so much easier and faster as simply ignored, swept under the rug, as it were, except that it was too much trouble to even bother with the sweeping. Her mother had always looked askance at the way she kept her house.

Thinking of her mother put her in mind of her child-hood in Plymouth. It had been a quiet life, pleasant but inconsequential. She was born shortly after World War II, among the first of the Baby Boomers, though she never thought of herself as such. She came of age in the midst of the civil rights movement, the Vietnam War, the sexual revolution, yet somehow those were all things that happened "out there," in some other part of the country or the world, in the newspaper and on the television, and not as part of her daily life, at least not so much that she could draw a direct line from them to herself.

It was true she had got pregnant, in her last year of college. So maybe she was part of the sexual revolution after all, though of course people had always got pregnant unexpectedly, whether or not they talked about it, whether or not it was acceptable or celebrated, scandalous or merely mildly shameful. In any case it wasn't as if she had embraced sexual liberation in any deliberate way, more that a liberated sexual mindset had impinged itself on her. She certainly didn't feel liberated to find herself pregnant with final exams and an uncertain future looming. Her parents had been surprisingly, thankfully, pragmatic about the affair, in that solid New England way. But the father of her child, a local Bridgewater boy who worked at the shoe factory, wasn't a candidate for a husband, not even for a moment. It was decided — Janet decided, though her parents as good as decided for her — that she would carry the baby to term and then give it up for adoption. He was a stout little boy, ten pounds three ounces, and the kindhearted nurse had allowed her to hold him for a few moments before she carried him away; her last vision of him was the nurse's receding back. She had felt such acute pain at the loss of him, even though she didn't want a child, not then. For days she cried bitterly and then for weeks she wept unexpectedly. But mostly she felt an emptiness, a hollowness, like a walnut that had gone bad in the shell, its shriveled core rattling minutely against the hard outer case.

She learned later that the father — Christopher Hodges, his name had been; she remembered thinking at the time that she would have liked the name Janet Hodges — had died in the war in Vietnam. So perhaps the war had touched her after all, though not directly, not in a way that really affected her life, that prompted her to march the streets of nearby Boston in protest, that led her to wear military-green fatigues from the Army-surplus store, that drove her to paint peace signs on her forehead or sit in a circle in a strange room of strangers and smoke pot or drop acid. So much of the late sixties and early seventies had seemed foreign to her, though she didn't remember it, as some people seemed to, as an era of bitter upheaval, of youthful rebellion and political strife. Rather, at the remove of decades, it seemed a time of optimism and aspiration, when people her age sought, however naively, to change society, or at least some part of it, in some vague way, for better. And it seemed a shame the time had passed.

Not that she had really been involved in any of it: she had been busy with her own life. She managed to finish college, before the baby was born, and then after a year of living at home with her parents she began substitute teaching. She was making arrangements to share an apartment with a college girlfriend, when she started dating Henry and her plans changed. Henry had been from Nova Scotia, originally, so he had avoided the Vietnam War, since Canada didn't fight it. Janet found herself remembering that Nova Scotia meant "New Scotland." New Scotland, New England: Europe trying to repeat itself, though she wasn't sure whether the Brits truly thought of themselves as part of Europe or whether the Scots truly thought of themselves as part of Britain, for that matter. Perhaps she could ask Ann.

She hadn't told Henry about the pregnancy, the adoption, when they started dating, or even after they were married, and it wasn't till years later that he learned of it. It was a milestone in their marriage, or a millstone, as she thought of it, as it precipitated a huge fight and a lasting, low-grade resentment — on Henry's part because she had become pregnant by another man, she assumed, and because she hadn't told him about it, on her part because Henry refused to accept the fact of it or to understand why she hadn't told him. They never had their own children, though she didn't think it was because she already had a child; they had never talked about not having children, and they had never tried not to. They had simply never gone ahead with it, the way most couples do, and eventually she was simply too old for it. She and Henry had always enjoyed each other's company, anyway, when Henry wasn't flying across the country, and soon the idea of children faded into their past. And then he had contacted her, her son, a young teenager already, as unexpected as an August hailstorm. Joseph Furze. It was the name of a stranger.

She had started wiping down the tables and chairs, but she noticed the floor could use a good cleaning, as well. She set her bucket and rag aside and got out the mop, one of those modern ones with an aluminum handle and a place for securing an inverted bottle of cleaner so that the detergent could be dribbled onto the floor. She wasn't convinced it was better than getting down on your hands and knees and using a sponge, though. Well, my cleaning habits, if nothing else, have certainly changed with the times, she thought, with whatever some unknown corporation, some commercial advertisement, has told me is new and improved. So perhaps I'm more influenced by the outside world than I realize.

11

Paula drove Ash's car to the teahouse. She wasn't sure it was even open on Sunday, but she didn't mind driving the few minutes to find out. She had looked without success for a Web site, and when she called 411 they didn't have a listing for anything like "teahouse" in Lower Slaughter. But she had decided she wanted the job, and she wanted to get things settled as soon as possible.

She and Ash had gone to pick up her car from the station parking lot early the day before. The teahouse was closed, but as there was no sign on the door listing hours, it could be that they opened later on the weekend. She had watched with proprietary admiration as Ash connected the jumper cables. But despite generating some spectacular sparks when he accidentally knocked the clamps together, after attaching one end of the cables to his car's battery, he couldn't get her car to start. He ended up calling AAA — which he referred to as "my drivers club" — to have them come tow it. He also called ahead to the garage, which said they would look at the car on Monday and call with an estimate. As they left, Paula had noticed the charred remains of an industrial toaster oven lying behind the teahouse, near the trash dumpster.

When Paula got to the teahouse she found the front door locked, but she could see someone moving around in the kitchen. Janet came to the door wearing yellow latex cleaning gloves. She hadn't been entirely sure Janet had meant it — meant her, that is — when she said she was looking for someone for the teahouse. But yes: Janet said her friend Ann had gone back to Scotland, where she was from, and she didn't think she'd be able to run the teahouse on her own, and she needed "a waitress." But surely it was much more than that, a store manager, really. Janet didn't seem to have any sense of what the wages should be, but to be honest neither did she; she had no idea what people made working at a coffee shop — sorry, a teahouse — in the United States. They settled on an hourly rate she felt certain was lower than it should be, but clearly Janet had no way of predicting what business was going to be like and how much she could afford to pay. It was a job, anyway, and Janet seemed more than willing to take care of any necessary paperwork for her work visa, though she got the sense she'd be the one actually filling out the forms. She agreed to start on Monday, the next day.

She left the teahouse and drove to Ash's parents'. After she got there Ash was going to take her back to her apartment. She was a little annoyed he hadn't come with her, but he had wanted to stay at home and play one of his online war-strategy games. She didn't like not having her own car, while hers was in the shop, likewise not having a job, not being sure how she was going to pay her rent, not being sure of her visa status — not having anything stable or certain. Oh, wait, she had a job now. At least that was something.

Stability and certainty had never been especially familiar. She felt relieved that Janet hadn't asked about her life
in Brasil. There were two versions of the story, depending
on how she wanted to present herself. The first version,
accurate if incomplete, was that she had grown up in an
orphanage, along with twenty other children, on the out-
skirts of Rio, in a ramshackle building of dirt floors and
corrugated-metal walls. The second version, more completely true, was that her grandparents ran the orphanage,
that she stayed there during the week, while her parents
worked, and went home on the weekends, or at least on
some weekends. Many of the children at the orphanage
did the same, though some truly had no parents and lived
there full-time. But for most of them it was like a boarding
nursery school.

She had lived at home with her parents till she was
seven, but she didn't have a clear image of what that earlier life was like. They had moved from apartment to apartment, and the memories of her early childhood were like
snapshots. She had never taken a real vacation trip, but she
had a college friend, Gabriela, who had gone to America,
to New York and Niagara Falls and Las Vegas. Gabriela kept
photos of her trips on her laptop, and she had showed them
to Paula. There was Gabriela in Times Square, Gabriela in a
boat shrouded in mist, Gabriela at a casino hotel. To Paula
that's what memories of early childhood were like, images
of a vaguely familiar face in various unfamiliar contexts.

It wasn't till she moved in with her grandparents, Avó
Mariana and Avô Victor, that her memories became clear
and continuous. Her father had gone off to work, suppos-
edly on an oil rig, though what he actually did was never
discussed, and she had always sensed he was involved in
something vaguely illegal. In any case she rarely saw him,
though he sent money from time to time. Her mother

worked as a maid and, with growing frequency, as a server at the dinner parties of wealthy Rio de Janeirans, and she was often too tired to care for Paula. But her grandparents, her mother's parents, were always there at the orphanage. Avô Victor had built the structure himself, or at least parts of it, digging the footings by hand, laying the concrete block of the central rooms, attaching the corrugated metal of the outer walls. It was a daycare, to start with, but soon the parents started leaving their kids overnight, and then some of them arranged to leave their kids permanently. There were fees involved, but she had the sense these were hard to collect, and she knew the orphanage depended on charitable donations.

Paula had always been the oldest by several years. Most of the children at the orphanage were two or three, many of them still in diapers. None was older than six, the year *Brasileiro* kids started school. Paula had had to change schools when she moved in with her grandparents. Her parents had never been strict about school, but Avó Mariana and Avô Victor made her study. She had to help out with the orphanage in the evenings and on weekends, when she was there, watching after the younger kids, putting on their pale-yellow smocks before dinner, cleaning up afterward. But her grandparents insisted that schoolwork come first; she could never use her chores as an excuse for falling behind in school.

Then, just before she started high school, her father sent a large sum of money, with instructions that it be used to send Paula to a private college-prep school. It wasn't till years later that she realized how consequential this development truly was. Only by attending a college-prep school was she able to score high enough on her *vestibular* exams for entry into the tuition-free Universidade Federal do Rio de Janeiro. After she started at U.F.R.J. she moved back with her mother, but by then they had grown apart. She always wondered if her mother resented that the money had gone to Paula's education and not to her.

She had liked living at the orphanage, the constant noise and activity, the exuberance of the children relieving the plodding quietude of Avó Mariana and Avô Victor. Her fondest memories were of hot summer days under the weak shade of palms in the brown-dirt orphanage yard, the kids clambering for a spot on an enormous seven-seat swing set. Avô Victor had installed the swing against the rear wall of the orphanage and painted it yellow, like the pale yellow of the children's smocks.

One day several Americans showed up to take photos. They were from a large corporation whose employees had collected a donation for the orphanage, and the Americans were there to take pictures they would put in a brochure, or something like that. The photographer wore a khaki vest with pockets, while the other Americans were dressed in business suits. They lined up the kids on the swing while Paula stood aside and watched. She had learned not to grow too close to the children, who seldom stayed at the orphanage for more than a couple of years. Their departures were rarely announced; they simply went home for the weekend and never returned. It had been the same at the cyber café, once she had become the manager. The girls — the vast majority of them had been teenage girls — would work there for six months or a year, and then abruptly they would be gone, with little warning or fanfare. When they worked there they spent all their free time at the café, but as soon as they quit they were never seen again, as if the café had become a place to be ashamed of. Or maybe it was simply no longer relevant. She learned later that the Americans were from Globanaut.

She turned down Ash's street. He would have to drive her to and from work till she got her car back from the shop. She didn't like to have to ask.

**

The Monday-morning air was damp and cold. A layer of frost, the first of the season, whitened the green lawns of Lower Slaughter. Paula didn't think she would ever get used to the American winters. When she arrived in January, the year before, the cold had been such a shock, especially in the mornings. She dreaded each colder day as winter approached. But she was happy to be starting her new job. Was *happy* the word? Well, content, at least for now.

The intention was that the teahouse would be closed for the day while she and Janet got things back in order and came up with a plan for who would do what and who would be in at what times. But when Ash dropped her off she found the front door was locked, Janet wasn't there, and there was no sign indicating the teahouse was closed. A clumsy line had formed of people expecting the teahouse to open at any moment. The morning commuters, cold and caffeine-deprived, peered through the door and windows and speculated as to what it might mean that no lights were on inside. Paula stood quietly to one side, not comfortable enough in her new role as teahouse employee to make any general announcements.

Janet arrived in a flurry about ten minutes later, parting the waters of the small crowd with her one-woman commotion and greeting the customers she recognized. "I'm so sorry," she said. "I had meant to put up a sign explaining that we were closed for the day. But Paula stopped by — Paula's my new employee; she'll be here today — and we got to talking, and after that I just went home and forgot about all the things I had meant to do. Oh, hello, Richard," she said to a middle-aged man who stood by the door quietly. He nodded hello.

"So are you, like, open, or what?" a woman asked.

"No, I'm afraid not, not today," Janet said. The woman made a sort of expression of rolling her eyes, without actually doing so, and walked off, her high heels clacking on the flagstones. The rest of the crowd likewise began to disperse.

"So is it just today you're closed?" a man asked.

"Oh, here's Paula now," Janet said, having just noticed her. The remaining customers turned to look at Paula, who smiled politely. "Yes, we're just closed for today," Janet continued, answering the question. "We had a fire, you see — just a small one; nothing was damaged — and we need a day to get things back in order. Oh, look, it's the Mochas," she said to an approaching couple. "I'm sorry, dears, but we're closed for the day."

"Did I hear you say there was a fire?" the woman of the couple asked.

"Yes, on Saturday night. I had left the oven on, and it caught fire, but the fire company came in time to put it out. But everything is covered in soot now. Paula, you need to meet Donald and Maria, who we call the Mochas. They come in almost every day." Janet had taken out her keys and was jingling them in the lock. "You're not usually here this early, though, are you?" she said to them. She didn't wait for their reply, or for Paula to say hello, but instead bustled Paula into the teahouse.

They spent the morning cleaning: wiping down the tables and chairs; mopping the floor, which Janet had never finished the day before; washing the windows, at least on the inside, which proved rather onerous in the kitchen, where the panes had been blackened by soot. When they had finished Janet said she wanted to go through the inventory to figure out what they needed for the week ahead. She had started keeping a written record of how much she sold of what, each day, tea or coffee or blueberry muffins, and what sort of supplies she went through, paper cups and lids and dish detergent, that sort of thing. It was all rough estimates, though, not accurate enough to really plan, Paula found. And there were stacks and stacks of plastic lids that were the wrong size for the paper cups.

"Well, Ann had been getting the lids," Janet explained, "and I thought I had written down which size to get, but when I got to the store I couldn't find it, so I guessed at the size, which turned out to be wrong. Actually, I think they're pretty close, but they're a different brand, so they're not quite right. I tried forcing them on the cups, but I found they popped off just as I was handing people their drinks, and after enough spills I realized they just weren't going to work."

Paula nodded.

About halfway through the morning Janet announced she was going to the post office to mail the card to Ann. "I have to stop at home, first," she added, "because I never did get around to writing the address on the card. I might as well take the curtains with me, so that I can start them in the washer." She left Paula in the middle of sorting through supplies. As Janet drove off Paula realized she had neglected to take the curtains.

Paula tried to keep herself busy while ignoring the commuters who pressed their face to the glass of the front door, surprised by the Closed sign that greeted them. She realized, as the middle of the day approached, that she hadn't thought about lunch. She hadn't brought anything with her, and she didn't have a car, and with the teahouse closed since the Friday before, there weren't even pastries.

But when Janet finally reappeared, a few hours later, she was laden with bags from Dunkin' Donuts.

"I left the coffee in the car," Janet said, heading back out the door. "I know we can make it here, but I just thought it was easier this way."

They spent the rest of the day planning. Paula explained to Janet that she could order her supplies from wholesale catalogs and have them shipped at regular times. She could do the same for things like pastries, ordering from local bakeries. She also hinted that it might not be a good idea for customers to see bags and coffee cups from chain restaurants lying around. It all seemed a revelation to Janet. Paula promised she would look up supply companies on the Internet.

"Now I want to talk to you about your work visa," Janet said. "I'll just pay you in cash for now, and I don't care if we have to keep doing it that way. But I do want to be sure your status is OK."

Paula agreed she would look into the details. At the end of the day, when Ash arrived to take Paula home, Janet had them lug the derelict oven from the back parking lot to the trash dumpster. They were just tipping it over the dumpster's edge as Janet drove off, toot-tooting her horn goodbye.

**

"So do you feel you've made the right decision?" Janet asked Paula. "I mean about working here."

"Yes, absolutely." It was Friday morning. Paula had been working at the teahouse for two weeks now, and she loved it. She had her car back from the shop, and it was at least starting, when she turned the key, if not running entirely smoothly. She had got Janet set up with regular deliveries of supplies and a growing assortment of scones and croissants and muffins and "hand-crafted doughnuts," which weren't different from any other donut, except they were more expensive. The pay at the teahouse wasn't what she had grown used to at Globanaut, but it was an income, at least. She had also convinced Janet to institute a tip jar, which daily overflowed onto the counter. Janet insisted that all the tips go to Paula.

Paula had already come to recognize the regular customers. There were the Mochas, who chatted briefly at the counter but then went off to sit by themselves. There was Richard, who came in every day at the same time and ordered the same drink, always clearly stating his order, even though there could be no question that he was going to get a "small Earl Gray with milk and sugar, for here, please." He sat alone, downing his tea in about two minutes before leaving without a word.

In the mornings, around ten o'clock, a group of three young mothers came in pushing baby strollers, each of which was larger and more elaborate than the next. They wore carefully coordinated plaid skirts and pink sweaters and bows in their hair, for God's sake, along with diamond jewelry and perfectly manicured nails. Mostly they nattered about baby poop and incompetent husbands. Even so, Paula would have been fine with them, except that they were specific with their orders to the point of absurdity. And they never hesitated to voice a complaint: "Excuse me. Excuse me. I specifically asked for my chamomile tea to be a hundred and thirty-five degrees. I'm quite certain this tea is under a hundred and thirty. Feel it. Feel it. It's cold."

Paula heard a clack of heels and a clatter of stroller wheels. "It's the L.I.C.'s," she said to Janet.

"The L.I.C.'s?"

"The Long Island Contingent." Paula had never been to Long Island, but she had heard Ash refer to it disparagingly, which she thought was funny, because she had met Ash's parents, and it sounded like they would fit in there perfectly. "You know, those three women who come in every day with their spoiled children?"

"Oh, they're insufferable," Janet whispered, as they came through the door. "They're not really from Long Island, are they?"

"No, I don't think so."

"A chamomile tea. No milk or sugar. And I want it a hundred and thirty-five degrees. Did you get that part? It's very important: a hundred and thirty-five degrees." The woman had a somewhat older child with her today, maybe three years old. "Billy, do you want a bagel? Billy, if I get you a bagel, will you eat it? Billy, put down those sugar packets, they're not for you. Now look what you've done, you knocked all the sugar packets onto the floor. Miss, can you clean that up? He knocked all the sugar packets onto the floor."

Paula glanced at Janet. "Insufferable," Janet mouthed, and Paula smiled.

12

The door opened, the bell tinkled, and a round body, followed by two overstuffed suitcases, shuffled into the teahouse.

"Ann?" Janet said.

"Hello, Janet," Ann said. She smiled wearily.

"Ann, what are you doing here?"

Ann wheeled her suitcases to the side and set them upright. "It's Logan," she said. "He's ill."

"Is he all right?"

"Well, I don't think it's grave. But apparently he's been sick for two weeks, and I just learned of it. So I thought I'd better come over, to be sure he's being taken care of."

"But you didn't call. You should have called me."

"I'm sorry, I know I shouldn't just arrive unannounced like this."

"No, I mean, I could have checked on him. But it doesn't matter; you're here now. Well, here, let me take your things," she said, extending her hand to indicate Ann's coat. "Come and sit down. Paula!" she called to

Paula, who was just coming from the kitchen. "Paula, you remember Ann. Her son is sick." She turned back to Ann. "Well, what's wrong with him, anyway?"

Paula said hello through their conversation. She went to help a customer who stood at the counter.

'It's the swine flu, apparently. Apparently all the monks got it."

"The swine flu? I thought that was over with."

"Well, it's still out there, evidently. From the look of it, someone brought it to the monastery, and of course once one monk came down with it, they all did."

"It's not serious, though, is it? English Breakfast?"

"Yes, that would do nicely."

"Paula," Janet said over the waiting customer, "can you get Ann an English Breakfast with milk and sugar?"

"Well, people still die from it, so I don't know," Ann said. "But they didn't seem to do anything about it, at the monastery, and he ended up with pneumonia. But apparently he refused to go in hospital. I spoke to him on the phone, but he could only whisper. And Father What's-His-Name, he was no help. So here I am."

"Well, I'm glad to see you, despite the circumstances. But wait, have you seen him yet?"

"No, I came straight here. I was going to impose myself and ask if I could stay with you?"

"Oh, of course you're staying with me. That goes without saying."

Paula brought over Ann's tea.

"Thank you, love," Ann said. "Just a second, that means you're working here now."

"Yes."

"Oh, Paula has been an absolute revelation. She's figured out our supply and inventory, and the customers absolutely love her."

"I got your lovely card, by the way," Ann said, "only I never had a chance to reply. Did you work something out with the coffee filters, then?"

"Well, Paula takes care of all that now."

"So business has been good?"

"Yes, I couldn't be more pleased. It's already to the point where Paula and I can't keep up with things."

Ann sipped her tea as Janet nattered on about the teahouse and the fire and the L.I.C.'s. A line began to form at the counter. "Should you be helping Paula, then?" Ann asked, interrupting Janet.

"Yes, you're right, I probably should."

Ann closed her eyes. "I think I'll just sit here and rest my eyes for a bit," she said, as Janet's footsteps receded.

She felt so tired. She had always been energized by travel. But her last two trips, this one and the last one, coming to see Logan, had taken so much out of her. Was it because the trips weren't on her own terms, weren't what she wanted to be doing? Was it because she couldn't go home, at the end of them, to be with Lionel? Lionel would have told her there was no reason to cross the Atlantic to check on a young man with the flu. But then he would have supported her completely, talking on the phone with her every day, taking care of things at home in the meantime. Life had been so easy to manage when she had Lionel. Since his death it seemed so out of her control.

She had always felt like she was in control of her life, even before Lionel was in it, and life had unfurled neatly and normally. She met Lionel in London, when they were both university students, and they found jobs and were married and had a child at the typical times and in the typical ways. She was surprised when he took a post at the University of St. Andrews, teaching European history; after she moved to London, she never expected to leave it. But then she found a job as curator of the tiny, nascent museum of the St. Andrews Preservation Trust, which had as its mission to preserve the integrity of the town's buildings and character. It was a position perfectly suited to her, and she had held it for forty years, more or less, except for a few years here and there when Lionel was on sabbatical and they went back to London. Control wasn't the right word, she thought; it made her sound like a mini dictator. What she meant was more like poetic justice, or perhaps the Buddhist law of kamma-vipaka, a kind of quid-pro-quo with the world. You have a certain level of intelligence and achieve a certain level of education, and so you move with a certain crowd. You put your time and effort and imagination into your work, and as a consequence you have work you enjoy and time off to travel and a retirement to spend with your husband and your garden. You raise a son with love and tenderness and instill in him a mindset you value, and then life owes it to you for your son to reach adulthood as a man you can consider a friend, or at least an intellectual equal.

Only it doesn't, apparently. After Lionel became sick he had to leave his job at the university. And then the stress of caring for him, even when he was in the hospital, when she wasn't actually providing care, when all she really had to do was stop in twice a day and sit with him: it became too much. She would take an early lunch and leave the museum to bring him his coffee, which he had always loved. But he never once drank it during his long, grueling sickness; it simply sat with her by his bed and grew cold. She would stop in again in the evening on her way home from work, parking in the dark and trudging in the rain. And then she would go home to a silent, drafty house, unable to travel, not that she would have wanted to anyway, while Lionel was ill, unable to cook or to read or even to think. After a few weeks she felt overwhelmed. She gave notice at the museum, and just like that forty years was over. The museum staff, along with other select members of the St. Andrews Preservation Trust, hosted a retirement party for her, with fairy cakes and ginger biscuits, like a scene from an outmoded television program on Life in the United Kingdom for an American Audience.

Then Logan rang to announce he was joining a monastery. A Coptic monastery, no less; she had to look it up on the Internet to even know what he was talking about. How could the son of two rational, educated people, who was himself educated if not, apparently, rational, embrace a lifestyle founded on a complex system of oddly specific beliefs fabricated from ideas that were so obviously false and expectations for which there was no evidence? Of course, people had been doing it for millennia, and they would continue to, ignoring the growing mountain of proof, or maybe she should say reproof, against them. It was like people on the highway rolling up the windows and pretending they didn't notice the stench as they drove past the city dump.

Logan was a disappointment, there was no other way to put it, not that she would ever say that to him or to anyone else, for that matter. He had been such a clever child, sunny and inquisitive, if a bit rigid, with overdeveloped scrupulosity and compunction. She remembered that he had always had a hierarchy for his toys — favorite to least favorite, largest to smallest, always some organizing structure — and punishments for toys that misbehaved. But he did well in school and had the usual allotment of friends and activities. He had grown a bit distant while at university and immediately thereafter, as many children do as they first reach adulthood. And he had never really found a career for himself, even though he had taken a degree in business studies. She was so pleased when he took up with Ainsley, his erstwhile fiancée, who seemed to steady him, like the extra hull that runs along one side of certain boats. They were soon living together and engaged to be married. Then he had called to say he had ended the relationship and was joining the Coptic Church. She had kept the news from Lionel, at first, but then it seemed he was going to recover, and it was such a relief to be able to share it with him. Then Lionel died unexpectedly, and Logan announced he was moving to America to join the monastery. She couldn't remember which had happened first. Isn't it strange, she thought, how you remember the tiniest details, but then major events get muddled? The clearest image in her mind from those days, from the endless weeks at the hospital, the pained phone calls, the wretched funeral, with practical strangers hoping a nonexistent God would bless her, was lying on the floor of their sitting room, alone and in the dark, hugging herself, on her side, facing the wall, sobbing, sobbing.

People talk about stages of grief, she thought, but they have it all wrong. What were they supposed to be? Denial, anger, depression, acceptance. There was a fifth one in there somewhere, what was it? Bargaining. Well, it must come before depression, because whom are you going to bargain with, and to what end? So naturally depression would follow. Except that in her experience bereavement didn't follow any sort of plan. It was all the emotions at once, and they kept recurring, like waves on the ocean, a constant pounding on the shore, or lapping lightly, almost imperceptible, till there came an engulfing, unexpected breaker, drowning all. And surely there was no such stage as acceptance, no tide going out, no remittance.

There was only longing. It was a physical pain, really, but an elusive one, one that seemed to move around the body, when you tried to isolate it, like squeezing a balloon. It was a unique kind of longing, too, different from the longing of new love, different from the longing for things, for a vacation trip or a cherished possession or a new situation, whatever it was that was going to make life better. It was different even from the longing of missing someone, which she had felt when she traveled without Lionel, as much as she enjoyed traveling alone. Those were longings of desire, of hope, of what could be. Grief was the longing of loss, of despair, of what could never be again.

"You must be exhausted," a voice said.

Ann opened her eyes to find Janet standing in front of her.

"Would you like me to run you home now?"

"No, not a bit of it," Ann said. "Let me just go freshen up in the ladies."

Ann wheeled a suitcase to the tiny restroom, which was just big enough for her to squeeze in herself and her bag. She emerged a few minutes later looking more hopeful if not entirely energetic.

"Were you planning to go see Logan today?" Janet asked.

"Well, I would like to see him as soon as possible. Only I'm not sure I'm quite up to it today. If it's all right with you, I'd just as soon stay here with you and Paula."

13

Ann once again found herself on the gray stone steps of St. Antony's. It was a different monk who greeted her at the door this time, upright rather than stooped, but he had the same benign facial expression, the same bushy beard. She was reminded of an old black-and-white short she had once seen in which a crotchety W.C. Fields pokes a shotgun at a decrepit man with a preposterous amount of facial hair, out of which fly two mallard ducks, which Fields proceeds to shoot at. She found herself glancing at the monk's beard as he led her across the courtyard to the visiting area.

She had been instructed on the phone that she wouldn't be permitted to see Logan in his cell but would have to commune with him through the metal grate, as she had before. He arrived in his black tunic, looking gaunt and rather unsteady on his feet. His beard was fuller than when she had last seen him, or at least as full as it probably would get, but it didn't mask his sallow skin.

"Hallo, Mum," he whispered. He seemed relieved to see her, and too run down for monkly propriety.

"Logan, you truly don't look well. How are you feeling?"

"As well as can be expected. Better than some of the brothers, certainly."

"Are you getting enough to eat? You're not still fasting."

"Well, we're not reckless about our health. But I do still try to observe ..." He broke off in a jagged cough.

"I don't think you're getting enough to eat."

"I have food to eat of which you do not know."

"Oh, Lord. Have you seen a doctor?"

"A doctor's concern is with temporal matters. But I'm taking an antibiotic, and I'm starting to feel better."

"I do dislike sitting across the grate from you like this. Although I suppose I should be keeping my distance in any case."

"I don't think I'm infectious any longer, although it is still going around the monastery."

"So do you feel you're finding what you were looking for here?"

"I'm not here to seek, Mum. I'm here to practice what I've already found. There's no sense believing if you don't practice your belief. Even the demons believe."

"I assume that's another Biblical reference. Logan, I guess what I want to know is, are you happy here?"

"Well, what does it mean to be happy? And how happy is anyone? How happy are you? I notice you keep coming back to the States. Are you finding what you're looking for?"

She wanted to say, I've just lost my husband. She wanted to say, I've flown all this way to see you. She wanted to say, No, I can see you're not happy, not at all.

Janet was waiting in the car by the curb; she had been kind enough to drive Ann to the monastery. Ann would have liked to have had some time to herself after the visit, to think things through. Why had she come to see Logan?

116

Was she merely concerned about her son, or was Logan some kind of connection to Lionel? Or was he an excuse to come stay with Janet again? Well, there was no time to think about it now; Janet wasn't one to leave you to your own thoughts. She eased herself into the car.

"How does he seem?"

"I get the sense he was quite ill, actually. But I also get the sense he's on the mend."

"What will you do, do you think?"

"What I'd like to do is stay awhile, just till I'm sure he's going to be OK. I'll visit as often as they'll let me. Well, maybe not that often; I don't want to overdo it. But I'll keep an eye on him."

"Well, you're certainly more than welcome to stay with me for as long as you'd like. Truly, I enjoy the company, and I really have plenty of room. Of course, I'm at the teahouse all day."

"I was hoping I could help out at the teashop. It would take my mind off things, for one thing."

"Oh, I could certainly use your help. For one thing, we need another server. Actually, more than one, because Paula and I are both working more hours than either of us can keep up with. But more than that, there are just so many decisions I have to make, and I just keep putting them off." She hesitated. "I'm not sure I can afford to pay you, is the thing."

"Let's not worry about that for now. I'm retired, after all, so I don't really need the income. It's just something to do, while I'm here. And I have to admit, I really do like the teashop."

"Oh, Ann, I'm so pleased. I really do think it will be good for you. Well, in any case, it will be good for me."

**

117

Ann ran the teahouse with authority. She convinced Janet to invest in a new commercial toaster oven and an automatic espresso machine and a station where patrons could fix their own drinks, if they wanted. She also saw to the smaller things, like pull-shades for the windows and the front door, a padded floor mat for behind the counter, and a regular routine — a revolutionary idea to Janet, apparently — for cleaning. That left Paula to be in charge of inventory and scheduling, and it allowed Janet to focus on more creative endeavors like picking out tea services — Paula had found her a catalog, and there were so many lovely designs to choose from, teapots with matching cups and saucers and dessert plates — and installing a little community area, with a cork bulletin board where customers could post announcements for things like the local middle school's production of "Glass Menagerie: The Musical" or ads for "Sushmita's Yoga Explosion: Tantric Yoga for the Full-Figured Woman."

Ann also convinced Janet, after much cajoling, to begin assembling a staff of part-time servers; there would be ample supply from the local Catholic college. Janet began to refer to the forthcoming young women — she anticipated hiring mostly young women — as "my posse."

"What is this word?" Paula said. "Did you say 'my pussy'?"

"Posse," Ann corrected gently, while Janet laughed till she cried. "It's like a group or a gang."

"What *will* we call them?" Janet asked, wiping her eyes. "They won't really be waitresses."

"Why not call them 'baristas,' like they do at coffee shops?" Paula suggested.

"I was thinking 'tea caddies,' maybe."

"What is a 'tea caddy'?"

"Well, it's a canister to store tea. But I was thinking more along the lines of a caddy at a golf course."

"I'm not sure they will want to be called 'tea caddies.' I think you should stick with 'baristas.'"

"Well, we'll see," Janet said, but she had as good as already decided.

They started with two, Daniela and Davina, both of them provocatively dressed and enthusiastic, like oversexed puppies. They were virtually indistinguishable to Janet, who couldn't keep them straight. Paula took on the task of training and scheduling them, which prompted Ann to suggest that a raise in wages might be in order. She brought up the topic during a lull late one afternoon, while the three of them stood in the kitchen.

"Oh, I agree, absolutely," Janet said. "I should have thought of it already myself. Paula, starting on Monday we'll double your salary."

"Double?" Paula said.

"Now, Janet, I'm not sure we need to go as high as that," Ann offered. She realized, now, that she shouldn't have mentioned it in front of Paula.

Janet hesitated. She knew she had been overzealous, and doubling Paula's salary was probably neither necessary nor prudent. But she had already said it aloud, and in front of Paula, so she couldn't very well take it back. "No," she said to Paula, "you should have been making more all along, and I want you to understand how important you are to the teahouse. To me."

Ann reminded herself to have a chat with Janet about impulsiveness and business plans. Still, she couldn't disagree that Paula was integral to the entire operation, and probably had more natural sense of how to run a teashop than did Janet.

There was a last-minute rush of customers, as there often was. Among them was Charles. It was the first time he had been in the teahouse since the night of the fire, and in

119

fact the first time he had stopped by while it was open for business. He waited in line along with the other customers, and Janet didn't notice him till he reached the counter.

"Ann," she called, after saying hello to Charles, "this is Dr. Grapnel, my landlord."

Ann emerged from the kitchen. "How do you *do*," Charles said emphatically. He seemed to Ann to be simultaneously formal and genuine.

"Oh, and you should meet Paula, as well."

Paula was busy fixing drinks for other customers. She smiled hello.

"And Janet, *do* stop calling me 'Dr. Grapnel.' It makes me sound like a country physician. Paula, *you'll* call me Charles, won't you?"

"Charles, then. Ann is from St. Andrews, and Paula is from Brazil, originally."

"Well, we have quite the international consortium," Charles said. "I've never been to Brazil," he said to Paula. "It just seems so *tropical.* And of course *filled* with exuberant young women such as yourself."

Paula laughed. "And flirtatious men."

"Yes, well. Now, Ann, are you *from* St. Andrews?"

"I'm from Winchester, actually, although I've lived in St. Andrews for forty years or more. But I must say, I always think of myself as a Londoner."

"Yes, of course, I do *too.*"

"Have you lived in London, then?"

"I used to stay there with a friend, in the summer. But of course that was *years* ago." He turned to Janet. "Now, does one have to know the owner to get a scone here? They say *scon* in London, don't they?" he said to Ann. "It always makes me thinks of *sconce.*"

A sour-looking woman had sidled up to Charles.

"Oh, Emily, you've come back. Charles, this is my neighbor, Emily Reaper."

"How very nice to meet your neighbor."

"Janet, I heard there was a fire," Emily said.

"Oh, that was weeks ago now."

"Well, you seem to have survived it."

"Yes, thank you, Emily."

"I know just what you've been through," Emily said. "I have a cousin out in Newcastle, and there was a woman who lived down the road from her, and she went to work one day, and when she came home, she found her entire house had burned to the ground. And her poor little dachshund dog had burned to a crisp. So I know just what you've been through."

There was a brief silence.

"That's not really the same thing, is it?" Charles finally said.

"Now who is this?" Emily asked Janet, indicating Paula.

"This is Paula, my employee. Well, my friend."

"Is she legal?"

Paula raised her eyebrows.

"Oh, Emily, really," Janet said.

They were interrupted by Davina, who had just come in.

"Oh, Daniela, what are you doing here at this time of day?" Janet asked.

"Davina," Davina said. "I'm here to get my paycheck."

"Didn't you get your paycheck yesterday, then?" Ann asked, glancing at Janet.

"I got a paycheck, only it turns out it was Daniela's."

"Oh, Janet," Ann said.

Davina traded in Daniela's paycheck for her own and left. Emily sniffed at the pastry case and wandered out as well.

"Why do you put up with her?" Ann asked, meaning Emily.

"Well, I have to. She's my neighbor."

"She's rather *grim*," Charles said. He noticed no one seemed to get the joke.

"She's what we would call a sticky beak in Scotland. You know, someone who sticks her nose in other people's business."

"In Brasil my friends would call her *cricri*."

"Klee klee? What is that?" Janet asked.

Paula hesitated. "You know what crabs are?"

"Crabs?"

Paula thought maybe she had gone too far. "It means a person who is — what is the word? — insufferable."

"Did you say *crabs*?" Charles asked. "Oh, I think I like *you*."

There was a lot of banging at the front door, the bell ringing out shrilly. The four of them, Janet, Ann, Paula, and Charles, turned to see Ben come in, lugging the sign for the teahouse.

"You've finished!" Janet exclaimed.

"Yes," Ben said. He stopped some distance from them and set the sign down.

"Well, turn it so we can see it," Charles instructed. Ben did as he was told.

"It looks wonderful," Janet said.

"Very nice indeed," Ann said.

The sign was almost square, just taller than it was wide. It was cream-colored, with simple black letters that read "The Teahouse by the Tracks," with "Teahouse" larger than the other words and in fancier type. In the middle was a teacup and saucer, green to match the teahouse trim, with a white curl of steam rising from it.

It hadn't come out quite as Ben had wanted. He had had the idea of painting train tracks, disappearing to a vanishing point, through the middle, but they had visually cut the sign in two and got in the way of the text. So he had painted them over, but you could still see the topography of their masked edges behind the cream background. In addition, he hadn't quite got the perspective right on the teacup, so it looked as if the cup were empty, the white curl of steam rising from nothing.

"I can hang it tomorrow," Ben said. "I just wanted you to see it now."

"You must let me pay you for all your work," Janet said.

"No, we've already decided that. You've paid for the materials, and that's fine."

"Oh, but there are some other things I wanted to ask you to do. I still need to have the window fixed in the kitchen. Oh, and the back door sticks. Can you do that sort of thing?"

"Well, not for free, Janet," Ann said.

"Of course not for free. The truth is, we could really use a handyman for the teahouse. You know, just part-time, but someone who could fix things when they broke, or make sure things were working properly."

"Ben, I've been saying to you that I need a handyman at my house, as well," Charles said. "You really must think about it."

"Well, I'll think about it. But I'm not sure I would want to be referred to as a handyman."

"Besides," Charles added, "it's a good idea to have a career to fall back on if your *graduate* studies don't pan out."

"Thank you for that, Charles."

"You did a good job with it, Ben," Paula said quietly. "With the sign."

"The teahouse is complete," Janet announced. "The sign completes it. Ben completes it." She realized, then, that these were the people in her life, all the people whose lives intersected with hers. And it was the first time they were together in the same room, in the light and warmth of the teahouse. She gazed at each of them in turn: at Ann, solid and substantial; at Paula, radiant and right; at Charles, charming and distant; at Ben, quiet and diffident. She gazed about the teahouse — as she thought of it, at what she had wrought.

14

Thanksgiving came to Lower Slaughter with a shock of cold, the frigid morning air quieting the winter birds and leaving hoarfrost on bare branches that stretched above the Wissahickon. All week long the teahouse regulars, running late, blew on gloveless hands after having scraped an unexpectedly icy windshield. They spoke urgently into ubiquitous cellphones as they hurried from their parked cars to the train, their vaporous breath trailing behind them.

Thanksgiving has become the neglected holiday, Janet thought, long since orphaned to the easy commercialization of Halloween and the weeks-long domination of Christmas, forgotten amid the taking down of cornstalks and jack-o-lanterns and the putting up of wreaths and colored lights and inflatable lawn ornaments. For Janet the holiday was a lean reminder of Thanksgivings past, of extended family around their modest dining-room table, abundantly if frugally set, the children at a separate table in an unheated sunroom, her father at the head of the grownups' table, carving a withered, stringy turkey. The sensations of those

Eric Schoeniger

days were keen in her memory: the feel of a shelled walnut; the hiss of roasting chestnuts; the tang of lemon-meringue pie; the smell of pipe tobacco and mothballed tweed. But the holiday had shrunk through attrition, as nieces and nephews grew up and moved away, as cousins divorced and remarried and embraced new traditions, as grandparents and aunts and uncles and finally her father passed away.

Janet wasn't sure what she would do for Thanksgiving this year. She would have Ann, and that was something. But of course Thanksgiving meant nothing to Ann. She suspected she would pick up some precooked, shrink-wrapped turkey from the Safeway, along with a jar of gravy and a can of cranberry sauce. She and Ann would have their Thanksgiving in mid-afternoon, and then she would stop over to see her mother at the home. There would be a Thanksgiving dinner at the home, too, but her mother probably wouldn't go. When she thought about it, she had to admit she was dreading the day.

Charles, likewise, would have liked to keep the holiday at bay. As a young man he had always gone home to Baltimore for Thanksgiving, for "the family abscess," as his father had referred to it. But once he was established at Grier & Buchanan he had created his own holiday traditions, with lavish dinner parties for colleagues and their spouses, for visiting writers and local artists. His bountiful entertainments had become things of legend, and invitations, limited by the constraints of his on-campus housing, were prizes to be envied. But that was all past, now. Probably he would make himself a small meal and open a bottle of Cabernet.

Ben had long since abandoned Thanksgiving. The fond memories he had of the holidays of his youth were marred by the inevitable fights between his parents. He and his siblings would be at play in the living room, or

126

watching television, already dressed for dinner, the boys in sweater vests and clean shoes, his sister in a velvet dress and white tights. His parents would be in the kitchen preparing dinner, silent and efficient. Almost imperceptibly the atmosphere would change, the familial warmth replaced by a flinty electricity. He would hear tension in his parents' voices, pleading from his mother, growing disdain from his father. Then abruptly, like a thunderclap on a clear day, there would be shouting, banging, slammed doors, things thrown. Through this storm he and his brothers and sister would continue to mime play, gazing intently at nothing. A little later one set of grandparents or other would arrive, or his childless aunt and uncle, and they would all gather around the table, tense, quiet, the fight ignored but not forgotten.

Paula could take or leave Thanksgiving. It was a relatively recent tradition in Brasil, and not one her parents had ever embraced. At the orphanage Avó Mariana and Avô Victor served turkey and sweet potatoes and jaboticaba sauce, but it never felt like anything much more than a regular meal. This Thanksgiving she was having dinner with Ash at his parents' house, just the four of them around Mr. and Mrs. Billington's mahogany dining-room table, long and imposing and impersonal.

"Do we have to tell them I'm working at a teahouse?" Paula asked as Ash eased his car up to the curb.

"You know they're going to ask, Parchy. You might as well just tell them and get it over with."

Paula sighed and swung open the car door. Ash's parents lived in the Chestnut Hill section of the city. Both sides of the family had lived there for generations, in what they never failed to point out was the wealthiest portion of Pennsylvania "per square foot," whatever that was supposed to mean. They lived in a low-slung, sprawling house of concrete-gray stone, which they had christened "Duchess II." The house was even grayer on the inside, with low, oppressive ceilings and narrow, miserly windows. The drabness was relieved only by the worn but brightly colored oriental rugs that covered every floor. When Paula had complimented the rugs and asked, simply to make conversation, where they had come from, Ash's father informed her gravely that "one *has* oriental rugs; one doesn't *acquire* them."

Ash's father was Ashford E. Billington III. He referred to himself as Trey and to Ash as Forty. He was an executive at Blandoleum, a maker of vinyl floors, about which he spoke passionately. Not that he would have had vinyl floors anywhere in his own house. When he wasn't holding forth on the virtues of fabricated sheet flooring he was meting out measures of wisdom from an imagined knowledge of Latin. "Do you know the word 'educate' comes from the Latin *educere*, which means 'to lead out'?" he would say. "So you see, education isn't so much about teaching as it is a matter of drawing out the knowledge that's already within us." He had taught this lesson on every occasion Paula had met him.

The Billingtons were big on education. It was a disappointment to them that Ash hadn't graduated from the University of Pennsylvania — *Penn*, they always called it, pronouncing the single syllable emphatically — but it was acceptable to them that he had attended Haverford. He quit in his third year, though, and his failure to graduate was a minor scandal that was pointedly ignored.

Ash's mother was Mitzi Pemberton Widener Billington the Third, as she invariably referred to herself. She had sallow skin and sunken eyes and a long Episcopalian nose, and she looked to Paula like nothing so much as a plucked pelican. When she conversed with people she spoke to them through her husband in a fashion that allowed her to avoid asking direct questions.

"Do you think she'll enjoy working at a teahouse, Trey?" she asked after Paula and Ash told them about her new job.

"I'm sure I don't know," Trey said.

Trey and Mitzi sat at opposite ends of the table. Paula and Ash sat across from each other. Before dinner Trey said grace, during which Mitzi liked for everyone to hold hands. Except that it was too far to reach, so they had all merely stretched their arms toward one another, fingers extended but not actually touching, like God and Adam on the ceiling of the Sistine Chapel. "Bless us, O Lord, this food to our use, and us to our loving service. Make us always mindful of the foods of others. In Jesus' name we pray. Ahh-men." Paula had heard a prayer like this before — it was similar to the Catholic prayer before meals she had said as a girl — but she was certain it didn't go quite like that.

Ash's parents seemed skeptical of their son's girlfriend's working "in a nonprofessional capacity," as Trey put it.

"Now this Janet who runs the place. Where did she matriculate?" Mitzi asked.

"Matriculate?" Paula said.

"She wants to know where she went to college," Ash said. "Mother, we have no idea. Does it really matter?"

"Charbray, did you say her name was? I wonder if we know any Charbrays. Is that French, do you think? Trey, do we know any French people?"

"Of course we don't know any French people."

Paula and Ash gazed at each other across the table, rolling their minds' eyes in shared sarcasm. As painful as dinner with Ash's parents was, Paula thought she never felt closer to him as when sitting across from him at his parents' dining-room table, unable to voice her thoughts but certain he understood them.

"Now is she from Philadelphia?" Mitzi asked.

"I think she said near Boston," Paula said.

"Oh, then she must have gone to a good school. Daddy always said, 'In New York, they ask, How much money does he have? In Boston, they ask, Where did he go to school? And in Philadelphia, they ask, Who are his family?'"

"I think he got that from Mark Twain," Ash said. "Although I think it's misquoted."

"Don't be surly, Forty," Trey instructed. "It doesn't suit you."

"Ash is a Haverford alumnus, aren't you, dear?"

"I didn't actually graduate, Mother, as you well know."

"Do you know that when you're invited to a dinner party," Mitzi said to Paula meaningfully, "you're meant to arrive fifteen minutes late? Except in Philadelphia, where the fashion is to arrive twenty minutes late."

"You say that every time you have someone to dinner," Ash said. "That's why Paula and I show up twenty minutes after you tell us to."

That's not the only reason, Paula thought.

"Do you know, I once hosted a dinner for one of your father's cousins. Who was it, Trey?"

"Crackstone."

"For his cousin and his wife, Bernie and Betty Crackstone. And would you believe it, they arrived a half-hour early? I mean, really."

"Mother, you've been telling that story since I was fifteen. Paula's already heard it, like, ten times."

"But *really*."

Paula was becoming familiar with Mitzi's litany of conversation, facts and anecdotes repeated every time she saw her. It was mind-numbing, on the one hand, but it relieved the necessity of having any sort of real conversation, which she assumed was why Mitzi recited it.

"Now, do you often not wear a skirt?" Mitzi asked Paula, glancing at the jeans she couldn't actually see, hidden as they were by the draping tablecloth. "Do you know, I've never worn dungarees in all my life. I still have my skirts made by the most lovely woman in Connecticut."

"In Brasil, women only wear skirts when they go out for dinner or to a club. In school or at the office, all women wear pants."

"Trey, did you hear that? Can you imagine?"

Trey continued eating without glancing up from his plate.

"Before Ash was born, his father taught at the University of Virginia. Trey, how long were you at U.V.A.?"

"Three miserable years. Damn liberal intellectuals."

"And I sewed suede patches on all his tweed jackets. He would wear the elbows right through. I don't know how he did it, I'm sure I don't."

Paula poked at the turkey on her plate. She didn't often eat meat, though she wasn't such a strict vegetarian that she would make a fuss if someone offered it to her. Ash was an ovo-lacto vegan, and he made a great show of avoiding the turkey and gravy. His parents pretended not to notice. He had given up reminding them of his eating habits. He seldom ate with them anyway, even though he still ostensibly lived at home. Over the past few months he had taken to eating most of his dinners with Paula at her apartment.

"Are you enjoying the bird?" Mitzi asked, obviously aware that Paula had reservations about it. "I have to do my own cooking, now, I'm afraid. When Ash was a boy, I had Odessa. Do you remember Odessa, Trey?"

"Of course I remember Odessa."

"Odessa was a black woman," Mitzi said. "She had to leave because of some family matter. The problem with black people is they can't chunk."

131

"Mother, what the hell are you talking about?"

"Forty, don't talk to your mother that way."

"I learned it in a class I took at Chestnut Hill College. They can't chunk. One area of their life gets all mixed up with the other areas."

"Mother, that doesn't make any sense. It's also racist."

"I'm not explaining it well. I'm not racist."

"Mother, you're aware that Paula has African ancestry."

"Well, that's not quite the same thing, is it?" Mitzi said. She smiled at Paula.

I can't think of a single thing to say to her, Paula thought.

"At the end of a meal, you never say you're full," Mitzi announced, placing her cloth napkin in her lap. "You say, 'I'm satiated.'"

Trey looked up from his plate. "No one cares, woman."

"It's important to know these things," Mitzi defended herself. "You never know when you're going to be invited to dinner at the White House."

I'm satiated, Paula thought.

15

Charles sat at his kitchen table in the fading afternoon light and sorted through the mail. It was mostly supermarket flyers and coupon mailers and other junk, the *New Yorker* magazine and *Newsweek*. Mixed in was an official-looking letter from the direct-lending company from which he had got his third mortgage. It was addressed to "Mr. Charles Grapnel," and he had to admit it always irked him slightly when he received a letter addressed to "Mr." instead of "Dr." He tore open the envelope and unfolded the single sheet of white paper.

November 30, 2010

Mr. Charles Grapnel
52 Station Ln.
Lower Slaughter, PA 19437

Dear Mr. Grappel:

This letter is to remind you that your one-year balloon payment, in the amount of $1,600,000.01, is due in full on Dec. 31, 2010.

Should you have any questions about your loan, feel free to contact a customer service representative Mon. - Fri. between 9 AM and 5 PM ET at 800-555-LONE.

Sincerely,

Rodney McAnally
Nimrod Lending, LLC

    As Charles read and re-read the letter, he had a sense of his ears being full, as if he were underwater, a sense of his field of vision narrowing, as if he were cupping his hands around his eyes. He stood and immediately sat again. He became aware of his heart beating.

    It must be a mistake, he told himself. He knew it had taken some clever financing to enable him first to renovate the barn and then to buy the train station. And he recalled something about a one-year term, a change in the loan after twelve monthly payments. But he thought it had something to do with the interest rate, with switching from a fixed to an adjustable rate, something like that. He hated numbers, despised money, resented all things financial, the crossroads of counting and commerce, all that he disdained. He paid his bills on time, every month; wasn't that enough? Beyond that he wanted to be left alone, to not have to think about making a living, the cost of living, paying for living.

The first panic of reading the letter was passing. Yes, it must be a mistake. He would look up the details and contact the loan representative. He climbed the stairs to his office, where he kept his records. The mortgage papers were in a hanging file somewhere, was it in the desk drawer? He searched in vain and then remembered he had put them in a separate folder in the closet. He rifled through old receipts, appliance warranties, instruction manuals for various things having to do with his computer. There was the folder from the bank, for his first mortgage; maybe the papers were in there. Yes, here they were. He hadn't remembered putting them in here. He squatted on the floor and spread out the papers, scanning for details that would explain the terms he had apparently agreed to, the obligation to which he had committed himself with signatures and initials; the yellow plastic tabs that indicated where he should sign were still affixed to the pages. Gradually, inexorably, like the livid rise of a bruised shinbone, the facts became clear to him. It was a fixed-rate mortgage but an interest-only loan. In fact, the monthly payments he had been making, close to two thousand dollars each month, didn't even cover the interest, and with each passing payment the amount he owed actually grew. At the end of the term, which was twelve months, the balance, the principal and interest, was due in its entirety. And there it was, clearly printed on the sheet, $1,600,000.01, the amount portended in the letter. It was almost the same amount he had borrowed, and he realized he must have been confused, he must have thought it was the amount of the original loan, not what was actually due in full.

How could this have happened? How could an educated man, and not a young one, intelligent and discerning, a lecturer at Oxford, the author of academic papers and books, for Christ's sake, be duped by a cheap-suited, tooth-whitened loan officer named McAnally?

There had to be a solution. What was it? Perhaps he could take out another loan. But of course the banks had become so tight-fisted since the financial collapse; those who had considered risk not worth the paper their actuarial tables were printed on were now petrified to let slip one errant dime. And what sort of loan would he get? Another mortgage with a balloon payment would only delay the inevitable, with the likely addition of more closing costs and assessment fees and penalties, surcharges that only members of a secret mortgage society could hope to understand. *Mortgage*, he thought: the dead pledge. If only he had held onto his inheritance from Alain, had purchased a house he could actually afford, in a more affordable suburb.

Why had he been so foolish? Had it been greed? He had simply wanted a source of income. Renting out his third floor wasn't enough to cover his expenses. He had had no other choice but to invest in real estate, and the train station had seemed so serendipitous an acquisition. *Serendipitous*: it was one of those words that had become popular within academic circles for a time, like *paradigm* or *capaciousness*. But really, he had wanted to stick it to his former colleagues, the sanctimonious bastards, to show them he could still have a life, unconstrained by the petty preoccupations of mid-western Pennsylvania's quasi-intelligentsia, their sparsely attended poetry readings and sad little art shows, their glum, decaying on-campus housing. The truth is, he missed it, the academic life: the familiar course load and time-worn lectures; the book-strewn office, seldom cleaned; the bad pay, which really wasn't all that bad; the endless, mindless committee meetings and equally endless and mindless conflicts with the administration; the lumpy, thrown-together outfits of people with more important things to think about; the idle gossip about who had put on weight, who wasn't getting tenure, who may or may not be having dalliances; the respect of his peers or, even better, their envy; the adulation, if that wasn't too strong a word, of young students newly besotted with literature and literary theory; the reliable, comfortable cycle of it: Labor Day, convocation, midterms, fall break, finals, a long holiday, the start of the spring semester, midterms, spring break, finals, commencement, Memorial Day, the summer off. When he started his career, in the mid-eighties, a tenured professor was still unimpeachable, unassailable, assured of a job no matter the circumstances, innocent till proven guilty, and usually even after. More than one of his aging colleagues regularly taught classes while drunk, served alcohol to underage students, had affairs with younger colleagues and even students. Such indiscretions were tolerated, if frowned upon, humanizing quirks, rites of passage. When had that begun to change, and why? Maybe it had to do with money: as the cost of education increased, parents demanded accountability, protection for their children, more for their dollar. Possibly it had to do with the empowerment of women, more female professors in higher places, with less need to indulge their patriarchal counterparts. But slowly, irrevocably, it began to change. Professors became professionals. They stopped drinking and having sex, or they kept both activities far more secret. They became responsible, boring.

For Charles it had never been an issue. He enjoyed drinking, and there was always plenty of liquor at his parties. But it never descended into abuse, if that were the word, and his parties were never for students. He had enjoyed relationships with several of his female colleagues, over the years. But they hadn't amounted to much more than companionship, someone to take to a concert or the theater or, more rarely, on a vacation trip. Perhaps it was because, even after his death, it seemed that to do otherwise, to become more involved than that, would somehow have been unfaithful to Alain.

He was certain most of his colleagues assumed he was gay, or perhaps bisexual. The possibility of someone's being other than heterosexual seemed to hold endless fascination for people. "Do you think he's gay?" you heard people whisper, or, "I heard she's a lesbian." Of course, it would be silly for people to point out who was straight, since most people were, or thought they were, or behaved as if they were. But still, why the keen interest?

But then one bad decision, one misjudgment, and it had all unraveled. Perhaps it was several misjudgments. He had been feeling depressed, for no particular reason, and waiting for the depression to reach its nadir and then lift, as depressions do. He had opened a bottle of scotch, late one evening, Laphroaig, as he recalled, peaty and irresistible. By bedtime he had drunk a good portion of it, and it was then he remembered he had left some papers in his office, forms he needed to fill out by the next day. It was a miserable late-spring night, warm but rain-ravaged, and it would have made more sense to wait till morning. But he had in his mind that he wanted the papers, so he grabbed an umbrella and headed across campus. He was trudging stooped against the billowing rain, the umbrella angled just enough that he could find his way along the asphalt path, when he practically ran into one of his students. It was Ms. Creasy, Lisa, a sophomore, and one of his favorites, astute if a little abstracted. She was in a class he taught called American Dreams, at eight in the morning, where she sat in the front row, gazing up at him dreamily, locking on his eyes whenever he glanced at her. What she was doing out on such a night he had no idea, but of course students were unfathomable. She had no coat or umbrella and was dripping wet, her soaked shirt silhouetting two perfectly formed breasts, the curls of her blond hair clinging darkly to her wet cheeks. He wordlessly offered his umbrella, and she took his arm. They ran together to the rear entrance of his office building, where an overhanging roof provided shelter from the weather. They stood close and talked of something, he had no idea what, and he could feel the warmth of her body, her breath. They kissed, then, unexpectedly, for no reason, long, luxuriant, like the kisses he remembered from his own days as an undergraduate, that he hadn't experienced in decades. They searched each other's eyes, and talked more, and kissed more, and held their bodies close. And then she said she should go, placing a finger on his lips to keep him from speaking. She turned and receded into the night. He went to his office to collect his papers. And that was it.

Except it wasn't. There was a tension between them, the next time he saw her in class, an imposed distance. He sensed that something was expected of him, that he had implicitly agreed to some unnamed obligation. But she wasn't in the next class, or the next. In fact, she never came back. He tried contacting her, and asked after her to her classmates, and checked with her advisor. She wasn't ill, and she was still attending her other classes, apparently.

But she never returned to his class, and when finals came and went he knew he'd have to give her a failing grade. It seemed such a shame, so unnecessary.

And then he was called to the dean's office. Ms. Creasy had gone to her resident assistant, and together they approached the department chair, who took up the matter with the dean. According to Ms. Creasy, she and Charles had had sex. By her account, he had lured her to his office, late one night, and the encounter had been so shameful that she couldn't return to class. She apparently had stopped short of calling it a rape, suggesting that he had overpowered her not with physical force but with professorial authority and wile.

He had felt much the same as he did when reading the mortgage letter, a sense of his ears filling with water, his field of vision narrowing, dark clouds gathering. He denied seeing her in his office, denied having sex with her, never mentioned the wet, rainy night of warm, luxurious kissing. And why should he? It was almost absurdly innocent, inconsequential. Besides, where was the proof, the supporting evidence? He was confident he would be exonerated by a stalemate of he-said/she-said, inconvenienced by accusation but ultimately untarnished.

Until the security video appeared, grainy and gray, shot from above and at an angle but unmistakably the two of them, professor and student, making out like two teenagers. Which, as it turned out, she still was, not yet twenty years old. Charles was suspended pending an investigation. The girl's parents agreed not to "press charges," whatever that might mean, if he were fired and she were given an A for the class. The video, inevitably, found its way to the Internet, where anyone with enough prurience could find it and view it, over and over, like an endless loop of bad film art.

But the worst of it, worse than the humiliation, worse than the loss of status, was the abandonment of his colleagues, every last one of whom remained silent, spoke neither for nor against him, turned a blind eye, turned for him his other cheek. The men and women he had worked with for two decades, who had been to his house and eaten at his table, with whom he had shared conversations, class loads, birthdays, bar mitzvahs, births, deaths, cancer treatments, did nothing. Not a single one called, or e-mailed, or wrote, or even spoke to him. So he tendered his resignation, and that was it: twenty years of work, of friendship, of life, gone.

And now financial disaster: more humiliation, more loss. What could he do? He could protest. He could get a lawyer and go to court and claim predatory lending, try to gain leniency, better terms, a lower interest rate. And be just one more of the sniveling indigent on the TV news, too ignorant or passive to make their own decisions or take their own actions, unless it was to blame others, the government or some hapless defendant, for whatever troubles befell them. It was always so unpleasant to see their images, to hear their stories, though it could be gratifying to think derisively or, in a more magnanimous moment, compassionately about them. No, he would not be one more sad case.

He would call McAnally at the Nimrod company, but he suspected he had little recourse, was already thinking about what the next steps would be. He could declare bankruptcy, try to weasel out of as many debts as possible. But surely he would lose both properties in any case, the house and barn, with its three all-but-finished apartments, the teahouse and its welcome income. There was no sense trying to sell; he had bought at the peak of the market, which now was glutted with homes selling for fortunes less than they had two years ago.

All this grubbing for money, he thought. He had counted on avoiding all that by studying literature, by becoming a college professor, by dedicating his life to an activity that was resolutely unnecessary and unproductive. He had always had such contempt for M.B.A.'s, for entrepreneurs, for people who seemed to think the purpose of life was to amass dollars. And yet here he was, acquiring real estate, renovating properties, leasing buildings, signing complex financial documents, in over his head. But that's what life is, after all: buying turnips.

He poured himself a half-glass of Glenlivet and took a sip. He thought, my drinking has become a cliché.

It was dark now. The teahouse would be closing soon. He slid into his loafers and headed out the door. For some reason, he took the letter with him.

The teahouse was brightly lit. Janet was seated at the table where she always was when there were no customers. Ann was busy in the kitchen. Paula wasn't there; she must have had the day off. Behind the counter was a young woman, Davida, something like that. She reminded him vaguely of Ms. Creasy, the blond curls, the eye makeup.

Janet looked up without speaking, which was unprecedented, but he must have had a look on his face that suggested urgency.

"I don't know how to say this other than to come right out with it," he said. "I'm going to lose the train station. The teahouse, I mean. The house, too. Everything. It's all gone now."

16

"Well, there must be something we can do," Janet said. She and Ann were in Janet's living room. She had been fretting about the future of the teahouse since Charles spoke to them the day before. She had taken out all her financial documents, pulled from various shelves and drawers and folders, and was sorting through them, creating piles based on some unknown organizing principle.

"We might be wise to wait till we have all the facts," Ann said. "Didn't Charles say he hadn't talked to the bank yet, or whoever it is?"

Janet sighed. Charles had explained the situation, the multiple mortgages, the balloon payment. The details were confusing, but the upshot was that Charles would lose the teahouse, and what would that mean for her? If nothing else, probably an interruption in her business. But more than that, she was fond of Charles, and things had just begun to settle down, to fall into place. She didn't feel like having to start over yet again.

"What is it again you're hoping to find in all those papers?" Ann asked.

"I was thinking maybe there was something I could do. Financially, I mean. I mean, I have retirement savings, so perhaps I could invest along with Charles."

"Didn't Charles say he owed something over one-and-a-half million dollars? Do you have anything like that kind of money? Sorry, I suppose it's not my business."

Janet sighed again. "Well, yes. No, don't apologize. I'm not sure how much I have. Henry took care of the retirement savings."

It had been a perfect arrangement, one of those rare marital compromises that works. With Henry traveling so much, for his job, it fell to Janet to take care of the day-to-day finances, budgeting for short-term expenses, paying the gas and electric and phone bills. But Henry was a man, after all, and he needed to feel like he was taking care of his household, like he had some control over their financial situation and wellbeing. So he invested all their retirement money. Which was fine with Janet, because she would have her teacher's pension and didn't really have to think about saving. So they lived modestly, if not frugally, and Henry put much of his pilot's salary into long-term savings. He didn't just park their money in some sort of index fund, either. He was constantly poring over reports and statements and prospectuses, or whatever they were. He seemed to know what he was doing.

"The thing is, this isn't making sense," Janet said.

"What is that?"

"Well, I get statements every year, or every quarter, or whatever, but I never really look at them. Henry always took care of all this, and until recently, it didn't even come to me. But it looks like all our money is in one account."

"Is that a problem?"

"Well, I always thought our money was spread around. You know, diversified. But it looks like over time he just moved it all to this one account, I suppose because he was getting the best returns from it."

"That makes sense."

"Except that the market crashed, if you'll recall."

"Yes, it did for us in Great Britain, too, although I think perhaps we're less reliant on personal savings."

"The thing is, I don't think I have any money left."

"What do you mean?"

"I mean, I'm looking at these statements, and it looks like the account lost all its value. Well, not all, but a lot."

"Are you sure?"

"No, I'm not sure. But that's the best I can tell."

"Well, let's not panic yet. For one thing, there must be protections against this kind of thing."

"No, that's just the point," Janet said, growing agitated. "It was a high-risk fund. I think it was some kind of derivatives; well, I don't even know what that means. But it made a lot of money. But then it lost a lot of money, a lot more than it made. And I guess that's the risk you take. There's no protections. There's no guarantees."

How could Henry have been so foolish? It was because of her pension. That was their safety net, so he felt he could gamble. And of course he was managing it actively, so if something went wrong, he would have shifted the money to somewhere else. Why hadn't she been more involved? She was angry, angry at Henry. It was strange thinking someone could do you this sort of wrong from beyond the grave. She felt guilty thinking of it that way. But it was his fault.

"Well, you say it lost a lot of its value. So you still have something."

Ann wasn't getting it. "I still have some, yes. But almost nothing. I have my teacher's pension, but it isn't much, not enough to live on, really. So that just leaves the money from the sale of our house, when I moved down here. Which isn't nothing, but it has to last the next thirty years. In any case, it's certainly not one-and-a-half million dollars."

"No," Ann said. She wasn't unsympathetic. She could hear the panic in Janet's voice. But she wasn't sure how to calm her. "Well, perhaps Charles needs to get all the facts about his situation, and you need to get all the facts about your situation. And then we can see where we are."

"You're very rational about all this," Janet said. "Which isn't an accusation. We need rational right now." Ann appeared to be thinking. "What is it?" Janet asked.

"No, nothing." She had an idea, but she thought it best to wait and see how things came out, for now.

**

Things came out much as Janet and Charles expected. Charles learned he had little recourse; he would lose his properties, and then some, because their value was less than what he had borrowed. Janet found that she was correct, that her retirement savings had dwindled to next to nothing. They met one evening at the teahouse, after hours, Janet and Charles and Ann.

"So: I appreciate your taking the time to meet and discuss the matter," Charles said, after they had exchanged pleasantries. He had reverted to the formal tone he had taken with her when they first met, Janet noticed. But he seemed diminished, withdrawn. Clearly it was painful to him to have to admit defeat, as it were.

She found herself compensating for his reticence. "Well, I know what it can be like to have financial difficulties. There's no shame in it. I know Mother and Daddy were never well-off, and they had to make some tough decisions over the years, to make ends meet. My father once invested in a timeshare property that never panned out. I think he took a bath, actually, and Mother was so cross with him over it, though I never did get the full story of what happened. He still talked about it till the day he died — he always referred to it as 'the campground' — but he had changed all the details in his memory, so that it became this idyllic place that he had wanted to move to, only Mother wouldn't have it. He had completely edited out the part about losing money." She paused. "I'm sorry, I realize I'm not being helpful."

"Yes," Charles said. "Well, here's what I think is going to happen. The lending company, *Nimrod*, or whatever they are, are going to foreclose on both my properties, on my house and your teahouse. I expect I'll put my things in storage and take an apartment in the city, or some such thing as that."

Janet noticed he was gazing past her, at an unseen horizon, as if self-consciously stoic, or wistful. "The thing is ...," she began.

"Now, about your *teahouse*," Charles said, cutting her off. "I don't think it should affect you, at least not in the short term. I expect Nimrod will just take over the property for a time, and then sell it, and then you'll simply have a new landlord. Of course, one can't know what the *new* owner will want to do with the property. But I can't imagine they'd want to make any changes."

Janet felt a new sense of panic at the mention of a future landlord. She supposed the new owner would have to honor the lease she had with Charles, but after that, who knows? The prospect of having to close down the teahouse, just as she was getting it going, was discouraging. She gazed around its interior: at the wrong-colored blue-checked curtains and, behind them, the pull shades Ann had put up;

at the tables and uneven chairs, made newly even by Ann, who had attached little caps to the shorter legs; at the fixings counter, as she called it, which Ann had set up to allow customers to fix their own drinks. It occurred to her that Ann had become indispensable, and the teahouse had become part of Ann's life, as well. But no, she was getting ahead of herself: it wasn't a foregone conclusion that the teahouse would have to close.

"The thing is," she said, "I had hoped to be able to help out in some way. That is, I had hoped to maybe invest with you in the teahouse. To try to keep things as they are now. But it turns out that I've had a bit of a financial setback of my own. It seems I've lost all my retirement savings."

"Oh, I *am* sorry to hear that," Charles said. "But I don't suppose there was anything you could do in any case."

They both seemed to sink into their own thoughts, as if searching their minds for a word they couldn't come up with, and then giving up on it. They sat in silence.

"What if I could?" Ann said abruptly.

It took a moment for Janet and Charles to resurface. They looked at Ann.

"Could what?" Janet said.

"What if there was something I could do?"

"What do you mean?" Charles asked.

"Well, here's what I'm thinking. I'm all alone in St. Andrews. I don't work, I have nothing keeping me there. Logan is over here, as well. I don't have a lot in the way of pension plans — retirement savings, I mean. But it's a historic home, it's quite spacious, for St. Andrews — it's quite valuable, actually. So what I'm thinking is, what if I sold my house and moved here, to Lower Slaughter? I don't think it would be quite so much as what you owe on your balloon payment, or whatever it is, Charles. But if Janet and I were to pool our money ...."

"But that's just it, I don't really have any money to pool," Janet protested.

"I doesn't really sound *practical*," Charles said distractedly.

"Well, I've thought a bit about this," Ann continued. "And I don't want to make any decisions for anyone, or suggest something they're not comfortable with. But what if I were to sell my house, and Janet were to contribute the money from the sale of her house, and Charles could throw in whatever savings he has, and we paid off the two properties, Charles' house and the teahouse? Then you could keep the teahouse, Janet, and Charles could stay in his house ...."

"Yes, but where would you and I live?" Janet broke in. "You're not thinking. ..."

"Oh, I see what you're saying," Charles said, newly interested. "I have my barn. You and Janet could each live in one of the barn townhouses. You haven't seen them, of course, but they're *quite* lovely. They're really almost complete. It's just a matter of the final details, like appliances and carpeting and what not. Oh, and then of course *Ben* could stay upstairs. In my upstairs, I mean."

"Yes," Ann said, "that's exactly what I was thinking. Of course, I'd have to look into the work-visa details."

They were quiet for a moment.

"Oh, but would you really want to give up your home in St. Andrews?" Janet asked. "It sounds so lovely."

"Well, perhaps it's time for a change. And it's a large house, more than I can really take care of myself. I wouldn't have suggested it if I weren't serious about it."

"Well, I think it's a *superb* idea," Charles said. He turned to Janet. "Janet, you seem skeptical."

"Well, Ann, I suppose if you're sure. And you'd have to move all your things over here, that isn't trivial. Oh, but

149

wouldn't it be wonderful to live next door to each other? And we could be partners in the teahouse. I've never been comfortable with your helping out without getting paid for it. Now, do you think you could sell your house quickly? Because I think we'd have to do all this very quickly. I'm sure I can sell Mother's condo. Those things seem to turn over very fast, even in this market. Oh, but I'd have to do something with Mother's things. I don't think they'd fit in very well in a converted barn, do you? Well, I guess I'm getting ahead of myself."

Charles and Ann looked at each other and smiled.

"I feel I'm being bailed *out*, though," Charles said. "I'm not sure I'm comfortable with that. Although perhaps I *need* to be taken down a peg."

"I wouldn't think of it that way," Ann said. "It's more that we're all three of us throwing in our lot together, in a sort of way."

"Like the council at *Runnymeade*," Charles said.

"Perhaps we should have a secret handshake," Janet added.

"Well, there are a lot of details to work out," Ann said, trying to keep them focused. "Charles, I suppose the first thing you should do is find out if you can hold off the mortgage people. And I need to think about getting myself back home. Or I should say, back to St. Andrews."

17

Things always seem to work out for me, Janet thought. I was a girl of slender means, yet I managed to go to college and have a career I enjoyed. I got pregnant in college, but I was able to give up the child for adoption and pretty much continue my life without interruption, and then even come to know him later as a young man. I had a decent husband and a long career and a comfortable life, in the town I grew up in and near the parents I loved. After all that I was able to start the teahouse, and it all just seemed to fall into place. And Ann just happened to walk through my door, a person connected to me by the slenderest of threads, stretched across forty-some years, and become my dear friend. And then just when it seemed like things were going to go all wrong, when it looked as if I had lost my savings and was going to lose the teahouse, Ann comes up with a solution to everything, and it all works out.

She realized that looked at another way, things always seemed to go wrong. She had grown up not poor but nearly poor, to be perfectly honest. Getting pregnant in college had been awful, and giving up the baby even worse, and then of course she had become estranged from her son, after having gotten to know him, which was probably worse than never having known him at all. She had soured on teaching, in the end, on the waning respect for teachers, on the growing demands of the administration and the parents, especially. She never did have what you'd call an ideal marriage, with Henry away so often, and he certainly wasn't someone you would describe as a soul mate. And then he had died suddenly, and it had been such a brutal shock. She had never really gotten used to living alone and being independent, being responsible for herself and her own decisions. On top of that, Henry hadn't managed their retirement savings very well, though perhaps she should say she was the one who hadn't managed them well, at least after Henry was no longer around to take care of things. Her father had died, too, as you discover everyone close to you does. Whatever the relationship is, it's going to end sadly, and the closer you are, the more important the person is to you, the sadder and more devastating it's going to be. Her mother had had the strokes, then, two of them, and it had been so exhausting taking care of her, she had become so difficult and so negative. And the whole idea of moving her to a nursing home — let's face it, of parking her in a room till she died — just wore on her, like a bad hip that you decide to live with but that you never get used to, that continues to cause you pain. And then it had been one thing after another with the teahouse, first her incompetence in getting it started, and then the fire, and then almost losing the place altogether.

But she preferred to look at it the other way, that things always worked out. And they were working out, in fact. She and Charles had been able to combine whatever savings they had — mostly from the sale of her house in Plymouth, two years ago — and keep the mortgage company at bay. Her mother's condo had sold quickly, to a Chinese couple with a young boy, or maybe they were Korean, she never did find out. Ann was already back from Scotland after arranging the sale of her own house, which was tied up with a historic deed, or something like that, though it looked like the transaction was a good as complete; her belongings were being shipped by a company that specialized in that sort of thing. In the meantime Charles was having the barn townhouses finished up, and workers were coming and going, putting on the final touches.

Charles was right, the townhouses were lovely. They were arranged side-by-side, the barn divided down the middle, so that each had two floors. The first floors were rather low-ceilinged and squat, but they had exposed beams and a sort of in-the-ground coziness to them. The upstairs had much higher ceilings and more exposed beams, and wide-planked wood floors that were newly finished. Charles had fitted the townhouses with the latest amenities, space-saving appliances and polished-stone countertops and modern accent lighting. They had a rather peculiar smell of old wood and new carpet, at once earthy and artificial. There was a loft apartment, too, up in the peak of the barn's roof, but they didn't have enough funds to finish that for the time being.

Janet gave Ann first choice of the townhouse on the right, which faced Charles' house and got much more light, even though it had the more northerly exposure. Janet took the townhouse on the left, which, though it faced south, for much of the day fell in the shadow of a low bluff that rose above the barn and house and teahouse.

Ben had explained to Janet and Ann that their new home was what was called a "bank barn." On one side of it the earth was mounded up to form an incline, retained by low walls of stone, that allowed the farmer, in a bygone time when the property was a working farm, to pull his hay wagon straight into the barn's second floor, where the hay would be stored over the winter. This had the effect of making the barn look almost like it had been built into a hillside. Ann said it reminded her of Mole End, in *The Wind in the Willows*. The name stuck, and the barn was christened Mole End, and Charles' house Toad Hall. There was speculation as to who was Mole and Badger and Ratty, but there was no question, at least for Janet and Ann, that Charles was Toad of Toad Hall.

The arrangement they came to was that the three of them, Janet and Ann and Charles, would own the deeds to the properties together. Charles would continue to live in his house and have the income from Ben's leasing his third floor. Janet and Ann would live in the barn townhouses and would jointly own the teahouse, from which they would split any profits. Ann was surprisingly nonchalant about pitching in the greatest share of the money, though it turned out the only way for her to get a work visa was if she were the controlling partner in the venture, so she had to contribute more than half anyway. Still, Janet couldn't seem to let go of her worry that Ann had made the wrong decision in giving up her home in St. Andrews.

"But as I've said," Ann repeated, "it really was too big a house for one person to be knocking about in."

"But it sounded so lovely, Ann, a historic home, near the water and the cathedral. I would have liked to have seen it one day."

"It just wasn't practical. And it was time for a change."

Christmas came and went in a blur. Janet had only two weeks to pack her things and get out of the condo before the closing date. She had left behind several boxes in the condo's makeshift attic, with a promise to the new owners that she'd be back for them soon. In the meantime her new home, in the barn townhouse, was only beginning to take shape, with most things still in boxes and most of the boxes not even in the right rooms. Getting ready in the morning, showering and dressing and fixing breakfast, had become a frustration of misplaced items and minor disasters, and she rarely managed to get to the teahouse on time.

Ann had moved into her side of the building, as well, but as most of her things were still in transit from Scotland, her new home echoed with emptiness and incompleteness. She had just enough clothes that she didn't have to wear the same outfits with too obvious frequency, though the compact washer and dryer had to run constantly. She had bought a new mattress set and bed frame, rather than shipping them over, so she at least had a nice bed to sleep on, and in American proportions, no less. But she was stalked by loneliness, in this new place, this new house and new country, and she found herself lying awake at night, listening to empty rooms. Occasionally she heard Janet, who seemed to be up at all hours, as she banged doors and drawers open and shut, as she stumped up and down the stairs. She would have found it annoying, under other circumstances, but in the foreignness of her situation Janet's invisible but audible presence was reassuring.

Janet had completely forgotten about Christmas presents, in the kerfuffle of moving, and she was a bit dismayed that Ann had actually thought to bring treats from Scotland, tins of shortbread, ceramic figurines. She had wrapped them neatly in paper that featured little cartoon Nessies, the Loch Ness Monster, wearing a Santa's cap. Charles, for his part, produced bottles of rather expensive-looking French wine, Château Margaux something or other, which he gave to Janet and Ann and Ben. Janet searched in vain for something she could give them in return, till she uncovered several old glass Mrs. Butterworth's bottles in a box of craft supplies, along with colored markers and ribbons and stenciling materials. She stayed up most of the night and used her stencil paints, complemented by glued-on clothing she fashioned from old wrapping paper, to transform them into reasonably recognizable facsimiles of Toad and Badger and Rat and Mole. She presented them, their paint and glue scarcely dry, the next morning at the teahouse.

"Now Ann, don't take offense, but you're Badger," she explained. "I thought you might make a good Rat, as well, since you're so practical, but that seemed better suited for Ben, so I've reserved Ratty for him. So you're Badger, because you're always in charge, and you always solve everyone's problems. Not that you're antisocial at all, like Badger."

"It's delightful, Janet," Ann said. "And he's got a dinky little walking stick, as well."

"Paula, I made you Mole. Not that you're really like Mole at all, I suppose. The truth is, I'm more of a Mole character, I'm sure that's the way Ann sees it. But then I'm not going to make one of these for myself. And I did want you to be included."

"What is 'Mole'?" Paula asked, regarding her gift skeptically. There had really been no way for Janet to give the Mrs. Butterworth's bottle a pointed nose, so Mole, with his little wire-rimmed glasses, came out looking more like an old woman with large hands.

"Oh, it's a character from *The Wind in the Willows*. They're all characters from *The Wind in the Willows*. It's an old children's book. I don't suppose you have it in Brazil."

"Now, what are these glass figurines?" Ann asked.

"Oh, those are Mrs. Buttersworth bottles. It's a kind of pancake syrup. You don't have it in Scotland? They're plastic now, and not the same, but when I was growing up they were glass and looked like this. I found a bunch of them in one of my boxes. I have no idea why they were there. Mother must have been saving them for some reason. Anyway, I suppose the joke loses something if you have to explain it."

"I think they're lovely," Ann insisted.

Charles and Ben would get theirs later. In the meantime they displayed Toad, Badger, Ratty, and Mole on top of the pastry case, to the delight of most customers if not Emily Reaper.

"Now what is this?" Emily demanded.

"That's a rat and a mole and a toad," Paula said. "Ann, what is the other one, a bastard?"

"Badger," Ann said.

"A badger," Paula said. "Janet made them."

"They're not for sale?"

"No, not for sale. For Janet's friends."

Emily sniffed at them and wandered out.

Christmas Day itself passed with Janet and Ann and Charles and Ben in their own homes alone. Ben hadn't thought to get presents for anyone and was somewhat abashed to receive gifts from the other three, especially the Mrs. Butterworth's Ratty from Janet; it was so personal a gift. But he didn't mind spending Christmas by himself. It's a day like any other day, he told himself, and whether you celebrate or not, or whether you celebrate on the day itself or some other day, really makes no difference. He hadn't bothered to decorate, other than to hang a rather anemic wreath on his front door. He noticed Charles hadn't decorated, either, and he didn't see much of Charles in the days leading up to Christmas, as if he were avoiding the holiday, or the awkwardness of two people finding themselves alone in the same house on the same day. He did see quite a bit of Janet, however, the source of a seemingly endless stream of requests for help moving furniture or hanging pictures or placing heavy objects on high shelves.

Paula spent Christmas at Ash's parents' house, Duchess II, where the four of them basked in the polyvinyl-chloride glow of a towering silver-and-blue Christmas tree. Billington Christmases were rather Spartan affairs, old money not-withstanding, and the gifts exchanged were on the order of fleece gloves and cheap cable-knit sweaters. At two in the afternoon they had a roast-goose dinner, for which they were joined by Trey's cousin and his wife, Bernie and Betty Crackstone, who arrived at one-thirty. Afterward they retired to the den to sip sherry under the apologetic gaze of a stuffed moose head that Trey had allegedly bagged in Maine some twenty years before. Mitzi joined them after giving instructions to a stout, silent Mexican she had hired for the day as kitchen help.

"She was loading Mother's silver in the dishwasher, can you believe it?" she said. "It's so hard to find people these days who understand the value of things."

"That's true," Bernie agreed.

"The Asians are the smartest," Mitzi said, pulling up a chair. "Do you think the young people know this, Trey? The Asians are the smartest, then the Caucasians, then whatever it is you call Spanish people, then the blacks. The blacks are the ... least smart. It's been proven."

Paula had heard about racism in America. Brasil was supposed to be the true melting pot, she had always been told, unlike America, which only pretended to be. But Brasil wasn't as egalitarian as it liked to think it was. And she had never actually experienced racism in America; she had never felt like she was being treated differently at Globanaut or the teahouse or anywhere else, for that matter, by people who thought she was black. But maybe this was what American racism was, a secret categorizing, a benign distance. Yet Mitzi seemed so frank about it, so innocently lacking in self-awareness. Perhaps she's just saying what some people actually think, even if they wouldn't actually say it, even if they wouldn't actually put it to themselves quite that way.

Ash, for his part, had given up trying to convert his mother, as he thought of it. He had heard her theory of racial intelligence levels so many times there was no point in trying to reason with it. The only hope was to chip away at the edges. "Hispanics," he said.

"What, dear?"

"You said, 'whatever you call Spanish people.' It's *Hispanics.* You know, Paula. ..."

"*All* Asians?" Paula asked, cutting off Ash.

"I beg your pardon?" Mitzi said to Paula.

"*All* Asians are the smartest? One billion Chinese peasants?"

"You know, the blacks ruined Chestnut Hill," Mitzi continued, ignoring Paula's question. "Mother said it was lovely when she was a girl. Then the Jews started to move in. Daddy said, as soon as the Jews move in, the blacks follow. And he was absolutely right."

"Mother, you realize that Paula is part Portuguese and part Amerindian and part African."

"You don't need to defend me," Paula said to Ash. "I can speak for myself."

"I'm only trying to help."

"I don't know what that is," Mitzi said. "Amerindian?"

"The point is, she has African heritage. Like African-Americans. Like blacks."

"Well, I don't mean you, dear." Mitzi turned to Paula and offered a Protestant smile.

On the ride back to Paula's apartment Ash agreed he owed her much more than the silver Tiffany earrings he had already given her. He pointed out that it was their first Christmas together and promised to make it special. Paula realized, then, that it was also her first Christmas in the States, her first Christmas away from home. She hadn't thought of it that way, because home was the orphanage, really, not her mother's house, and because she had spent so many holidays at college, in the few years just past. She felt an aloneness, then, as she gazed out the window and Ash continued the conversation on his own. She had been thinking of her home as being in America, even though her work visa wouldn't let her stay here permanently; she had been thinking of her home as being Ash, as the one person, however unlikely, she had chosen to be with. But did she have one, really, a home?

18

Janet was up early the day after Christmas. She had planned to close the teahouse for Christmas week, but Ann suggested they should take advantage of commuters riding into the city for last-minute shopping and after-Christmas sales. Besides, they could use the income, having essentially just depleted their life savings. It had proved to be a good idea in any case, because the activity, the need to get up in the still darkness, the hubbub of a long line of customers, the constant demands on her attention, were a welcome distraction from what she had to admit had been a rather disappointing holiday, her new townhouse notwithstanding.

Daniela and Davina had the week off, so it was just Janet and Ann and Paula. There was the usual throng of customers in the morning, the regulars who still had to work plus early-rising shoppers hoping to beat the rush. Later there was a procession of family clusters, most often a father with two or three young children, presumably banished to the teahouse by a weary mother tired of scolding and

161

cleaning up after them. These were challenging, because they took minutes to decide what they wanted and even longer to actually order, while a line formed behind them, impatient commuters shifting from one foot to the other, and because the children, some of them still in pajamas, most of them with uncombed, pillow-ruffed hair, were over-animated by a day full of presents and sugar. After leaving the counter they crammed noisily around a table, having snatched extra chairs from neighboring tables, till the children began getting up to explore the teahouse and generally get in the way of the other patrons. When they finally went, after a protracted corralling, they left behind half-empty cups and crumpled napkins and scatterings of pastry crumbs, which other customers then complained about before Janet or Ann or Paula had a chance to clear them.

The day was beginning to drag, for Janet, though someone had left behind a magazine in which she found an interesting article on Oliver Platt; he was handsome in such an agreeable way. Then Charles made a rare appearance.

"Oh, *good*, you're all here," he said. "Well, Ben isn't here, but I can speak with him later."

"Do you want me to see if Ben is at home?" Paula asked.

"No, I won't stay a minute. I just wanted to — Ann, this is for you, too," he said, getting Ann to stop what she was doing and pay him attention. "I've decided I'm going to host a New Year's Eve dinner. And you're all invited. No, you're all *required*. I would have sent formal invitations, but there isn't time."

"Oh, that sounds lovely, Charles," Janet said.

"Now, what can I bring?" Ann asked.

"No, no one is to bring anything. Just come around six o'clock for cocktails, and then we'll have dinner around seven, and who knows if we'll make it to midnight. But in the intervening hours we'll *live it up*."

"And who all will be there?" Janet asked.

"Well, I think just you three and Ben and I. Can I count you in, Paula? It will give you an excuse not to have dinner with those awful *Billingtons.*"

Paula had told Janet and Ann and Charles about Thanksgiving dinner at Duchess II. "Yes, I will come," she said. "I don't think I could stand another evening with Ash's parents so soon after yesterday. I haven't even told you about that yet."

"And you can certainly bring your young Ashford, of course," Charles said on his way out the door.

It felt like a big step to Charles, to host a dinner party, the first he would have had since leaving Grier & Buchanan. But he felt he owed it to Janet and Ann, after all they had done for him. And Thanksgiving and Christmas had been so awful, so drab and gray and alone. He didn't think he could spend another holiday staring at his kitchen television, slowly getting drunk on vodka martinis, while Proust paced about his feet and reminded him that the only living thing he had any meaningful interactions with had four paws and a tail.

He was aware that his frequent entertainments, the dinner parties and brunches and holiday gatherings for which he had become famous at Grier & Buchanan, were merely rather paltry attempts to re-create the festivities he had enjoyed with Alain. Alain applied himself to a dinner party the way a business tycoon takes on a merger, the way a professional athlete approaches a championship match, as if nothing else in the world were more important, nothing else mattered. It helped that he had the money to stage them properly, with a full-time Italian cook, Agostina — "Ms. Botticello to you, Agostina to me," Alain would say — matronly and regal, who oversaw his culinary endeavors and who seemed similarly to superintend his dual excesses, cheap liquor and ill-advised affairs.

He had met Alain during his first year in London, when he was a Rhodes Scholar. One of his professors invited him and two or three other students to a party at the home of "the notorious bon vivant" Alain Lallemand. None of the other students showed, and Charles found himself there alone and with no one to talk to, till Alain — more than twenty years his senior but suavely dressed and professionally polished and looking much younger — buttonholed him and plied him with sidecars and kept him till most of the other guests had fallen asleep or gone home. And so he was "in": he became a regular visitor to the sprawling Victorian flat at 52 Brompton Road, to elaborately choreographed dinner parties, replete with crystal and silver, to more loosely organized evening parties that seemed never to end. There he met writers, of varying repute, as well as artists, filmmakers, musicians, wealthy hangers-on. Alain was a commanding host, adeptly orchestrating entrances and introductions and interactions, putting his guests at ease yet somehow managing to remain the center of things, like an even more extravagant bird in a den of preening peafowl. Or at least he managed this till he got tipsy enough to start pursuing his young male and female guests alike and then carelessly drunk enough to start skewering anyone he felt had overstayed his welcome. "*So* sorry you can't stay," or, "Will you have a *long* drink?" he would say, taking an elbow and guiding his hapless interlocutor out the door.

But with Charles he was tender and solicitous. Guests arrived late — even dinner parties didn't start till well past eight o'clock — but Charles was always expected hours earlier. He would sit at the round oak table in Alain's generous kitchen, sipping a gin and tonic, while Agostina cooked and Alain hovered, mostly getting in the way. They felt a kinship, certainly on Charles' part, but surely on Alain's, as well, despite that, or maybe because, Alain had never chased him the way he chased other bright young men. Perhaps it was because they both were foreigners — Alain was Belgian; *Lallemand* was French for "the German" — at home in but transplanted to London. "*Luxe, calme, et volupté*" — luxury, peace, and pleasure — he often proclaimed, quoting Baudelaire, which presumably was what London afforded him.

They remained friendly while Charles was in college, in the way a student and professor can sometimes develop a lasting rapport. They stayed in touch after Charles returned to the States for his doctoral degree, and Charles visited Alain in London from time to time. But when, after Charles finished his schooling, Alain invited him to stay with him at his flat for the summer, their friendship entered a new phase: they became, approximately, a couple.

For the next ten years Charles spent every summer and every Christmas break in London with Alain. They ate their meals together and shopped together and went to the theater together. They consulted each other, often, on important decisions, such as where Charles would spend a sabbatical. And they were expected to be seen together at Alain's parties, where Alain would introduce him meaningfully as "my friend Charles."

But their mutual attraction had never been overtly physical, and their relationship never became sexual. He knew, or at least sensed with near certainty, that Alain took lovers, or gentleman friends, as he would have called them. But even on those occasions when Alain was thoroughly drunk, when his inhibitions presumably would be at their lowest, he had never urged their relationship further, had never initiated physical contact, other than, perhaps, a rather delicious lingering of a hand on his shoulder or a grasping of his wrist during conversation. In hindsight he felt some regret at this, or a sense of implied rejection: why *hadn't* Alain made a pass, in all their years together? Had they been a couple, then? He never thought of himself as gay. Or was it that he never allowed himself to think of himself as gay? The truth was, he had always been more attracted to women than to men, though certainly not in a way that led to anything like marriage. Rather, perhaps, he enjoyed the company of both women and men, but women more so. In any case it seemed to him that all friendships were sexual, to some degree, that you wouldn't invest in a friendship with anyone, man or woman, unless you felt at least some measure of sexual attraction to them.

What would their relationship have become, had it lasted longer? By the time he was in his early sixties Alain was losing his passion for parties if not for luxury. Would he have become a dull rich man, consumed with decorating his sitting room and having his nails done and buttressing his financial assets? Would he have become faithful to Charles, in the sense of investing more in the relationship, emotionally, of revealing secrets, of wanting to know Charles'? Even after ten years of friendship he maintained a certain distance, a formality, that kept him at arm's length.

Charles had been hopeful. But there wasn't to be more than ten years with Alain. There had been a night of drinking. A fall in the shower. A fractured sternum. A stay in the hospital. A respiratory infection, pneumonia. A severe allergic reaction to the antibiotic. The revelation of a preexisting problem with his kidneys, which began to fail. And in six weeks, Alain was dead.

Charles had rushed to London immediately after the mishap, fitting in the visit just before spring-semester finals. That was before the pneumonia, before the antibiotic, and while Alain had been miserable, unable to breathe without a respirator and therefore unable to speak or get out

166

of bed, it all seemed under control, a terrible episode but one that would be over in a week or so. But then one thing after another had gone wrong, like a frustration dream that won't end. As soon as the semester was over he returned to London, where he had to battle the doctors for the right to see Alain, to learn about his condition, to manage his affairs. Alain had no family in London, no one but Charles to look after him, and the few friends who had visited him after the accident, who had sent abundant flower arrangements or left outrageous, optimistic phone messages, mysteriously vanished when his health declined, like birds scattering from a suddenly electrified wire. It emerged that Alain's will had been revised so many times over that it was a complete muddle, and there was required an excruciating session, with hospital administrators and lawyers present, during which a doctor lifted the fog of morphine and allowed Alain to dictate his last testament. He left what remained of his depleted estate, after a generous concession to Agostina, to Charles, dear, sweet Charles.

And that was it. He was lowered back into his morphinic dreams — or were they nightmares, as from the hand of Phobetor? — and in three days he was gone. Charles oversaw the cremation and the pathetic, pallid funeral and the disposition of Alain's things. He met with officials and signed documents and went home, home to Grier & Buchanan, home to Falmouth, Pennsylvania, home to his empty, silent house.

His colleagues would have been disappointed to learn that he and Alain had never been lovers. Oddly, though, they never seemed to question the possibility that he had had an affair with a female student.

Proust mewed for his dinner.

"Yes, Marcel, I know," Charles said. "I wonder if I should serve a paté with dinner on New Year's."

19

The night was deep and crisp, the stars clear, the chill wind in repose, as the revelers made their way to Charles', Ben from upstairs, Janet and Ann from next door, Paula in her car, the short drive from her apartment, all arriving almost at once. Inside, fires cracked briskly in the fireplaces, warming the Turkish marble, brightening the rooms. Proust greeted the guests at the side door off the dining room, animated yet apprehensive, and every so often withdrew to a safe distance before returning again to their company. Paula had never been in Charles' home before, and it was the first time she had met Proust.

"Your cat is so handsome," she said.

"Yet he's not the least bit *vain* about it."

"Oh, Charles, everything looks wonderful," Janet said.

Charles had laid the dining-room table with silver and crystal, which reflected the tinkle of the cut-glass chandelier. A bowl of wild pink roses — where could he have got them? — floated at the table's center. The sideboard was spread with boughs of pine and spruce and warmed by the glow of stout candles. Pichl drifted cheerfully from ancient stereo speakers as the guests unburdened themselves of coats and hats and scarves.

Charles, on the other hand, was not himself so well put together. He had put on an old gray sweatshirt, instead of his usual white oxford, and it had got rather splotched with his dinner preparations. He had meant to go upstairs to change it, before the guests arrived, and to shower, for that matter. But the more vodka martinis he drank the less imperative it seemed to be, and now it was too late.

"Well, let's everyone come into the library for drinks before dinner," he said. He led them to a room lined with books, their multicolored spines reaching the twelve-foot ceiling, and stuffed with low, comfortable sofas. "I've set out some *very* expensive artisanal cheese — which I don't think Proust has eaten *too* much of — though I have to warn you it smells suspiciously of wet cow. To drink I've made hot-buttered rum and *Glühwein* — which is a sort of German mulled wine — although of course I can offer pretty much any sort of liquor you can imagine."

"Oh, hot-buttered rum for me," Janet said. "Although I should warn you all that even a half-glass of wine makes me rather foolish."

"I refuse to believe you have *ever* been foolish, Janet. Certainly not foolish enough."

When they all had been sufficiently lubricated that conversation began to flow, Charles disappeared to the kitchen to finish dinner. He had decided on a roast turkey, as all but Paula hadn't had a real Thanksgiving, along with a supporting cast of vegetables: mashed potatoes, yams, haricot beans, Brussels sprouts, succotash, a personal favorite. He had also made fresh bread and a cranberry sauce and a rather disappointing aspic. He had added a vegetarian main course, in deference to Paula, and he had decided against the paté, for the same reason, though he supposed the aspic was as good as. He had meant to get pickled gherkins — another favorite — but had forgot. When everything was fully ready — the turkey let to stand, the potatoes doused with butter, the beans just cooked — he called in everyone to the dining room and appropriated Ben as his assistant in serving. Ben set out the serving dishes to enthusiastic comments while Charles rather approximately filled the water glasses.

"For you, Paula, I've made *Moros y Cristianos* — Moors and Christians," he said. "Which is black beans and rice, of course. It's *Cuban*. And I've thrown in shrimp; you'll eat that, won't you? I assure you I used *vegetable* stock, not chicken."

"Yes, we have something like this in Brasil. But we would call it *feijão com arroz*. And yes, I like shrimp."

"Oh *good*. Now where is your young Ashford?"

"He ... couldn't come tonight. He decided to have dinner with his family. It's OK."

"Well, too bad for *us*," Charles said, obviously not meaning it. "Now, Ben, you'll carve the turkey."

"Why do I have to carve the turkey?"

"Don't worry, no one's watching. Don't fuck it up, though."

"Charles!" Janet said.

"Oh, Janet, after teaching sixth graders all those years, surely you're familiar with the word *fuck*. Now," he said, addressing all of them, "I know some people say grace before meals, but I do *spirits* before meals, and we've done that already — although I *am* trying, in a New Year's resolution sort of way, not to drink spirits before noon, which is a bother, but of course it's well past noon now, isn't it? — so I will simply say: dig *in*."

171

"Oh, Charles, that wasn't much of a speech, was it?" Janet said.

"Heaven forefend: no speeches," Charles warned.

"Well, Happy New Year, everyone, then," Janet said.

Happy New Years were exchanged, napkins unfurled, plates passed, dishes served, wine poured, forks lifted. There was the slathering of butter and the clinking of crystal and the pouring of more wine. Janet sat back, quiet for once, and surveyed the happy scene, the warmth and conversation and goodwill.

"Oh, I'm almost forgetting," she said. "Paula needs an apartment. And I have an idea."

"Now what is this about?" Ann asked.

"My lease is up at my apartment next month," Paula explained. "In January. And anyway, I can't really afford it anymore, now that I'm not working at Globanaut. No offense, but the teahouse doesn't pay quite as much."

"But then I thought about the apartment in the barn," Janet said. "You know, the one above us, Ann, on the third floor. Why couldn't Paula have that?"

"Yes, that's a wonderful idea. Charles, is there a lot of work left to finish it?"

"No, not so much. It needs appliances and things. Oh, and I never did have the bathroom done. Well, it needs *some* work."

"But if the three of us pitched in together, we could finish it?"

"Yes, of course."

"Oh, but Ann must get the rent payments," Janet said. "After all, you put in the most to buy the properties."

"But do we even need to charge rent to Paula?"

"Yes, I would have to pay the rent."

"And Ann must get it," Charles concluded. "That's *that* settled."

"I think I will like living here," Paula said. For one thing, it had turned out there was a problem with her work-visa paperwork, and it was better not to have to deal with a new landlord.

"Welcome to the compound," Ben said. He recalled from his days as an anthropology student that *compound* came from the Malaysian *kampong*, a group of dwellings within a circumscribed space. Like a Lenape village. Like Toad Hall and Mole End and the teahouse.

Paula smiled.

"Is that what we are now, a compound?" Janet asked.

"Well, *something* like that. Now, Paula, you were going to tell us about Christmas and those dreadful Billingtons."

Paula told the story of Christmas day with Ash's parents, their condescension to the woman they had hired to help in the kitchen, Mitzi's ranking of race by intelligence.

"And didn't she say something before about 'chunking'?" Ann asked.

"She says that black people can't chunk. I don't know what that means."

"I suppose she's talking about something like compartmentalization," Charles said. "The ability to relegate things to categories. Like she does with people, apparently."

"I didn't think people were still so blatantly racist," Janet said.

"Well of *course* they are. They just usually keep it to themselves."

"I thought America was meant to be the melting pot," Ann said. "It's not that we don't have racial conflict in the United Kingdom, of course. But it does seem somehow more fraught over here. Or maybe just more present."

"I suppose it's the history of it all," Janet said. "You would think it would all be behind us by now. But it's not. It's just that people don't talk about it."

"Really?" Ann said. "It seems like Americans talk about race all the time."

"Oh, the blatherers on the TV, yes. But not regular people. I sometimes hear people making veiled references to race — you know, kind of talking in code. But no one really *talks* about it. I mean, I don't think I've ever had a conversation about race with a black person, or an Asian, or an Indian, someone from India. Now what about you, Paula? Do people ever talk to you about race?"

"No, not really. I don't think people are sure what I am anyway."

"Well, now, what do you consider yourself?"

Paula was never sure how to answer that question. Americans seemed to assume she was black, presumably because she looked black. But she didn't think of herself as black. She was Portuguese and African on her father's side and Portuguese and *Indios* on her mother's side. Or at least that's what her mother had always told her. "In Brasil I thought of myself as *mulata*. But I don't think people use that word here. So I guess I think of myself as a *Brasileiro*. A Brazilian. Living in America."

Why, she wondered, was race such a big deal? As if that's all you were: black, brown, white. What did it mean to be white, anyway, since weren't people who thought of themselves as white from, what, she didn't know how many different countries? And she had read somewhere that Hispanic was considered an ethnicity, not a race, though she had no idea what the difference was. She wasn't sure how to fill out the census form, when it came in the mail. She skipped the boxes for both black and Hispanic, instead checking "Some other race" and writing in "Brazilian." It felt as if she was being disloyal to her heritage, as if she belonged to nothing: "Some other race."

"I wonder if things will start to change now, now that the country is becoming more multicultural," Janet said. "I guess it always has been, but I mean out here in the suburbs. I mean, just look at the people who come into the teahouse. It seems that half of them are Asian or Indian — or I guess they could be Pakistani, or whatever. But the suburbs seem to be much more multicultural than they were even just a few years ago."

"I wonder if it will make people more accepting of other races, or if they'll start to blame problems on them," Ann said. "Of course, I notice I say 'people' when I mean 'white people.' I guess that's an Anglo-Saxon perspective."

"Oh, I would think it would make things better. Maybe race won't matter so much any longer, and the differences will become less."

"Well, I wonder if that's also an Anglo-Saxon perspective," Ann said. "Maybe racial groups don't want there to be less differences. They want to keep their black culture, or Chinese culture, or whatever."

"I see what you're saying. I guess the difference is that there's no such thing as white culture. Is there? It's just everything that isn't some other culture. Oh, I guess that is a white perspective."

"The conversation has degenerated into *seriousness*. Doesn't anyone have anything *inane* they want to add? How about more wine?" Charles got up to open another bottle.

It occurred to Janet that this was the first serious conversation they had had. Well, she and Ann had talked about their husbands' deaths, at times, and Ann had talked about Logan. But really, so much of conversation was about whatever the task at hand was, who should open the teahouse or whether they needed more scones, or else it was idle chitchat, did you hear what so-and-so celebrity did and do you think we're going to get snow? But this was the first

time they had all sat and talked about something of consequence, she and Ann and Charles and Paula and — wait,
where was Ben? "Has anyone seen Ben?" she asked.

"I was just wondering that myself," Paula said.

"Now where did the boy get to? Benjamin!" Charles bel-
lowed, to no response. "Well, he's going to miss pumpkin
pie."

Ben had slipped out of the dining room while the others were just finishing their dinners and still engrossed in
conversation. He was enjoying the evening, and their company, but he could take a roomful of people for only so
long before feeling exhausted. He felt tone deaf to group
dynamics, as if not all the frequencies were reaching him.
He would have no idea what to add to a conversation, and
then when he finally did speak, it would be just as the conversation broke up, so that his words hung in the air awkwardly, like a lone audience member clapping at the end of
a movement of classical music.

He had wandered upstairs to Charles' study. He had
been in the house a hundred times before, had helped
Charles with things like programming his DVD recorder,
had spent weekend mornings at Charles' kitchen table discussing literature or what he was studying in grad school
over wickedly potent vodka martinis. But he had never
seen the second floor, and he thought he might as well
use the excuse of finding an upstairs bathroom to explore.
The study was dark and dusty and lined with more books,
though not neatly organized, as in the library, but in random piles and mixed in with folders and papers. He knew
Charles was fond of him, that they shared a sort of kinship;
maybe it was their peculiar sense of humor, or maybe it
was their jaundiced view of the world. Still, Charles allowed
him only so close. Or was it he who maintained the distance? There was a manuscript on the desk, cross-stacked

papers covered with double-spaced words in Courier New. He read a page, lifted it and read another. It looked like Charles was writing a book on Muriel Spark. Or had been writing: the top sheet of the manuscript carried a film of dust. He had read one of her books in Charles' class as a freshman. What was it? Remember you must die. That was it: *Memento Mori*. She seemed to share Charles' sense of humor as well; if Charles wrote a novel, it would be like hers.

He began to feel like he was prying, so he wandered back downstairs. The party had retired to the drawing room to enjoy their pie and coffee. Charles had dropped off in drunken sleep, hugging a velvet cushion, on a rather uncomfortable-looking Victorian loveseat. The others talked quietly so as not to wake him.

"There you are," Janet said. "We had begun to think you had fallen in."

"There's coffee and pie in the kitchen, if you want some," Paula said.

"If you're going, love, could you bring me another piece?" Ann asked. "I do like pie."

He went to the kitchen to get a slice of pie for Ann. He hadn't had much dinner, actually, and was still hungry. He pried a decadent chunk of turkey skin from the bottom of the roasting pan and popped it in his mouth before making his way back to the others. He paused in the dim hallway outside the door and listened to their murmuring voices. We *are* a compound, he thought, liking the idea. Or maybe that wasn't quite the word. Haven. Harbor. Sanctuary. He turned the corner into the room, into the voices and light.

.

20

The teahouse was operating at full steam. Ann and Paula had fine-tuned their roles and tasks to a level of concision and efficiency and specificity of purpose, like an intricate machine designed by Germans, that they both found satisfying. Janet hovered and got in the way, often, but more frequently she simply waited at the uneven table for customers and then kept them entertained after they arrived. Each had found the thing she was best at.

Ben had begun to do small jobs here and there at Janet's request, and though he hadn't become the teahouse handyman in any formal way, he was doing regular enough work that he had a steady if modest income and passed an agreeable amount of time at the teahouse. He had hung the sign, of course, and later installed a pair of spotlights, one on each side of the sign, to illuminate it. He also resized the back door so that it no longer stuck, though it still made a distinct *shunk* when you opened it. This was most welcome to Janet and Ann and Paula, because it meant they could come and go from the back door, which was nearer the parking lot and trash dumpster and on the whole made life easier. Ben was equally pleased, for from his overheated apartment, its windows always cracked, he could hear the ringing of the teahouse bell as customers came and went and also as Janet sneaked in and out at seemingly all hours. It was a relief to no longer have to hear, at eleven-thirty or so at night, just as he was dropping off to sleep, the little tin tinkling of Janet's scattershot memory as she slipped into the teahouse to retrieve whatever she had forgotten.

Daniela, unfortunately, had quit, or maybe it was Davina, Janet wasn't certain. But Ann and Paula had found two new tea caddies to replace the lost Daneila or Davina and to keep up with the ever-growing throng of customers. One was Kirsten or Kristen, she could never remember which, though in any case she looked exactly like Shawn Johnson, the gymnast from the last Olympics, so Janet simply referred to her as Shawn Johnson. The other, Melissa, reminded her, with her smoker's sallow skin and throaty voice, of her late Auntie Tudy, even though she couldn't possibly be a day over eighteen, so she naturally became Auntie Tudy. It was some time before Ann and Paula figured out whom Janet was talking about when she referred to Shawn Johnson and Auntie Tudy, and after that Paula kept finding herself addressing Kirsten as "Shawn" and Melissa as "Tudy," to their great perplexity.

Paula handled all the scheduling, thank the Lord, because Janet couldn't keep track of it, no matter how hard she tried. All the tea caddies were students near the start of their college careers, undeclared of major and rapidly putting on unexpected pounds and often bleary-eyed from a late night out, and though they had the same class schedules from week to week, for some reason they never seemed to be available for any predictable day or time. It became a sort of game for Janet, guessing who would be in each day, and she was almost always surprised by the result. Paula scheduled her and Ann, as well, though Janet didn't pay much attention to it, instead just coming in pretty much every day to see how things were going and to lend a hand, if one were needed. Sometimes this approach didn't work out so well, though, because on certain days she was scheduled to open the teahouse, and she would arrive a half-hour or so late to discover several disgruntled customers and one or two even more put-out tea caddies waiting for her. Eventually the staff, as well as the regular customers, figured out which days Janet would be opening and planned their mornings accordingly. Ann and Paula overlooked her rather casual acquaintance with a fixed schedule, because they recognized that, as Ann jokingly put it, "she brings a certain what the French call 'I don't know what' to the teashop."

Mostly she got to know the customers. She found out where they lived and where they worked, where they had come from and what they hoped to do in the future, who their families were and what particular problems they were facing at the moment. For some reason she could never seem to remember what drink they ordered. But their personal details she could easily commit to memory.

"Now, this is Richard," she said to Auntie Tudy on her second day at the teahouse. "He comes in almost every day and gets ... oh, I'm sorry, Richard, I can never remember what it is you order."

"A small Early Gray with milk and sugar, for here, please," Richard said clearly and quietly. He waited for his drink by the counter after paying.

"If you're getting it for here, I can bring it over to you," Melissa said.

"No, Richard likes to get his drink himself," Janet explained. "Then he'll go sit by himself over at that table."

Richard smiled wanly.

"Now how is your mother?" Richard had told Janet that his mother was having a knee replaced.

"She's OK. I'm having a hard time getting her to do her rehab."

"Oh, now that's important. Tell her that one of the women at my mother's nursing home never did her rehab, and her knee froze up on her, and now she has a terrible time getting around. It's so hard as our parents get older, isn't it? I think I told you that my mother was in a nursing home. She's at Heavenly Passage, which really is an awful name for a home, when you think of it, and on top of that, it's on Hemlock Drive. Now, in her case she had a stroke, so she just can't get around in general. Or really care for herself, for that matter. I feel so guilty putting her in a home, but I tried taking care of her at home, truly I did, and it was just too much. I do go over to visit her when I can, but I have to say, she's just become so negative, it's really hard to spend any time with her. Her mind is as sharp as it ever was, I'm sure of it, but she just sits there moping and doesn't say much. Of course, it's hard for her to speak after the stroke."

Richard had collected his tea from Melissa and was eyeing his table.

"I'm sorry, I'll let you go, I know you want to go have your tea. Oh, I know what I wanted to ask you: Did I see you talking to that attractive young woman who comes in? Tracey, I think her name is."

"Um, which one do you mean? I don't think so."

"Well, then, I should introduce you. You're single, aren't you?" she asked, though she didn't wait for a reply, as she thought she knew the answer. "Do you know, she's an aerobics instructor? She's the one who comes in wearing the black leggings. You can't help but notice her; her rear end is just kind of out there."

A sheen of sweat had formed on Richard's upper lip. "I think I've seen her," he said. He bobbed his head in a gesture of departure and made his way to his table. Two minutes later he was gone.

"I really do think they'd make a good couple," Janet said to Paula, who was replenishing stacks of paper cups.

"Are you sure he's not? ..." Paula said.

"Not what?"

"I think Richard might play on the other side."

"Oh, you mean Richard is gay?" Janet said loudly. A few customers turned to look, so she brought her voice down to a whisper. "Do you think so? I never can tell. There's a man who comes in all the time, Evan, I think his name is. Anyway, he has a mustache, and he's very tan, and he wears leather driving gloves — I'm sure you've seen him. Anyway, I was certain he was gay, and then he came in with a woman and a boy who were clearly his wife and child."

"That doesn't mean. ..."

"Oh, Paula. But I know what you're saying. You never can tell."

There was a lull in customers at the counter, and Ann came over to join them. "Now what are you two conspiring about?" she asked.

"We're deciding people's sexual orientation," Janet said.

"I always wonder," Paula said. "Do you think Charles and Ben are a gay couple?"

"Do you know, I wonder that, too," Janet said. "I truly don't know. They don't seem to be a couple, per se."

"Is it really important?" Ann asked.

"No, not that it makes any difference," Janet said. "But I just wonder, out of curiosity. For one thing, if they were a couple I'd want them to feel comfortable telling us."

"But they might not want other people to know," Ann said.

"Well, I guess that's true. You know, Paula, I've often thought Ben would be perfect for you. If you didn't have Ash, I mean. You know he's not that much older than you."

"I never really thought about it," Paula said. She turned back to her cup-stacking.

"Now how old are you, dear?" Ann asked.

"Actually, today is my birthday. I am twenty-five today."

"Oh, you should have told us," Janet said. "We could have had a party."

"Ash is taking me out to dinner tonight anyway."

"Well, that's good. But we'll have a party, sometime soon. I should write down everyone's birthday, so I have them. Everyone in the compound, I mean. On second thought, Ann, you should write them down and then remind me, because I would simply lose them."

Charles made an appearance, which Janet had noticed was becoming less unusual, though his visits were often under the guise of some other intention. "I was hoping to find Ben here," he said, glancing around the teahouse. "I do wonder where that boy gets to sometimes. I know he doesn't have any classes today. He seems to go off on a lot of long *walks*."

"Charles," Janet said, "today is Paula's birthday."

"Happy birthday to *you*." Charles joined their circle and gave Paula a kiss on the cheek. "Be careful not to get *old*."

"I was saying to Ann that we should have a party."

"Yes, we must do *something*."

A woman approached the counter, and Melissa went to wait on her. Janet had seen the woman many times, though she hadn't yet introduced herself. She had a prominent nose and a bemused smile and wore her gray hair in flip-ups, and she always had on a loud floral-print dress. She looked exactly like the woman in the Victoria Roberts cartoons in the *New Yorker*.

"Oh, here's the New Yorker Lady," Janet said to her small party, quietly enough that the woman couldn't hear her. She smiled to the woman in greeting.

The New Yorker Lady was followed by the Mochas, Donald and Maria, who were followed by the Long Island Contingent. Ann and Paula stepped in to help Melissa with the onslaught.

"It's looking like Old Home Week," Janet said to Charles. "Now all we need is Emily Reaper."

"Not *her*."

The L.I.C.'s stood at the counter in their tennis skirts and diamond-stud earrings while the younger children squirmed in their overpriced baby strollers and the older, ambulatory offspring chased one another around the teahouse in anticipation of sugar.

"Ethan! Ethan!" the blond L.I.C. shrilled. "What do you want? Do you want a croissant? Will you eat a croissant if I get one for you? Ethan! All right, forget it, you're eating whatever I get you."

"Are you ordering?" the other blond L.I.C. asked her. "Are you ordering for all of us?"

"Yes, I'm ordering for all of us."

"You'll get me my chai, my black-eye chai?"

"Yes, I'll get you your black-eye chai." She turned to Paula. "I want a medium decaf one-pump two-Splenda no-foam soy vanilla latte, a four-pump raw-sugar one-percent hazelnut coffee, small, a four-shot black-eye chai, medium with skim, but make two of the shots regular and two of the shots decaf, two child-size Dutch-chocolate two-percent hot chocolates with extra whip and drizzled caramel, and a two-percent chocolate milk. And three chocolate croissants.

"No, Mommy, I don't want a croissant. I want a donut."

"Too bad! I asked you before, and you pretended to ignore me. So you're getting a croissant." She turned back to Paula. "You know what? For that first one, make it caffeinated. And did I say a hundred and thirty-five degrees? It has to be a hundred and thirty-five degrees."

Paula and Ann scribbled furiously, taking down the order. Melissa stared in stupefaction.

Next were the Smellies, a cycling group that met at the teahouse on weekend mornings and, in smaller configurations, sometimes during the week. They came in at the end of their ride, dripping with sweat and reeking of aged Lycra. They pushed a few tables together and appropriated chairs from a few others and in general took the place over, though few of them ever bothered to order anything. After a few minutes the customers sitting closest to them would have migrated to the other side of the room, where the air was less pungent.

The Smellies were followed by a couple who were members of a group Paula had taken to calling the S.I.C.'s, for Staten Island Contingent, a sort of low-budget wannabe version of the L.I.C.'s. They drove American cars, rather than German, and looked like they shopped at Macys instead of Nordstrom, but they nevertheless managed to be annoying. The husband ordered a large coffee, and the wife ordered a large rooibos tea, both of them to go. They always ordered their drinks plain and then added cream and sugar themselves at the fixings counter. The woman didn't have exact change, so she fished some from the tip jar.

"Those are tips for the staff, dear," Ann told her.

"No, I come in here all the time," the woman said, as if by way of explanation.

Ann and Paula looked at each other and decided to let it go. Paula brought over her large rooibos in a paper cup and set a plastic lid next to it. The woman grabbed the cup and in the process jostled hot water over the back of her hand.

"Cold water! Cold water!" she screamed.

Ann and Paula and Melissa stood motionless behind the counter, not immediately certain what the woman was asking for.

"Move, people! I need cold water!"

Paula was the first to leap to action. She filled a paper cup with cold water and brought it to the woman. The woman poured it over her hand and all over the counter.

Janet came over to see what was going on. "Is there a problem here?"

"You burned me! You burned me!"

"I don't think we burned you, dear," Ann said, mopping up the wet counter. "You picked up your cup of tea and spilled some on yourself."

The woman tried to speak but seemed unable to adequately express her exasperation. She glared at Ann and Janet and then clapped the lid on her tea. She handed the tea to her husband, who had been standing by silently, mortified. She then marched out of the teahouse, followed by her husband, who, when he got out the door, threw her cup of tea onto the train tracks. The two of them made their way to the parking lot, exchanging unheard epithets.

"Well, that was a bit of excitement," Janet said. The other customers, who had turned quiet in the uproar, went back to their conversations. The Mochas sat smiling to themselves, and when Janet caught their attention they made wide eyes and a sort of shrugging motion, which Janet returned. She found it unsettling when customers were unhappy, but on the other hand it gave her and Ann and Paula something to talk about, during the slow times. It also gave her a sort of us-against-the-world feeling, the teahouse, the compound, on the one hand, the customers on the other.

When she first opened the teahouse the customers had mostly been train commuters, and there had been a distinct rush at the beginning and end of the day. But by now the teahouse was attracting people from throughout the neighborhood, the L.I.C.'s and the S.I.C.'s and the Smellies, the Richards and the Emily Reapers, the Mochas and the New Yorker Ladies. She always thought "neighborhood" was rather loose usage when referring to the Pennsylvania suburbs, at least in and around Lower Slaughter. There was no sense of a town, really, just houses densely scattered, and there certainly was no town center, just a few businesses, an odd mix that included a notary, a beer distributor, a running-shoes store, a couple of forgettable restaurants. There were few streets with sidewalks where you could take a stroll and run into someone you knew. In fact, she knew precious few people, and even at the places she frequented, the Safeway and the Walgreens and the Target, a ten minutes' car ride away, she never ran into an acquaintance, never saw anyone she even recognized from the teahouse. It was off-putting. What was the word she wanted? Alienating.

She had been thinking about their conversation about race, at New Year's. More and more of the teahouse customers seemed to be minorities, Chinese or Korean, she guessed they were, Indian or Pakistani. Or maybe the Asians were Japanese; was there a way to tell? In any case, everyone seemed to get along fine; there was never anything remotely like racial animosity. But she noticed they all kept to themselves, the Asians to the Asians, the Indians to the Indians, the Caucasians to the Caucasians. If a group of teenage girls came in, if one of them was Asian, they all were Asian. The next time they came in it might be a different combination of girls, but they still were all Asian.

It had been the same at her mother's condo community. Her next-door neighbor had been a Pakistani family, the parents and five children crammed into four rooms and a bath. She had met them when she first moved in — all their names seemed to be multi-syllabic and start with the letter "M"; she forgot them immediately — and then she never saw them again, except around Ramadan, when they had friends and relatives over, all of them dressed in white robes, all of them Pakistani. Likewise all the condo lawn-care workers were Hispanic, she assumed Mexican. No one ever spoke to them, and they never uttered a word. She wondered where they lived. Certainly not in Lower Slaughter.

Maybe it was because they were recent immigrants, this desire to stick together. They missed their homeland, their culture, the familiar. But there were blacks in the neighborhood, as well, and they also seemed to keep to themselves, and surely they weren't recent immigrants. Few of them ever came into the teahouse.

She wondered if Paula had heard anything about her immigration status. Would she be considered an illegal alien? "Undocumented worker" was the more acceptable term, she had read somewhere, although that didn't sound much better, suggesting as it did that one's purpose was labor. Alien. Did Paula feel alienated, living on her own, all these miles from Brazil, from her home? Maybe not so much now, now that she had moved into her new apartment, into the compound. Did she, too, feel like it was us against the world?

21

Paula left the teahouse early to get ready for her birthday dinner with Ash. Ash's parents had very helpfully suggested dinner with them at the Philadelphia Cricket Club, which they were members of, but there was no way in hell she was spending her birthday with Trey and Mitzi, the uptight *babacas*. Instead Ash was taking her to Alma de Cuba, a pricey Cuban restaurant in Center City. It was one of her favorites, but she could afford it only when Ash was treating. There were *Brasileiro* restaurants in the city, some of which she had tried, but they all seemed to be *churrascarias*, which wasn't exactly the best choice for a couple of vegetarians.

Eating out had become a rare occurrence, as she had pretty much run out of the money she brought with her from Brasil. She almost hadn't taken the job at Globanaut's U.S. headquarters, when it became available, because she didn't think she could afford the move. She had no savings, and her grandparents certainly couldn't afford to help her, and her mother wasn't inclined to give her money, even if she had any to give. Then her father appeared again — she hadn t seen him since her college graduation — with several thousand *reais*, which he insisted she take. She had felt conflicted about it, because of his rather intermittent support for her mother, because she wasn't certain the money hadn't been obtained by illegal means. But she accepted the gift, and it was a good thing she did, because America had proved so expensive, and getting a lease, acquiring a bare minimum of furniture, buying the cheapest car that ran — a necessity in the suburbs, she discovered — had wiped out almost all of it. Even with the steady income from the teahouse she was pretty much living paycheck to paycheck.

She took a long, hot shower. She was as accustomed to the North American winters as she was going to get. Not that she missed the forty-degree heat and ninety-five percent humidity of Rio, though forty was better than minus ten Whatever that was in Fahrenheit. But long, hot showers helped, and she loved her new bathroom, with its gleaming-white porcelain and brushed-nickel hardware. Its newness still felt like a luxury.

She turned off the shower and realized her cellphone was going off. She wrapped a towel around herself and ran to answer it. It was Ash. He had to work late. He had to get some marketing videos ready for a customer conference that started the next day, an event they held every year and knew about fifty-one weeks in advance yet somehow never managed to be ready for. He was really sorry to have to cancel dinner, especially on her birthday, but there was nothing he could do. What if he came over later and they just ordered in Chinese?

It was OK, she told herself. They could go to Alma de Cuba another time. It was more important that she be with Ash on her birthday. And anyway, he had already given her

her birthday present, a Tiffany necklace in sterling silver. He had bought it for her months ago, before Christmas, and he couldn't wait any longer, so he gave it to her a week early. It was a pendant necklace, an old-fashioned key with a little diamond inset. She loved it. And it was sweet that he couldn't wait.

She hadn't had time to dry off before she answered the phone, and now she had a chill. She returned to the steamy warmth of the bathroom and pulled shut the door behind her. She dried her hair with the towel and then stood naked in front of the sink mirror, which was fogged and opaque. She turned sideways and pulled her shoulders back, viewing her breasts in profile. She stood on her tiptoes to better see her torso and sucked in her stomach. She hadn't put on weight, according to her bathroom scale, but it felt like she was getting a tummy. When did people start to put on weight? She was still only twenty-five.

Ash had given her lingerie for her birthday, as well, a red lace-and-mesh teddy from Victoria's Secret. She was flattered that he thought of her in that way, as being sexy, and by the intimacy of the gift. But it wasn't particularly comfortable, and anyway, when was she going to wear it? It wasn't at all her style. It occurred to her that maybe he had bought it just to start getting the Victoria's Secret catalogs, but probably that was unfair. Of course, they would come to him at his parents' house, where Mitzi collected the mail. The thought of Mitzi paging through the catalog, aghast, and then seeing Ash's name on the address label made her smile.

She really did have a chill, now, so she ran to her bedroom and dressed quickly. At least she'd be able to dress casually now that they were staying in, in jeans and a soft sweater. She liked the idea of being sexy, of being attractive, but more for herself; she had never been comfortable with other people seeing her that way. When did she start noticing it, the way men looked at her? Not all men, not all the time, but a lot of them. Not when she was an adolescent, because she had been skinny, with no figure. It must have been in her last year of high school, when she finally got breasts. She had wanted to show them off. Not that you could hide them anyway, because everyone in Brasil wore tight clothes, especially jeans; your ass was always out there. *Brasileiros* weren't supposed to be shy. It felt empowering, sometimes, the way men responded to her, attentive and accommodating as soon as they noticed her. But just as often it was annoying, their obsequiousness, she thought that was the word, or worse, revolting, fifty-year-old men flirting with her and, what, thinking she was going to flirt back?

But she missed Brasil. She missed the food, she missed the warmth, she missed the people. The *Cariocas*, as Rio de Janeirans called themselves. *Brasileiros* were friendlier than Americans, there was no question. They made friends more easily. Of course, it's not like she had had a million friends in Brasil. For one thing, when she was growing up she was often busy at the orphanage. And then when she got to U.F.R.J. she felt sort of out of place, like she wasn't meant to be a college student. But she had had friends, and it hadn't been hard to meet people. But here in America she had made no real friends, other than Ash. Her last birthday had come right after she moved to the States but before she and Ash started going out, and the loneliness caught her by surprise. Her department at Globanaut had a sheet cake for her in the afternoon, vanilla with white icing and pink letters that spelled out "Happy Birthday Paula." But at the end of the day she went home to her empty apartment. She called her grandparents, the first time she had talked to them in more than a month. Avó Mariana said they would have sent a present, but it probably would just have been stolen at the post office, as packages often were. She didn't even hear from her mother. It was the first time it occurred to her that she didn't have any friends. And now a year later, had anything really changed? Well, she had the people at the compound, as Ben called it, Janet and Ann and Charles and of course Ben. They counted as friends.

There were other *Brasileiros* in Philadelphia. There was supposed to be a large community in the northeast part of the city. She and Ash had driven around there once, but she was less than impressed. It didn't look like the kind of place you'd want to walk around by yourself at night, though you could have said that about her old neighborhood in Rio. Plus, she had heard that most of the people there were from rural areas, from places like Minas Gerais and Goiás. There was also supposed to be a town in New Jersey, Riverside, she thought it was, where a lot of *Brasileiros* lived. But somehow that seemed like the immigrant thing to do, to only have *Brasileiro* friends, to go to *Brasileiro* markets and shop at *Brasileiro* stores. She knew that a lot of *Brasileiros* were just passing through, staying in America long enough to earn money to afford a better life back in Brasil. She wasn't sure she wanted to stay in the United States permanently. But while she was here she wanted to experience America, not Brasil in America.

There was so much about Brasil she missed, though. She missed stores that sold jeans shaped to actually fit her body. She missed *telenovelas*, the guilty-pleasure soap-opera miniseries on Rede Globo. She missed impromptu games of *futevôlei*, which she was good at, a kind of beach volleyball played with no hands. She missed the more casual social life, the informality of going out, of not rushing at restaurants. She liked efficiency and punctuality, it was true; she wasn't a good *Brasileiro* when it came to her strict adherence to schedules. But that was when she was at work, when she had a job to do. She couldn't understand why for Americans going out, for drinks or to a restaurant or a club, had to be an event, with a schedule and an agenda.

Food was what she missed most, real *Brasileiro* food. *Bobó de camarão*, shrimp in yucca cream. *Pão francês*, a kind of short baguette. Authentic *feijão com arroz*. Maybe it was because food was such a fundamental thing, something you remembered from your earliest years, that called to mind childhood. Oh, and *brigadeiros*, one of her favorites, a chocolate candy made from cocoa powder, condensed milk, and butter. Avó Mariana used to make them at the orphanage. She remembered that in Brasil they were almost always served at kids' birthday parties. *Que saudade.*

She glanced at the clock and realized Ash would be arriving soon, which was good, because she was hungry. She decided she would light some candles. She loved this apartment, up near the peak of the barn's roof, for its clean white walls, for the sprawling view out the gable-end windows, for the massive exposed beams — hewn from chestnut trees, Ben had told her — that bisected the vaulted space of the living room. She had placed votive candles along the beams, which she could just reach by standing on a kitchen chair, and as she lit them they cast watery, flickering shadows on the room below. She heard the crunch of Ash's footsteps on the gravel walkway. He rapped on the door and then opened it.

"Hey, Parchy!" he called up the stairs. "It's me."

She lit the last candle and blew out the match, which had burned down to the tips of her finger and thumb.

"I'm up here," she said.

Ash had brought a bouquet of flowers in a cone of paper, which was sweet. He hugged her warmly, and they remained in a swaying embrace. The local jazz station played softly in the background, a tune she didn't recognize. Ash was asking her how she was while he kissed the side of her neck and behind her ear. He slipped a hand under the back of her shirt. It looked like dinner was going to wait. They began to kiss and then sort of shuffled together to the couch, beginning to shed clothing as they went. She would have liked to have turned off the radio, but she didn't want to interrupt the mood. She found music distracting during sex.

Paula wondered how much of people's ideas about sex were influenced by movies. Certainly not by books, because sex scenes in books were so uncomfortable as to be almost embarrassing. Writers seemed always to try to treat sex subtly, or reverentially, and the result was either prudish or ridiculous, like a middle-aged man trying to be cool in front of his teenage daughter's friends. Sex in movies was more successful, more believable, maybe, but it was always so stylized, so smooth and choreographed and well-paced. Unless it was a movie about a geeky teenager, in which case its awkwardness, the fumbling and the sheer work of it, was emphasized to comic effect. But that's what real sex was: awkward, fumbling, effortful. Of course, no one wanted to admit that, because everyone wanted to pretend their sex was like the sex they saw in movies.

She was glad she had lit the candles. When they first started going out, Ash always wanted to have sex with the lights on, because he had some idea this was grown up or sophisticated. But she had convinced him it was better in the dark or, more ideally, by candlelight. She tried to be straightforward about what she liked and didn't like in sex, but Ash didn't like to discuss it, so talking about it required a deft touch. Some things she just put up with, like Ash's preference for doing it doggie style, which she didn't like at all; rather than confront the issue, she tried to simply redirect Ash's interest. But he never seemed to quite get it. That was kind of a joke, wasn't it, "confront"? What was the word? A pun. "In a sort of way," Ann would have said in her English accent. She realized she was letting herself get distracted.

He was above her then, kissing her eyelids and her temples and the sensitive underside of her jaw. He unclasped her bra with a pinch of his thumb and forefinger, and Paula slipped it forward off her shoulders. He moved down her neck to her cleavage, briefly, and then attached himself to her left breast, above her beating heart. She wrapped her arms around his head. His hair was getting long. Ash's hair was so thick that if he didn't keep it cut short it stuck out in all directions, like a porcupine. She returned her focus to her left breast. She loved it when he drew her into himself in this way, drawing at her breast, though sometimes he got carried away and it turned into a sort of painful sucking. She tried guiding him gently, but he didn't seem to take the hint. Lately Ash's love making had grown hurried, almost furtive, as if he had become uncomfortable with intimacy and just wanted it over with. She managed to dislodge him, and he moved rapidly down her stomach, kissing her lightly. He hooked his fingers around the top of her panties and slid them down her legs. She squirmed a bit to get the panties over and off her feet. Ash pushed open her legs. She closed her eyes.

He was briefer than usual. In a few moments he was above her again, on his elbows, pushing his pelvis against hers. He tried to kiss her, but he should do that before, she thought, not after, and she turned her head away. He hadn't taken off his pants yet, and he tried to remove them without getting up, balancing on one hand while using the other to push the top of his pants down past his knees. But they got caught in a knot around his ankles, and he fell forward onto his shoulder, lightly knocking his head against Paula's. She smiled at him in the dimness, but he was obviously frustrated, so she tried to use her feet to disentangle his feet from the knot of his pants. It didn't work, though, so he had to stand up, skinny and stark in the candlelight, and pull them off.

He slid back on top of her and rubbed against her. Then he raised himself up and tried to find his way in without using his hands. Paula moved beneath him and angled her pelvis to try to accept him. This was always the awkward part of sex with Ash; he could never find his way on his own. He tried to look where he was going, and in so doing dangled his hair in her face. She turned her head to the side. His hands were outside her shoulders, his elbows locked to hold himself upright. He began to whimper a bit with the effort. Paula decided to take things into her own hands. That's funny, she thought, "take things into my own hands." She reached down and pushed him inside herself. Ash released his breath, which she realized he had been holding, and lowered himself onto her.

They began moving together, slowly, evenly. In this they were compatible; they both liked to do things slowly, and quietly. And then all at once Ash stiffened and stopped moving. His mouth was in her ear, wet and whimpering, and he shuddered against her. He made a final, deep thrust, and then his body relaxed. So that was all it was going to be. *Comme ci, comme ça,* she thought.

She really was hungry. How long would she have to wait till she could suggest to Ash that they order the Chinese food?

22

Ann pulled out of the compound parking lot. She was at the wheel of her new car. She had grown tired of having to borrow Janet's car, so she decided to get one of her own. She and Lionel had always had Fords at home, in St. Andrews, so she got herself a Ford. But this was a proper American-size car, not at all like the cramped, jarring sub-compacts she had driven in the past.

She was on her way to visit Logan at the monastery. She hadn't seen him since moving to the States permanently, since buying the teashop and Toad Hall and Mole End with Janet and Charles, since selling her home in St. Andrews. She had visited just before Christmas, at the tail end of his bout with the swine flu. He had seemed so much better then, if still oddly distracted, unfocused. But she had been able to reassure herself that he would make a full recovery, at least as far as his health was concerned, despite his apparent lack of interest in getting proper medical care.

She had been meaning to go see him for six weeks or more. But she had been so busy with the teashop and with settling into the compound, into Mole End. And she had to admit that her past visits with him had been so distressing, so estranging. Maybe now that he was fully ensconced at the monastery, and feeling better physically, he would be more pleasant, more the Logan she thought she knew.

She had told him, the last time she saw him, that she was selling the house and moving to the States. He had seemed indifferent on both counts. But it had been a rather studied indifference, as if he thought he wasn't supposed to respond with emotion or didn't want to show the emotion he felt. She had hoped he would have been pleased that she would be living nearby, though perhaps that was too much to wish for. She was more surprised that he had no reaction to the news that she was selling his childhood home. In the past, when he had been a business-studies major at university, he would have protested that giving up such a historic home was unwise, or asked after the selling price, or offered unsolicited advice on finding a good estate agent. But setting that aside, did he feel no emotional attachment to the place where he had grown up, where they had all had so many happy years? And they had been happy years, too, the three of them as normal and stable and close as any family she knew.

Selling the house had been harder, emotionally harder, than she anticipated. Not making the decision to sell it; that had been surprisingly easy. She had been in such a torpor since Lionel's death, lonely and depressed and rudderless. She needed to start a new chapter, and she needed to be with people. She needed to press on. And then the opportunity at the teashop had presented itself, to run the business with Janet and invest in the properties with her and Charles. And Lord knows they had needed her — Janet because she had an almost preternatural lack of common sense, bless her, and Charles because he truly had made a mess of his financial situation and was about to lose every-thing. It had felt good to be able to help them, to iden-tify the problems and define the solutions and take action. And into the bargain she could relieve herself of her old house in St. Andrews, a house too big for her in a city not of her own choosing, full of drafts and damp and ghosts.

Only when she got back to St. Andrews she hadn't wanted to let go. The familiar street; the red-painted front door; the narrow entrance hall, with its wood floor tilted with age; the low doorways, sized in an age when Scots were a foot shorter; the tiny, cozy kitchen where Logan had sat in his highchair as a toddler: it was all so dear to her. She wandered the rooms without purpose, as if seeing them for the first time. They were filled with a lifetime of belongings, so many of which she wouldn't have room for in America and would no longer be hers. It was like visiting the Preservation Trust Museum, where she had worked all those years, with its exhibit of a nineteenth-century chem-ist's, a snapshot in time, a slice of life, all painstakingly pre-served yet fake, a facsimile. Her things had abandoned her. Like Logan. Like Lionel.

She wanted to remember all the happy times. When they were first married they had to be particularly frugal, with only Lionel working, even though they were both from respectable families. They had lived in a tiny flat in Paddington, near Hyde Park. Logan would have been too young to remember it. She went from memory to memory, the milestones in their lives: their quiet, no-frills wedding in Winchester; a honeymoon trip to Barbados they could scarcely afford; moving into the house at 52 North Street, in St. Andrews; Lionel getting tenure at the university, which meant they would stay; starting her job at the museum; the ticking clock of Logan's childhood, marked by the hours of first tooth, first word, first step, first day at primary school, and so on till he went on his first date and learned to drive a car and got accepted at university. She pictured Christmases by the hearth, vacation trips to the countryside, a teary rush to the emergency room after Logan fell and cut his chin. The time Lionel took a five-year-old Logan fishing on the River Spey and the poor boy was tugged headfirst into the freezing water by a truculent trout.

But try as she might to reconjure them, these images were pushed aside by more recent events, by Lionel's sickness, his suffering, his wasting away. She wanted to picture Lionel young and vibrant, but all she could see were the sunken eyes, the yellow skin, the distended abdomen of his illness. The waiting and hoping, the boredom of sitting by his silent bedside relieved only by the crushing weight of worry. The doctors, the diagnostic tests, the decisions. The news of his death, the slow-marching awareness that his death was cruelly real, and horrible, and permanent. The mind-numbing facts and responsibilities of buying a coffin, scheduling a funeral, arranging for a burial. The silence afterward. The vacant feeling, as if her soul had been excised. The memories were spectral in her mind's eye, like black-and-white photographic slides projected from an ancient magic lantern.

Had she and Lionel been soul mates? She probably would have said yes at one time, though she was no longer sure what it meant, "soul mates." Certainly they had been in love. When they were first married they would lie in bed together, she on the left, Lionel on the right, and turn to face each other, their noses almost touching. Then they would cup their hands at their temples, like blinkers on a horse, and stare into each other's eyes to the exclusion of all else. It had been both intensely intimate and enormously expanding, each becoming the other, two becoming one. She still lay on the left side of the bed.

When had they stopped doing that? The sex continued, she found, though not as frequent, but the appeal,
the romance of it lagged. Perhaps it was merely a matter
of waning attraction as their bodies first grew familiar,
routine, and then increasingly paunchy and pallid. And
let's face it, the human body could be something less than
appealing, up close — in the flesh, as it were — hairy and
smelly and rather disappointing. Kissing, when you came
to think of it, was fairly revolting, involving as it did teeth
and tongues, saliva and bacteria and dental plaque. Maybe
it was all just a matter of biochemistry, the brain no longer telling the body to reproduce. But they had remained
as close as ever, she and Lionel, companions, confidants,
best friends. It had been a wonderful marriage, a long marriage. As if that could be any consolation. As if that didn't
make the pain worse.

And then the actual business of selling the house had
felt like an infidelity, the prospective buyers like illicit lovers, something to be ashamed of. She had resented their
presence in the house, as they toured the place, her solici-
tor pointing out the historic features, the upgrades, their
solicitors raising questions about woodworm, dry rot, rising
damp. Mostly they were wealthy young couples, the only
people able to afford the property at today's prices, and
they wielded their privilege like a blunt weapon, tsk-tsking
her decorating choices, disparaging the very intricacies and
idiosyncrasies that made a house a home. But it was worse
after they left, after the light faded, and she was left once
again alone. She resumed her watch, wandering the rooms,
catching her shadowed image in dim mirrors, filling herself
with fright. She wouldn't miss the early Scottish twilights,
this time of year, which left that much more time for ghosts.

But she had to press on. She had a new life, now, in
Lower Slaughter, at the teashop, at Mole End. It wasn't what

she had expected, but it was what she had been able to salvage. And she felt deep affection for Janet, and for Charles and Paula and Ben, for that matter. Logan remained a disappointment, an unsolved problem. But at least he was nearby, now, where she could keep an eye on him, where she could try to restore their relationship.

She eased the Ford up to the curb and switched off the engine. She sat for a moment, aware of her breath. Press on, she thought.

She sat in the upholstered chair by the metal grate, waiting for Logan to appear. For Brother Michael, she thought ruefully, or Mikhail, whatever it was. And then, instead of appearing behind the grate, Logan surprised her by coming in through the outside door.

"Hello, Mum," he said. He took the wooden chair from the corner and sat down opposite her.

"Well, it's certainly nice to be able to speak to you face-to-face," she said. "Not through bars of steel, that is. How are you feeling?"

"I feel well."

"You look well. You look like you've fully recovered."

"Yes, I feel well," he repeated. He smiled, then, and it occurred to her that it was a real smile, not the benign smile he had inherited from Father What's-His-Name.

"Well, I'm back from Scotland, of course. And I've sold the house. And I've moved into Mole End — into my new house. I don't know if you're allowed 'out' at all, but I'd love for you to come see — just a minute," she interrupted herself. "Why *aren't* you on the other side of the grate?"

"Well, it didn't seem necessary at this point. I've decided to leave the monastery."

So Logan was full of surprises today. "Really?" She hoped her voice didn't betray too much enthusiasm, but she couldn't help smiling. "What led to that decision?"

"It wasn't any one thing. It wasn't the illness. It's not that there's anything wrong here. It's not that I've lost my faith, either, although I think I'm seeing my faith in a different light. But I realized I don't think this is what God wants of me. Well, I don't know what God wants of me, to be honest. But it's not what I want for me. I haven't told anyone at the monastery about this yet."

"Well, I can't say I'm not pleased. Not that I was opposed to your joining a monastery per se; it's your life to do with as you please, after all. But I never sensed that you were particularly happy here."

"Well, I think I was happy initially. But it's not about happiness anyway. Or maybe it is, at least in part, I don't know. I think I realized that my interest in religion is more intellectual than a matter of believing. I'm very much interested in religion as a field of study. But I'm not convinced I was put on earth to serve God, whatever that even means, let alone live in seclusion for no clear reason. To no apparent end."

"Well, you had been through so much, Logan. First ending your relationship with Ainsley and then losing your father. And I'm afraid I wasn't in much of a position to offer much support at the time."

"No, I think that's too simple, to suggest that I came running here as a replacement for Ainsley or Dad. It was a decision, and I think it may have been the right decision at the time. Or at least a necessary phase to have gone through. And now I'm making a different decision."

"What will you do, then? After you leave the monastery."

"Well, there will be the unpleasant matter of telling Father Anastasi and the others here. I expect I'll be shunned, in some sort of way. And I've grown close to many of them. There's a peculiar kind of oneness that's achieved, an unexpected democratization, when you spend time with others in silent meditation."

"And then?"

"And then I'll go back to Scotland, I suppose."

Ann felt a sort of sitting loss of balance, like when you hit turbulence in mid-flight and your seat drops from under you.

"I'll have to get a job, of course. But I have my business-studies degree. I'm sure I'll find something."

Logan was moving back to Scotland. Just after she had moved here to be with him. After she had sold the house. After she had left Lionel in his grave and, presumably, left Scotland forever.

"But I'm here now," she said. "This is where I live."

"I know that. I'm not moving back to get away from you, if that's what you think. It's not like we won't be in touch."

"Be in touch?"

"What I mean is, we can talk on the phone and send letters and keep up by e-mail. We did before. And you like to travel; surely you can come visit. But I want to go back. And this is your home now."

This was her home now. Had it been a mistake, to uproot herself, to leave the place she had lived in for forty years, to throw her lot in with the teashop, with Janet, with the others in the compound? Had it been an awful mistake?

23

Ann saw Logan once more, briefly, before he left. It was only a week after he had told her of his plans, though she supposed that once you announced you were leaving a monastery there wasn't much to do but leave. He decided he would find a flat in London, initially, rather than St. Andrews, and then figure out what he would do from there. She didn't ask what he was doing for money in the meantime, but he had a modest inheritance from Lionel, which she assumed he had kept in a bank account even after joining the monastery.

Janet had been wonderfully understanding about her worries and uncertainties, of course, a welcome ear to bend. But you could get only so much mileage out of a conversation with Janet before her interest began to wander and she was talking about something completely unrelated. It was just as well, because Logan was going to do what he was going to do, and she was busy with the teashop, with her own life. One of the tea caddies, as Janet called them, had quit unexpectedly, as they seemed to do, and she needed to find a replacement quickly. But she had interviewed a delightful young man, Tommy, his name was, another college student, and she was quite certain he would be a perfect fit. She wanted to call him today to offer him the job.

She had woken up with a sore throat, which she hoped wasn't the start of a cold. She needed her energy today, because tonight they were having a belated birthday party for Paula. Janet was organizing it, which meant most of the details would likely fall to her. They would have it at Charles', which was the best venue for a gathering of any size. And she hated to be sick. Not that anyone likes it, obviously, but some people just seem to roll with the waves, whereas for her even a minor illness was disconcerting, felt like a setback. Maybe it was because she was almost never sick and had never had any sort of lasting illness. Well, that wasn't entirely accurate. She had been a smoker in college and for the first several years of her marriage; it seemed like everyone was at the time. But at some point she developed a lasting lung infection, an experience unpleasant enough to put her off cigarettes for good. That seemed to be the end of her respiratory troubles, thankfully, except that years later she had a bout with bronchitis, and a doctor told her she had early signs of emphysema. A measuring device — a spirometer, she thought it was called — showed that her lung function had been compromised. It had been frightening, hearing the word *emphysema* uttered in connection with her own health.

Yes, she definitely had a sore throat. And she thought she might feel a bit tired; not sleepy-tired, but run down. Fatigued.

When she got to the teahouse she found Janet was as talkative as ever, not least because she was excited about the upcoming party. "I think it's important that we make it really special for Paula," she was saying. "It can't be easy being all alone at her age, and so far from home. I meant to order a cake from the Safeway, but it slipped my mind until this morning. But I'm sure they can just decorate one for me while I wait. And look," she said, rifling through a worn-out shopping bag, "look what I've made for her." She drew from the bag a shoebox diorama, a tiny-scale replica of the teahouse. There were the little tables and chairs, and there were the tall Victorian windows with their blue-checked curtains, and there was the black-slate counter with its cash register and the pastries in their case. There too were Janet and Ann and, working the register, a slightly out-of-scale Paula. The people were achieved with cutout photographs glued to something like ice-lolly sticks. What did they call them over here? Popsicles. Janet had recently started taking Polaroids of the teahouse staff, herself and Ann and Paula, Daniela and Kirsten and Melissa, and, for good measure, Charles and Ben — much to their chagrin — and she hung these on a bulletin board by the counter, so that customers would know who was who. The diorama was rather roughly made, but it was unmistakable as the teahouse, and Ann had to admit it was rather clever, even if she wasn't certain Paula would want a miniature reminder of work in her apartment. "The glue isn't quite dry yet," Janet said as the cutout photograph of herself peeled from its popsicle stick.

"Is there anything else we need for the party?" Ann asked.

"Well, I got streamers and paper plates and matching napkins. I also got plastic silverware," Janet said, reaching again into her shopping bag. "Oh, shit, it's just knives. I thought I was getting knives and forks and spoons. But it's just knives."

"Oh, Janet, you could have just grabbed a few plastic forks and spoons from the teahouse. But anyway, Charles will have real silverware. It's just the five of us, right?"

"Six, actually, because Ash is coming."

"Really?"

"Well, I thought it only fair to invite him, and Paula said he said yes. It will be nice to finally get to know him."

"I suppose so. Anyway, what about food and drinks?"

"I hadn't really thought about that."

Ann sighed. She definitely was feeling run down. "It's all right. I'll take care of the food and drinks."

The denizens of the compound, plus Ash, gathered at Charles' around seven. Charles gently overruled the paper plates and napkins — "They *are* lovely," he said, wistfully eyeing his own plain-white Wedgwood — and set his table with crystal and silver and linen napkins. Ann had picked up hors d'oeuvres from a restaurant in Chestnut Hill, shrimp kabobs and mini quesadillas and tortellini salad. Charles produced several rather expensive-looking bottles of Bollinger champagne to get things started. "Perhaps young Ashford would like to pour," he said.

Ash seemed to take his assignment seriously, carefully examining the bottle before he uncorked it. "Have you tried the 1999 Special Cuvée?" he asked Charles. "It has a hint of pear."

"I don't think I have. Although I suppose I never thought of a non-vintage wine like Bollinger Special Cuvée as being associated with a particular *year*."

"Oh, right."

Charles turned to Ben and rolled his eyes.

When the assemblage was fully enjoying the glow of the lights and drink and one another's company, Janet slipped off to the kitchen to light the cake. She brought it into the dining room with candles ablaze, and Ben doused the chandelier, and they all sang a rousing "Happy Birthday to You." Then Paula blew out the candles, revealing that the iced lettering on the cake read "Happy Birthday Paul."

"Oh, Janet," Ann said.

Charles redeemed the moment by bringing out a Brazilian dessert he had made, *olhous de sogra*, mother-in-law's eyes, prune candies each with a clove stuck in its center. The reference to Ash's mother went unstated.

"Charles, that is so sweet of you."

"Don't mention it, *Paul*."

As the partiers ate their cake and sampled the *olhous de sogra*, Janet wondered if any of them had vacation-travel plans.

"I always did like to go somewhere warm this time of year," Ann said. "But I don't think it's in the cards this year."

"Now where do you like to go?" Charles asked. "I think you once mentioned Australia."

"I've been there, yes. But I have to say my favorite warm-weather place is the French Riviera. Anywhere in Provence. I'm a bit of a Francophile, I'm afraid."

"Oh, the Côte d'Azur," Janet said. "I've always wanted to go."

"I prefer the Amalfi Coast," Ash said.

"Now what do you like about it?" Charles asked.

There followed a long pause while Ash seemed to search for words. There was a dawning realization among the others that perhaps Ash had never actually been. "Oh, pretty much everything," he finally said. Janet noticed that Paula seemed to shrink in her chair.

The group discussion broke into several smaller conversations. Janet and Charles chatted about French cooking. Paula sat, observing, with Ash and Ben while they debated early acoustic blues.

"But the complexity of Blind Blake's compositions are so superior to Blind Boy Fuller," Ash was saying. "And Fuller obviously stole the thumb roll from him. He's really a Blind Blake wannabe."

"I'm sure you're right," Ben said dryly.

"I don't know what she *sees* in him," Charles said quietly to Janet.

"Well, he is interesting."

"He has a lot of *interests*, yes. But being *interested* isn't the same thing as being *interesting*."

"I wonder if people who have a lot of interests, in the way he does, aren't simply afraid of being bored."

"Well, yes, but boredom gets too much credit as one of the signature afflictions of modern life. It's not boredom that's unforgivable as much as being *boring*. Although perhaps that's 'boredom' in a different sense."

The conversations reconfigured themselves once again, and Ben realized he hadn't seen Ann in some time. He found her sitting quietly by herself in the kitchen. "I've never known you to disappear during one of Charles' soirees."

"The truth is, I feel a bit rough."

He noticed, then, that she looked ashen and tired and not at all well.

"Do you think it was something you ate?"

"No, I woke up with a sore throat this morning. I'm probably just coming down with a light head cold. I'm sure that's all it is."

"Can I get anything for you?"

"No, no. But I should be thinking about making a move."

He walked her out to the dining room, but the others had apparently reconvened elsewhere, their voices drifting from one of the front rooms.

"Well, I'll just be off, then."

It was uncharacteristic of Ann to just slip out; she must really be feeling unwell. "Let me at least tell the others, so they can say goodbye," Ben said.

He disappeared down the dark hallway. Ann steadied herself by leaning on the back of a dining-room chair. She felt cross-currents of nausea and light-headedness, like two waves colliding. Then Janet appeared, followed by the others, cluck-clucking in the way women her age do. There was a barrage of run-on sentences Ann couldn't exactly follow, concluding with something like "let me walk you home."

She wanted to protest, to tell them all to stay and finish Paula's party. But the waves of sickness seemed to be over her head, now, and she thought perhaps it best if someone accompanied her. After much seemingly unnecessary discussion it was decided that Ben would walk her home while the rest stayed to clear up.

The walk home with Ben, brief as it was, was a blur, and she hazily left him at the door, which she pulled shut on a darkened house. She felt feverish now, and a growing pressure behind her eyes. Whatever it was, it was definitely something more than a cold. She felt her way through the pitchy rooms, not bothering to turn on any lights, and managed to take off only her glasses and shoes before lying down on the bed. The last thing she remembered was thinking she would never fall asleep.

She awoke in what must have been the wee hours. She stared at the digital clock, which without her glasses was blurred, but she couldn't make sense of the time. She still had a headache, sharp and insistent, and now other symptoms emerged as from a murky pool: sore throat, congestion, body aches, fever. She realized she had been sweating profusely and now felt a damp chill. Her heart was beating rapidly, too, as if trying to compensate for her overall sense of enervation. She hoisted her feet over the edge of the bed and sat up. She waited for the dizziness to settle, when all at once she became aware of an abdominal imperative. She leapt up, ran to the bathroom, and vomited. She thought she might feel better, then, but all her symptoms seemed to coalesce and overwhelm her. She lay down on the cold tiles of the bathroom floor and, using a crumpled bath towel as a pillow, fell back asleep.

She awoke some hours later to the gray light of a February morning. She was stiff from spending the night on the floor, but at least her nausea was gone. As she got to her feet, though, she realized her other symptoms had grown worse. She still felt feverish, though it was now a sort of dry heat, her skin fiery to her own touch. But in particular she felt like she couldn't catch her breath. She leaned against the bathroom sink and inhaled deeply, which brought on a horrid cough, phlegmy and raw. The coughing shook her whole body, and as she stood there hacking she became aware of a similarly percussive sound emanating from downstairs; someone was knocking at her front door. When she had got her coughing under control she shuffled into her dressing gown and made her way down the stairs.

It was Janet. "Oh, Ann," she said. "You look awful."

Ann smiled wanly. "No, really," she said, and then was bent over by another coughing jag.

"Oh, dear, you sound awful, too."

The truth was, she couldn't remember having felt this bad before. She nodded while she caught her breath.

"Have you thought about seeing a doctor?"

She hadn't, actually, in part because she hadn't even chosen a doctor since moving to the States, let alone gone in for an office visit. She was able to get health insurance, with her work permit, through the teashop. Janet had seen to that; she was remarkably on-the-ball with the important things. "Why don't we just wait and see," she said.

"Well, in the meantime, let's get you sitting down," Janet said. She let herself in and walked Ann to the sofa. "I'll put on some tea. Anything else?"

Ann shook her head no. Janet disappeared to the kitchen, where she could be heard putting on the kettle, banging open and shut doors and drawers, rummaging in the silverware tray. Ann leaned her head back and tried to catch her breath. Her chest felt tight, her throat sandpapery. When Janet returned with the tea, English Breakfast with milk and sugar, she continued her interrogation.

"When did you start noticing you didn't feel well? You seemed fine yesterday at the teahouse."

"Last night at Charles' party. Paula's party. Actually, I felt run down all yesterday, and I had a bit of a sore throat. Last night was awful."

"You're sure there's nothing else I can get for you?"

Ann shook her head no again. She lifted her cup and took a sip of tea, but it didn't taste at all appealing, so she set it back on the coffee table. "I think I just need to rest."

"I'll leave you alone for a while," Janet said. "You should go up to bed. And make sure you're drinking lots of liquids. I'll stop back in the afternoon, OK?"

Ann nodded and closed her eyes.

She awoke to more knocking. She was upstairs again, in bed. It was late afternoon, judging by the waning light. She heard the door open. "Ann?" Janet called up. "Are you all right?"

She opened her mouth to speak, but no sound came out. She cleared her throat. "I'm up here," she called, though she realized she probably wasn't loud enough to be heard. She made her way downstairs to Janet.

"You don't look any better than before."

"I don't feel any better." In fact, she had woken up several times throughout the day, and each time she felt worse. She had managed to get down some tea and toast, but that was it. It occurred to her that maybe she should take something for whatever she had, but she had no idea what.

217

"I think you should see a doctor. I can make an appointment with my doctor for you, if you'd like."

"I don't want to be any trouble."

"It's not any trouble at all, Ann."

"Why don't we just wait and see."

"Well, if you're not any better tomorrow, I'm going to make an appointment."

Ann nodded and sat down.

"Now, can I make you something to eat?"

"I can manage, Janet," Ann said. She hoped she didn't sound shirty, but at the moment she didn't feel well enough to care all that much. But she didn't really want Janet banging around in her kitchen, breaking things and leaving messes.

"I'll just go, then," Janet said, sounding a bit put out.

Ann nodded again and closed her eyes. She heard Janet let herself out.

24

Ann woke later that night, immediately aware of her breath. Each intake of air was a raspy struggle. She felt horribly hot.

I need to get to the emergency department, she thought. She rolled out of bed and felt her way downstairs. She found her keys on the kitchen table and then realized: she didn't know where the hospital was. Stupid, she thought.

She would have to get Janet to drive her. She opened the front door and felt a blast of February air that told her she was still in her pajamas. Her dressing gown was upstairs. The phone, she thought. She could call Janet on the phone.

It seemed to take Janet a dozen rings to pick up the phone and then another fifteen minutes to walk the few steps from next door. When she finally appeared Ann realized she hadn't bothered to get dressed in the interim.

"Oh my God, Ann," Janet exclaimed. "You're really sick." She sounded a bit panicked. "I'm going to call Ben."

"No, we don't need Ben. Just drive me to emergency."

After seemingly endless confusion about whether they should call Ben or Charles, whether Ann should get dressed or take extra clothes, there was a knock at the door, and Paula appeared.

"What's going on?"

"Ann is very sick. And I'm not sure whether to wake Charles or Ben, and I was just saying she should probably take extra clothes with her, but you never can be sure what they want you to do. I know when I took Mother to the hospital after her second stroke, there were all sorts of rules about what she could and couldn't bring, and it was hard to keep track of it all. How did you know we were up?"

"Let's just say there isn't much sound-proofing. Ann, do you need me to drive you to the hospital?"

"Oh, now that probably is a good idea for you to take her," Janet answered for Ann. "I'm not sure I'm much good in cases like this."

'Then let's go," Paula said to Ann. "You should put on your coat. We can get clothes for you later."

"Yes," Ann said, going rather shakily to the coat closet.

"Do you have your glasses? Do you have your health insurance card?" Paula asked.

Paula went upstairs for Ann's glasses while Ann put on her shoes and collected her wallet from the kitchen table. Paula then helped Ann to the car while Janet bustled around them, keeping up a constant stream of conversation.

"It took me a while to realize it was the phone that was ringing when I first woke up, and then I couldn't imagine who would be calling so late at night. I had just been having the oddest dream. I was teaching sixth-grade social studies again, only it was in the teahouse, and I was also in sixth grade, and all the students were my actual sixth-grade classmates. And they all wanted to leave, and I was having the hardest time getting them to stay. Now you know where you're going? You know where the hospital is?"

"Yes," Paula said, pulling shut the car door and turning the key. She gave Janet a kind of half-wave and started backing up, when Janet stepped forward and opened the back door.

"I think maybe I'll just come with you after all," she said, climbing in.

The emergency room was empty except for a greasy-haired man who from what they gathered had burned his hand while uncapping an overheated car radiator. He alternated among moaning and watching late-night television and complaining to the admitting nurse. Paula helped Ann fill out a medical-information form. After a short wait Ann was wheeled to an examination room, where she had to change out of her pajamas and into a paper gown. She was joined by a pleasant young doctor, who asked questions and listened with his stethoscope and said he was going to order up some chest films.

"Have you been exposed to anyone who had the H1N1 virus?"

"Well, my son had the swine flu. But that was weeks and weeks ago."

"Well, then, you probably didn't catch it from him. It could have been anyone, of course."

"Do I have the swine flu, then?"

"It's a reasonable assumption, given your symptoms. We'll have to verify that with a lab test. I also think you may have pneumonia. And you're certainly dehydrated. In the meantime I'd like to keep you here for a few days for observation."

"How did I get so sick?" Ann said, more to herself than to the doctor.

"Have you been under any unusual stress?"

The doctor didn't wait for an answer before he left. A nurse began arranging for her admittance, and someone was sent to fetch Janet and Paula from the waiting room. Ann was thinking it would be most appropriate for Janet to be the primary contact for the hospital, but on the other hand she knew Paula, as young as she was, would be much more competent in the role, better able to follow the details and help with any decisions. She thought of Logan, but it just wasn't practical, with him so far away. And then she realized the solution was to name Janet, because the details and decisions would fall to Paula anyway. She wondered if Paula was able to get her own health insurance, if Janet had ever worked out the details with her immigration status.

She signed some papers, and a nurse hooked her up to an I.V. Janet and Paula stayed with her till she had been settled into a room, and then they left, with a promise to visit the next day. She had some relief now that she was in the hospital and knew she was being looked after, but still she felt miserable. She tried to sleep, but the fluorescent lights and unfamiliar noises, the staff coming and going in the hallway, the I.V. and the uncomfortable bed let her doze only fitfully.

The next day the lab tests and chest films confirmed the doctor's diagnoses: swine flu and pneumonia, and of course dehydration. She would be on an antiviral and an antibiotic and an I.V. for fluids, and with any luck she'd be home in a few days.

But by that afternoon her condition had taken an unexpected turn: she developed respiratory failure. The effects of the flu, the pneumonia, the lingering, latent harm of her long-ago cigarette smoking, had deprived her body of oxygen, had loaded it with carbon dioxide. She became confused, sweaty, cold, her breathing rapid, labored, ineffectual. She could only lie in the uncomfortable hospital bed, frightened and miserable, while medical workers scurried around her. They transported her to the intensive-care unit, the orderlies banging her rolling bed into doorways, the white-tiled hospital ceiling sliding above her. In the I.C.U. they put a tube down her throat to deliver oxygen directly to her lungs, a procedure for which she was, thankfully, anesthetized.

Janet and Paula arrived in the early evening to find Ann's room empty. Janet had called earlier in the day but had only got a ringing phone; she assumed Ann was asleep. They asked at the nurses' station and were told that Ann had been transferred to the I.C.U., and in the ensuing panic Janet had a difficult time explaining who she was and why she should be told more about Ann's condition. At last they found the nurse who had been on duty the night before, and she gave them what details she had. When they got to Ann's new room and had suited up in paper gowns and masks they discovered that Ann had been sedated and was unable to speak.

Ann spent several days in intensive care before she was moved back to a regular room. It was a few more days till she could return home. Her time in the I.C.U. was actually less awful than the rest of it, because she was under sedation and the nurses were so gentle and the experience seemed to pass like a fevery dream. It was only when she was back in a regular room that she realized how sick she had been and still was, that she felt miserable and fearful and unmoored. But Janet and Paula and Charles and Ben, in one combination or another, came every day to visit bearing cards and flowers and friendship. She thought of calling Logan but decided to wait till she was back at home. She already had her family with her.

It was Paula, though, who visited most often. She came with Janet several times in the evening, and once with Ben.

But she came every day at lunch, as well, alone and without telling the others. She made sure Ann was as comfortable as possible and asked questions of the nurses and doctor, when one was available, to be sure both she and Ann had the latest details of her treatment and her condition. It's interesting, Ann thought, that you never know how people are going to respond in a time of need. You never know who's going to panic or who's going to vanish or who's going to be compassionate and attentive and reliable. How strange to think that three or four months ago she didn't even know Paula, and now here she was at her hospital bedside. Of course she and Paula had already formed a kind of bond, working closely as they did at the teashop, both of them efficient and practical and competent. She sensed that Paula understood how unusual it was, how difficult, for Ann to lie prostrate in bed, unable to function, while others hovered about her, their own health and decisions and actions firmly in hand.

"It's OK that you're away from the teashop?" she asked Paula. It was her last day in the hospital, and she was feeling well enough for some semblance of conversation. The truth was, she didn't much care about the teashop at the moment. It was just something to ask, what she would have been expected to ask before she became ill. She didn't know what she cared about now. She felt exhausted but also somehow disillusioned — of what, she wasn't sure.

"Don't worry. Janet is there. And Kirsten and Melissa know what they're doing. So you should not worry about that. You should only get better."

"I'm accustomed to thinking of myself as the one who takes care of things. Not the one who needs taking care of." She sighed. "I suppose all this has made me feel rather out of sorts. Getting sick, I mean, and Logan leaving." She was surprising herself by confiding in a twenty-five-year-old.

"Life is not just about working." Paula said.

"Well of course not. But I'm no longer certain what it is about. If I ever was."

"Perhaps it is about less tangible things. Our connections with others. The things we believe." Paula wondered at her own words. She found in situations like this in the past — when a child at the orphanage had been sick and needed comforting, when one of her friends had broken up with a boyfriend and wanted sympathy — words of advice simply came to her, words she hadn't prepared and wasn't even certain she believed herself. Was she connected to others? To Ash? Besides Ash, to anyone?

Ann often found it interesting how ready young people were to offer advice, as if they had lived long enough, had experienced enough and learned enough, to have wisdom. Although surely Paula was older than her years. And of course no one gained wisdom with age anyway, unless it was to recognize there was no wisdom to gain.

"I suppose it's about those things as much as anything," Ann said. "I'm sorry, that sounded dismissive. I'm not sure what you mean by 'the things we believe,' though. You mean religious beliefs?"

"It could be religious beliefs."

"You're Catholic, yes?"

Paula smiled. "In Brasil, everyone is Catholic. But I'm not talking about Catholicism or religion. I guess I mean spirituality."

"Oh, Paula, I don't know about spirituality. You know I'm an atheist, yes? Does that offend you?"

"No, not at all. I respect that as I would any belief."

"But atheism isn't a belief. It's the lack of belief."

"Really?"

Isn't it interesting, Ann thought, how these sorts of conversations always seem to arise when you're least able to do them justice, when you're lying in a hospital bed recovering from a grave illness, for instance. A Christian would likely say that was no coincidence, as it's in our weakest moments that we turn to God for succor. But that's a rather paltry recommendation for belief, if you need it only when you're at your worst. And the whole "it comforts me" or "it inspires me" notion isn't much of an argument for religion in any case, because people could be comforted or inspired by all sorts of things, as often as not the very things religion condemned. Not that there was ever a good time to talk about belief. She had loved discussing religion and philosophy in college, so many years ago, when she and her fellow undergraduates discovered they could read books and parrot back ideas to one another as if they were their own. But as you grew older you began to realize you really had nothing new or enlightening to say, and neither did anyone else, so you might as well keep your opinions to yourself and hope others did the same.

"OK, I see your point," she finally said. "And I wouldn't want to dissuade anyone from their own beliefs. But you're an intelligent person. Do you really believe there's a God who has always existed, and suddenly he decides to create an earth and all the things in it, but then he steps back and lets evolution take over, and then a man named Jesus is born of a virgin, and he rises from the dead? And this God is loving and all-powerful, yet he lets millions of children die horrible, painful deaths? And there's no evidence for any of it, because for some reason this loving God wants to keep it all a big secret? I could go on, but I think you get the idea."

"Yes, sure, but that is more religion than spirituality. But anyway, does it have to be factual for you to believe it?"

"Certainly it has to be factual for me to believe it."

Paula thought for a moment. "Well, for example, the days of the week. There is no such thing as the days of the week. They're a human ... I can't think of the word. Human construct. But you wouldn't say they don't exist. They are real. There is Sunday, Monday, Tuesday. So you could say, maybe, that there is the Father, Son, and Holy Spirit. They exist as much as the days of the week exist. You see?"

"Well, it's not fair to argue with someone in hospital. But I suppose thinking of it in that way does at least make some room for beliefs that one can take comfort in, even if they aren't necessarily true in any rigorous sort of way. But the spirituality part." She paused and closed her eyes. She wasn't quite up for this long a discussion.

"You don't believe there is a spiritual world?" Paula asked. "Or at least that there is something like fate, or destiny?"

"Not really, dear."

"So you and Janet crossing paths after all these years. That was just a coincidence? And all of us coming together at the compound, as Ben calls it. And our friendships. That is not a spiritual connection?"

Ann reopened her eyes. "It would be lovely to think there were such a thing as fate or destiny. Well, actually, depending on what your fate was, it might be awful. But I suppose it would be comforting to believe there was someone or something guiding all this, and a reason for it."

In the absence of that belief it was comforting to have someone to talk to about it. People didn't have these sorts of discussions any longer, she thought. Honest discussions, without rancor or judgment. Or at least reasonably honest, and reasonably free from judgment. But perhaps Paula was right, perhaps there was room in her life for spirituality. Not religion, not the sort of absurd beliefs and rules that Logan had been clinging to. But there could be mystery and even magic in the world, in art and literature and music, in love and friendship. And even if it was merely a human construct, like Paula's days of the week, or a bio-chemical thing in the brain, could she not still embrace it, this notion of connectedness, of purpose?

"We'll talk about it more when I'm better. When I'm home."

**

Ann was welcomed home warmly by her friends, Janet and Paula and Charles and Ben. They brought her flowers and food, casseroles and soups and homemade breads, and they fussed over her till she had to shoo them out the door. After a few days she insisted on coming into the teahouse, but once she got there she realized she had no strength and resignedly returned home. It was another week till she felt well enough to actually work again, and then only for brief, rather slow-paced spells.

After another week Charles invited them all to a Sunday brunch to celebrate Ann's recovery. Ann and Paula worried about leaving the teahouse in the hands of the tea cad-dies for the day, but Tommy, their newest employee, had started, and Janet assured them that among Shawn Johnson and Auntie Tudy and Pooh Bear, as she called Tommy, they would be fine, and anyway, they were just next door and could easily stop over if something went wrong. Charles served cheese omelets and home-fried potatoes, peach crepes and fresh-fruit salad and pumpkin bread, along with wonderfully strong bloody marys, which he himself took without tomato juice.

"It *is* such a relief to have you back," Charles said to Ann. "You did *worry* us so."

"Well, I won't say it wasn't a horrid experience. But you all were so wonderful and thoughtful and supportive. Every one of you. Paula especially."

"Well surely Paula is the most *saintly* among us."

"Talking of saintly, Paula and I had a long talk about belief and spirituality. And while I can't say I had any kind of life-changing epiphany, I do perhaps see things in a different sort of way, now. As if perhaps there's room for more possibilities, do you know. Or at least for mystery."

"I sense the conversation is veering toward the *significant*."

"And why not?" Janet said. "I like our conversations. I like that we feel we can talk about anything."

Could they talk about anything? wondered Ann. She supposed yes, as much as any such group of people could. And she felt she could be honest with the others, or at least as honest as she would want the others to be with her. In general she found forthright people off-putting, hiding as they did behind the shield of candor. And that of course assumed you were being honest with yourself. Did she really think it would be comforting if there were such a thing as faith or fate or destiny? How comforting was it to think that the course of your life was beyond your control, that you were helplessly floating downstream? Maybe it was that very relinquishing of responsibility that people found comforting. And of course there really was no such thing as being in control anyway. As much as she liked to feel her hand was on the wheel, there was little she found more infuriating than those small-witted people who advised that one should "believe and achieve." Become a child prodigy! Cure yourself of cancer! Bring back your dead loved ones! So then, had Lionel's death been fate? In a sense, yes, because after all everyone was fated to die.

Janet and Ann and Paula began to discuss religious faith. Paula was describing her Catholic upbringing, and Janet was explaining how she never had had much in the way of religious belief, though she did think about it quite a bit. Ben found his mind wandering. He had grown up in a fundamentalist Christian household, his parents and siblings born agains who believed that Balaam's ass actually spoke and that the sun stood still for Joshua and that the great day of the wrath of the Lamb was imminent. To Ben such beliefs were largely a method of avoiding anything that resembled thinking as well as a means of preventing others from any thinking of their own. How anyone could buy into the malarkey was beyond him, and why even atheists expressed respect for religious belief, for those who so willfully abandoned all reason, was equally perplexing. But of course most opinions, which surely is what religious faith came down to, were held in the absence of knowledge and evidence alike.

Charles recognized Ben's reticence and understood it. He had little time for religious debate, as people seemed to cling so resolutely to their opinions, however ill-begotten, especially when it came to faith. Religion itself, and Christianity in particular, Biblical studies, at least from a literary or historic point of view, he found fascinating. But to discuss such things with any degree of success your interlocutor had to be an atheist or, at worst, an agnostic. To Charles Christian faith was nothing so much as a widespread manifestation of Stockholm syndrome, the development of an emotional attachment to and even adulation of a God who appears to give life simply because he isn't at that moment taking it. God's beneficence is nothing so much as an apparent withholding of suffering, the absence of abuse conflated with kindness. People experiencing Stockholm syndrome were believed to regress to a state of infancy, he seemed to remember, in which they became completely dependent on their captor. No wonder Christians think of God as the father and they themselves behave like his dim children. Of course, all that had probably been thought of before, by many people many times over. He'd have to look it up on the Internet. No matter what seemingly new idea he might have, when he checked on the Internet, it turned out someone else had already thought of it, and often as not had honed it to a finer edge. It was one of the reasons he was relieved to be free of academic life, of research and papers and publishing. If the Internet didn't reveal there was nothing new under the sun, academia surely did.

He was about to bring the conversation around to something more frivolous when he realized it was shifting of its own accord.

"Did they ever figure out how you got the pig flu?" Janet asked. "Or whatever it is, swine flu. Was it from Logan?"

"He had it too long ago for me to have gotten it from him. But of course there are people coming into the teashop every day, and who knows what they could be carrying? There's really no way to escape it."

"One thing I don't understand," Janet said. "I thought the people who got really sick with it always had some 'underlying medical condition,' or something like that."

"Well, I think that may be a bit of a misapprehension," Ann said. "I read up on H1N1 when Logan was sick with it, and apparently in many cases that turn serious there is no underlying condition. But I think in my case, the reason I went into respiratory failure was because I used to be a smoker. Apparently I have some early form of emphysema."

"Now, I don't know about that, do I?" Janet said.

No, Ann didn't think she did. She hadn't started smoking yet when they were pen pals, all those years ago, and the subject had never come up after they found each other again. It occurred to her that this behavior from the past, the decision to smoke, which she thought she had left behind, had returned unexpectedly. It had threatened her life, really, and in fact had affected them all. She noticed Janet had turned quiet.

Janet was thinking. She felt not hurt, that wasn't the word, but perhaps just a little surprised, or maybe disappointed, that Ann had never told her that she had smoked, that she had emphysema. Of course, there were things from her own past she didn't often discuss. She hadn't told Ann and the others much about Joseph, for instance, other than the mere fact of having given him up for adoption. But certainly not about who Joseph was, who he had become when she knew him as a teenager; the ache of letting him go, the reopened wound of losing him a second time. For that matter what did she really know of any of them? Of Paula's childhood in Brazil? Of the supposed scandal that had brought Charles to Lower Slaughter? And of Ben, what did she know of Ben at all? They had become her dear friends, but they remained inscrutable as strangers.

Charles turned to Ben. "I think another pitcher of bloody marys, don't you?"

25

Winter was relinquishing its hold on Lower Slaughter. What snow had massed along the sides of roads and in the drifted shade of evergreens had all but melted. White-breasted juncos busied themselves in preparation for their springtime journey north, while Canada geese paired off and settled over meager nests. The brown suburban lawns now wore a hint of chlorophyllous green, and in the air there wafted smells of life, sodden, urgent, not spring, not yet, but nearly. Ben sensed it as he walked the road from the compound to the Wissahickon, where he would take a trail that ran along the water's edge. He liked this time of year. All spring and summer lay before him, and their familiar advance: redbud, dogwood, cherry; honey-bee, firefly, cicada; verdant fields of goldenrod and foxtail, humid and sweet like strawberries; daylight creeping further into night.

He was happy to be rid of February, the longest month. He had always dreaded Valentine's Day, a reminder that he was, in fact, alone. Yes, he had his friends at the compound,

Charles and Janet and Ann and Paula, and he valued them, cherished them, even loved them. But surely they didn't love him in return, not really. He was an afterthought, a fifth wheel. There was no one to whom he was truly special, no one about whom he could say "we."

How had this come to be? He had had crushes, obsessions, love interests. But he had never had a long-term relationship. In high school he hadn't even dated. He had been afraid to ask girls out, afraid of their rejection, afraid of their acceptance, too, afraid of spoken words. He believed on some fundamental level he had nothing to offer them. In any case he would have been embarrassed to bring them home, to the working-class squalor of his family's house, to the intellectual poverty of their Christian fundamentalism. And so through high school and into college, through a seemingly endless procession of parties, dances, Homecomings, Prom Nights, Valentine's Days, he had watched from a resentful distance while others experienced pleasure, intimacy, love. It wasn't till his last year in college that he had his first sexual experience. What had changed? He had found a cadre of students, previously unknown to him, who thought of themselves as Young Intellectuals and had Deep Discussions about Important Topics. They also had parties, sustained by quantities of alcohol and pot and other less familiar substances, where the hazy sexual pairings were based less on physical attraction than on cognitive affinity. In short, he had discovered philosophy majors.

But his foray into coeducational relations hadn't extended into graduate school. In part that was because his philosophy-major friends had all graduated and taken jobs at Barnes & Noble. In part it was because he had always commuted to school, driving the hour from his mother's house to G&B, and so was less likely to form bonds outside the classroom, in dorms and off-campus. He had always felt like an outsider, as if he were auditing his entire college experience. And now, far into adulthood, he still bore the leaden affect of alienation.

It had taken him six years to complete his undergraduate degree, largely because he had had to work his way through college and couldn't afford to go full-time. He felt vaguely ashamed he hadn't finished in the traditional four years. He had started as an English major, but after a year he switched to anthropology. He had enjoyed literature, poetry and drama and short fiction and novels. But he began to find the stories of imaginary characters less compelling, whereas with anthropology you were learning about real people who had lived real lives, even if you didn't know who they were as individuals. But even before that he had begun to wonder if he were a better consumer of literary data than producer of it. For one of his first papers he had decided to write about *The Waste Land*. But at the library he discovered more than a hundred books of literary criticism on Eliot, and those were just the ones in English. He felt certain he had no way of finding anything new to say on the subject, no means of breeding lilacs out of such thoroughly tilled land. He couldn't even remember what *The Waste Land* was about, or if he ever knew.

When he finished college he discovered there wasn't much he could do with a degree in anthropology except get into graduate school. He would have to save for it first, though, to supplement what student loans he could get, so it was another two years before he started. He chose Maximus University, in the bowels of Philadelphia, because it had a program he wanted to get into, not because an urban university with tens of thousands of other students was at all appealing to him. And so here he was, thirty years old, living alone in a third-floor apartment, a student of

Native American studies, of all things. And no clear end in sight.

He had chosen Native American studies because he had an interest in the Lenape, the people who had lived in what became Pennsylvania and New Jersey and Delaware and New York. It turned out they weren't so much a single tribe in any political sense as scatterings of bands of fifty to several hundred people who shared a cultural heritage and spoke varying dialects of the same language. They had lived here for at least five hundred years before the arrival of Europeans, and their forebears for at least ten thousand years longer, abiding in relative harmony among themselves and neighboring tribes. They were by nature democratic and egalitarian, respecting one another and respected by others. To Ben the most interesting aspect of the Lenape was a society organized by matrilineal phratries, or groups of clans: Wolf, Turkey, Turtle. A man married outside his phratry, and his children belonged to his wife's phratry. The children's maternal uncle, their mother's brother, and not their father, was considered their closest male relative, because their father belonged to a different phratry. Such a societal structuring had perplexed the European invaders.

And invade the Europeans did. At the time they started sighting European ships in the early to mid-sixteenth century, the Lenape of the Delaware and Hudson river valleys numbered at least ten thousand. Within two centuries ninety percent of them were gone, victims of warfare, slavery, displacement, and, especially, introduced diseases, primarily smallpox. Then began the push west, the remaining Lenape cheated out of their ancestral lands, forced into Ohio, into Indiana, into Wisconsin, into Ontario, into Missouri, into Oklahoma. By the time of the Revolutionary War they were all but absent from their homeland.

Their descendants persisted, however. They established recognized tribes in Oklahoma and reserves in Ontario. They endeavored to preserve the language and revive old customs. They were called the Delaware now, a designation derived from Baron De La Warr, governor of the Virginia Colony. To Ben that seemed about equivalent to referring to Congolese as "the Leopold," after Belgium's Leopold II, but who was he to dispute the name they now claimed?

But Ben had no interest in the Native Americans of today, in their economic struggles, their legal battles, their disenfranchisement, their casinos. He was concerned only with what he admitted was an idealized, sanitized past, of an aboriginal people living in harmony with the world around them. He believed emphatically that humanity's most intractable problems would be solved if it could somehow return to an imagined paradise of Lenape society circa 1500 C.E. This was not an opinion he could share with his colleagues in the Native American studies program at Maximus.

He wondered what he would do with his degree if he ever finished the program. He had an acquaintance at Maximus who was a classics major, studying ancient Greece and Rome. There were five students in the program. They all planned to become classics professors at universities, where they would each teach five other classics majors, who would also become classics professors, and so on in an endless loop, a closed system, like breeding fish in an aquarium, equally self-perpetuating and self-terminating. He didn't want that as his future. Instead he had a vague notion that he would work in the field, where he might be free of the intrusions and judgments of colleagues and students and other people in general.

When he started graduate school he still needed to earn an income, but he had had enough of manual labor, of sign painting and quasi-carpentry. He thought he would try working in an office, so he took a job at an insurance company. The position he applied for had been indeterminate, but after doing well on an aptitude test, and because he had a four-year college degree, he was placed in a supervisory role. His charges were all twenty-somethings, some with Associate's degrees, some college dropouts, who had responded to an ad for MANAGEMENT TRAINEE! and whose task it was to process insurance claims. His staff never seemed to be certain what their purpose was, though, nor was he certain, of their purpose or, consequently, his own. None of that seemed to matter, however, as the imperative was volume: more claims, faster. And so they moved stacks of paper with admirable speed, boxes checked, forms stamped, copies routed to their destinations by color: white, canary, pink. Each day he was newly amazed, in this age of computers, of electrons and photons and magnetization, how much data was recorded on paper. After a year he got a bonus and a raise, for an uncertain job well-done, and he realized it was time to quit.

But the most distressing aspect of the job, the most perplexing and alienating, had been the constant, endless conference calls, groups of largely unfamiliar people communing telephonically, each sitting alone, sharing their disembodied voices, for no discernable reason:

SCENE ONE

(Int. nondescript office building. BEN sits in a tiny cubicle, facing the wall. He sets his phone on Speaker and dials. We hear a dial tone and then eleven beeps as he punches in the number.)

FEMALE VOICE
Thank you for using Qwikie-Con, the conference-call solution that works at the speed of business! Using the

touchpad of your phone, please enter your thirty-digit Qwikie-Con participant code now, followed by the pound or hash key!

(We hear thirty beeps as BEN painstakingly enters the code.)

FEMALE VOICE
You are the ... first ... caller in the conference! The host has not yet joined! You will be placed on hold until the host arrives! While you wait, you will hear music! To stop the music at any time, using the touchpad of your phone, please enter the fifteen-digit stop-music code! Remember, Qwikie-Con is the conference-call solution that works the way you do, to empower you to achieve the results you want!

(We hear an endless loop of annoying music. After a few moments, we hear a series of beeps.)

MARK
Hello? Who's on the call?

BEN
I'm here. This is Ben Shriver.

MARK
Hi, Ben. Thanks for joining the call.
(There's a long pause.)
Is anyone else on the call?

BEN
I think I'm the first one.

(We hear a series of beeps.)

JACK
(After a pause)
Hello? Is anyone there?

MARK
(After a pause)
This is Mark. I'm the host for the call.

JACK
(After a pause)
Hi, Mark. This is Jack.

MARK
(After a pause)
Hi, Jack. Glad you could make the call.
(There's a long pause.)
Ben is also on the line.

JACK
(After a pause)
Hi, Ben.

BEN
Hi, Jack.

(We hear a series of beeps.)

JEFF
This is Jeff in Atlanta.

MARK
(After a pause)
Hi, Jeff. We also have Jack and Ben on the call.

JEFF
(After a pause)
Is that Jack?

JACK
(After a pause)
Yeah, I'm here.

JEFF
(After a pause)
How you doin', man?

JACK
(After a pause)
I'm good.
(There's a long pause.)
How are you?

JEFF
(After a pause)
I'm good.

(We hear a series of beeps.)

MARK
(After a long pause)
Who just joined?

PAM
(After a pause)
This is Pam.

MARK
(After a pause)

Hi, Pam.
(After a pause)
We also have Jeff and Ben and Jack on the line.

JEFF
(After a pause)
Hi, Pam.

PAM
(After a pause)
Is that Jeff?

JEFF
(After a pause)
Yep.

PAM
(After a pause)
Hi, Jeff.

JACK
(After a pause)
This is Jack. Hi, Pam.

PAM
(After a pause)
Hey, Jack.

Mark
(After a pause)
We're still waiting for Jen and Ted.
(There's a long pause.)
Well, why don't we just get started, then. The reason for ...

(We hear a series of beeps.)

MARK
Who's there? Who just joined the call?

JEN
(After a pause)
This is Jen.

MARK
(After a pause)
Hi, Jen. We were just getting started. The reason for ...

JEFF
Hey, Jen.

JEN
Who is that?

JEFF
It's Jeff.

JEN
(After a pause)
Hi, Jeff.

MARK
OK, we're going to have to get started.

JEN
Is Ted on the call?

MARK
(After a pause)

No, Ted hasn't joined yet.

JEN
(After a pause)
Well, we can't do this without Ted's input. He's the primary stakeholder.

MARK
(After a pause)
OK, then why don't we just wait a few minutes and see if Ted joins.

(There's a long pause.)

JACK
Hey, Jeff. Jeff, you there?

JEFF
(After a pause)
Yeah, I'm here.

JACK
(After a pause)
How's the weather in Atlanta?

JEFF
(After a pause)
Oh, it's good. Warmer than where you are, I bet.

JACK
(After a pause)
Don't I know it.
(There's a long pause.)
Hey, how're the Braves gonna do this year?

JEFF
(After a pause)
Well, we'll see. They got no pitching.

MARK
(After a pause)
Look, we're gonna have to do this without Ted. So, the reason for ...

(We hear a series of beeps.)

TED
Hi, this is Ted. Who's on the call?

MARK
We have Jen on the line. Also we have Pam, Jeff, and Ben.

TED
Jack isn't on?

MARK
Sorry, I was forgetting Jack.

JACK
(After a pause)
I'm here.

TED
Who is that?

JACK
(After a pause)
This is Jack.

MARK
Sorry, Jack, didn't mean to leave you out.

TED
OK, listen, I have a hard stop in ten minutes, so we're gonna have to move quickly on this.

MARK
Ted, we were just getting started. I was gonna start by running through the numbers, but since you're the key stakeholder on this one, why don't I turn the call over to you?

(There's a long pause.)

MARK
Ted? Ted, are you there?

(There's a long pause.)

TED
Sorry, I was on mute. OK, here's the four-one-one.

(We hear a series of beeps.)

MARK
Did someone just join the call?

JEFF
(After a pause)
No, I think that was someone dropping off.

MARK

(After a pause)
Who dropped off the call? Jack, are you there?

JACK
(After a pause)
I'm here.

PAM
(After a pause)
I'm here.

JEFF
(After a pause)
I'm here.

MARK
(After a pause)
OK, Jen must have dropped off the call.

JEFF
(After a pause)
Should we wait for her, because ...

TED
Look, we have to move on this, so Jen will just have to get up to speed later. So like I was saying ...

(We hear a series of beeps.)

JEN
Sorry, I got bumped out.

MARK

That's OK, Jen. Ted was just telling us ...

TED
(Quieter, as if he's not talking directly into the phone)
No, you know what? Just make it a turkey club, and tell them to be sure to hold the mayo this time. And can you get me a real Coke? I'm tired of that diet crap.

MARK
Ted, are you talking to us?

TED
(Louder, as if he's talking into the phone again)
I talked to the DWK people about the G-lat initiative, and they want to know when we're gonna have feet on the ground. I told them I want to look over the KPIs first to be sure we're trending in the right direction. But penultimately I think we can leverage our synergies in a win-win value proposition. Anyway, you all know your MBOs. We need to reduce spend while grabbing a bigger share of wallet. If we don't make this work, people, we're gonna be four paws to the moon. That's the short and end of it.

MARK
I hear what you're saying, Ted.

(There's a long pause.)

TED
OK, look, I've already run into my eleven o'clock, so I gotta go.

MARK

All right, then why don't we plan to ...

(We hear a series of beeps.)

JEFF
Was that Ted leaving?

(There's a long pause.)

MARK
OK, I think Ted dropped off. So why don't we plan to reconvene in about two weeks? Pam, can you set something up?

PAM
(After a pause)
You want me to set it up?

MARK
(After a pause)
Yeah, is that OK?

PAM
(After a pause)
Yeah, I can set it up.

MARK
(After a pause)
OK, then we'll meet again in two weeks.

JEFF
OK, bye.

MARK

Thanks, everyone.

JEFF
Thanks, Mark.

JEN
Bye.

(We hear a series of beeps.)

JACK
Bye.

JEFF
Bye.

(We hear multiple series of beeps.)

In his mind's ear, Ben could hear Peggy Lee singing, "Is that all there is?"

26

With April came a week of rain. The trail along the Wissahickon had grown muddy, in some places nearly impassible, so Ben decided to walk along the bluff above Mole End. He had to pass through the few acres of woods behind the teahouse to reach it, and then, at the edge of the woods, through a tangle of brush, which even at this time of year, before the leaves had fully formed, was a thicket of thorns and cockleburs. But he liked the view from the bluff, and he welcomed the change from his usual route along the stream.

There wasn't much in the way cf real woods left in the Philadelphia suburbs, even at this far reach. What remained was a patchwork, a few or several acres here and there, like leftovers on a buffet table. He missed the ampler sweep of trees, broad expanses of hickory and ash and walnut, he had grown up with farther north, where state game lands and remoteness combined to thwart development. Here there was less. Fewer. Fewer small mammals, raccoons and red squirrels and grey foxes;

fewer amphibians, toads and newts and salamanders;
fewer insects, June bugs and leafhoppers and katydids. Yet
the suburbs were where he had chosen to live. They were
where a lot of people had chosen to live. People liked
to disparage the suburbs, he thought, for lacking character or color, for hiding shadowy secrets behind good-
neighbor fences and curb appeal. But the suburbs were
no less parochial and no more sinister than the city where
he went to school and the country where he had lived as a
boy. Both city and country felt claustrophobic to him, the
urban streets hedged in by concrete, the rural lanes over-
populated with ignorance. What the suburbs lacked was
locus. They offered no sense of place, of people belong-
ing — to the land, to a town, to one another. They were
comfortable yet common, but in the sense of ordinary,
not community, like a junior suite at a mid-tier chain
hotel. They were much of a muchness, numb. Perhaps
numbness was the ransom paid for convenience, for con-
formance, for absence of pain.

The bluff had been carved by the flow of the
Wissahickon. There was a craggy outcropping of sedimen-
tary rock, beyond which lay a narrow plateau of fallow
field, maybe sixty acres, a rare expanse of open land that
hadn't yet succumbed. In an earlier era it may have been
a natural clearing, kept free of trees by fire and shallow
soil. More recently it had probably been cleared by human
hand, perhaps more than once as it was tilled and left to
nature and then tilled again. Ben had no idea who owned
the property, as he never came across anyone up here, and
what houses could be seen lay in the distance, the nearer
ones shrouded by trees. It was easy to cross the field at this
time of year, the grasses low and brown, the Queen Anne's
lace and milkweed still dormant. The ground was fairly dry,
even after all the rain. He thought he'd walk to the top

of the bluff, where he could survey Lower Slaughter and glimpse his own house, Charles', below.

And then he saw them, surveyor's stakes, squat lengths of lumber hammered into the ground and beribboned with fluorescent marker tape, polyvinyl chloride, pink and dirty. So it had succumbed, after all: a development must be going in. The developer was probably trying to finish up the planning while the weather was still cold and damp, before people emerged from their houses and noticed yet more open space was disappearing. Soon the graders and loaders and block trucks would arrive, rumbling and scarring the earth. He wondered if he'd hear them from the compound.

As he neared the overlook he came upon a rectangular trench, presumably carved by a backhoe. It was about six feet long and maybe four feet wide and deep. Heaped beside the trench was the soil, red and raw, that it had held. They must be checking the drainage, he thought. But of course the drainage here would be quite good; the soil was shallow and shaly. He noticed, then, the wide tracks where the equipment had come through, flattening the weeds and leaving lumpy ruts. He would have thought he would have heard them, the excavators, but maybe they had come while he was away from home, in class, perhaps. He approached the hole and peered in.

He stood for a moment, idly thinking what a shame it was but aware there was nothing he could do about it. He turned to continue, but as he did his eye was caught by an object in the mound of dirt, a small triangle, butterscotch in color, roughly hewn. It was a Lenape projectile point, possibly, or, more likely, some kind of scraper. He bent to pick it up. He turned it in his hands. It was Late Woodland, from the shape of it, having been fashioned maybe four hundred years ago, just before the Lenape began to use metal tools traded from the Dutch and Swedes and English. It was made of jasper and would have been affixed to a wooden handle and used to deflesh animal hides before tanning or to shape implements of wood or bone. It was dulled from use and probably would soon have been discarded.

It had become rare to find Lenape artifacts here, where most of the land had been farmed at one time or another, where repeated turning of the earth had already uncovered much of what had been left behind. But maybe this was in fact a natural clearing; maybe the soil was too shallow to support agriculture, at least this close to the bluff's edge. He pocketed the stone tool and eased himself down into the hole. It rose above his waist, and at its bottom it scraped the bedrock of red shale. It gave off the earthy smell of freshly dug soil, like wet stone and old manure.

He surveyed the walls of the trench, though he didn't know why he bothered. It would be too much to hope for something like obvious strata in the soil or bits of black that suggested charcoal, shells or grinding stones or anything else that might point to a permanent human settlement. Besides, it was assumed the Lenape built no villages this far north on the Wissahickon, instead preferring the floodplains of the Delaware and Schuylkill rivers, where resources were more plentiful. He stood passively, staring, till the image before him blurred. And then he realized he was looking at a profile of ochre-colored material in the brown-dirt trench wall. He instinctively reached out and pried it from the earth, instantly realizing that it was the wrong thing to do, that he should leave it in place till he could get a better sense of what he was looking at. But it was too late, for in his fingers was a potsherd, about six inches long, an inch or so wide, a quarter-inch thick. One end of the sherd was clearly the lip of the pot, and the incising on it, at least at first glance, also evoked Late Woodland, like the scraper. The length and thickness of the sherd suggested it was from a large pot, perhaps one that would have been used for cooking over an open fire. It might also indicate a longer-term settlement, as it wasn't the sort of thing that would be carried on a hunt or used at a temporary campsite.

Of course, it wasn't much to go on. But while it was merely interesting to come across a scraper, it was almost exhilarating to find a potsherd, as it suggested there was more to look for. He would have to move quickly before the developer did further damage. They should have requested an archaeological assessment before they started excavating, but it's possible they did and got the go-ahead; there was no reason to expect to find anything of value here. Would a stone tool and a fragment of pottery be enough to stop the construction? It might at least prompt another assessment. He wasn't sure whom to contact. One of his professors would probably know.

He stood leaning against the trench wall. The earth was still cold, and he could feel its chill seeping through the seat of his pants. He removed his glasses and perched them on top of his head. He held the fragment of pottery close to his face, where he could focus on its detail. There weren't large caches of Lenape pottery lying around, and while he had seen plenty of it, in museum collections and photographs, he had handled only two or three pieces. It was a thrill to touch something so old, something that had been created and used by a person who stood on this spot maybe four centuries ago. Maybe on a raw, early-April day very much like this one. He took the piece of jasper from his pocket and gave it an equally close inspection. It had come from the earth and returned to it, and now it had come from the earth again.

He put his glasses back on. He thought he'd take another look around, just to see if there were anything else to be found, another artifact exposed to view. No, nothing in the hole itself. But maybe in the mound of dirt outside of it, where he had found the scraper. He recalled from his fundamentalist Christian childhood that the walls of the New Jerusalem were to be made of jasper. The Mormons believed Native Americans were a lost tribe of Israel. He supposed you could make up anything.

There was a discoloration on the opposite wall of the trench, starting about eighteen inches below the surface and extending almost to the bedrock. It was just an area of darker soil, really, about eight inches across at the top and narrowing almost to a point at the bottom. It looked a bit like a giant tea stain. Strange, he thought. And then he realized what he was looking at. It was a post mold, the archaeological remains of a wooden post. It was what was left behind after the post had rotted away, the subtle evidence of what had once been. It was a telltale, and extremely rare, sign of a Lenape settlement.

The Lenape of the Late Woodland lived in houses framed with slender wood poles. The poles, typically fashioned from saplings, were inserted into the ground at close intervals. They were long and flexible enough to be bent into an arched roof. This framework was covered with broad panels of bark stripped from large trees. Another course of poles would then encircle the house, helping to secure the bark siding and provide stability. Such houses would be scattered over a broad clearing, with new houses added as the band's population grew and old houses discarded if they were no longer needed. But because they were fashioned of wood, with no excavation or stonework, physical evidence of them had long since disappeared. All that remained were the ghostly stains of post molds, like shadows in an old photograph.

What was the chance that the developer would dig a hole that made a perfect cross-section of a post mold? But of course so much archaeological discovery was by chance. And there could be post molds scattered all over the clearing. He climbed from the trench and gazed out over the field. If this had been a natural clearing, it would have been the perfect place for a small village, enough area for ten or so houses, plenty of acreage for planting maize and beans and squash. It was near enough the Wissahickon for easy access to its resources, but set high up enough that flooding would never be a concern. It would have allowed a clear view of looming storms as well as approaching visitors or intruders.

It was a potentially significant find, one that could be meaningful to his academic career. He would definitely have to stop the housing development, but that shouldn't be a problem now, now that he had clear evidence of a Native American settlement. He noticed the surveyor's stakes extended in a long line, receding into the distance. Where they ended he could see a narrow swath of trees had been felled. It struck him as odd, because he assumed developers would want to retain such mature trees, especially at the tract's edge, where they would shield the construction from onlookers and later provide greenery and soundproofing for prospective homebuyers. He realized, then, that the surveyor's stakes described a long, broad path and that the trees and undergrowth had been cleared in a similar fashion.

It wasn't a development. It was a roadway. He knew a four-lane highway was going in, a long-delayed bypass, planned for decades, that would connect Norristown, south and west, with Doylestown, north and east. But he had no idea it was intended to pass through here. So close to the teahouse. So close to the compound. Right over the archaeological site he had only just discovered.

So now instead of fighting a local real-estate developer he'd be fighting the state department of transportation. That could make it easier, because surely it would be more visible, of interest to more people. But more likely it would make it harder, much harder. The state had been struggling to put in the bypass for thirty years or more, quashing lawsuit after lawsuit as residents up and down the highway's length tried to redirect it from their own back yards. At last it had been approved, the final legal battles waged and won, the land acquired and cleared, the work already started. There was no turning back now.

He started walking. He would have to think this through. He continued past the bluff, down a gentle slope and through a scrim of trees to Station Lane, the road that ran past the teahouse. He supposed an overpass would have to be built, launching the new highway off the end of the bluff and bearing it over the road he was now on.

He wondered if he could stop it, somehow, the bypass. Would his feeble protests be enough to dull the momentum of modernity, the received wisdom of progress? Would the fact that he had discovered the scarce remains of a Native American village make a difference? Probably not. The New World had long since forsaken its first people. America had long run roughshod over Native Americans and felt little compulsion to remember what it had done to them or even remember them at all.

He had always been vexed by small-witted people who parroted claptrap about how one person could make a difference. One person made no difference whatsoever. Well, a murderer could surely make a difference, destroying the life of the murdered and, quite probably, the lives of the murdered's loved ones. A Stalin, an Amin, a Kim could destroy the lives of millions, but of course dictators only dictated; they needed their executioners, willing or unwilling. But otherwise? An Alexander Fleming, a Jonas Salk, a Mother Teresa could certainly ease suffering, but to what end? Would not all those whose suffering they eased merely one day suffer in some other way, physically, mentally? And for how long would their suffering be eased before they died? Would not a more effective way of easing their suffering be for them to die now rather than later, or never to have lived at all? And if each person whose suffering had been eased made no difference anyway, then was the purpose of existence merely to avoid suffering? It was another endless loop, another closed system. More to the point, perhaps, what was the purpose of his own life? Did he ease the suffering of or bring meaning to or otherwise benefit even one other person? If he had never lived, would anyone have noticed? If he died sooner rather than later, would it matter?

It was interesting. He seldom went up to the clearing above the bluff. It was interesting that he would go up there just after they had started excavation but before they had made irreversible progress. Almost anyone else who had passed the trench wouldn't have noticed the jasper tool, wouldn't have seen the potsherd, wouldn't have recognized the post mold for what it was. Had he been fated to discover them? He didn't believe in fate, of course. He wondered if the Lenape did. They believed in a creator spirit, apparently. They also believed that all living things possessed a spirit, and that the spirits of other creatures weren't necessarily more or less important than their own. He wondered at the perspective of a people who believed in spirits. He had once hiked, alone, in a remote Pennsylvania forest, and got lost. He had been walking for several hours when he realized he didn't know where he was, that the trail he was looking for wasn't where he had expected it to be. He hadn't panicked, exactly, but he had felt threatened, as if danger lurked nearby. It was another several hours till he found his way. As he wandered, following a shallow stream, he passed through a deeply riven valley shrouded by towering hemlocks. It had been a clear summer's day, stark and hot, but in the basin of the valley he was engulfed in a crepuscular gloom. The chill air was utterly silent. The presence of spirits then had seemed not only plausible but also reasonable, logical, likely.

Perhaps in discovering the settlement he had also assumed a responsibility to protect it. He often wondered what his responsibility was to the world, to others. He saw images in magazines, on Web sites, on the news, of people crushed by an earthquake in Haiti or drowned by a tsunami in Indonesia or starving in Somalia. The countries varied, slightly, from disaster to disaster, but the regions didn't change much, nor did the victims: the already-poor, the equatorial, the dark-skinned, the Not-European and Not-American. Although of course there had been Hurricane Katrina, just a few years ago, bodies in the flooded streets, the third world lapping at America's shores, the nation's most singular city apparently deemed unworthy of redemption. But then people from around the country had rushed in to help, had taken time away from their jobs and their families to deliver supplies, serve meals, clear debris, begin to rebuild. He had thought about going.

The problem was that once you saw, once you knew, it was difficult to close your eyes, to turn away. An earlier generation may have had an excuse. Before journalists and TV cameras and the Internet reached into every corner of the world and displayed every tragedy and injustice, before international aid organizations and global supplies distribution and instantaneous money transfers made it infinitely more possible to redress distant wrongs, before so many millions of people enjoyed security and comfort and wealth while millions more did without, it was easier to ignore, easier to forget, easier not to act. At G&B he had met a woman who as a girl had escaped the Khmer Rouge, had fled with her teenage brother through the jungles of Cambodia to eventually make her way to America, leaving behind the ghosts of her mother and father and beloved uncle, who had been brutally killed before her young eyes. He had been horrified to learn the events took place just two years before he was born, but he also took comfort in it, because it absolved him of responsibility. But now he knew. He knew car exhaust and plastic packaging and wanton development were destroying the earth. He knew chickens and cows and pigs — conscious beings, and in the case of pigs, at least, highly social and intelligent, capable of remarkable feats of memory — were kept in horribly abusive conditions. He knew cheap manufactured goods were available only through the exploitation of poor people in far-off lands. He knew millions of children — some of them likely just a few miles away, in Philadelphia — lived in poverty and fear and abuse, lacking health and help and hope. Yet he still drove his car. He still drank his bottled water. He still shopped at Wal-Mart. He still ate chicken salad and cheeseburgers and sizzling brown sausages. He still drove blindly through the slums of Philadelphia, locking his doors and keeping his eyes on the car in front of him as he urged himself toward the lush green campus of Maximus. Perhaps it wasn't so difficult to turn away after all. One's character, whether good or bad, compassionate or cruel, was a reflection not so much of one's action as one's inaction.

He became aware that at some point he had turned around and was headed back to the compound. He hadn't come up with a solution, though he wasn't certain what he was seeking a solution to. Ahead of him on the edge of the road lay a small domed object. As he drew nearer he saw it was an eastern box turtle, exquisitely figured in orange. If you found one in the road you were supposed to carry it to the other side in the direction it was pointing. But as he bent to lift it he realized the top of its shell had been shattered, and the turtle was dead. He wondered how it had happened, as a car would have crushed it completely. Perhaps it had been struck by a lawnmower and then crawled here and died slowly, or perhaps someone had harmed it intentionally. He would have expected it to have died drawn into its shell. Instead its legs and tail and neck were fully extended, its head upright, frozen but defiant in death.

27

The next day, a Saturday, there was a dinner party at Charles'. Ben wasn't sure what this one was intended to celebrate, but the soirees were becoming more regular, and it seemed there no longer needed to be a reason for them. It was just for the five of them, Charles and Janet and Ann and Paula and him, and there was no question that they all would come. Likewise there was no question that no one else would be there, that no one from outside the compound would be invited. Having Ash join them was an experiment that wasn't likely to be repeated soon.

He felt nervous, getting ready upstairs in his apartment beforehand. Normally he would have been recruited by Charles to help with the preparations, making fresh bread or releasing a terrine from its mold or mixing some new alcoholic concoction, but he had begged off with a weak excuse about having to work on a paper. He wanted to tell the others about what he had found, the day before, but he wanted to explain it to them all at once, not one at a time. Besides, Charles tended to be dismissive of his graduate studies, and he was potentially less likely to make cutting remarks in front of the others. He was glad it was the weekend, because he assumed the workers wouldn't return to work on the bypass till Monday at the earliest. That didn't necessarily give him a lot of time, but it would at least allow him to discuss the situation with the others, to see if any of them had any ideas about how he might stop the bypass, or at least divert it. He waited till he was certain the others had arrived, till he could hear their voices — primarily Janet's — drifting up from the first floor through the air-return grates. Then he made his way down the stairs, out his own front door, and around to Charles' side door.

"Here's Ben," Janet said. "I've never known you to be fashionably late for one of Charles' dinner parties."

"He claims to spend all his time up on the third floor, studying his *Indians*. I was beginning to think he had a *girl-friend*. But I know what he's really doing is taking too many long walks alone, communing with nature."

"Charles, I'm sure Ben does spend a lot of time studying," Paula said.

"Thank you, Paula. Charles, you're just miffed that I wasn't here to carve your roast for you."

"As it happens, I managed perfectly well on my *own* with the roast-carving. Although I did spend an hour searching for my electric carving knife, and never did find it. But just for that you don't get any sidecars, of which I made not one pitcher but *two*."

"Now, Charles, let him have his sidecar," Ann said. "Or three or four, if I know your dinner parties at all."

And so the conversation continued through cocktails and dinner and desert, the five of them becoming in equal parts friendlier and sillier as the pitchers of sidecars and bottles of wine and, for Charles, martini after martini were drained away. Ben helped himself to far more than his usual quantity of liquor and was feeling numb enough that he could have said anything, revealed that he had an embarrassing medical condition or admitted that he had shoplifted or confessed his undying love for Charles.

"So, I went on a long walk yesterday, as Charles accuses me of doing too much of, and I found the most extraordinary thing," he began.

"It wasn't my electric carving knife."

"No, Charles, it wasn't your electric carving knife. It was a Lenape settlement. Right here in Lower Slaughter."

"You're certain it wasn't American Indian Day at the local Boy Scouts? Were there *teepees* and *tom-toms* and what-not?"

"Oh, Charles, I'm sure he's talking about something archaeological," Janet said. "You are talking about something archaeological, aren't you?"

"Yes, I am. Yesterday I was walking up above the bluff, and it turns out they're putting in a road up there. It's where the bypass is coming through."

"Is it really?" Janet said. "I knew it was coming by here, but I didn't realize it would be so close. Oh, now, you don't think we'll be able to hear it from the compound, do you? Because that really would be a shame."

"I understand they'll be putting in those *noise* barriers. I do hope that's enough."

"Well, it can't be too close," Ann said. "After all, there's the train tracks, and the stream, and of course Station Lane. It can't come right through all that, can it?"

"Ben is trying to tell us about what he found," Paula interrupted.

"Sorry, Ben, what was it you were saying?"

"The bypass will come close to us, but not right past us," he continued. "It looks like it's going to come through the clearing above the bluff and then cross Station Lane with an overpass. So if they do in fact use sound barriers, I don't think we'll hear it that much. But that's not the point. Charles, are there any more sidecars?"

"You've emptied *both* pitchers, I'm afraid. Martini?"

"Yes, that would be lovely. Only regular-size portions, not a yard glass filled with vodka."

"Would I ever? *Would* I? No one's answering."

"Yes, Charles, you do all the time," Paula said. "But let's get back to Ben's story."

"There's a clearing up there?" Janet asked. "Sorry, I never have reason to go up there, of course."

"Yes, about sixty acres."

"Well it's nice to know there's still some open space in Lower Slaughter. Although I guess it's not going to be open for long, from what you're saying."

"Thank you, Charles," Ben said, accepting a highball glass of vodka with a few cloudy ice cubes and a twist of lemon in it. "Yes, that's exactly what I'm saying." He took a long drink and felt a renewed numbness, in his lips and behind his forehead. "The bypass is coming right through the clearing. But the thing is, I've found the remains of a Lenape village."

"How do you mean?" Ann asked. "How do you know it's a village? Was a village."

"Well, they had done some excavating up there, maybe to test the drainage, or perhaps it's the start of the footings for the overpass. Anyway, they had dug a trench. And as I was walking by I came across a stone scraper. Well, it could be a projectile point — by that I mean an arrowhead — but more likely it's a scraper. A stone tool. And then I found a shard of pottery, which isn't necessarily significant, but it suggests something more than a campsite. But the most extraordinary thing was that I found a post mold, which is the remains of where a wooden post would have been.

The thing is, they're all consistent with the Late Woodland period, one thousand to four hundred years ago, and the potsherd and post mold were at a depth of about eighteen inches, which suggests they had been there for a while. So it's not like the post mold would have been from a farmer's fence, or something like that."

"How exciting," Ann said.

"Well, yes, it is exciting. The only thing is, the bypass is coming right through the site."

"But surely they'll have to stop, now. There must be rules about this sort of thing."

"There are, naturally. But you don't understand. This bypass has been in the works for years and years. And there's been lawsuit after lawsuit from people who wanted to keep it out of their own neighborhood. Now that the state finally has it all hammered out, now that they're actually starting to go ahead with it, they're not going to want to stop it. So I'm sure they'll find a way around it. Or should I say, through it."

"Surely one of your professors would know what to do," Janet suggested. "I mean, they must work on archaeological sites. They must know what to do in situations like this."

"The thing is, I'm not sure I want to tell any of my professors or colleagues just yet. This could be really big for my academic career. I mean, this could be the rest of my career altogether. But I'm just a graduate student, and I don't have a strong background in archaeology. So I'm a little concerned that someone from the department would just sort of take over the operation, and I'd be pushed aside. What I'd like to do is get a better sense of what's up there first, kind of establish it as my own site, before I make its existence more widely known."

"Ooh, that's devious," Charles said. "Now you *are* thinking like an academic."

"Which reminds me," Ben said. "I'd appreciate it if you all could keep this under your hats for now."

"Well, now, who are we going to tell, anyway?" Janet said.

"Well, someone like Emily Reaper, for example. If she found out, it would be on every local news program before the day was out."

"Oh, you're right about that. Well, I think we can all agree to keep this to ourselves. You can count on us."

"I also wanted to ask you all a favor. I wondered if anyone would have any ideas about how I might go about stopping the bypass. Well, not necessarily stopping it, but getting it redirected so that it doesn't come right through the site. Of course, without revealing that it is in fact an archaeological site."

"That does sound like a bit of a pickle," Ann said.

"I'm afraid *I'm* no help to you. I've spent my entire career in academia, and while we academics generally are in fact good at preventing things from getting done, I'm afraid I don't know anyone in any position of power who would know how to stop your *bypass*."

"I wish we could help you, Ben," Janet said.

"No worries," Ben said. "I didn't really think there was an easy solution." The effects of the liquor, at least the pleasant effects, were wearing off, and he was left with the vague headache that was precursor to a hangover. He realized he felt terribly dehydrated.

"I might be able to help," Paula said. "Ash's father, Mr. Billington, knows a lot of people at the Cricket Club. People in government, or people who have money. I could talk to him about it."

"Yes, he's *just* the sort of person to meddle in something like this."

"I'd really appreciate that, Paula. Just be sure not to mention anything about an archæological site. Maybe just say we wanted to get the bypass moved farther away from the compound."

"Yes, that wouldn't be such a bad thing in any case," Janet said.

**

The night sky glowed as Ben made his way up to the clearing. He had decided the best time to explore was at night, when there was less chance he'd be found out. He had meant to come up here the night before, the night of Charles' dinner party, but the festivities had run too late and he had drunk too much to make it feasible. Anyway, he had had to go to the Home Depot for supplies: shovel, hand scoop, bricklayer's hammer, pointed trowel, brushes. He carried all but the shovel in an old book bag; he had to walk softly to keep the tools from clanking together. He would have to do without larger items such as a shaker screen for sifting soil. He'd also have to do without a flashlight, as it would draw attention. He had hoped for moonlit nights, and tonight, at least, he had got one, the full moon unobstructed by April clouds.

This wasn't the right way to approach an archaeological dig, he knew, in so haphazard a fashion. But he wouldn't be able to do much in the way of digging anyway, as the *shunk* of a shovel, turning the soil, would likely carry across the clearing and attract as much attention as a flashlight. Instead he would sort through what ground had already been disturbed by the road crew, to see if he could find additional artifacts. He thought he might also try to locate other post molds, which might begin to describe the perimeter of a dwelling.

He had been a little disappointed by the reaction of the others. Well, Paula had offered to help. And Janet and Ann did in fact seem pleased for him. But they had immediately begged off any involvement and without much thought concluded there was nothing they could do. He would have thought, or at least hoped, they would have recognized how important it was to him and, consequently, considered it important to themselves as well.

He had waited till after midnight, to be sure Lower Slaughter was fully asleep, before starting, and then worked till the sky was lifted by the grainy light of pre-dawn. Disappointingly, he uncovered no more post molds or pottery, but he found enough other artifacts to strengthen his hypothesis that there had in fact been a Lenape settlement here. The first were two projectile points, both of jasper. More significant was a celt, an ungrooved, tapered axe blade typical of the Late Woodland. It had been pecked into shape and was finely polished on its bit end. But most promising were two halves of a nearly round stone, rubbed smooth by flowing water, that surely had come from the Wissahickon. It was the sort of stone that would have been used in a cooking fire. Three or four such stones would have been placed in the fire pit, where a round-bottomed ceramic cooking vessel would have balanced on top of them. The stone had broken in two, but from the looks of it not recently; most likely it had cracked centuries ago as it had heated and cooled in the fire.

He placed the artifacts with the tools in the book bag and started the short walk home. As he walked he gazed up at the sky, tilting in what stars remained in the rising light. There weren't nearly as many as he remembered from his childhood farther north in the Pennsylvania countryside, where there were fewer shopping malls and car lots to gray the nighttime darkness. On a moonless winter night the sky

would actually have depth, as if you could tell just by looking which stars were comparatively close and which were
infinitely more distant. They had been enrapturing but
also dwarfing. They were uncountable and unaccountable.

He had always had a hard time conceptualizing infinity. Future infinity, infinity going forward, maybe wasn't so
difficult to imagine: something started and just kept going.
But past infinity, infinity going backward, that just didn't
compute. Something could have no end, perhaps. But how
could it have no beginning? He wondered if you could
think of infinity in terms of halving. You took one second
and cut it in half. You took the resulting half-second and cut
it in half. You took the resulting quarter-second and cut it
in half. And so on. You could keep cutting the halves in
half, and you'd never run out of halves. Was that infinity?
What else could you keep dividing and dividing and never
run out of? You could do it with time, perhaps, but could
you do it with matter? Wouldn't you eventually get down
to a quantum, a subatomic particle? Perhaps he could ask
a physics professor at Maximus. They'd probably think he
was an idiot.

28

Paula and Ash sat within the gray stone walls of Duchess II, the Billington's Chestnut Hill residence. Paula hadn't been here since Christmas, but she accepted an invitation to "a luncheon" with Ash's parents so she could talk to Trey about the bypass. Paula had told Ash about it, and about their interest in getting it rerouted, but, as promised to Ben, she didn't mention the Lenape village. Ash seemed particularly energized by the prospect of fighting the state; he had said something about "stickin' it to the man," though Paula didn't know what that meant and didn't bother asking. He had agreed not to broach the subject directly with his parents, instead waiting till Paula came for lunch so they could talk to them together.

Trey was in a rare pleasant mood, which was promising sign, while Mitzi was friendly as always, in her backhanded way.

"It's nice to see you again, Paula," Trey said. It occurred to her that it was the first time she had heard him use her name. The first time she had heard either of Ash's parents use her name.

"Well, Trey, of course she has her own young life to lead. And as lovely as it was to see Ash's friend over the Christmas holidays, I'm sure she has her own South American traditions to celebrate."

"Girlfriend, Mother. Paula is my girlfriend."

"South American traditions?" Paula asked.

"Now what do you suppose she's doing with her hair?" Mitzi asked Trey.

Paula usually wore her hair pulled back, but today she had let it take its natural shape. "I'm sorry?"

"Mother, enough. Let's just have lunch."

They sat in their usual places at the mahogany dining-room table. They were served by Mitzi's predictably Mexican kitchen help.

"I thought it would be fun to have chicken Wellington," Mitzi said as lunch was brought out. "You know, like beef Wellington, only with chicken."

"What is beef Wellington?" Paula asked.

"Mother, you know we're both vegetarians."

"But this is chicken Wellington. That's why I had Rosalinda make chicken."

Ash sighed. "Chicken is not a vegetable."

"But it's not beef."

"Damn right it's not beef," Trey said.

Now it was Mitzi's turn to sigh. "Well, there's also stewed plums. Will you eat that?"

"Fine, Mother. I guess that will have to do."

"You're sure you won't have chicken?" Trey asked Paula. "It's free-range."

"No, thank you. I'll be OK with the plums." Paula wondered why, since he lived here, Ash didn't simply offer to go to the kitchen and make something for both of them.

"The young people will just have the plums," Mitzi said to Rosalinda. "So you can take away their chicken. Oh, and don't forget the Mai Tais."

"Mai Tais?" Ash asked. "Since when do you drink?"

"I don't drink in the evening. But for lunch I think there's nothing like a pitcher of Mai Tais. Although I have to confess, I've already had two, before you arrived. Cocktails, that is, not pitchers."

Lunch proceeded blandly, like the plums, and Paula wondered when she should bring up the bypass. It probably would have been helpful if Trey had had a Mai Tai, as well, but Mitzi didn't offer one to anyone but herself. She wasn't sure exactly what a Mai Tai was. The pitcher had a little blue paper umbrella in it. She was about to mention the bypass, when Mitzi, loosened by the liquor, launched into a monologue about, of all things, her and Trey's sex life.

"Trey, did I ever tell Ash's friend about the time with the maple syrup?"

"Mother, you're not telling that story. Please."

"Now, Ashford. This is a grown-up conversation. When you're married, you'll understand."

Ash put a hand over his eyes. "Here we go."

"Heh-heh-huh," Trey chuckled.

"When Ashie was little, Trey and I were having the master bedroom redone. And for a lark we thought it would be fun to sleep in the den, in front of the fireplace, rather than in one of the guestrooms. So we had the workmen bring down the king-size mattress."

"Heh-heh-huh."

"Now you know what a married man and woman do with honey, don't you? Well, we had never done anything like that, but we had heard of it. So we wanted to experiment."

"Please, Mother. Stop right there."

"Heh-heh-huh."

"Well, it turns out we didn't have any honey. But we had some pancake syrup. Miss Butterworth's, if I'm not mistaken. So we used that."

"I don't understand," Paula said.

"Really, Parchy, don't ask her to explain."

"Anyway, the next morning, little Ashie comes downstairs, and he sees the Miss Butterworth's bottle. And he says, 'Mommy, why is the syrup out? Did you and Daddy have pancakes?'" And of course I couldn't tell him what we had been doing with it. So I said yes."

"I'm still not following. ..."

"And bless his little heart, he was so cross with us for not telling him we were having pancakes. So I had to get up and make him pancakes for breakfast."

"Heh-heh-huh."

"Well, I don't have to tell you we were both nude."

"OK, Mother, that's enough. Story's over."

"You still seem confused," she said to Paula. "What we were doing with the pancake syrup, is. ..."

"No, Mother! Please. Don't explain."

"Well, you have to move with the times, Ashie."

There was a moment of silence while Trey chewed his chicken Wellington and Mitzi poured herself another Mai Tai.

"Trey," Paula began. "Mr. Billington. ..."

"Trey."

"Trey. I wanted to ask you something. Do you know about the bypass that's going in in Lower Slaughter?"

"Yes, sure. They've been working on that for thirty years now."

"Well, it's coming right past the teahouse."

"Is that right?"

"The thing is, it's coming really a lot closer than we expected. It's going in the buff, right behind where I live."

"In the buff?"

"She means bluff, Dad. There's a small cliff behind where Parchy lives, and they're going to build an overpass off the cliff and over the road she lives on."

"I thought we agreed I was going to do this," Paula said to Ash.

"So what about it?" Trey said.

"Well, I know you know a lot of people at the Cricket Club. We were talking at the teahouse — Janet, the woman I work for, and the others there — and we thought you might know of someone you could talk to about it, to see if there was a way to get the bypass moved. You know, so it doesn't come so close to the teahouse."

"Now where has that Rosalinda got to?" Mitzi said. "There was supposed to be a fruit tart. Rosalinda!"

"I'm afraid there's nothing to be done for your teahouse," Trey said. "That highway has been being argued for decades. You wouldn't believe the lawsuits. In fact, it was on hold for so long that people put in new houses right along where it's going to go. Too bad for them."

"Really?" Paula said. "There's no one you could talk to? Maybe someone in the government?"

"Well, it doesn't work that way. Yes, I know people of influence. But there's nothing to be done in this case." He turned to Mitzi. "Did you say fruit tart? I thought we were having apple pie. There's nothing like a slice of apple pie and a tall glass of cold milk for dessert."

**

Paula didn't report back to Ben till the next day. She could have called him that evening, but she was disappointed she hadn't been able to help, and she knew Ben would feel let down, as well. She had to work a full-day shift

277

at the teahouse, and she was relieved he didn't come in for a cappuccino, as he often did. At the end of the day she stopped at home for a quick dinner of Safeway sushi. Then she crossed the lawn and knocked on Ben's door.

It was a minute, maybe, before she heard him coming down the stairs. He came to the door in a faded blue tee shirt, and Paula noticed his hair was rumpled, as if he had been running his hands through it or had recently taken a nap. It hadn't occurred to her that he didn't work full-time and might not have had class today, and so wouldn't necessarily be dressed for company.

"Oh, hi, Paula."

"Sorry, I hope I'm not bothering you. I had lunch with the Billingtons yesterday."

"No, not at all. Would you like to come up?"

Paula followed him upstairs. She noticed he was trying to comb his hair with his hands as he went.

"Can I offer you something to eat or drink?"

"No, that's OK. I won't be long. I don't have much to tell you, unfortunately."

"Please, have a seat." He indicated his rather unwelcoming Ikea couch. Instead of taking a chair himself he sat cross-legged on the floor.

Paula explained that she had told Trey about the bypass and asked if he might know anyone who could help, but to no avail. Ben didn't allow his facial expression to change, but she could tell he was disheartened.

"Well, I really appreciate your trying. I know you're not a huge fan of Ash's parents."

They sat quietly for a moment, gazing toward but not actually at each other.

"Have you been back? To the site?"

"Yes, a couple of times now. I've been going at night, so as not to attract unnecessary attention."

"Have you found anything more?"

"Yes, a few more things. Mostly I've just been mapping things out and recording what I've found. There seems to be a bit of a lull in the construction, which seems to be how road construction works. I'm trying to find out from the department of transportation when they're going to start up again. Sorry, this is probably boring you."

"No, not at all. I actually think it's very interesting."

"Would you like to see what I've found?"

He showed her the jasper tools, the scraper and the arrowheads, as well as the potsherd and the celt and the two halves of the cracked stone, explaining the significance of each item. It felt good to be able to share them with someone. To be able to share them with Paula.

When he had finished, the conversation seemed to reach its natural conclusion, and they found themselves not looking at each other again.

"Have you had dinner?" Ben asked.

"Yes."

"Oh."

"But I could have a drink."

"That's a splendid idea. I don't know that I have much to offer, though. Some scotch, I think, and a couple of bottles of cheap chardonnay.

"We could go out for drinks," Paula suggested. "I can drive."

They ended up in the bar of a local country inn that catered to white-haired couples who sat sullenly over prime rib au jus or veal parmigiana or calf's liver with onion, add bacon for one dollar extra. The bar was all dark-wood Formica and black-vinyl seat cushions, wagon-wheel light fixtures with amber-glass shades. The blunt waitress, dressed in a tuxedo uniform with a frilly white waist apron, brought them watered-down drinks and then disappeared for the night.

They talked. They talked with the ease and pleasure of two people who have just discovered each other and, somehow as a consequence, have re-met themselves and like what they've found. Ben talked about his childhood in the thickets of rural Pennsylvania, his family's working-class conservatism and born-again zeal; about how he came to know Charles and what kind of professor he had been; about his vague ambition to be an independent field archaeologist. Paula spoke of her life in the orphanage with Avó Mariana and Avô Victor; of her mother's cool disregard and her father's secretive, presumably illicit, business dealings; of her worries about her still-unresolved immigration status and her uncertain plans for the future. They were unaware of the passing of time, of other patrons coming and going, of their drinks having run dry. They stayed till the place closed, the blazer-clad men and rinsed-and-set ladies long since departed, the wait staff already vacuuming the low-pile carpet.

**

Ben decided his last best hope of halting the highway construction, without revealing the existence of the archaeological site, would be to muster the support of local residents. Perhaps if he could get enough people to sign a petition or contact their state representative or attract the attention of the news media, they could persuade the state to consider their wants. He pictured public speeches, roadside protests, bake-sale fundraisers, the citizens of Lower Slaughter united in their opposition to the bypass. He knew it wasn't very realistic, however, as he had never got a strong sense of active community involvement in Lower

Slaughter, though of course he wasn't at all involved in the community himself, so maybe such things went on that he wasn't aware of. He knew there had been legal challenges to the bypass in the past, but he had no idea from where along the highway's proposed length they had sprung, no sense of whether his unknown neighbors resented the prospect of the new highway or simply accepted its progress as inevitable.

It occurred to him that the best place to start would be with an organization called Wissahickon and Space Preservation, otherwise known as W.A.S.P., a well-healed advocacy group formed by wealthy Lower Slaughterers who liked to think they were maintaining a "greene countrie towne" by setting aside an acre or two here or there for public use. Although they were largely passive in their efforts to protect what little open space remained, they were fairly militant in their opposition to anything — land clearing, new houses, commercial development — that might impinge the Wissahickon's flow. If he could convince W.A.S.P. that the highway's close proximity to the creek could adversely affect it, he might be able to mobilize its considerable financial and political clout.

But he got quite a different response, when he finally caught up with W.A.S.P.'s executive director on the phone. It turned out W.A.S.P. was the very reason the bypass would run through the clearing, over the bluff, and across Station Lane. The original plans had brought the bypass on the other side of the compound and directly over the Wissahickon. When W.A.S.P. learned of it, it immediately filed a lawsuit and, after much wrangling, got the highway rerouted. There was no way, the director assured him, that W.A.S.P. was going to get involved in any effort that might undo its previous work. Running the bypass through the clearing was precisely what the residents of Lower Slaughter wanted.

So: one person indeed could make no difference. In the meantime construction had begun to move ahead, the chainsaws felling trees, the bulldozers leveling the landscape. Thankfully, they had not yet brought in the diggers and graders to excavate the footings, carve the berms and swales, pave over the remnants of a civilization with crushed stone and crude oil. He wondered if he were being reckless in not telling anyone, other than the denizens of the compound, about what he had found. There still was time, he reasoned. There still must be a solution.

29

Ben stood in his kitchen, leaning against the counter, and ate slices of Mandarin orange from a can. It wasn't much of a dinner, really, but it was reasonably healthful, and as it was late he didn't feel like bothering with cooking. He had spent a tiresome Saturday afternoon at the library at Maximus, finishing up his final paper for the semester. The days were lengthening as springtime crept into May, but the sun had long since gone down, and the sky was now dark with an invisible new moon.

He read the can as he ate the orange slices. The can was labeled "Dole," which he had always associated with bananas. It was strange to think that bananas came all the way from Costa Rica. He had heard somewhere, or read, that the most common variety, Cavendish, was headed for commercial extinction in the next ten years or so. It occurred to him that Cavendish was a British name. He saw from the can that the oranges came from China: "Manufactured for Dole Packaged Foods." It was strange to think of fruit as being manufactured.

He had left the window partly open to relieve the perpetually overheated apartment, but the night air had turned cold, and a draft stood up the hair on his arms. In the near distance, below him and across the lawn, he heard a bell ring out sharply: the little brass bell of the teahouse. Janet must be working late.

He finished his oranges and set the can and fork in the sink. He crossed to the window and slid it shut. He peered out to look for Janet walking to her car. He thought it funny that she drove to the teahouse instead of crossing the lawn or even walking down the driveway and then along the road; it couldn't be more than an eighth of a mile door to door. But he didn't see her, and there was still a glow of light from inside the teahouse. Odd, he thought. There was always the *shunk* of the back door and then Janet crossing the parking lot to her car.

Wait. There was no *shunk*. It was the bell of the front door. Why would she use the front door at this hour? Not that she had used it, as far as he could see. He continued to watch from above.

Perhaps I'd better go check, he thought. Well, it's probably nothing. He sighed. I'll just go check. He first dropped the empty can of oranges in the recycle bin and set the used fork in the sink.

He crossed the lawn reluctantly but quickly, anxious to get it over with and get back upstairs. It was colder than he had expected. As he approached the teahouse he thought he saw shadows across the windows, suggesting interior movement. Did he hear voices coming from within? Was there a man's voice? He couldn't quite see through the teahouse windows from where he stood in the parking lot, which was slightly lower than the floor inside.

The front door was partway open. Well, Janet was leaving things open all the time, doors and windows and drawers. Why, then, did he feel apprehensive?

He pushed through the door at the same time he became aware there was in fact a man's voice, at the same time he realized a man occupied the middle of the room, at the same time he noticed Janet was standing defensively, backed up against the counter, and wearing a look of tense surprise, of confused concern.

Janet shifted her eyes from the man to Ben. "Joseph," was all she said. Something in the way she said it made Ben realize this must be her son. She had once told him that she had a son whom she gave up for adoption and that his name was Joseph. What was his last name? He could only remember "Joseph."

Joseph spun to face Ben. "This has not to do with you," he hissed.

"Janet, are you OK?" Ben asked. The words sounded hoarse in his throat. There was electricity in the air.

"He wants money," Janet said meekly.

"What's going on here?" Ben asked, now looking at Joseph squarely. The teahouse was dim in the fluorescent glow of the kitchen light, but he could see that Joseph was solidly built and that he wore a heavy denim coat.

"This is a family matter," Joseph said. "I suggest you stay out of it."

A family matter. It was the sort of thing Ben had heard growing up among rural clans, who preferred to settle disputes without outside interference. Regardless of the situation, irrespective of who might be on the right or wrong side, whether or not laws had been broken, the claim to "a family matter" was unassailable.

The truth was, he wanted nothing more than to stay out of it; he already regretted having come down from his apartment. And yet he sensed that the right thing to do, or the expected thing, was to remain, to insert himself into the situation, to become involved. He willed himself, as laying the weight of his body against an immense lever, to take a step forward.

Joseph took a corresponding step back. He simultaneously reached into his coat and, without speaking a word, produced a blunt black-and-silver object.

It was, Ben realized, unbelieving, a .38-caliber revolver. And it was pointed at him. His instinct, his immediate urge, was to flee. He had to consciously will himself to hold his ground.

"Joseph," Janet said again. She remained unmoving against the counter.

Joseph stood dumbly, pointing the gun at Ben. Ben was uncertain what to do. He noticed that the hand that held the gun was trembling. He's afraid, he thought. He's got himself in too deep. He extended his left hand.

What happened next unfolded slowly in an instant. Joseph jerked back the gun from Ben's reach. Ben felt a burning pain in his extended left hand and a tightness in his chest, as if he had been kicked there. A blast, like a gunshot, seemed to come a moment later. On television guns always seemed to be going off accidentally, and it didn't seem very likely. Janet's mouth was open, a look of horror on her face. The pain in his hand was searing, like having a fingernail ripped off. He looked at the hand, which was bleeding, as from a distance. He felt a rising panic, like when you're underwater and you need to breathe, to get to the surface, immediately, now. Yet all he wanted to do was to close his eyes, to sleep, to escape the pain in his hand. Joseph looked puzzled, or frightened. Furze, Ben thought.

30

The midmorning sun was already warm and bright. Janet woke in her bed. She had the briefest moment of innocence, of forgetfulness. She sensed the instant slip inexorably through her mind's fingers, like a vanishing dream, like something intricately small and precious dropped, irretrievable. The events of the previous night rushed in, filling the fleeting void. She felt sickened, not just physically but also emotionally: she felt an emotional nausea.

She closed her eyes and began to turn over the events in her mind. She had left the teahouse early in the afternoon, in the capable hands of Ann and Tommy, the new tea caddy. She spent the early evening puttering around her house, doing what, she didn't really know; time seemed always to slip away from her. She realized she had left some mail at the teahouse, in a pile somewhere, probably in the kitchen. She went to pick it up, entering through the back door as usual. While she was there she thought she would just straighten up behind the counter a bit, and then she noticed it seemed unusually dark out front. She went out to check and discovered one of the spotlights that illuminated the teahouse sign had gone out. Maybe the bulb had come loose, but more likely it had blown. In any case it was too high for her to reach. She would have to have Ben fix it. She went back inside, pulling shut the door behind her.

She got to reading *Time* magazine, which was mixed in with her mail. There was an interview with Tom Hanks she found interesting; he seemed like such a nice man. She had just finished when the train arrived. She heard the familiar clang of the crossing signal, the *ho-oot hoot* of the horn, the rumble of the cars, the hiss of the brakes. There was almost never anyone boarding at this time of night, especially when the train was heading away from the city, and especially on the weekend, but there were always one or two stragglers debarking and returning to their parked cars. Sometimes she would hear the *clack clack* of a woman's high heels.

What happened next was as sudden as slipping on ice, and as jarring. The door lurched open and the bell rang out, shrill in the night air. A man filled the doorway, motionless but threatening. Janet gasped.

I must have forgotten to lock the door, she remembered thinking. After I went out to check the spotlight, I must have forgotten to lock the door behind me. She was always forgetting that sort of thing. She realized, then, that the man looked familiar, something about the slouched posture, the wiry blond hair.

"Mom," the man said. "Mother."

It was Joseph. She wondered how he had found her. But of course you could track down anyone on the Internet these days. Where she lived, the compound, the teahouse, wasn't a secret.

"Joseph," she said. What was he doing here?

She couldn't remember exactly what he said next. Something about needing money. Something about her owing him after all these years, that she hadn't had to pay for his childhood, for anything, so she owed him. He was agitated and inarticulate, but he managed to make clear that he wasn't so much asking for the money as coming to get it, as if this were as good as a robbery. He didn't look well.

He would be forty now. An adult, not a child. Old enough to have his own child, for that matter. What was he doing asking for money, demanding recompense for a childhood long past? Although our childhoods are never really over, are they, when it comes to our parents.

She hadn't seen him, talked to him, heard of him in twenty-two years. Twenty-two years of his life, of her life, they hadn't shared. The truth was, the only portions of his life she had been part of were the nine months of pregnancy, the twelve hours of labor, the four minutes of holding his little body, and then later, when he was a teenager, an hour or two here and there on the phone, over lunch, for an afternoon. It added up to less than one of his forty years, of her sixty-two. And it had all been a lifetime ago.

She wanted to ask what he was doing, how he was, who he was. She wanted to suggest they sit down and talk or make plans to meet another time and talk, like two rational people, though these kinds of family confrontations always seemed to take place without warning or planning, at importune times and places. She wanted to say she'd be happy to lend him money, even give him money, that they could discuss how much he needed and what he needed it for. But she found herself backed up against the counter, bracing herself with both hands on the counter's edge, with Joseph now occupying the middle of the room, advancing as his words rambled. He seemed to think she had a stash of money hidden somewhere in the teahouse, as if it were a bank and this were a stickup.

And then Ben arrived, the bell again ringing out. She felt relieved to see him but also apprehensive, as if she sensed it was unwise, unfortunate, for him to be there at that moment. She heard a few words. She saw a subtle movement. And then there was the gunshot, shockingly loud. Ben crumpled to the ground, staring at his hand. Joseph fled without a sound, without even glancing at her or at Ben. He was gone as abruptly as he had arrived, a shadow, an apparition.

Her first instinct, absurd as it was, was to call Ben. Her next thought was to call Charles, but she didn't know whether to call Charles first or help Ben first. But she was already rushing to his side, on her knees beside him, calling his name, Ben, Ben. She could see the blood now, on his hand, soaking his blue tee shirt. She had a fleeting thought that it was a crime scene and she shouldn't touch him, but she reached out and searched his wrist for his pulse. She thought she felt something, but she wasn't certain. Was he breathing? Maybe she should give him mouth-to-mouth. She realized she was still calling his name, Ben, Ben.

She didn't want to leave him, but she struggled back to the counter, for some reason crossing the room on her hands and knees, and dialed 911. She was surprisingly focused, then, panicked but focused enough to provide all the relevant information in a logical order. When she hung up she immediately called Charles, but there was no answer; he often didn't pick up. She had started to dial Ann when Ann's redeeming round frame appeared in the doorway. She saw Ann size up the situation and rush to Ben's side, just as she had done.

All her focus left her as she tried to explain to Ann what had happened. She was aware that her words were

rapid and high-pitched and shouted and that Ann probably wasn't comprehending the chain of events. Ann had
the presence of mind to ask whether Janet was OK before
returning her attention to Ben. They both knelt over Ben's
body, and Ann felt for a pulse at his wrist and at his throat.
He had collapsed forward and partly on his side. Ann
rolled him limply onto his back. Janet could see the hole
in his blood-soaked shirt, in his chest, and the realness of
the situation struck her like a physical pain, like a boot in
her own chest. She screamed, frightened, angry, horrified.

She opened her eyes to the morning light and shoved
the image from her mind. She could not think about that
now.

It must have taken many minutes for the first police officer to appear, but it seemed like he was there moments later.
He was young and small and not very effectual-looking, but
he confirmed that Ben had a pulse and watched over him
till the ambulance arrived. But the E.M.T.'s, when they got
there, immediately started chest compressions and applied
a sort of face mask with a squeeze pump. They scooped
Ben onto a stretcher and carried him away. More police
had shown up by that time, large, blue-uniformed men
with guns in their holsters, slow and ponderous, now that
the victim was in hand and, at least for them, the crisis was
over. The teahouse was filled with their presence, with the
flashing lights of their squad cars, with the screaming siren
of the ambulance as it receded into the night. The floor of
the teahouse was stained with Ben's blood.

She shrank into a shocked passivity. Ann said they
should drive to the hospital, after the ambulance, but
the police had questions. Once they realized that Ann
hadn't been there when the shooting occurred, that she
had come later, they let her go. Janet wanted to go with
her, to be there with Ben, but two policemen were already

interrogating her, right where she stood, in sight of Ben's blood on the floor of the teahouse. Couldn't they at least let her sit down, at least let her escape the image, the waking nightmare, of what she had seen? But she continued to stand there, to answer their questions, explaining who Joseph was, that she didn't know how he got there, didn't know where he lived, didn't know what he wanted, didn't know a single thing about him, really. They wanted to know what he looked like, but the only photo she had was of Joseph as a teenager, and who even knew where she had stashed it away? The other policemen were milling about, talking among themselves, taking notes, cataloging minutiae. They had switched on the lights, and the room was now stark. She described the succession of events, as best as she could organize them, though she still couldn't fathom the gunshot. It had to have been an accident. To suggest that Joseph had shot Ben without provocation meant implicating her son in a crime. To imply that Ben had provoked Joseph meant blaming her dear friend for his own tragedy. She wanted to go to the hospital, but the policemen seemed unconcerned. As if they already knew.

Time had dragged, then, the police doing she knew not what. She sat at a table in the corner, as far removed as possible. The flashing lights of the squad cars continued to red and blue the teahouse walls. The sputtering bark of two-way radios rudely invaded the air. Then Charles appeared, somehow evading the scrum of police. He was obviously drunk, visibly willing himself to understand what was happening. She started across the room to him but stopped halfway, sobbing out details. He seemed frustrated he couldn't snap himself into sobriety, and he feebly made as if to go to the hospital. Instead he returned her to the corner table, where he sat with her, glancing about the room, occasionally asking a question, gazing at his usual unseen horizon. One of the policemen began stringing up clichéd yellow crime tape. She and Charles were told that they'd have to leave, as if they were intruders, that the teahouse would have to remain closed for the investigation. They stumbled out to the station parking lot, and one by one the police cars drove off, till she and Charles were left alone under the vaporous glare of the streetlights.

They were crossing the overgrown lawn to Charles' house, when Paula's car pulled into the driveway of Mole End. Paula climbed from her car slowly, gauging them, as if she sensed something was wrong. She met them at Charles' side door.

Janet had the sense of watching the scene from above, from the safety of the night sky, as she told Paula what had happened. It was already the fifth time she had had to recount the ordeal, and she didn't know which was worse, reliving the pain or seeing the pain, the shock, the fear in Paula. As soon as she comprehended the facts Paula announced she was going to the hospital. Janet had thought she also wanted to go, before, but now she decided to stay with Charles. She entreated Paula to do the same, but Paula was already racing away, her car clattering into the darkness.

The call from Ann came just before midnight. There had been no hope. Ben was gone.

Janet had already known. He had already been gone. He left them as he lay prone on the teahouse floor, perhaps even as she knelt over him, cradling his still hand. The last time she would see him was when they bore him out the teahouse door. The last words she would hear him say were, "What's going on here?"

31

Janet got out of bed. She wanted to stay in bed. She wanted to suspend this moment of glorious morning, the spring air soft and warm, even indoors, the cerulean sky glad and bright, even through the closed window. As long as she could suspend the moment she could negate the events of the previous day, she could defer what would surely come the next day and the next and the next: funeral, family, investigators, lawyers, sadness.

She knew it was a false hope. For as long as she lay in bed she could only turn over the events in her mind. She had to get up, she had to do ... what? Eat breakfast? Turn on the television? Make a grocery list? But that's what life is, isn't it.

The morning brought to mind that September day everyone now referred to as 9/11. It had been just such a day as this: clean, clear, calm. It had been a school day, of course, at the start of the school year yet far enough along that her kids were already settling into the routine. She was starting a lesson on geography: land and water forms, topographical maps, latitude and longitude. She was interrupted by a knock on the door, a furtive beckoning into the hallway. It was Betty Lou, one of the school secretaries, her face stricken. Betty Lou spoke not a word but instead handed her a folded sheet of paper. The nation appeared to be under attack, the sheet said. Planes had struck the World Trade Center and the Pentagon. The school would follow the procedure for early dismissal, sending home students at eleven-thirty, but of course they had to scramble buses and make sure the kids weren't delivered to locked houses. In the meantime teachers were cautioned not to convey the news to students and not to turn on any televisions.

Her first thought was of Henry, who was still a pilot. He was on the other end of a leg to Chicago, returning to Norwood. But of course the airlines would be the first to know anything, so if there were a problem they would either keep him grounded or divert him somewhere out of harm's way. She wished she could talk to him, but it had been before she carried a cellphone, and in any case he probably didn't know much more than she did.

Of course the school was a madhouse, the students asking questions, the parents showing up to cart their children away, rumor and speculation running wild. The television was on in the teachers' lounge, and colleagues reported what they could when they could. The principal had thought about assembling everyone in the auditorium, but he decided it would be wiser to keep the students in whatever classroom they already happened to be in. She was stuck with them, then, till they could be sent home. The last didn't leave till well after noon, by which time she had learned that one of the planes had flown out of Boston, not forty miles away.

Her colleagues gathered in the teachers' lounge, but Janet rushed home. She wanted to be alone. Well, truthfully, she wanted to be with Henry, but in lieu of that she wanted to be by herself, to learn what she could and understand the situation in private, in her own way. She switched on the television and stood there, transfixed, watching the endless loop on CNN, one tower billowing smoke, a speeding jet slamming into the other, the second tower collapsing, the first tower collapsing. She dropped to her knees and sobbed.

She didn't know which were more horrifying, in the days that followed, the enormity or the specificity. The scale of the calamity, the proportion, was hard to fathom; she could only think of a line from a Richard Hugo poem: "The loss is so damn gross." But it was the individual stories that were so wrenching: the wife calling her husband from the plane just before it crashed, the young father rushing into the tower moments before it crumbled. The whole world, like her, was stunned, but it was nothing when held up against the pain of those who had lost wife, husband, mother, father, sister, brother, daughter, son.

But then. Then things continued. Yes, school was closed the next day. Yes, Henry was delayed in flying home. Yes, it was all anyone could talk about. And thousands lost their lives. Thousands lost their loved ones. New York was forever altered. Air travel was never the same. One war was launched, and then another. Hundreds of thousands more, soldiers and civilians, lost their lives, and their bodies, and their loved ones. A nation's treasure was depleted. A shameful president was re-elected. Xenophobia was enflamed. And lines could be drawn: to mounting violence, to societal division, to growing hatred, to economic collapse. The ripples were ever-widening, and as complex as hydrodynamics.

Yet things continued. She went back to work. Everyone went back to work. They shopped. They went to movies. They kept up with the Joneses. They traded office gossip and nursed petty grievances and frittered away their savings. Despite all the horror, despite all the repercussions, their lives didn't change, not in any way that was meaningful. Most strangely, she thought, living near Boston, living near New York, she didn't know a single person who had died, or even a single person who knew a single person who had died — in the attacks, in Iraq, in Afghanistan. It was something that happened "out there," in some other part of the country or the world, in the newspaper and on the television, and not part of her daily life, just as it always had been.

Of course she couldn't say any of that to anyone. It would be considered heresy, sacrilege, even ten years later, especially when there were so many soldiers, young men and women, who had given their lives or whose lives had been forever ruined. Yet she had to think other people, millions of other people, thought the same thing, felt the same way. It didn't penetrate. It didn't connect.

And now Ben was dead. She felt guilt for thinking of 9/11, for thinking of anything else, just hours after he had died. She felt guilt that anything should continue, when he could not.

Why had Joseph come back into her life, like a wrecking ball swinging, its mass and force smashing through all that was dear to her? She thought she had left him behind, twice, once when he was an infant, again as he was on the cusp of adulthood. She thought he was part of her past. She wished she had never known him.

But the past never leaves us, does it, and we never leave the past. It's always there, like an endless tune we can't get out of our head, like the rough edge of a chipped tooth, forever at the tip of our tongue.

She still thought about Christopher Hodges, more often than she liked to admit. He had been thin and slight, with narrow shoulders and childlike, rather wistful blue eyes. They had met at a party; he was a friend of one of her classmates. He asked her out, and their first date, if you could call it that, was on a Saturday afternoon. He drove from Bridgewater to her home in Plymouth, and they took the T into Boston and strolled around the Common. It was a late-September day, dry and warm, and he bought her flowers from a street stall. For the rest of the day she had to carry them around, and they became a nuisance.

But they had a lovely time, though they had little to talk about. He worked as a trimmer at the Bridgewater shoe factory — she couldn't remember the name of it, though she could picture the building; it had closed only in the past fifteen years or so — and his ambition was to become floor manager. She had found this both admirable and sad. She knew there was no future for them, yet she found herself agreeing to another date, to his wistful, childlike eyes.

It was on their third date that they slept together, that they conceived Joseph, as it turned out, in the back of Christopher's aging Chevy Biscayne. The car had been covered in dust, she remembered, and he had fingered their initials in it. It was such a cliché, she felt, the furtive coupling in the backseat, the pregnancy on the first try, despite his having used a condom. He had called it a rubber — or "rubbah," in his Brockton accent. It hadn't been her first time, but he was only the second boy she had ever had sex with. And the last, actually, till she met Henry. It hadn't been especially transcendent, though Christopher surely had more of a knack for it, a better natural instinct, than Henry ever did.

It was also their last date. Thanksgiving got in the way, and then she learned she was pregnant, and she used the Christmas rush as an excuse till she was ready to confront him. He hadn't bought her a present; he must have sensed something had come between them. He seemed relieved to learn she had decided on adoption, almost eager to absolve himself of any responsibility. They agreed it was best, for their families' sakes, for them no longer to see each other, and he simply receded into his shoe factory, into his own life. It was only years later she learned he had gone to Vietnam, had died there. She never found out whether he had volunteered or been drafted. He would have made an unlikely soldier, with his slight frame and narrow shoulders.

The pregnancy had seemed interminable, even in her last semester of college, which itself hurried by in a blur. She tried to put on weight, which she didn't find difficult, to hide her swelling belly, and it was only in the final weeks that people seemed to notice she was expecting. Why was there shame in having a baby without being married? There was then, and there still seemed to be. In retrospect it seemed odd that she had given the baby up; she was twenty-two, after all, and already finished college. Today most women would have kept the baby or had an abortion.

Her mother stayed with her through the delivery while her father worried in the maternity waiting room, most likely smoking Tiparillo after Tiparillo, as he always did. They had been there for her, yet they had seemed detached, practically formal, during the birth and for a time after. Was she there for her mother now, at the end of her life? Well, it's different with our parents as they age. You care for them with affection for years and years, but then finally they seem almost like strangers, chronically ill and befuddled and unpleasant. You become detached, practically formal.

She hadn't really regretted giving up Joseph, not in a deep, abiding way. But she carried the guilt of it around with her for years. It was like an unsightly birthmark, just hidden by your clothing, that you were forever afraid was going to somehow show. In class, admonishing her unruly ten- and eleven-year-olds, she often felt like an imposter, as if she had committed some grave crime and was in no position to dole out punishments for gum chewing or note passing or talking out of turn. A birthmark, yes.

And then of course she had kept it from Henry. It wasn't the sort of thing you told someone when you first started dating, and before she knew it they had decided to get married, and then there was the engagement and the wedding and the moving into their first home. By then the time for telling had long since passed. In the movies and on television that sort of thing was a setup for a comedy of errors, but in her case there had never been anything funny about it. It really was awful when Henry found out, the low point of their marriage, and at a moment that should have been joyous, when she was re-meeting this child, her child, now a young man, this part of her that had left her and come back, that had seemingly returned to the earth and sprung from it anew. Curiously, by the time she lost touch with Joseph again Henry was over it, and all the emotional upheaval, the storm and stress, seemed distant and unnecessary.

It hadn't been a great marriage, she supposed. By that she guessed she meant that she and Henry hadn't been anything like kindred spirits; Henry hadn't been her One True Love. Had she ever hoped for such a thing? Perhaps she had, in a sort of idealized way, but she had never really sought it out or expected to find it. But after ten years of so or marriage she realized Henry was, in fact, her best friend, even if she wasn't inclined to use that term, and she was his best friend as well. They felt more like roommates than a married couple, at times, especially with Henry coming and going, so often, for his job. But there was no one she was closer to, or probably ever had been closer to, and at the end of decades there was no one she could imagine being closer to.

She almost never spoke of him, now, even to Ann, but she still thought about him almost monotonously. Mostly she wanted his input, his involvement. Should she think about taking the car in for a service? Should she try moving the sofa to the other wall? Should she talk to Ann and Paula about starting to offer finger sandwiches at the teahouse? She wondered what he would have thought of the teahouse, of her new home at Mole End, of Ann and Paula and Charles and Ben. He would have loved Ann, surely, and he would have been charming and solicitous to Paula. Charles he wouldn't have taken to, at least not readily. He would have largely ignored Ben, probably, or made disparaging comments to her in private about his lingering academic pursuits. Of course, the teahouse, the compound, her friends there — well, her family, really — would never have existed if. ... She couldn't finish the thought.

People liked to say we sugarcoated the past, calling to mind only the fond memories while ignoring the unpleasant ones. But it seemed to her the opposite was true. What we ruminated on, what we turned over again and again in our mind, were the old pains and insults and injustices, the petty grievances and profound griefs, the might-have-beens and could-never-be-agains. It was like working a crossword puzzle, and you overlooked the answers you had already solved, instead going back to the squares that were still blank, trying desperately to fill them in. You kept returning to the past, or the past kept impinging on your present. Which is what Joseph had done. He was the history that had caught up with her, that had become her here and now.

There would be more police, surely, and news reporters, more people asking questions. Would there be a trial, a hearing, an inquest? She didn't know what the right term was. But surely there would be prosecutors and judges, court appearances. The teahouse would remain closed, at least for a while, and she'd have nothing to distract herself with. And of course there would be a funeral, a dreadful, miserable, painful funeral, and soon. Ben's family would have to be there. He hadn't talked often about his family, but she got the impression he didn't much like them, wasn't much like them.

She had never been especially afraid of death. But then she had never been close to death herself, had never had a serious illness or accident or found herself in a life-threatening situation. But she had lost friends, and family, and now Ben. People's deaths affected you more than other events in their lives, more than births or marriages or new homes, more than relocations or new jobs or illnesses. What led up to their deaths was about them, but once they had died, once they were gone, their deaths were about you, because you were the one left behind.

What did it mean that Ben had died? He had died trying to protect her. But what had he actually done? Nothing, really, just stood there and got shot. It seemed so unnecessary. Not that she was blaming him, not at all, but if he hadn't been there, Joseph wouldn't have shot him.

It occurred to her, as if for the first time, that Joseph had committed murder. But it wasn't really murder, was it, because she couldn't think for a moment that it had been intentional. It was more like manslaughter, involuntary manslaughter. So it wasn't murder, her son wasn't a murderer. *Manslaughter* was such an awful word, when you thought about it.

Why had Joseph had a gun? Was he planning to use it against her? She couldn't imagine that were so. But there he had been, in her teahouse, demanding money, a weapon concealed in his coat. So maybe Ben had in fact saved her. Maybe Ben had died in her place.

But even if you considered Joseph to be a murderer, he wasn't really her son, not in any real sense of the word. They shared genetics, nothing more, not the same values, the same experience. It wasn't necessarily your blood relatives who were your true tribe. Her real family, the family she had finally found, late in life, were the others in the compound, Ann and Paula and Charles and Ben.

She realized, all at once, that it was Ben. It was Ben who was her son.

32

Ann woke later than usual. She hadn't got home from the hospital till after one in the morning. She had expected Janet and Charles and Paula to wait up for her. But Paula's car wasn't in the driveway; maybe she was still at the hospital, or maybe she had gone to see Ash. Charles' house was dark except for the blue glow of his kitchen television; probably he had been at his kitchen table, drinking, and had passed out. High up near the roof's peak, Ben's kitchen light was still on. How crushing it was to see that light and know Ben wasn't there.

Janet's house was also dark, and Ann didn't hear her through the common wall. Why hadn't she waited up? Could Janet really be sleeping on this night? But of course she had been traumatized and was probably devastated. Who's to say how someone should behave in such a situation? It was just as well. She didn't feel up to reliving the experience, so soon, nor to Janet's scattered mind and emotional need.

She was exhausted but felt too agitated to sleep. She hadn't had any dinner and realized she was hungry, despite all she had just been through. She put on water for tea and made herself some buttered toast.

It had been a long day at the teashop. Paula had the day off, and Janet left early, just as the late-afternoon rush was starting, as she so often seemed to. Tommy was with her, and while he was one of the more competent tea caddies he was still new and could be impossibly slow filling orders. She was in a bit of a foul mood when she got home and decided to clear her mind by reading the *Times Literary Supplement* instead of having dinner. She must have dozed off, because the next thing she knew she was awake and sitting up, aware she had heard what she could only assume was a gunshot. She wasn't accustomed to guns, though she had discovered that here in Lower Slaughter you could sometimes detect the report of a distant hunter. But it was springtime, now, surely not a time of year when hunting would be allowed. And this had sounded close by.

It was probably nothing, but guns disconcerted her so. She decided she'd just pop over to Janet's to see if she had heard it. She rang the bell and waited. She knocked and poked her head in the door and called for her, but there was no answer. It was odd, not because the door was unlocked and the lights were on, but because she hadn't heard Janet go out, and her car was still out in front. She was standing outside Janet's door mulling this over when she noticed the interior lights of the teahouse.

She hadn't gone to the back door, as she normally did. What had compelled her to go around to the front? What subtle cues we instinctively pick up, we human animals. But no instinct could have prepared her for what she found, for what she saw. There was a pallor to Ben's face, and a slackness, that, while it could simply mean he was unconscious, suggested the situation was grave. She wanted to smack Janet, who was blathering nonsensically, to shock her back to coherence. But of course she had already been shocked. Janet kept saying something about "Joseph," and she realized she was talking about her estranged son. So Joseph had been there, and there had been a gunshot, and Ben was lying on the floor soaked in blood, and there apparently was some connection among these things.

The details, as they tumbled out, as she was able to piece them together, weren't much more enlightening. Joseph had wanted money. So why had he come to the teahouse? Couldn't he simply have called Janet, or gone to her house? None of it made any sense.

She must have arrived at the hospital not long after the ambulance got there, but she couldn't locate the emergency department. When she finally found it, the admitting nurse, or whatever she was, an unpleasant black woman with a nametag that read "Cordelia," wouldn't let her see Ben and couldn't give her any information about his condition. She explained that no one knew who or where Ben's family were and that she was as close to family as they were going to get, but it was another hour before a doctor, or maybe it was some kind of hospital administrator, finally told her that Ben was dead, that he had already been dead. She didn't weep, though she felt so sad, so painfully sad. Paula had shown up then, by herself, and she sobbed and sobbed when she found out. Ann surprised herself by wanting to hold her, but Paula had pulled way, had dropped into the vinyl embrace of a waiting-room chair, where she curled into a ball of sorrow.

She didn't have any information to give the people at the hospital, other than Ben's name and address, which they already had from his driving license. She did think to give them Charles' address and phone number, and let them know he was Ben's landlord. They all considered themselves such close friends, at the compound, such a tight-knit group, but at the end of the day they knew so little of the practical things about one another. Yet Paula seemed to know the name of Ben's G.P.; how had she known that? Paula said goodbye, then, saying she wanted to be by herself. But she must have changed her mind, because Ann saw her being led by the doctor through a set of doors to the patient area. Apparently she had talked her way into seeing Ben. Into seeing Ben's body. Perhaps she thought it was the only chance she'd have to say goodbye. Ann could have tried to follow, but she had already seen Ben dead, and she didn't want to reinforce the memory. She remembered that she had to call Janet and Charles.

She lay on her back and stared up at the ceiling. She thought she heard Janet through the common wall now, banging open and shut drawers and cabinets in her kitchen. So she must be up. She wasn't sure she was ready to go see her. Probably all of them could use some time alone. She assumed Paula had come home, though she didn't hear her upstairs.

There had been too much of hospitals, first Lionel's long slog and then her wretched time in the I.C.U. and now Ben's dying in emergency. There had been too much of leaving, first Lionel leaving her a widow and then Logan leaving for the monastery and next her leaving St. Andrews and finally Logan leaving again for London. There had been too much of death, first Lionel, for her, and before that Henry, for Janet, and now Ben, for both of them, for all of them.

Ben had been so young. Why was that upsetting? Why did we feel bad for people who didn't live into old age? It didn't really matter, once they were dead, didn't make any difference, not for them. It was as if we needed people to reach a certain age for the their lives to have been valid. As if the last man standing was the winner. Of what? Of nothing. Still, it was sad.

We think of life as a journey, but it isn't. We're not really going anywhere. No matter how busy we might keep ourselves, no matter what effort we might put into moving our bodies or our relationships or our fortunes from one place to another, we simply were, while things happened around us and time wore on. The only real traveling we were doing was in hurtling ever farther from the center of the universe, from the origin of space and time. And now physicists said the universe itself was expanding, which meant everything was gaining distance from everything else, everyone was growing farther from everyone else. Of course, that was while we were alive. What happened after we died was unknown. Did we travel then? Had Lionel gone on to exist in some other dimension? And Ben? She longed to believe so.

There was mystery in the world after all, in the conjuring of life, in this collection of atoms, molecules, cells we call the body, these randomly assembled motes of the universe, in their disintegration after death. Death came before the disintegration began: the atoms and molecules and cells remained, even after life was gone. Or maybe they had already begun to change form, loosening their bonds. But the component bits, presumably, were still there. Like Ben on the floor of the teashop.

There had been mystery, even magic, inside her when she was pregnant with Logan. It was one thing to understand the biology behind it but something wholly different to feel the quickening of new life within you. It was nothing less than extraordinary. Had Janet felt that with Joseph? Of course she would have. The experience would have been no less exceptional, even if she knew she was giving up the baby for adoption.

Birth and love and death always seemed exceptional to us, and surprising. The new mother and father believed nothing was ever so singular as their own baby, nothing was ever as delightful or captivating or clever; the world till now had not served its true purpose, which was to provide for their offspring. The man newly in love held there was nothing so perfect as his beloved, except maybe his love for his beloved, which was as pure and substantial and well-formed as a figure in marble. The woman betrayed thought no one had ever suffered more acutely, no person had ever given more of herself to another and yet been so wretchedly abandoned. The griever who lost friend or companion to death clung to the notion that no other had ever experienced such searing pain, no insult or injustice had ever been graver. How could God, how could the universe, allow any such thing to happen? Yet birth and love and death were so ordinary. They were experienced by every one of us. They were almost beneath mention.

Humans were getting ever closer to answering the questions of life, ticking off the answers like filling in a crossword, one solution leading to the next. Knowledge was an antidote to faith, facts a call not to prayer but to recognition that there was nothing to pray to. If the earth was billions of years old, and the universe billions of years older, if every thing that creepth upon the earth had not been created but had so obviously, so irrefutably, sprung from the elements and evolved over eons, then you had to reexamine your image of a creating, omnipotent God, reassess your assumptions about a human soul.

But even if we could one day create life as easily as we could now destroy it, even if we could piece together a living thing and biochemically breathe into it life, the mystery would remain: the mystery of what life is, of where it comes from, of where it goes, of what it is that quickens.

And beyond the mere fact of death, of the disappearance of life, was the loss of the person, the individual. She had been so struck by this when Lionel died. All he knew, a vast knowledge of European history amassed over decades of study; his quick, punning humor, which he revealed to almost no one but her; his idiosyncrasies, those quirks that were in turn endearing an annoying; his understanding of her own character, her dislikes and desires and weaknesses: all gone, irretrievable, irreplaceable. How could that be?

Perhaps the hardest thing about losing Lionel to death was simply that she still wanted to tell him things, about an article she had read that would interest him or someone she had run into that they both knew. Most of all she wanted to talk to him about his own death. She wanted to tell him how sick he had been, how awful it had been for her, to see him in pain, to worry about him, to anticipate his dying. She wanted to tell him how he had got better, unexpectedly, how the morning sun had been so warm on her face, as she strolled down North Street toward St. Andrews Cathedral, how even the cutting wind had been welcome. She wanted to tell him that he had died, suddenly, that it had been such a mean trick, to give them both hope like that but then snatch it away. She wanted to tell him about the awful funeral, about the relatives who had shown up, people she scarcely knew, whirging on about what a shame it was that he didn't have any religious faith; she had wanted to smack their sanctimonious faces. But if she could simply tell Lionel about it, it would set the whole thing right, it would make the entire ordeal retroactively bearable. They would have had a good laugh about the funeral. Losing Lionel to death, she thought. It works both ways, doesn't it?

It occurred to her that she would experience the same thing with Ben. She and Ben would have marveled that he had been so brave to confront Joseph. They would have commiserated about the awful experience in the emergency department. They would have expressed regret that his life had ended so unexpectedly, and so early.

She had always enjoyed traveling, being on the move. She had always liked to drive, and to drive fast, to get wherever she was going as quickly as possible. But why, when she enjoyed traveling, when she liked to drive, was she so eager to reach the end point? For the end point always came too soon.

She heard a thump from upstairs. So Paula must be up. She wondered who among them would be the first to emerge to greet the others.

33

Paula stood under the welcome spray of the shower and let the water run. She felt simultaneously enervated and agitated. The events of the previous day played ceaselessly in her mind.

She had taken the day off to go with Ash to a blues festival in central New York. She didn't particularly like blues, and she wasn't wild about the idea of driving four hours each way, but Ash had been so excited, so insistent. She felt bad about asking for the day off at the last minute. Janet had offered to go in to the teahouse to help Ann and Tommy in her place, but she knew Janet was likely to leave early, and it was as good as having only two people on the schedule for the entire twelve-hour shift.

The festival had been fun, in a festival sort of way, meaning there were lots of people, and multiple stages where you could hear various acts, and vendors' stalls where you could buy things like tee shirts and C.D.'s and harmonicas as well as all kinds of greasy, decadent, cooked-in-animal-fat food. But it was too early in the year for an outdoor festival, and while it was a gorgeous, sunshiney day, the ground was damp and the blanket they had brought quickly soaked through. Which meant they had to spend the afternoon standing.

The theme of the festival was acoustic blues of the twenties and thirties. Most of it involved a single singer with a single guitar belting out songs with monotonous melodies and a mind-numbing number of verses. Ash couldn't have been happier, though, and spent the day explaining the finer points of the performances and describing, yet again, the history of blues, the disparate styles and influences that had coalesced in a uniquely American musical form. The vast majority of early blues artists had been black and male, and Paula had long since become familiar with their names: Mississippi John Hurt, Blind Blake, Blind Lemon Jefferson, the Reverend Gary Davis, Blind Boy Fuller, Robert Johnson. At some point it occurred to her that there wasn't a single black person at the festival.

They got back to Ash's parents' around nine-thirty that evening. Ash had wanted to leave from his house, which hadn't made a lot of sense, because it meant she had to drive south first before they headed north. She was tired and wanted to get home, so she gave him a quick kiss good-bye and left. Her mind was almost blank, the way it can be after a long day, as she pulled into the driveway of Mole End. And then she saw Janet and Charles crossing the lawn. What was it about the way they were walking, the way they stopped and watched her, as she drove up, that gave her a feeling of dread?

Her first thoughts, as she rushed to the hospital, were that she couldn't understand why Janet and Charles weren't coming with her, weren't already there. Maybe older people reacted differently in this kind of situation. From what Janet said it sounded like none of them had really done anything for Ben before the ambulance finally got there. If only she had been there. If only she hadn't gone with Ash to that stupid blues festival. She might have been able to perform *ressuscitação cardiopulmonar*— whatever they called that in English. Or maybe it didn't even have to happen. Maybe she could have stopped the shooting from ever taking place. If only she had been there.

When she got to the hospital, to the emergency waiting room, Ann was just standing there, talking to a doctor. She looked pale, pale and resigned. The doctor spoke in low tones she couldn't hear, and as she approached he turned and walked away. When she saw her Ann visibly braced herself, as if she didn't want to talk to her, didn't want to have to say what she was about to tell her. "He's gone," was all she said. Paula had the briefest moment of thinking that maybe she didn't understand the meaning of the word in this sense, that maybe "gone" meant something other than what she knew it to mean. But then Ann had added, "Ben's dead."

Janet had said Ben had been shot. She hadn't said "shot dead." She hadn't said "killed." People could be shot and recover. They could be treated and sent home. Why was Ben dead?

Ann reached out to her, but she wanted to be alone. She wanted to be by herself. She didn't want to be at a hospital. She wanted to be with Avó Mariana and Avô Victor. She wanted to be home.

The hospital was trying to get information. They wondered if she might know who Ben's closest relative was or if she might know of any friends who might know. But she had no idea. It had once come up in conversation which doctor's office he went to, so she told them that. It was the only thing she knew about Ben that was useful, a single piece of information she just happened to remember. The

315

hospital had checked his cellphone and found numbers for only four people: Janet Charbray, Ann Firth, Charles Grapnel, Paula Pereira. Were any of them his family? No, she said. Yes, she wanted to say.

She told Ann she was going home, but she changed her mind. She wanted to see Ben. She wanted to say goodbye. To say goodbye in private, when it was just the two of them.

The woman at the front desk was no help. But then she saw the doctor, the doctor who had been talking to Ann. After some pleading she convinced him to take her back to see Ben. He was about to be wheeled away by an orderly.

Ben's eyes were closed. His face was ashen, empty. She felt like she should say a prayer, but she didn't know what to say, or to whom. So she simply stood there, looking at his closed eyes. She hadn't noticed before that he had such long eyelashes.

She turned off the water, stepped out of the shower, and wrapped herself in a towel. She wished, now, that she hadn't gone to see him. She wanted the last images of Ben to be the night they had had drinks at that country inn, the night they had talked and talked. He had been so shy and earnest. But all she could see now was Ben lying on the gurney, shrouded up to his neck in a white sheet. There had been partially dried blood in his ear.

She hadn't seen a lot of death, which was remarkable, given where she grew up. Rio had more than its share of shootings, and a girl she knew had been killed when rival drug dealers started spraying bullets at each other. Rio also had a lot of fatal car accidents, and three kids she went to high school with, a girl and two boys, had died in a head-on collision. But she hadn't lost anyone she was really close to. No one she really loved. She had always assumed that Avó Mariana and Avô Victor would be the first among those she really cared about. She never thought she would come to America and, a year and a half later, lose the person she cared about most.

People thought they wanted adventure. They traveled to Brazil to encounter an exotic culture. They moved to America to experience the world's richest country. But what they really wanted was the semblance of adventure. They wanted to take a guided tour of a favela and then return to their luxury hotel room. They wanted to get an American job and find an American boyfriend, without having anything ever go wrong. It explained the popularity of reality shows, of *telenovelas*. People thought they wanted interesting things to happen. But what they really wanted was for interesting things to happen to someone else, while they sat and watched. What they really wanted was for nothing to happen at all.

She surprised herself by thinking Ben was the person she cared about most. Shouldn't that be Ash? She would have to think about it. But not right now. She couldn't think about it right now. She still felt the blunt pain of Ben's death, like when you've been hit hard in the face, and all you can comprehend is the blow.

She got dressed. She guessed she would have some breakfast. She assumed the teahouse would be closed for the day, but she didn't really care one way or the other, and she didn't plan on finding out.

She wished she had spent more time with Ben. She wished she had gotten to know him better before now.

34

What did it mean, Charles thought, that Ben had died?
That is, what did his death mean? Had he died in Janet's
stead? Had he sacrificed himself, an atoner, a scapegoat, a
burnt offering? It seemed rather more like an accident, a
mistake, a random event. But then all events were more or
less random.

He once taught an undergraduate creative writing
course, a distasteful experience he thankfully never had
to repeat. One earnest young student submitted a short
story about a man who operated a railroad drawbridge
that spanned the Mississippi. The man's job was to ensure
that the drawbridge was up when ships passed under it
and down when trains crossed over it. One day the man
brought his eight-year-old son to work with him. They ate
lunch on an observation deck that overlooked the river,
watching as ships sailed beneath them. Suddenly they
heard a train whistle, and the man realized he hadn't
been watching the time. The Memphis Express, carrying
four hundred passengers, was fast approaching the open

bridge. Instructing his son to remain on the observation deck, the man rushed to the control house. Before lowering the bridge, he scanned the water for ships. To his horror he saw that his son, in attempting to follow him to the control house, had fallen into the massive gears that worked the bridge. He quickly realized he had only two options. If he took the time to rescue his son, the Memphis Express and its four hundred passengers would plunge into the Mississippi. If he lowered the bridge, his son would be crushed by the gears. The man made his decision. He pulled back on the lever and lowered the bridge, sacrificing his beloved son to save the lives of the unwitting train passengers.

There were several problems with the story. First, it was plagiarized; he had come across it, and its various permutations, numerous times before. Second, it was usually presented as being factual, which was highly unlikely, in part because the details seemed to change with every telling. Third, no one ever seemed to notice that the man was responsible for his own cruel dilemma, both for leaving the bridge up as the train approached and for allowing his son to fall into danger.

In some versions of the story the bridge operator was compared to God, who had sacrificed his son, Jesus, for all us thankless sinners. In others the implication was that we should each be like the bridge operator, willing to sacrifice what was dearest to us in order to serve others, or at least to serve God. In one version the commuters on the train were sinners bound for hell, the storyteller apparently failing to realize that the sacrifice would let the train continue to its fiery destination. He had even come across a version that placed in the gears an adult son who insisted that his father kill him to save the train passengers, as well as a version in which the adult son somehow managed to turn the gears himself, actively effecting his own demise. Apparently custom could not stale mutilation's infinite variety.

One problem with apocryphal stories was that they weren't true. They might contain truth, which was fine, but if they weren't true then they should be presented as fiction. And if it wasn't important whether they were true stories, then why were they sold as such? It annoyed him how blindly people clung to such stories, how credulously they insisted on the stories' being factual. He once had to sit through a sermon in which Jesus was reported to be such a talented carpenter that you could go to Israel today and find window sashes he had crafted that still slid up and down in their frames. The congregation marveled at this and praised God for it, never pausing to contemplate how it was known that Jesus had constructed the windows, whether there were in fact windows with moving sashes built in the Middle East circa, say, 33 C.E., or what any of it had to do with religious faith.

The bridge-operator story was of a piece with the Genesis story in which Abraham binds his only-begotten son on an altar and comes shockingly close to stabbing him to death and then burning his body. Many Christians accepted this story as factual. Were they truly comfortable claiming as a patriarch someone crazy enough to believe God had told him to kill his son and heartless enough to be willing to do it? Did they truly want to worship a God who would demand such a thing, and for no good reason? The idea — of such a God, of worshipping such a God — was repugnant. Of course, he could understand how this might have been an effective recruiting tool for the early Hebrews. In a time and place where human sacrifice wasn't uncommon, the Jews could argue that their God was as formidable as other gods but also merciful, requiring the shedding of human blood but ultimately sparing the sacrificial lamb.

But the biggest problem with such apocryphal, absurd-choice, blood-lust stories was that they cheapened the real choices and real suffering faced by real people. It was like taking those "which would you rather be?" questions seriously. Which would you rather be, a painter who went blind or a composer who went deaf? Which would you rather be, a boy who was crushed in a giant machine or the father who crushed him? Which would you rather be, an elephant that doesn't like peanuts or a mouse that's afraid of elephants or an elephant shrew that ate a bad peanut? Stupidity isn't a crime, but it's surely an indictment.

Had Ben had to make a choice, like the bridge operator, or rather, like the adult son in the gears? Had he chosen to thrust himself between Janet and harm, and, if so, had he been mindful of the consequences? He wondered if, in the same circumstance, he would have done the same.

He had heard the gunshot, but he hadn't thought much of it. It wasn't hunting season, not that there was any place to hunt in Lower Slaughter anyway, but one did occasionally hear the sound of a gun being fired. There were two or three small farms, maybe fifteen miles away, and he wondered if perhaps it came from one of them. Would you be able to hear a gunshot from that distance? Or maybe there was a practice range somewhere nearby. People certainly did like their guns.

Anyway, he had been drinking. He decided to have some wine with dinner, which he almost never did, and ended up drinking the whole bottle. Somehow this put him in the mood for Islay scotch. He had an old bottle of Port Ellen he had been saving for no good reason, so he opened it, and one glass led to another. He hadn't intended to get drunk. The phone had rung, then, but he didn't answer it and didn't bother to check the caller I.D. If somebody wanted something, they could leave a message.

He fell asleep, and into a dream, and in the dream there were police sirens and flashing red-and-blue lights. At some point he surfaced and perceived there actually were lights and sirens, and a few minutes later he was awake enough to realize something was going on at the teahouse.

He had that off-balance, walking-on-a-pitching-ship feeling too much alcohol gave you, which could be fun if you were strolling aimlessly but was frustrating when you were trying to get someplace with purpose. There were several parked squad cars, and police coming and going, but in a plodding manner that suggested whatever was happening had already happened. He entered the teahouse. There was a large bloodstain on the floor. Janet was sitting in the opposite corner, looking distraught. There was a large stain on the floor, and it looked like blood.

Janet explained what had happened. He wanted to go to the hospital, but clearly he couldn't drive. Time passed. They exchanged a few words. The police asked some questions. The police told them to leave. They stumbled back to his house. He wished he hadn't been drinking.

When the call finally came from Ann, to Janet's cellphone, Janet wept. She wanted to be comforted, to be held. But he wanted to be alone. Women liked to huddle in their grief, to seek the solace of others who can share their pain. Men wanted to find solitude, to withdraw into the cave of their own injured minds.

He had felt so alone after Alain died. He had in fact been alone. To start with, there was no one else who understood their friendship, no one else who knew how much they meant to each other, or even that they meant anything to each other. Yes, there was Agostina, Alain's longsuffering cook, silent observer of their slow-blooming relationship. But after Alain's death she retreated to her official capacity as employee, and his interactions with her turned formal.

Yes, there were Alain's friends, and they were legion, but they were older, and detached, and mostly absent, and while they had met him at Alain's parties, while they had seen him with Alain at restaurants and at the theatre, they thought of him simply as another of Alain's toy boys. And then when he returned home to Grier & Buchanan, to Siberia, it might as well have been, there was no one that even knew who Alain was. He had spoken of Alain, and his colleagues knew he spent the holidays and summers in his company. But they didn't know a thing about him, didn't know what he looked like, what he talked about, how elegantly he could orchestrate a dinner party, how much he adored cut flowers. Alain might as well not have existed. In fact, he no longer did.

When he first knew Alain, when he was a young man in a foreign city, he wanted to be protected by him, to find in him shelter, sanctuary, comfort. But that wasn't the kind of companionship Alain could offer, and he had to make do with his almost grudging affection, his friendship more lean-to than gambrel roof. After the accident, as Alain lay dying, it was he who wanted to do the protecting, to relieve his pain, to shield him from the horror of his bedsores, his ventilator, his feeding tube. But there was nothing he could do for him. He couldn't ease his suffering. He couldn't make him whole. He couldn't stave off death. And now once again he had failed the person he most loved.

Oh, Ben. Oh, Ben, why have I forsaken you? If only I could just hold you, protect you from harm, shelter you from the world. If only I had told you that I loved you.

There's a kind of sobbing that's more rage than grieving, a raging grief, that comes rarely and only briefly, that wracks the body and then abruptly leaves it.

He closed his eyes. He had a sense of falling backward into inky darkness, into infinite night.

35

Charles got a call from Ben's mother. The people at the hospital had tracked her down through Ben's doctor and provided her with Charles' phone number, which they had got from Ann. Apparently Ben's mother hadn't even known where Ben lived. But now she wanted to collect his things. She agreed to stop by the next day. She sounded oddly dispassionate.

He hung up the phone. He found the key to Ben's empty apartment, let himself in the door, and climbed the stairs.

The apartment was hot. The kitchen light was still on. There was a single fork in the sink. The rooms were possessed of an eerie stillness.

He went to the bedroom, to Ben's desk, and rifled through drawers till he found what he was looking for: Ben's will. Of course Ben would have a will. He was only thirty years old and still single, but of course he would have a will.

The will had been drawn up just over a year ago. It was notarized by an attorney and witnessed by a name he didn't recognize, probably the attorney's secretary. It left everything — his sparse furniture, his carpentry tools, his collection of books on anthropology and Native American history, a very meager savings account — to Charles. It also named Charles executor. That was very like Ben, to have named him executor but not to have asked first, not to have mentioned it. There was a codicil, in Ben's scrawl, that left the recently unearthed Lenape artifacts, the shard of pottery and the stone tools, to Paula. As if he had somehow known.

He had been standing, leaning over the desk drawer where he found the will, which was mixed in with college transcripts and odd receipts. The document was brief, though leavened with legal jargon, and as he scanned the pages he lowered himself to sit cross-legged on the floor. Why had he left the artifacts to Paula? Why had he left all his banal belongings to him, yet the Native American objects, the things that surely were most precious to him — why had he left them to someone else? It felt like a reprimand, a censure, from beyond the grave.

He called Janet, and she wisely suggested they all meet at her house that evening. She would tell Ann and Paula. He would have had them to his house, but the only times they gathered there had been for his soirees, for brunches and drinks and dinner parties. It would have been so dispiriting, the four of them sitting around his kitchen table, no food, no drinks. No Ben.

When they got to Janet's house none of them seemed to know how to behave around one another. They sat brittly on the edge of the sofa and chairs in her living room. Charles described Ben's will, though he didn't show it to them. He explained that the majority of Ben's belongings would go to him, while the Native American artifacts were set aside for Paula. He added that Ben had left Janet and Ann each a keepsake of their own choosing. It was only appropriate, it seemed to him, and in any case Ben's things were really his now, to do with as he saw fit. It seemed the kind of thing Ben would have done anyway.

"So that's it, really," he said.

"He left nothing to his family?" Ann asked.

"Apparently not."

"Well, I know he didn't much care for them," Janet said. "But it doesn't seem quite right."

"Well, I think we have to respect his wishes."

"Oh, naturally."

"What does it say about the funeral? Or does it say anything?"

"He says he wants to be cremated and interred."

"Can you be both?" Ann asked.

"I suppose what he means," Charles said, "is that he wants to be cremated, but then rather than have his ashes kept in an urn or spread somewhere, he wants them interred in a cemetery, with a gravestone."

"Does it say where he wanted to be buried?"

"No, though he says he doesn't want to be buried in his family plot. He wants to be in a completely separate graveyard. He's very clear about that."

There was a space of silence as the four of them gazed distractedly.

"I've always said that I want to be cremated," Janet finally said. "And I want my ashes scattered over George Clooney's body."

The others looked at her with held breath, and then they all burst forth in laughter.

"Oh, Janet," Ann said, her round body shaking with mirth.

"It is good to laugh," Paula said. "Ben would have wanted us to laugh."

Charles was tempted to disagree with that last statement. But Paula was right, it was good to laugh.

**

Ben's mother came the next day, showing up early. Charles found her on the front porch, rapping on the double front doors. She was short and stout, with sloping shoulders, rather like a Postal Service mailbox, and she had raw skin that was simultaneously red and dull; she looked nothing like Ben. Charles invited her in, but she was only interested in gaining access to Ben's apartment and was going to waste no time with the landlord. Charles went to get the key and a copy of the will, which he had placed in a large envelope, and then led her upstairs.

Ben's mother surveyed the rooms, picking up two or three objects and turning them over, as if inspecting items at an estate sale.

"There's not much here," she said.

"No."

"I'll have my sons clear it all out," she said. "They can do it after the funeral."

He noticed she said "my sons." She didn't say "my other sons" or "my older sons." "The thing is," he said, holding up the envelope, "there's a will."

The will didn't go over big with Ben's mother. She seemed skeptical, especially of the fact that Charles was both executor and beneficiary. She studied the text myopically, frowning, her nose almost touching the pages. After a minute she seemed to give up.

"Well, I guess I can't say I'm surprised," she said. "He didn't have that much stuff anyway." She added, "Who's this 'Paula'?"

**

But while Ben's family seemed ready to concede the will, they were not about to surrender control of the funeral, which they guarded as "a family matter." They swooped in from out of town, the father and older brothers and younger sister joining the mother, and insisted on making all the arrangements. There was talk of having it in Ben's hometown, farther north, where his mother still lived; the family plot was there, Grandma and Grandpa Shriver already having taken up permanent residence. But Charles was firm on this: if Ben wanted not to be buried there, as his dying wish, as his desire after death, then there was no way he was going to allow it. The family balked, till lawyers were mentioned, and then just as quickly as they had engaged the battle they backed down. They still handled the details, the funeral home and flowers, the gravesite and headstone. But the ceremony would take place just outside Lower Slaughter, "if he wanted to be here so bad," as one brother put it. The family did instruct Charles, as executor, to ensure that payment was rendered "from Ben's estate," which of course was all but nonexistent. Charles willingly paid for everything himself.

Janet had expected to be involved, had wanted to be involved. But when the family sort of took things over she readily stepped back, thankful not to have to deal with the depressing details of death. It turned out to be a mistake, though, because the funeral was a dismal affair. She had braced herself for something overtly religious, held in some evangelical church or other, with a heavy-handed message of repentance and salvation. But apparently the family resented Ben's rejection of their beliefs, so they arranged for the ceremony to take place at the funeral home, a sagging, windowless building smothered in pale blues and golds, like her mother's nursing home. There were few people in attendance — just the four of them from the compound, plus Ash, along with Ben's extended family and some of their friends and neighbors, as well as a few of his graduate-school professors and colleagues — yet the room they were assigned to was so confining that it couldn't accommodate even their small party. The overflow was relegated to an annex, where the proceedings apparently were piped in over loudspeakers.

Janet and the others sat in the second row, behind Ben's immediate family, his divorced parents separated by their three remaining children. There was no coffin. Instead, Ben's ashes resided in a rectangular wooden box, which had been placed at the front of the room. It looked like a miniature casket, as if for a small pet; as if for a bad joke. Also in attendance were an aunt and uncle, the latter apparently an ordained but churchless minister. He offered a bland, monotonous eulogy full of backhanded compliments, noting that Ben had had "a great head knowledge of Christ," by which she supposed he meant that Ben was well-educated but lacked a spiritual awareness. She was sorely tempted to stand up and object, to protest this travesty of a celebration of her dear friend's life by people who were virtual strangers to him or, worse, the source of his ill-deserved diffidence. But she wasn't going to make a scene.

Thankfully, there was opportunity at the end of the program for people to step forward and offer remembrances. All of them, she and Ann and Paula and Charles, found it within themselves to speak, and in so doing were able to hijack the service and turn it into something that truly honored their friend. Charles was eloquent, of course, though she noticed he spoke without his usual italics. Ann was pithy, and Paula was sweet and tearful and hopeful. She had no idea what she herself said, rambling on as she always did, but it didn't really matter; it was the emotion she felt that was meaningful. She managed to remain composed till the very end, when she broke down and blubbered like an idiot. But she couldn't have cared any less, really, as the day was for Ben, and the least they could do, all they could do, was to honor and indulge in his memory.

36

The funeral was over, the family had gone, but Ben's death was still present. For one thing there were the local news reporters, like bees at the end of summer, insistent and annoying and bearing the threat of stinging pain. Janet and the others refused to talk to them, though they persisted, though they went away for a time but reappeared whenever there was a development in the case. The story was all over the local papers, the suspicious death of a young man in Lower Slaughter the biggest news since the opening of the Trader Joe's. Janet refused even to look at the papers, at first, and she assumed the others did as well, as they never mentioned anything they had read. But she was, after all, almost desperate to understand what had happened, what was happening, and before long she found herself trying to absorb as much information as she could.

Between the news reports and brief conversations she had with investigators she was able to piece together at least some of the details. The police had quickly tracked Joseph down. How and where, she had no idea, but apparently he had fled on foot, so he couldn't have got very far very fast. In his denim coat was the gun, recently fired, a spent round in one of its five chambers.

He lived in Middletown, Pennsylvania, now, out near Harrisburg. His life had evidently ambled along with reasonable grace but had recently become rather hobbled. There had been a live-in girlfriend, with whom he shared a house, but she had left, pretty much disappeared, from the sound of it, not to be seen again. He had had a decent job, working as a security guard at the Three Mile Island nuclear power plant, right there in Middletown, but he had lost it after an ongoing conflict with his supervisor reached a fury. He had taken another job, then, any job he could get, and was working part time driving a wholesale delivery truck for a local ice-cream company. The pay wasn't adequate, however, and he was behind on his mortgage payments and in danger of losing the house, his sole investment, his nest egg. On top of that his car had been impounded as a result of his failure to pay a multitude of parking fines, and he had been reduced to riding a bicycle. Well, that explained why he had come on the train.

It turned out he had a permit to carry a concealed weapon, though Janet had no idea why he needed one or why he had the gun with him when he came to see her. Maybe it had something to do with his former job as a security guard. Security guards didn't carry guns, though, did they? But from what one of the policemen told her, it was decidedly easy to get a concealed-weapon permit in Pennsylvania, requiring only the filling out of a simple form, the submission of a couple of references, and the payment of a twenty-dollar fee. How many of her neighbors were walking around with guns strapped to their ankles?

But the bigger question was what Joseph was doing here in Pennsylvania. He had lived in Massachusetts when she knew him, out toward the western part of the state. What had brought him here? Maybe his girlfriend had family in the area. Or former girlfriend, whatever she was. But here he was. Here they were, she and Joseph, both in the same state, not a hundred miles from each other, unknown to her and, presumably, at least until recently, unknown to him.

Of course there would be a trial, which she was dreading. Would she have to testify? How could she say anything against Joseph, her son, how could she suggest or even believe he meant to take money from her, meant to harm Ben? Yet how could she defend him, how could she take sides against the innocent life he had taken, the man he had killed, Ben, her dear friend and, she now felt, also her son? She met, reluctantly, with the district attorney, who would prosecute the case, and with Joseph's lawyer, both of whom wanted her side of the story, to their own ends. She told them she didn't know whether Joseph had planned to rob her, didn't know whether Ben had provoked the shooting, didn't know whether Joseph had fired the gun intentionally, didn't know whether any or all of it could have been avoided by one side or the other. All of which was the truth, really.

Joseph had been assigned a public defender, as he lacked the wherewithal to pay for his own lawyer. Janet wondered if she shouldn't step forward and offer to hire someone who would be more effective, or at least have more of an interest. But she wanted to stay out of it, as much as she could, to remain a neutral observer, if that were at all possible.

But then he copped a plea, as they said on the TV detective shows. On the one hand there was no way to prove a robbery was in progress, no way to show any sort of premeditation, in terms of shooting Ben, no way to argue he had acted with malice, no concealed-weapon violation to charge him with. On the other hand there were the facts that he had showed up under somewhat suspicious circumstances, that he had drawn a gun, when there was no clear threat to his wellbeing, that he had failed to assist the man he injured, that he had fled the scene. So they allowed him to plead guilty to involuntary manslaughter, and in so doing avoid a jury trial and any additional charges. He would spend fifteen months in jail.

So her son would go to jail. Her son was a convicted criminal. Her son was in jail.

Of course, with the investigation over, the teahouse was once again open. Ann wisely arranged for professional cleaners to come in, after the police took away their crime-scene tape, to remove any trace of that awful night. All the tea caddies came back, as did the customers, and only two or three asked anything about the incident, the rest simply returning to their places in line, their usual orders, their regular routines. Here was Richard, ordering his "small Earl Grey, with milk and sugar, for here, please"; there were the Mochas, sitting in their seats by the window, talking quietly; here were the L.I.C.'s, ignoring the misbehavior of their spoiled children; there were the Smellies, making space for themselves with their invisible force field of acrid Lycra. Janet and Ann and Paula quickly fell back into their familiar roles, each of them thankful to be busy again, to have something to turn their minds from what had happened.

It wasn't long before the grim Emily Reaper made an appearance. "I read all about it in the paper," she said to Janet as soon as she saw her.

"Oh, did you?"

"And I came right over to see for myself. But it was all closed off. You couldn't see a thing."

"No, I suppose not."

"Was there a lot of blood?"

"You'll forgive me if I say I'd rather not talk about that."

"And he was your son, no less. The man who shot him."

"The son I gave up for adoption, yes."

"I see he got jail time."

"Yes."

"It's only right, I suppose. But such a shame about the daughter."

"Yes. I'm sorry, what? What about the daughter?"

"I mean it's a shame that she has no parents now. The daughter. Well, your granddaughter."

"My granddaughter?" What was Emily talking about?

"Since the mother didn't want her. Does that mean she'll go to an orphanage?"

Janet stared at her uncomprehendingly.

"Surely you knew, Janet. That your son has a daughter. That you have a granddaughter?"

Except she hadn't known. She hadn't known that Joseph and his erstwhile girlfriend had had a child together, that the girlfriend had left them when the child was three, that Joseph had been raising her himself for the past year, that the loss of his job and car, the potential loss of his house, had been that much more wearing, that much more troubling, because he had this four-year-old daughter to care for.

It must have been in the papers. How had she missed it? Well, she hadn't read the papers at first, and then shortly after she started reading them she stopped, because it was just too distressing, too painful. And the others in the compound, Ann and Paula and Charles, hadn't been reading the papers, either. You'd think one of the investigators would have mentioned it, at some point, or the prosecutor or the defense lawyer, but maybe they thought it was too a delicate topic. Or maybe it just never came up.

So she had a granddaughter. Her name was Lily. She had a granddaughter, and her name was Lily.

"Where is she now?" Ann asked. They were in Ann's living room. Janet had rushed out of the teahouse, following the Emily Reaper revelation, and spent the afternoon searching the Internet, scouring back issues of local newspapers, calling the attorney general's office, calling the public defender's office, calling Child Services. She resurfaced at the end of the day, after the teahouse had closed, and came knocking on Ann's door.

"She's up in Worcester, now, with Joseph's parents. Apparently Joseph left her with a neighbor woman while he was at work, who had a sort of daycare set up in her house. So that's who had her when he came here. I don't know what exactly happened to her when the police first had him in custody. It must have been so frightening for her, the poor thing. But the mother is out of the picture. I don't know whether they couldn't track her down, or they tracked her down and she didn't want anything to do with it, I never did get a clear answer to that. Apparently she's from Pennsylvania, originally, and her parents were down here, I guess, but it sounds like there are no longer any living relatives on her side. So they shipped Lily up to Joseph's parents, but that's just a temporary thing. I think they're a lot older. I mean, I think they were in their fifties when I knew Joseph, so they must be close to eighty now." She paused for a breath. "Worcester is in Massachusetts," she added, realizing Ann wouldn't know it.

"What will happen to her, in the long term?"

"The thing is, I just can't believe Joseph would just abandon her like that. I mean, I know his life hasn't been going smoothly, and obviously he had a lot of things on his mind. But I can't believe he would just leave her with the neighbor woman, and not make any arrangements for her. Of course, he didn't plan on going to jail."

"No."

"That must sound strange, coming from me, to say I can't believe he abandoned her. Considering I gave up Joseph for adoption."

"Well, it's not really the same thing, is it?"

"I can't think what Joseph was trying to achieve by coming here, I truly can't. I can't think he was in his right mind. But maybe his intention was more in the way of just trying to reach out to me."

"I think you're probably right."

"And in his defense, apparently he was trying to make arrangements for Lily. But I don't think he has any say in the matter. The state just sort of steps in and takes over."

"What was he trying to arrange?"

"Well, my understanding is that he wanted Lily to come live with me."

"Really?"

"The thing is, that's exactly what I was thinking. That was my first thought, when I found out she even existed and needed a place to stay. Well, needed a home."

"Really? Sorry, I should stop saying 'really' like that. I don't mean to sound surprised. It actually sounds wonderful. That is, if that's what you want."

"Well, I've given it a lot of thought, and yes, absolutely that's what I want. Can you believe it, Ann? I have a granddaughter."

"What will happen next? I assume it can all be arranged."

"Apparently there will be some sort of court hearing. And I imagine there will be a lot of forms and paperwork, and some kind of background check. But assuming everything goes smoothly, then Lily will move down here. Well I suppose I'll go up there and get her. But Lily will come live with me here."

She wondered what that would mean in the long term. Would she have Lily just for the year or so that Joseph was in jail? Would she be responsible for her from now on? Certainly she would be responsible for her for a while, for providing food and clothing and everything else she needed, for finding her a pediatrician and getting her registered for school, whenever that would start — next year? — for raising her in general; it's not as if Joseph could sponsor her from jail. But beyond that, she'd probably take care of her, be a part of her life, for a long time, maybe for the rest of her life. Would she have to think about saving for college? Perhaps she was getting ahead of herself.

It would also mean she would be a part of Joseph's life. Assuming he wanted that. But surely the dynamic would have changed, with her taking care of Lily. Although how would he ever forgive himself for what happened to Ben? How would he ever get past feeling he was secretly resented if not despised? Still, their lives would come together, at least to some degree, because of Lily. Because of Ben, really.

So Lily and Joseph were her family now. She had thought of Ann and Paula and Charles and Ben as being her family. She had thought of her friends as being the family she chose. But it turned out your family isn't the family you choose. Your family is the family you're born with, the family that's born to you. Like it or not, they're the family you end up with.

37

Lily joined Janet at Mole End at the start of summer. Following a series of meetings with Child Services and a parade of paper forms and a home inspection by some kind of social worker, Janet made the trip up to Worcester to get her. She had hoped Ann would have been able to join her, but of course she had to stay back in Lower Slaughter to see to the teahouse. It was a nerve-wracking journey, not least because she got lost not once but twice along the way. She stayed overnight in a cheap motel and went to collect Lily in the morning.

Joseph's parents were docile and cooperative. That might have been effected by the presence of a narrow, angular woman from the Massachusetts Child Services who was there to ensure Lily's uneventful transfer, but Janet got the impression the fallow soil of their quiet lives had been rudely turned over by Lily's arrival, and they were more than a little relieved to see her go. They had only ever had Joseph, and he had moved out some twenty years ago, and now they lived in an oddly shaped single-story house that was scarcely big enough for the two of them and not really set up to accommodate a young child. They mentioned to Janet that Lily seemed often to withdraw, and pout when she didn't get her way, but they appeared more concerned than critical in their observations. Lily called them Grampy Dick and Grammy Hildie. They had that old-person smell about them, like stale sweat and dry leaves.

It was strange to think this was now her family, Joseph and Lily and by extension Joseph's parents, Lily's grandparents. But no, Joseph's parents weren't actually blood relatives, so they weren't part of it. She realized it was unfair of her to think of it that way.

Lily did seem withdrawn, at first, and skeptical of this loud woman who was going to take her away, who was not significantly younger than her grandparents though certainly more talkative and, one could only hope, at least marginally more cheerful. But she didn't seem at all traumatized by what she had experienced, the disappearance of her mother, not a year before, and then of her father, just a few weeks ago, the interference of social workers, the faltering care of her grandparents, whom she apparently had met on only a few earlier occasions. Mostly she seemed pliable, agreeing to whatever was asked of her if not fully embracing it, like many children in such situations. You'd think they'd resist, or cry, or act out in some way, and she supposed some children did. But just as many seemed simply to flow in and out with the surf, treading water if not entirely buoyant.

In fact, some children seemed almost to wish for unfortunate circumstances, to expect the worst and then welcome it. She had experienced this once herself. Her parents had had a marriage like many of their generation, frank and uncomplicated, not openly solicitous or tender. They said what they thought, without excessive introspection or hindsight, and while this meant they were sometimes brusque with each other, the harsh words usually were brief. But she remembered a time when the lukewarm resentments of their leftover disagreements somehow became overheated. It must have been over the campground, the timeshare investment in which her father had lost their savings. There was one fight on top of another, till one night her father erupted over dinner. He thundered at her mother with anger, even hatred, ending his tirade by sweeping his full dinner plate from the table. The plate shattered and the food scattered, roast beef and mashed potatoes and gravy all over the cabinets and floor. After her father stormed out she helped her mother with the mess. By the time he returned there was no trace of his outburst save a dent in the cabinet door where the plate had exploded as it struck.

The thing is, as horrible as it had been, as awful as it was to experience, a part of her had wanted it to happen. As her parents' bickering intensified, a part of her hoped there would be a real blowup. She later felt guilty about this, and the mar in the cabinet door was a constant reminder, an ongoing reproof, as if it had been her fault, as if her wishing for it had caused it to occur. She had wondered if it might be some kind of masochistic tendency or victim mentality. But now she believed it had more to do with a desire to get past the conflict, a hope that the animus would boil over and be done with, like tripping the pressure-relief valve on an overheated furnace. She wondered if other children ever felt that way. She wondered if Lily had felt that about her own situation.

The grandparents had told Lily she was going away to camp. What a stupid thing to have told her. She had no time for people, especially parents, or in this case grandparents, who blatantly and needlessly lied to children.

343

They introduced her as Janet and explained to Lily that she was going to take her to camp. Lily asked if the camp were called Camp Janet. They got a good laugh out of this, at Lily's confused expense, and said, Yes, you're going to Camp Janet. Then the child got into her head that Janet's name was in fact Camp Janet, and that's what she began to call her. That actually was fine, though, because what else was she going to call her? Grandmom? Auntie Janet? Neither quite fit. Camp Janet, then.

Lily was silent on the ride home, which, with stops for lunch and several potty breaks, took nearly eight hours. She gazed out the window, the way children do, at the streaming landscape, entertained or bored by her own imagination. She had brought so few belongings with her, just a small collection of toys and a wicker hamper full of her clothes. The outfit she had on was threadbare and stained.

So Janet was left to her thoughts. She had planned to visit Joseph before she went to pick up Lily. Ann was going to go with her, for moral support, just as she had driven Ann to see Logan at the monastery, back before Ann had her own car. She remembered reading somewhere that the American prison system, when it was established by the Quakers, was intended to compel criminals to meditate on their transgressions. It was for this reason prisoners were confined to a "cell," which was meant to evoke a monk's cell.

But she decided not to go. She decided she would see him after she got Lily, after she had got Lily settled in. She'd have something to report, then, for one thing. And maybe Joseph would be more inclined to talk to her. The last time she actually spoke with him was twenty-two years ago, when he broke off contact. Unless you counted the night he appeared out of nowhere and shot Ben.

Should she take Lily to see him in jail? She thought not. On the other hand, it would mean she'd go more than

a year without seeing her father — a very long time for a
child her age. By that time he would have become almost a
stranger to her, at least in some ways. And surely she must
have grown acutely dependent on him in the months since
her mother disappeared. But it would likely be upsetting
to her to see her father in jail, and then she'd be stuck with
the memory, probably for the rest of her life. It wasn't an
easy decision. She wondered if Joseph could demand that
she be brought to visit him, or if the Child Services people
could insist on it. She hoped Lily wouldn't feel like a pris-
oner at Mole End.

How awful it must have been, must still be, for her to
have lost both mother and father, even if only temporarily.
How could the mother have left her child like that? She
realized this sounded hypocritical, even ridiculous, coming
from her. But to be fair, giving up Joseph wasn't quite the
same thing. She hadn't actually known him when she gave
him up. How could a mother know her daughter for three
years, how could she raise her, nurture her, hold her for all
that time and then leave her? Well, people were unfathomable. You couldn't judge. Well, you could judge, and she
did. But it probably wasn't fair to.

Lily was asleep when they got home, in the early evening, and when Janet woke her she could tell Lily wasn't
sure where she was and was frightened. She tried to carry
her, but the girl wanted to walk, which was just as well, as
she had all the luggage and things to bring in from the car.
Thankfully neither Ann nor Paula made an appearance,
as Lily had enough adjusting to do without a barrage of
strangers. She carried Lily's things upstairs and showed
her to her room, which had already been decorated, if a
bit sparsely, with a child's bed and bureau and matching
lamp. There wasn't much hung on the walls, yet, and there
still was a stack of boxes in the corner, from when Janet

had moved in, but it was a start. Lily seemed not to quite comprehend that it was her own bedroom, or maybe she simply wasn't interested, so they went downstairs to find some dinner. She turned out to be a picky eater, despite having devoured her french fries on the ride home, and rejected everything Janet suggested, till Janet turned up a can of SpaghettiOs she didn't even know she had. She was aware of being artificially enthusiastic and knew Lily probably wasn't buying it.

But Lily made the transition quickly, over the next few weeks, and in fact faster than Janet, who had to get used to the idea that there was this other presence in the house, and a constant one, and a rather energetic one. She was a delightful little girl, really, unaccountably sunny and almost always pleasant. She was a wonderful addition to Mole End and a welcome distraction from the memory of Ben. She had Joseph's blond, wiry hair.

Lily took up a lot of her time, naturally, though Ann and Paula were wonderfully understanding about her not being able to put in as many hours at the teahouse. But she brought Lily to the teahouse nearly every day. Ann and Paula delighted her and delighted in her. Even Charles, who could be so intimidating and remote, was gentle with Lily, solicitous and adept at drawing her out.

Janet avoided the difficult conversation, about where her father was and when she could see him and how long she would be at Mole End, for as long as she could. She assumed it would come up on its own, as it did one day at the breakfast table.

"Camp Janet, what are you?"

Janet thought she knew where this was going. Well, it would be good to get it all out. Lily might not fully understand all of it, but there was no reason not to be straightforward. "What am I?"

"Are you my mom?"

Ohh. You're going to make me cry. "No, honey, I'm your grandmom."

"But I never had you before as a grandmom."

"Well, that's because I didn't know you before."

"Are you my dad's grandmom, too?"

"No, I'm his mother. I'm your dad's mom, and I'm your grandmom."

"But I thought Grampy Dick and Grammy Hildie were my dad's mom."

"Well, they're his parents. That is, they're also his parents." She might as well dive in and see how it went. "I was your dad's mom when he was very little. But I couldn't take care of him. So I gave him up for adoption. Do you know what that means?"

"Yeah."

She could tell she didn't. "It means I gave him to your Grampy Dick and Grammy Hildie. So they could take care of him."

"Like they gave me to you."

Ohh. "Well, not exactly. You'll just be staying with me for a little while, while your dad's away."

"But where is my dad?"

"He had to go away for a little while. Something bad happened, and your dad got in trouble for it, so he had to go away. It wasn't his fault, but he had to go away for a little while. But he'll be back. It won't be for a while, but he'll come back for you."

"Am I in trouble, too?"

Ohh. "No, honey, no, not at all. You didn't do anything wrong."

"It's OK, Camp Janet. I like it here at the campground."

It was a term she had used before. She must have heard one of them, Ann or Paula or Charles, refer to the compound. Janet couldn't use the word any longer, to describe where they lived, because it was what Ben had called it. She wondered if she could get used to "campground."

"I'm glad you like it here."

"I love you, Camp Janet."

"I love you too." Ohh.

38

Summer was passing quickly, as summer does. Ben's apartment sat empty. No one wanted to talk about it or even think about it. You expected an awful situation to be over with, Janet thought, once the actual events of it were past. But it doesn't work that way when someone has died. You get up the next morning, and the next and the next, and the tragedy is still there.

She had been so busy with Lily that she hadn't allowed herself time for Ben. But now she permitted herself to be reminded of him. For one thing, the bypass was going in, and from time to time she could hear the construction equipment rumbling in the near distance. It was a shame he hadn't been able to stop it, to save his Indian village, and more and more she thought maybe they should try to do something about it in his memory. She mentioned this to Ann one day at the teahouse.

"I can't say I haven't often thought the same thing," Ann said. "But I thought Ben had already examined all the possibilities, and there was nothing to be done."

"Well, there was nothing Ben could do. But surely there's someone with money or power or influence who could get some results. It's just a matter of finding the right person."

"What do you recommend, then? As a next step."

"Why don't we all discuss it? It will give us a reason to get together, if nothing else. I almost never even see Charles, any longer. There's no sense pretending we don't all live next door to one another. We'll have to get over it eventually."

"Yes, I suspect you're right. Let's do it, then."

They met at Janet's house, as she had Lily now, and it made the most sense to go there. Janet had made a lemon-merengue pie and offered tea and coffee. They all seemed just a bit abashed, in one another's presence, but it wasn't as awkward as she had feared.

She had told each of them what she wanted to talk about, of course, and had encouraged them to come with ideas. They had all been enthusiastic, and they all claimed to have given it a lot of thought. But no one seemed to have come up with a solution.

"I hate to be a wet *blanket*. But I'm not sure there's anything we can do that hasn't already been *tried*, and to no effect."

"But Ash says these things are all done by politics and money. You just have to know the right people."

"I agree with Paula, there must be something we can do," Janet said. "And I think we can all agree that we owe it to Ben's memory to at least try. It feels like unfinished business, for one thing. And there are so few causes like this that one feels compelled to rally around. Here's something we all have a vested interest in, and it's right in our back yard, and we're the only ones who know about it."

"Now, Paula, what about Ash's father?" Ann said. "Didn't you say he knew people at the Cricket Club? I wonder if that's an avenue."

"But I already talked to Mr. Billington, and he said he couldn't help."

"Yes, but maybe we should try again," Janet said. "Charles, what if you were to talk to him? You can be very persuasive, when you want to be."

"Well, I suppose it can't hurt to *try*. Paula, I assume your young Ashford can put me in touch with him?"

"Sure, whatever. You can try."

"Now, I do think this will be a good idea," Janet concluded. "At least it can't hurt."

Paula talked to Ash, and Ash mentioned it to Trey, and Trey reluctantly agreed to meet with Charles. They engaged on neutral turf, in the bar of the Chestnut Hill Hotel. Charles arrived first and waited drinkless till Trey showed up in a navy blazer and rep-stripe bowtie, looking like a Brooks Brothers ad. In short order they had exchanged introductions and sat down to double bourbons.

"Now what's this about?" Trey asked, betraying little real curiosity.

Charles explained the situation fully: the existence of the archeological site; the progression of the bypass; Ben's tragic death; their interest in getting the bypass rerouted. "Ben originally didn't want to reveal the presence of the artifacts, for his own *academic* reasons, but I suppose that's neither here nor there at this point," he finished. "We were going to make the case that the bypass was coming too close to our properties and our *business*, but I suspect the archeological site is the more compelling argument."

"Doesn't matter," Trey said. "The reason isn't important. I'm sure I can get results on this. Let's just say I know people who know people, and certain parties owe certain other parties a favor. Consider it done."

"We are all most *grateful*, I don't have to tell you. And of course we're aware there may be a some kind of *remuneration* required."

Trey looked self-consciously aghast. "I'm sure I don't know what you mean."

Charles abided his false opprobrium and nodded without speaking. Trey rose to leave. "You're the professor, no?" he said. "Forty's friend speaks highly of you."

"I'm sorry?"

"Forty's friend. Paula."

"Ah. Yes."

"You know, you should have come to me before about this."

"Yes."

Weeks went by with no word from Trey. But just as Charles was beginning to resign himself to failure, Trey called with news.

"I think I have a solution to your bypass situation," he said without introduction.

"That *is* good to hear." Charles found himself wondering why they couldn't have conducted their last conversation over the phone, instead of over drinks, and how Trey had obtained his number. Probably from Paula, through Ash.

"Unfortunately, the cure may be worse than the disease."

It seemed there were three viable options for the bypass, from an engineering perspective. It could pass over the Wissahickon, the approach blocked by W.A.S.P., the preservation group. It could traverse the plateau above the bluff, where the archeological site lay. Or it could run between those two courses, which would bring it alongside the train tracks and directly through the compound, through the teahouse and Toad Hall and Mole End.

"So the only way to save your Indian relics would be to lose your property," Trey said. "Of course, you'd be compensated royally for it. If that's what you want to do."

"*Really?* You're sure there's no other way."

"Those are your choices. Either where it is now, or through your front yard. It's up to you, though I sure as hell would never give up my Duchess II. But if you want to move forward, I can set the wheels in motion."

Charles sighed. He suspected that it was a ruse, that it was proposed as a solution only because it surely wouldn't be accepted. But perhaps it was a genuine alternative. Would he be willing to give up his home to honor Ben's memory? Well, he'd report back to the others and see what they thought.

"Let me get back to you," he said to Trey.

He told Janet, who of course told Ann and Paula. They all gathered the next day at Charles' house, under the bank of windows in the sitting area of his kitchen. Lily wandered off in search of Proust, who wisely was in hiding.

"So: does anyone have any initial thoughts or *feelings?*" Charles asked.

"I have to say it's up to all of you," Ann offered. "I probably don't have the same connection here that Janet and Charles do. I do have to think about my work-visa status, of course. And of course I did just relocate here from St. Andrews. But as I say, it's up to all of you."

"Well, I've been thinking about this quite a bit, naturally," Janet said. "And I know it was my idea, really. But I suppose there are lots of things that sound good initially but turn out to be not entirely practical. On the one hand it would be lovely to do something for Ben. But I do have Lily to think of now, and it's a responsibility I take seriously."

"I have to say I agree with you, Janet. Perhaps there's a more *symbolic* way we can memorialize Ben that would in fact be more *meaningful*, in the long run."

"It just wouldn't make a lot of sense, at the end of the day, would it?" Ann said.

"It's just not *practical*."

"Are we sure there's no other way?" Janet asked.

"That's what Billington told me," Charles said. "Either where it is now or through the compound."

They were all quiet for a moment.

"Well, I don't think Ben would have wanted us to give up our homes," Janet said. "And he was so fond of your house, Charles, and the teahouse, for that matter. They meant something to him, I think. So I really think we should do what Ben would have wanted, which would be for us to stay here at the ... at the compound."

"I notice you've been conspicuously *silent*, Paula."

"No, whatever you think," Paula said quietly.

"I think it's *decided*, then."

Ann nodded.

Janet gazed out the bank of windows. It had been a sweltering day, and the late-afternoon sky was turning livid with the threat of thunderstorms. From where she sat she could just see the back door of the teahouse. "Yes," she said. "I guess it's decided."

39

Paula could feel changes coming, the way she could feel autumn approaching by the thinness of the air. The seasons were all backward here, but you could sense when they were changing.

The compound hadn't been the same since Ben. She still loved her apartment. She still liked her job at the teahouse. She still had her friendships with Janet and Ann and Charles. But it wasn't the same. For one thing, they no longer had parties at Charles', they no longer spent time with one another outside the regular routine of the teahouse. But it went beyond that. Before it had felt like they were more than simply neighbors, more than merely co-workers, more than just friends. It had felt like the five of them somehow formed a whole. Now they were just four people — neighbors, co-workers, friends, yes, but four separate individuals.

She couldn't understand the way the others had acted about Ben's archeological site. It's true Janet got them all together and suggested they do something to preserve it.

But the only thing they tried was to talk to Trey, which she had done already. And as soon as they discovered that the solution would affect them, would require them to make some kind of sacrifice, they immediately abandoned the idea. Yes, it would have been a lot to give up their homes and the teahouse. But they could find new homes and open a new teahouse. Yet they didn't even consider it. Not a single one of them even suggested they think about it. As if they no longer cared about Ben. As if now that he was gone, he simply didn't matter.

Not that she had done anything, either. But what could she do? She didn't own the properties. And her work-visa status hadn't been settled, so she had to be careful. Besides, they were all older than her. She had never felt that way before, but now she did. Those all sounded like excuses.

She would have to think about her job at the teahouse. From what she could determine, there was no way for her to keep her work visa unless she got a job in the same field she went to college for, like the job she had at Globanaut. And even if she got a job for a company like Globanaut, that had offices in Brasil and America, she might have to go back to Brasil. She didn't think she'd be able to convince the immigration people that she was a communications specialist for the teahouse.

Why had Trey agreed to help Charles, when he hadn't helped her? Was it because she wasn't American? Was it because she wasn't white? He had acted like there was nothing he could do, like it was ridiculous of her to even ask. But then as soon as Charles approached him Trey immediately knew who the right people were and met with them about it and came up with a solution. Not that it had made any difference.

She had talked to Ash about it. He tried to explain it away, which wasn't like him; he didn't usually defend Trey.

Anyway, Ash seemed to have forgotten all about the bypass and was obsessed with some new cause, toxins in plastic water bottles or hormones in cow's milk, something like that. That would last till the next enthusiasm came along.

But how long would they last? What was their future, as a couple? It concerned her to think of it that way. When they first started going out, they were simply together. They were attracted to each other and enjoyed each other's company and simple were. Now it felt like they were "a couple," like they had to think about being a couple and self-consciously act like one. What was she even doing with Ash?

She could feel changes coming.

**

The changes came. Or maybe, she thought, it was more accurate to say that she made the changes, that she brought the changes on herself.

The first was that she broke up with Ash. She hadn't really planned to, at least not yet. He had taken her out to dinner, to an out-of-the-way vegan place he had heard about, just off South Street in Philadelphia. Except that it was closed when they got there, the boarded-up windows already covered in graffiti. They eventually found a Thai restaurant, which was quite good, actually, but only after walking almost clear across the city, which they would have to do again to get back to their car. Over red and green curry they got to talking about their relationship. Ash was worried about whether he was a good boyfriend, whatever that was supposed to mean. He wondered if perhaps she'd be better off without him.

For some reason it really annoyed her. Maybe it was just another instance of his habitual self-focus. He was always going on about his interests and enthusiasms: acoustic blues or micro-brewed beer or his latest obsession, custom-built bicycles. He had told her all about the materials they were made from, molybdenum and niobium and titanium and vanadium; about their various aspects, double-butted tubing and asymmetrical chain stays and forged dropouts; about how the builders were the last of a dying breed, craftsmen, artisans, artists; about how there was something truly Zen in a handcrafted bike frame, the coalescence of natural elements and human senses, the always-there and ever-present, the phenomenon of existence. She had never even seen him ride a bike.

But it was more than that. She had always admired Ash's easygoing self-confidence. Lately, though, he seemed to need constant reassurance. It had started when he met the others in the compound, as if he wasn't sure where he fit in, of his position in the constellation of their friendships. It felt like Ash had become dependent on her, as if her purpose in life was to make him feel good about himself. To go with him to his stupid blues festivals. To tell him, when he said she'd be better off without him, that he was the best thing that ever happened to her.

But what had really come between them, she realized, was that she couldn't talk to him about Ben. About how much she missed him. About how the loss of their new-dawning friendship was the forfeiture of something precious and a regret she would carry with her for the rest of her life. It was something personal and private she didn't want to share with Ash. As if talking about Ben would somehow be a betrayal of him.

She supposed they should discuss it, try to work through it, strive to save the relationship. But she didn't want to discuss it. She didn't want to work through it. She didn't think there was much of a relationship to save.

So she took him up on his suggestion, that maybe she would in fact be better off without him. For a second she thought he was going to choke on his lemongrass. He recovered quickly, but she had the sense that he was suddenly in a dark room and groping blindly.

"You mean you think we should break up?" he asked.

"Well, maybe we should."

"But I don't understand. I thought we were in love. I thought we loved each other."

"I do love you, Ash. I'm just not sure I'm in love with you." It sounded so conventional, predictable. "It's not that. I'm just not sure we should be together."

"Do you mind if I ask why?" He sounded disconcertingly calm and measured. Feeling his way with his toe in the darkness.

"I'm just not sure the same things are important to us."

"But don't we always do fun things together? Don't we always have a good time?"

"Yes," she said, meaning no. "But that's not really what I'm talking about."

"Do you mean just for a while? Maybe you need some time to think about it."

"I have already thought about it a lot."

Ash seemed to move rapidly through a series of psychological stages, going from denial to anger to bargaining in a matter of seconds. Finally, he said, "I'm just trying to understand. I don't mean to be a bastard about it." Apparently the final stage was patheticness. Was that a word? The state of being pathetic.

They would remain friends, he said. Who knew, maybe they would. He was surprisingly pleasant on the drive home.

The second change was that she got a new job. She had been looking vaguely online, just to see what was out there. She had even sent out a couple of résumés, without luck. But then she came across a listing for a communications specialist at a large company in Center City. The company had offices in several South American countries, including one in Sao Paulo. They needed someone at their headquarters who spoke *Português do Brasil*. She had two interviews, which went well, and they offered her the job. They said they'd work out everything with her visa status. In fact, they'd have to before they could hire her. She hoped she wouldn't have to go back to Brasil. It would feel like giving up ground.

She had felt guilty asking for time off from the teahouse to go on the interviews. She hadn't told Janet or Ann that she was looking for a job, because there was no sense creating a commotion if she didn't end up getting hired anyway. But now that she had the job, she'd have to tell them about it. There was no immediate rush, as she wouldn't start for another six weeks. She brought it up the first chance she had, on an evening when it was just the three of them closing the teahouse.

It was one of those things you couldn't just come out and say, and she found herself circling around it, like a vulture hovering above a carcass. She watched the comprehension of what she was saying gradually become visible on Janet's face. When she was finally done, Janet looked as if she had been slapped. As if she had been slapped gradually.

"I don't know what to say," Janet said, apparently at a rare loss for words. Or maybe it was that there were so many words they had got stopped up at a mental bottleneck, and she didn't know which to force through first.

Ann stepped in, ever Janet's practical, rational counterweight. "You've obviously given it a lot of thought," she said. "And it's probably a wise decision for your career, long-term."

"I don't know what to say," Janet repeated.

Paula explained, as best she could, why she wanted a new job, that it was good for her career, that she needed a position that would allow her to stay in the United States. She didn't mention her feeling that things had changed at the compound.

"Does it have anything to do with your breaking up with Ash?" Janet asked. Paula had told them about ending the relationship. "Well, I guess I can understand that," she went on, not waiting for Paula to reply. She seemed to latch onto the idea, then, and the words broke free. "Yes, certainly when you make a big change like that, it can seem like the right time to make other changes. I know after I broke things off with Joseph's father, I really felt I needed to make some changes in general. Of course then I had Joseph, and gave him up for adoption. And I was just finishing college, and I got my first teaching job not long after that. So there were all these changes happening anyway, which I think was a good thing. So that need was met just in the course of things. Of course, that was a long time ago. But people don't really change over time, do they?"

Well, Janet didn't really change over time, Paula thought, which somehow was reassuring. But giving notice at the teahouse was proving to be more unsettling than breaking up with Ash, which surprised her. She would have thought something to do with love would have been more emotional. But maybe leaving the teahouse had to do with love, as well, only a different kind of love, possibly a more important kind of love. She realized, then, that she loved Janet and Ann, and Charles, for that matter, all of them. They were her family as much as any of her real family had ever been, even as much as Avó Mariana and Avô Victor.

She started crying, despite her best efforts not to. And then so did Janet, and so did Ann, the three of them standing in the kitchen of the teahouse and looking from one to the other, weeping silently. They came together in a brief three-way embrace, hot and teary, and then stepped apart as their tears subsided. She expected Janet and Ann to ask about her new job, where it was and what she would be doing. But they had grown quiet and awkward and began fussing about the teahouse, making themselves busy.

The final change was that she decided to get a new apartment. She couldn't explain why she felt the need for this, really, especially as she adored her place high up in the peak of Mole End. But it would be a long commute to her new job, and there was no reason for her to stay at the compound, once she was no longer working at the teahouse.

She found a place in Northeast Philadelphia, near the *Brasileiro* community that had somehow congregated there. It was cramped and airless and in need of fresh paint, but it was cheap, and she would fix it up and make it her own. She could move in in another week. There had been something reassuring about seeing other *Brasileiros* on the street when she went to sign the lease.

She lay on the floor and gazed up at the exposed beams and vaulted ceiling of her apartment. Of her old apartment, she reminded herself. She was surrounded by boxes, which she had been packing bit by bit in the evenings. Janet and Ann had offered to help, but she had declined. It would have been too uncomfortable. Besides, this was something she felt she had to do herself.

She would miss the compound. She would miss everyone in the compound, Janet and Ann and Charles and of course Ben. But it wasn't like she wouldn't keep in touch. It wasn't like she would never see them again. Well, except for Ben.

But she realized it would never be the same. She felt regret, now, for having decided to leave. But sometimes leaving can't be helped. Life flows along, like a coursing river, and while it's always the same river, it's never the same water.

Among all of them, she thought, she probably had grown closest to Ann. But she realized it was Janet she would keep in touch with. It was Janet who had brought them all together, after all. It was Janet who had always been at the center of things, of the teahouse and the compound and the five of them.

40

Janet trudged uphill, through a dense tangle of underbrush long red and gold with autumn. It was an unusually warm day for October, and beads of sweat gathered at her temples and trickled down her cheeks. Indian summer, people called it.

She emerged onto a long, narrow clearing. The goldenrod was tall and woody after a full season of growth, and much of its yellow had already been shaken to the earth or borne away by the wind. As she walked, the stalks crackled beneath her footsteps, releasing a faint odor of stale coconut.

The construction equipment, the diggers and graders, sat idle, like sleeping behemoths. The road bed had been carved and crushed-stone substrate spread along its length. In the distance, where the road approached the clearing, the asphalt had already been laid. So this was Ben's archeological site, she thought. His Indian village. Already buried. Like him.

And now Paula, too, was gone. Not in the same way, of course, but it might as well be. There had been no big sendoff. Instead, Paula had said goodbye to each of them separately. Janet was the last to see her. Paula left her with the key to her empty apartment and loaded the last of her belongings into her rattling old car. They both cried, then, and Janet believed her when she said that she would keep in touch, that she would write and come to visit, that she could call or send e-mail whenever. And she was sure she would, at least for a while. But Paula had life ahead of her. Who knew where that life would take her, and in five years, or ten, would she remember them? Well of course she would remember them. But how often would she summon them to mind? Would she think to send a Christmas card? Would she call to tell about a new job or a new boyfriend or a good book she had read? To find out how things were going at the teahouse?

The October sun cast long thin shadows across the dry scar of the new roadway. Janet turned and walked downhill, back through the hedge of witch-hazel and winterberry and redbud, back within the compass of the compound, of the teahouse and Toad Hall and Mole End.

**

Ann was pleased to have begun a correspondence with Logan. It started soon after he left for London, just as she was beginning to think she wouldn't hear from him. "Dear Mum," his first letter opened, "I've found a job. And would you believe it, it's in Winchester." He would know Winchester from his childhood, from trips home to see her parents. Her father had died when Logan was a baby, but he remembered her mother, who lived long enough to see him start school. It was so long since she had been to Winchester.

Logan had finagled a managing director position at a wildlife park, in the countryside south of the city. They had all sorts of creatures, lemurs and zebras and roos and red pandas and cheetahs. She wondered if their enclosures made him think of his monk's cell. But of course he wouldn't actually be caring for the animals; he'd be running the wildlife park from a business perspective, making sure it was fiscally sound and accomplishing its mission. He was living in town in Winchester and enjoying himself immensely.

She wrote to him of her time in the hospital, of her conversations with Paula about religion and belief. Thus commenced an extended dialog on faith, the two of them sharing their knowledge and thoughts and experience. He had read more widely on the subject than she, Kierkegaard and Chesterton and Lewis, and while he tended to get carried away with Christian apologetics, she found his observations and digressions edifying. More welcome, though, and comforting, was the undercurrent of interest and concern: the casual questions about how the teahouse was faring; the subtle advice on how she should invest her savings or when she should have the car serviced; the solicitous inquiries after her health and happiness.

Lionel would be content, proud that his son had grown into a fine young man and relieved that he was looking after his mother, even if from a great distance. "Would be," she thought. Not "is"? If only Lionel was still with her, if only she could share with him her new home and new friendships and new relationship with her son, their son. She liked to think he lived on in her, whatever that might mean, in what she did and in who she was. Sometimes it helped; sometimes it made the pain worse. But she had found her way, she felt, without him. She wouldn't have expected it, this life she now had, but she was finding her way.

**

The young people were gone, Charles realized. Ben and Paula were gone. And his students, they were gone, too. He had always felt connected to young people, through his years of teaching, to their eagerness and optimism and vibrancy. It had made him feel young, as well, as if life could continue without changing, adulthood some sort of never-ending postgraduate school. As if his drinking were merely a vice of youth. As if the image he saw in the mirror, the stooping shoulders, the widening waist, the thinning lips, the tired brow, were a kind of science project, a test subject to be observed, one of those time-progression films in which a rose emerges and blooms and fades before your eyes. As if time didn't apply to him.

He had started teaching a class, and about time, too, he thought. It was an evening adult-education class, Women Writers, at the local Catholic college. The students likewise were all women, middle-aged stay-at-home moms whose children were finally out of the house or at least off to college. They showed up in their Lexuses, giddy to be free of their husbands and dull routines, nattering on at seemingly supernatural levels of pitch and volume and speed. They took turns bringing in treats, coffee cake or brownies or iced cupcakes. None was a standout student, even though all were college graduates, but they applied themselves with more interest and industry than any of his charges at Grier & Buchanan ever had.

It wasn't an illustrious career, by any stretch. He couldn't flatter himself that he was a tenured professor at a private college, respected if not widely then at least by his small community. But it was something. It was teaching. It was literature. And he did like teaching, for the pleasure of it, and literature, for the pleasure of it as well.

Life was a repetition of starting over: after leaving home, after finishing college, after losing Alain. And now, after abandoning his career, and when he thought it was perhaps too late, life was starting once more. How many times would it have to start again? But it did no good to think about that now. It was enough to be ... what? Well, it was enough to *be*.

**

Janet and Lily sat at the uneven table, Lily drawing a rather approximate picture of a pumpkin, Janet idly observing the steady stream of customers. She and Ann had their hands full, now, and it was nice to be able to sit back, when there were enough tea caddies on staff, and simply watch the gears turning. The tea caddies were all doing wonderfully, though one of them had recently given notice. Davina, was it? No, she had been among the first to go. Anyway, they would have to hire a new one. But that was just part of the routine.

Ann seemed to be recovering from the loss of Paula, which surely had been harder for her, at least when it came to the teahouse. And she was getting regular letters from Logan, which seemed to cheer her so. She thought they had grown closer in the past weeks, she and Ann, and the events of their lives intermingled so that it felt like they shared in everything, she in the transformation of Logan, Ann in the buoyant joy of Lily, both of them in the pleasure of the teahouse.

Charles, too, was much of his old self, perhaps even more than his old self. He was teaching again, just one class, but it seemed to invigorate him. He came into the teahouse almost every day, now, and he was speaking in italics again. He had even talked about hosting a dinner party or Sunday brunch, though he hadn't gone so far yet as to actually plan anything.

Lily was thriving. She was a constant struggle to keep track of and keep up with, of course, but she brought to each day a sort of haphazard structure, a spontaneous direction, that nothing else — not marriage, not teaching, not the teahouse — had ever quite provided. She still hadn't taken her to see Joseph, or gone to visit him herself. There was also the question of when she should introduce Lily to her own mother at the nursing home. These were things she would get to. For now she simply wanted to bask in the warmth of her granddaughter.

What would Henry have thought of what she was doing, of what her life had become? It was strange to think that all she was now taken up with, Joseph and Lily and the teahouse, had nothing to do with him. But she liked to think that even though he was no longer part of her life, even though he was gone, the memory of him, the way she had been shaped by their years together, had something to do with who she now was and what she was doing. Would he have embraced Lily as his own? She felt certain he would. But maybe it was better that he was gone for this portion of her life. Maybe Lily was something, was someone, that she alone had to see to, for herself and for her son and most of all for Lily.

So much had happened, and so quickly. You go along and nothing happens, nothing happens, and then suddenly it does.

The teahouse had never become quite what she had intended. She had wanted to create a cozy little haven where thoughtful people could stay for a quiet afternoon tea. Instead she had ended up with a loud, bustling café, where people came and went and drank coffee from paper cups. Still, there was always time to try new things.

And the compound: what would become of the compound? It felt almost sacrilegious to think about filling Paula and Ben's apartments, but they would have to sooner or later. And the three of them, she and Ann and Charles, were still there, and Lily as well. They could create it anew, the compound, a place for five people, six now, a place where the six of them could find comfort, where they could be separate, where they could be together.

The little brass bell tinkled as the door swung open. Into the teahouse stepped a lucid young woman, perhaps in her mid-twenties, with ripe-persimmon hair pulled back in a ponytail. As the woman approached, Janet thought her eyes were a clearer blue than any she had seen before. She had a smile that quickened all her features.

Janet thought, Tinkle.

About the Author

Eric Schoeniger has been a professional writer for more than twenty years. He holds a master's degree in creative writing from Temple University. For the past decade he has been an independent writer and marketing communications consultant specializing in business, information technology, life sciences, and alternative energy. He resides in Southeastern Pennsylvania with his wife, Jill, and their two cats, Bonobo and Cabbage. *The Teahouse by the Tracks* is his first novel.

www.ingramcontent.com/pod-product-compliance
Lightning Source LLC
Chambersburg PA
CBHW070400260626
47161CB00001B/218